HOW TO STAY

A BAD GIRLS OF CHERRY LAKE NOVEL

CHRISTINA MITCHELL

PIGASUS PEN PUBLISHING

First paperback edition September 2019.

Cover design by Evatalia
Formatted by Vellum

ISBN: 978-0-578-54394-9

www.christinamitchellbooks.com

For Josh
You're my home.

NORMAL PEOPLE CRIED at times like these. But Adelia Winters hadn't cried in fourteen years, and today wasn't looking any different.

She tossed her key ring from hand to hand as the backhoe dropped rich, dark earth into the grave. It was against the rules for her to be there after the cemetery closed, but she'd bribed the groundskeeper. She wanted to watch that casket disappear.

Her phone, snug in the back pocket of her jeans, shouted the opening riff of "So What?" The superior Metallica cover, of course. Not that tinny original by Anti-Nowhere League. She let the call go to voicemail. It was the third time her manager, EJ, had called and the third time she'd ignored it. He was the last person she wanted to think about.

Her gaze dropped to the grave. Maybe second to last.

Come to think of it, he was third if she counted Con—nope. She didn't want his name rattling around in her head either.

Man, she was up to her eyeballs in shit she didn't want to think about.

The backhoe driver finished and gave her a nod as the machine lumbered away. She adjusted her baseball cap and pushed her sunglasses high on her nose. How were you supposed to say goodbye to someone who was already dead? In movies people cried and picked up dirt to pat on the grave, a last loving gesture to the person they lost.

Whatever. She kicked a wad of dirt and grass onto the rectangle of freshly turned soil. "There you go, asshole."

Welp, that was all the wailing and gnashing of teeth she had in her.

A musky-sweet scent drifted along with the breeze, promising a heavy evening storm. The cemetery was silent as she wove between the headstones. The quiet—so different from the constant buzz of L.A.—grated on her nerves. There wasn't enough noise. There wasn't enough anything in Cherry Lake.

At the gate, something tugged at the back of her hooded sweater. "Motherf—" She spun with her fist raised, forgetting that she was in a tiny Michigan tourist town. There were no fans or photographers grabbing at her. It was just an Angel of Grief, resting a heavy head on one arm as the other dangled over the edge of a tomb, the back of her sweater caught in its outstretched hand. She pulled the fabric free and skimmed the cool granite with her palm. There was no name on the tomb. No dates. Just an angel, stained and green, mourning every soul buried there. Whether they deserved it or not.

Beyond the slope of the hill, she could still make out the mound of soil and the empty place where her father's headstone would go once the ground settled. She clutched the hand of the statue and tried to remember what it felt like to cry. Her grip tightened until it hurt so much she had to let go. She rubbed at the angry red tents on her palm and gave the grave one last glare.

What a waste of good dirt.

She threw herself into her '67 GTO and jammed the key into the ignition. "Come on, baby," she whispered. The engine screeched but refused to turn over.

Dammit, she really should have taken it in for that overhaul before driving across the country, but after what she did, getting out of L.A. as soon as possible seemed like a better idea.

Whispering a plea to the universe, she pulled the key out and slid it back in. The car had been a dumb idea. One of many. The purple beast weighed a ton and ate more gasoline than all the other cars in the U.S. combined. The steering wheel vibrated. The front end clunked. Everything under the hood was rusted and worn, waiting for her to give it the restoration it deserved.

She twisted the key again. Finally, the car roared to life, the radio blasting the tail-end of some cock-rock song she already hated without hearing the words.

"Thanks for tuning into *Saturday Rock Magic*," the DJ said. "Unless you've been living in a cave for the last few days, you've probably heard about Lia Frost assaulting the president of Gyroscope Records. I've been hearing some crazy stories about what happened. And now Lia's MIA."

Adelia flexed her bruised knuckles. Punch one CEO of a major record label in the face and no one would let you forget it.

"Don't know about you, but I don't mind old, rich guys getting knocked out." The DJ laughed. "Anyhow, we got a bunch of tweets requesting this gem, so Lia, wherever you are, this is for you. Here's rock's favorite bad girl with 'Two Hits.'"

She snorted. "Oh, you're funny."

The song howled into existence. It was a basic drop D with some palm-muting, a few bends and a shitload of thrash. It was inspired by a little Skid Row and a lot of Megadeth. She listened closely, still unhappy with some of the production. The studio's jackoff music producer hated the song and hadn't wanted it on the album. She'd fought him and mostly won, but his greasy fingerprints were still all over it.

Tapping her palm to the beat, she backed out onto Livia Lake road and hit the gas, putting the cemetery in her rearview.

A week in Cherry Lake, maybe two, to screw her head on straight. That's all she needed. Then she'd be ready to put the past behind her, drive back to California and deal with whatever was left of her career.

"Throw enough punches at shadows," her voice growled from the radio, *"you're bound to hit something that deserves it."*

IT TOOK a long time to get anywhere in a town that had more water and trees than people. Beyond the dreary woods, Adelia passed rows of lakefront mini-mansions and crossed the covered bridge to the town center. She pulled up to Keys Market and went around the back. Only down-staters, the forever-underfoot tourists, went through the front.

The run-down seventies vibe of the shop was gone now, along with the ugly yellow linoleum that she used to make fun of.

She wandered around the shop, grabbing handfuls of junk food off of the whitewashed wooden shelves. A gossip rag on the magazine rack caught her eye. Her picture was in the sidebar, above a headline shouting, *Rocker Lia Loses Control!*

She checked her sunglasses and the zipper on her sweater.

Should have worn a scarf, too.

"Hey, Mister Keys!" a girl shouted. The back door slammed against the wall, rattling the beer coolers.

Mister Keys? As in Old Curtis Keys? Adelia grabbed a packet of beef jerky from the shelf and peered around the corner for a better view. How the hell was he still alive? He'd been ancient when she was a kid and that hadn't changed. He was a grinning wrinkle of an old man, with bony shoulders and blue eyes so sincere it made her itch to look at him.

"You look like you're in a hurry," Old Curtis said to the girl, his voice still as creaky as an old porch swing. "What do you need?"

The girl—maybe a teenager, Adelia sucked at guessing that stuff—shifted a cheap, pink camouflage backpack from her shoulder to her back. "Fountain pop thing broke again," she said. "Mom needs two-liters. She said to put it on the tab."

"Go right ahead." Beneath the buzzing fluorescent light, Old Curtis nodded and went back to counting the cash spread out on the counter. He glanced up at Adelia and smiled.

She turned to the shelf beside her, studying jars of dilly beans, cherry jams, and canned peaches from the farms out on Lakeland Drive. It'd been years since she had to shove food in her pockets and sneak out the back door of the market, but her stomach ached as if the gnawing hunger of her childhood had never left.

Along with the guilt.

Needing to get the hell out of there, she spun toward the door. But a blur of black hair, sharp elbows and dirty sneakers slammed into her side, flinging the shopping basket out of her hands.

"Oh, damn, I'm sorry," the kid said, as she scrambled for the two-liter bottles rolling all over the floor.

Adelia rubbed at her sore side. "It's cool. You okay?"

Little Miss Cyclone nodded and dropped to her knees, picking up fallen junk food. "Yeah, I'm fine. Happens a lot."

Old Curtis shuffled slowly from behind the counter. "Everyone all right?"

Kneeling beside the kid, she grabbed the wayward bottles of pop and sat them upright. "We're good."

The girl blinked huge eyeliner-caked eyes at her and brushed a chunk of ratted black hair away from her face. Adelia had never seen hair dyed like that. It was so uniform and matte it absorbed all the fluorescent lighting. Like a black hole. She had to give the kid credit for being committed to looking that awful.

"Sorry again." The girl held up a couple squashed candy bars. "I gotta go pay for the ones I wrecked."

"No need, I've got it." She snatched them away and headed for the cash register before the human cyclone could argue.

"How ya doing today?" Old Curtis asked.

"Fine." She stared at the scratched-up counter.

He sifted through her junk food. "Looks like you've got a sweet tooth. Do you like pie?" From the display, he grabbed a plastic box with a slice of drippy, glistening cherry pie in it. "This is the best I've had. Just don't tell my missus I said so."

Was this never going to end? "Sure. I'll take it."

He slid it into a bag. "Oh, you're in for a treat, my dear." Moving slower than any human possibly could, he bent, disappearing beneath the counter, and reappeared with a plastic fork and a napkin. "Here. In case you can't wait to get home to dig into it." He squinted at the cash register. "Okay, that'll be twenty-four—"

"Thanks" she interrupted. "Keep the change." Tossing a couple twenties on the counter, she grabbed her bags and rushed out.

Patters of rain plinked onto the windshield of her muscle car as it sputtered to start yet again. The girl with the black hole hair emerged from the market, hefting a cardboard box full of two-liters. She adjusted the box and stopped in the middle of the sidewalk, staring at the car.

"Comeoncomeoncomeon," Adelia said. Finally, the car gave a delicious growl and started. "Good job." She patted the dashboard and pulled out of the parking lot.

In the rearview mirror, the girl, who'd been so frenetic before, was there, still as that Angel of Grief, before vanishing behind the blur of rain and the people rushing to their hotel rooms to escape the sudden storm.

2

CONOR ROSS WALKED the last customers out of Razzle Dazzle Glamor and Costume Photography. His umbrella wasn't much protection against the sudden downpour, and the elderly women squealed as their shoes filled with water.

"They're great pictures, aren't they?" Mrs. Babinski hollered over the rain, remnants of a molting red feather boa still in her hair.

No. Not at all. They were terrible pictures. But he couldn't tell her that. "They're gorgeous because you're in them," he said, with a wink and a smile.

She gave a coquettish shrug of her likely-arthritic shoulder. "You're a liar. But you are so handsome, you can just keep on lying to me."

He helped her into the car and then ushered Mrs. Davis to the other side.

"You're such a gentleman," she said, fluttering her heavily mascaraed eyelashes up at him. She put her arm around his waist as if seeking balance, but her hand slid lower and lower still and then her fingers went somewhere unexpected. Conor lurched forward with a bark of surprise and the old minx grinned saucily as she climbed in the car.

Once they pulled away, he ran back inside and locked the door. "Those two were something," he said.

"Yeah. When I put on her foundation, Mrs. Babinski asked me if I was 'one of them drag queenies' she's heard about." Andrew, Razzle's makeup artist, gave Conor a traumatized look over the edge of his blue plastic glasses.

"To be fair," Conor said, trying to hide a fond smile, "you're wearing a lot of lip gloss right now."

"And I'm *rocking* it." Andrew shook a lock of dark hair off his forehead and fluffed the gaudy floral cushions of the waiting area couch. "I swear I'm gonna look for another job."

Conor pushed aside the frizzle of anxiety Andrew's words gave him. Working at Razzle without the kid would be miserable. Luckily, Andrew was nineteen and all talk. "You love this job and you know it," Conor said. "Anyway, count your blessings. Mrs. Davis just goosed me and she uh, got right in there."

Andrew shuddered dramatically. "Please open your own friggin' studio already," he whispered. "Think about it. No boss. No sexual harassment. And you'd never have to take another picture of a down-stater dressed like a bordello madam."

Conor closed his eyes. What a dream that would be. A clean, crisp studio where he could take photographs that actually captured people's spirits. He glanced down the hall to make sure their boss, Keith, was out of hearing range. "I'm working on it, but my business plan's not there yet."

"You've been working on it for, like, three years."

Five actually. But he didn't correct him. "Most small businesses fail. If I'm going to do it, it needs to be perfect. Failproof. So, until it is, I'll stick to what I do best." He headed for the computer station. The photo proofs from the last session were still on the screen. It was a sepia-toned wasteland of elderly ladies in corsets, feather boas and Razzle Dazzle-sanctioned poses that approximated—but never landed on—sexy.

Andrew wrinkled his nose. "That isn't your best."

Yeah, not even close to it. Those women deserved more than musty, over-processed glamour photos. Mrs. Babinski, with her striking pale eyes and salt and pepper waves, should have been photographed like an ancient sea siren. Mrs. Davis, with her deep eye wrinkles and sly grin, like the goddess of chaos, Eris, come to life. There were stories hiding in every line, every look, and he was talented enough to capture them. But that wasn't what he was paid to do. His job was to charm tourists into buying expensive photos of themselves painted like sad clown hookers and posed like glassy-eyed mannequins.

He sighed and shut the computer down. Razzle sucked, but for a small town like Cherry Lake the money was decent, and the work was steady. Even when tourist season ended, they did brisk business with wedding photo booths.

And anyway, it was temporary.

After locking up, he waved goodbye to Andrew and made his way through the downpour, following the old train tracks to Littlewood's Railway Diner. The garishly painted red and yellow restaurant used to be a train depot and water stop. Ninety years ago, steam locomotives ran through Cherry Lake picking up lumber, and the memory of it lived in every building and street in the town. You could dress like a train conductor or pose in front of a painting of a locomotive at Razzle, visit the tiny Iron Horse Historical Museum or attend the annual (and controversially named) Steamy Nights Train Festival, which was really just a model train show with a contest tacked on. You could even take your selfies in front of the old water tower. It stood beside the diner, the name of a long-gone rail company peeling from the wood. Down-staters loved the quaint nostalgia of it all. Charming on the outside, stuck in a rut on the inside.

Seven-thirty. Right on time, the dinner crowd clogged the

entryway as they left. Rather than push through, he walked around to the kitchen entrance. The rain couldn't erase the greasy waft of diner food pouring from the place.

"Hold the door!" Jo, his best friend's daughter, barreled through, soaking wet and toting a box full of two-liters.

He grabbed it from her and gave her a smile. "Your arms are going to fall off, Flash."

"I'm stronger than I look." She shook the circulation back into her limbs and then spun to snatch a fry from a red plastic basket on the counter.

Conor shook his head. "That's not yours. And it's gross to touch other people's food."

"I was just in the rain! It's like I washed my hands the whole way here."

Laughing would only encourage her, so he kept his expression serious. She made a face and slowly reached toward the basket.

"Do *not* put that fry back."

She shrugged and shoved it in her mouth. "Can you tell Mom I'm heading home?"

"In this storm? Wait a few and I'll drive you."

"Nah, that's okay. Fresh air is, um, good for me. Healthy." She backed toward the door and he held an arm out, blocking her exit. Jo was a brilliant, scheming thirteen-year-old, but she was also a terrible liar. Always had been.

"We talked about this, kiddo. I know how much you love Lia's music, but funeral or no funeral, she's not coming here. You're going to make yourself crazy looking for her."

"I'm not looking for her. Anymore." She gave him a suspiciously bright smile. "I swear." She slipped under his arm and raced across the back lot.

"Stay away from the motel," he shouted as she disappeared.

The kitchen staff grunted hellos as he walked through. In the dining area, dusty framed photos of steam engines dotted the faded yellow walls. The décor was as dated as Razzle's business model.

"Hey, Shan," he said.

Shannon Cooper pulled a pen out of her mess of strawberry curls and grabbed her notepad, throwing him a sunshiny grin. "Conor, I'm not going to marry you no matter how much you beg. Don't make me file a restraining order."

He dropped the box next to the pop fountain. "You think you're funny. You're not."

"Oh, shut up, I'm hilarious." She jerked her head toward the back booth before turning her attention to her customer, Georgie, owner of the Cherry-On-Top ice cream parlor.

The old man grabbed his arm. "How'd my pictures come out, eh?"

Conor patted Georgie's wrinkled hand. "They came out great. I'll bring them by the parlor as soon as the newsletter goes out." His contract with Razzle didn't allow him to charge for photography outside of the studio, but he sometimes donated his services to the Cherry Lake Express newsletter. It reminded him that photography was fun. It also gave him work he could actually put in his portfolio.

Georgie swung toward Shannon. "He took my picture for the parlor's 100th anniversary." He puffed himself up, the tuft of white hair on top of his head bobbing like a cupcake decoration. "I'm going to be online the webernet."

Shannon laughed and filled his coffee cup. "That's awesome."

Conor made his way to the back booth. He brushed flakes of vinyl off the peeling mustard yellow seat. Shannon slid in a moment later.

"How's it going?" he asked.

"I killed it today." She tossed her apron off. "Great tips, and between you and Georgie, I'm clocking my second marriage proposal of the day."

"Are you sure he wasn't saying *hello*? You have trouble differentiating between the two."

"*Hello. Get me coffee. Can I have pie?* When men talk, it's all blah-blah-blah. It's easier to hear what I want." She covered her mouth and yawned. "Where'd Jo go?"

"A safe guess is that she's snooping around The Dive."

Shannon snorted. "Like Adelia would show her face here after all this time."

Conor tried not to waste thoughts on Adelia or Lia or whatever she called herself now. She used to be easier to avoid thinking about, but that was before she turned up on his favorite radio stations. And before her dad died. He rubbed his forehead. "What have you heard?"

"Not much. One of the kitchen kids said they saw a Porsche at the gas station in Brightwell, but Jo said that was, 'Totally not Lia's style, Mom! God!'"

Shannon's coworker, Dany, jiggled over, her tight Railway shirt emphasizing her bountiful curves. "Heya Conor. Decaf?"

At his nod, she filled the chipped ceramic cup. "Want your usual? Veggie egg white omelet, no cheese, and a whole wheat English muffin without butter?"

That sounded nearly as depressing as thinking about Adelia. "Perfect," he said, giving her a slow smile. "You know what I like."

She flushed and bit her lip as she headed for the kitchen.

Shannon snorted. "Don't you ever turn it off?"

"Not usually." Flirting was fun, for a minute. Though lately the thrill of watching women light up with interest was fleeting. Sometimes he missed the anonymity of being a fat guy. Back when no one expected him to be anything at all.

"Could you plow her and get it over with so I don't have to hear her going on about how hot you are? It nauseates me."

He grabbed a napkin and wiped a drop of coffee off the side of his cup. "Nope. Not interested." He folded the napkin into a perfect square, running his finger along the seams. "I don't do casual."

"Yeah, but you don't do serious either."

Behind him, the door whooshed open, bringing a chill into the diner, followed by the clack of high heels. He didn't bother turning. The blast of ice gave her away every time.

"Hello, sweetheart." Maureen Ross patted his cheek with a cool palm and gave Shannon the side-eye. "I'd like a cup of hot coffee with cream. The real stuff, not that horrible creamer."

"She's on break, Mom," he said.

Shannon arranged her face into sunny professionalism and stood. "That's okay. I'll be right back with that, Mayor Ross."

Maureen waved Shannon away without looking back. She brushed some invisible fuzz off his shoulder and clicked her tongue. "Did you see your brother on MSNBC today? His pinstripe Armani oozed class."

He tugged at the neck of his t-shirt. "And isn't that just what class does?"

"Your sarcasm is exhausting." She sat down. "Did you have a stressful day taking pictures of grandmothers in corsets?"

"Don't start."

She tapped her shiny beige nails on the table. "You've made it perfectly clear that you won't entertain the idea of doing anything valuable with your life beyond taking your little pictures, so I'm trying to be supportive." She pursed her lips. "Your brother runs an empire and you run...laps."

Dany slid his plate onto the table, giving him a flirtatious smile and a long, purposeful look at her cleavage, sparing him from saying something snide about his perfect brother with his perfect business acumen and his perfect life.

His mother snapped her fingers in front of his face. "Focus please."

Shannon returned to the table, shooing Dany away, and topping off his coffee. She gave his mother a sweet smile.

"Mayor Ross, your usual table is ready. You've got hot coffee with real cream and I took the liberty of ordering you the whitefish special with greens. I know how much you love it."

Maureen bored into Shannon with glacial eyes. "Please spare me your liberties. I would like the glazed salmon with pilaf."

Shannon's smile wattage increased in proportion to how much she looked like she wanted to punch his mother in the nose. "Of course. Please forgive me."

The creak of the door caught Maureen's attention and her lips thinned as a woman took a seat at the front table and waved. His mother's table.

She stood and smacked his cheek. "We'll talk later." Her surgically tightened face bent into a warm laugh as she crossed the room. "Grace, my dear, if you wanted to sit at *my* table, all you had to do was ask."

Shannon left and then returned from the kitchen. "I told them to make both. She hates the salmon. I give it five minutes before she sends it back and orders the whitefish." She dropped into the booth. "Remind me to poison her coffee next time I get up."

"It won't work. My mother, like most supervillains, is immune to pedestrian forms of murder. You'll need something more elaborate. A meteorite. Perhaps a vat of acid." He rubbed at his tired eyes. "Do you have anything stronger than coffee?"

"I think Dany takes Xanax. Want me to ask her for one? Maybe two?" She slipped a piece of broccoli off his egg and popped it into her mouth.

"Liam was on MSNBC today, probably hocking a new book." He lifted his voice in a well-honed imitation of his mother's. "*In a pinstripe Armani suit.*"

"Ah," Shannon said. "Definitely two, then."

3

THE DIVE INN wasn't a bad motel. Not that Adelia had many choices. It was the only motel in the area that accepted cash and didn't require an ID. She dropped her duffel bag and wandered the room. A Jacuzzi tub so small that it would overflow if you dipped a toe into the water. Faded artwork on the walls. A sign beside the television declaring, *We now offer free cable!* It was no Sunset Marquis Villa, but she'd slept in worse places.

She dumped the grocery bags on the table. Candy. Chips. Beef jerky. Dilly beans. Cherry pie. All the food groups. She ate the pie for dinner. Old Curtis was right; it was the best she'd ever had.

Licking the pink syrup from her fingers, she collapsed on the bed, moaning as she sank into it. A warm, soft bed was one of life's greatest pleasures.

Her phone rang. EJ again. She couldn't avoid him forever. Or could she?

Nah, probably not. She answered it. "Hey."

"Hello, duck." The rough silk of EJ's voice slithered through the phone.

"Don't call me that."

"Where are you?" he asked, still dangerously soft. If she didn't know him, she might have mistaken it for care, but it was cold, British fury.

"Bahamas."

"Without your passport?"

Shit.

"Also, you withdrew plenty of cash, but not enough to charter a private flight, and I'd certainly see a charge for it if you flew commercial."

"Breaking into my bank account is a crime," she said. Not that she was surprised. That's why she was using cash and not her credit card. She didn't want him tracking her down by her charges.

"I'm pretty sure punching Rod-bloody-goddamn-Norris was illegal too! What the hell were you thinking?"

"He deserved it." She stared at the greying oil painting that hung beside the bed. The blobby, crooked house in the center looked ready to collapse, as a strong wind sucked the dingy curtains out of an open window.

"He doesn't see it that way and now that vindictive cock is threatening to drop all my other acts." He caught his breath. She could almost hear his fingers scraping their way through his short black hair. "You humiliated him. He wants an apology. A public one."

"Fuck him and fuck you. I don't need Gyroscope Records."

"Let me remind you of who and what you are, you gutter slag—"

She hung up. Exhaustion settled deep into her bones. She was so tired of everyone telling her who and what she was. Especially EJ.

She turned off her phone.

The room was too warm. The AC gave nothing but a death rattle followed by silence. Sighing, she cracked the door open and stood in the doorway, letting the storm wind wash over her.

The rain was coming down so hard she half expected to see an ark in the parking lot.

She unbraided her long, dark hair and scratched her scalp. It was time to hack it all off and dye it back to her signature fiery red. Guess she'd put it on her to-do list, right after *un-tank career.*

A van pulled into the parking space next to her car. Adults and an army of children poured out, shrieking and racing for their motel rooms. Was it one family or two traveling together? She could never tell. Down-staters all looked the same in their khakis and capris, tugging at sticky children. She and her best friend, Conor, had spent countless nights on the curb between Keys Market and Cherry Moon Gifts. Drinking beer hidden in pop cans while he studied the tourists, figuring out their life stories by the way they dressed and moved and smiled. That was his gift. He saw the fine details, stuff no one else would think to look for. It was what made him so special.

No, dammit. She couldn't think about Conor. That would only lead to thinking about what she did to him, and that hurt too much to recall.

The thunder rumbled like a double-bass drum and she leaned against the doorframe, eyes closed, humming a melody to match the staccato beat of rain on the overhang. Lightning flashed so bright she could see it behind her eyelids. She blinked to clear her vision and locked onto huge grey eyes looking up at her from a pale specter of a face.

"Fuuuuuuuuuuuck!" She jumped backward, heart threatening to slam out of her chest.

The girl from the store, now with rain-flattened hair and eyeliner flowing down her cheeks, shoved past her into the motel room. "You scared the crap outta me," the kid said, panting for air.

"I scared *you*? What are you doing running around at night

in a storm, looking like that chick from *The Ring*? You almost made me swallow my tongue."

"I knew it," her intruder said, making a noise somewhere between a gurgle and a shriek. "You're Lia."

Fuckity fuck fuck.

"Don't know anyone by that name. Get out."

"I was like, almost a hundred percent sure at the store." The kid's backpack thunked on the floor. She dropped to her knees and rifled through it. "No one else sounds like you." She yanked out a copy of *Hardkor Rock* magazine and pointed a chipped black fingernail at the snarling redhead on the cover. "You're her."

"Nope."

The intruder's face pinched up. "Yup."

"Get out."

"Why're you in Cherry Lake?"

"Get out."

"Why'd you punch that guy?"

Adelia growled.

"This is like—I can't—" The girl shook her head. "I'm, like, your biggest fan. Well, maybe not your biggest. But you're my favorite singer." She waved the magazine at her. "I have every song you've ever made. Even the bonus tracks. Hannah—she's my best friend—her cousin stole 'em off the internet for us. I didn't think you'd mind cuz you're like, a bajillionaire and we're broke. Anyway, you have to admit, they're not that good or they'd be on the album." She paused to catch her breath. "You're like, a *total* genius."

"Please leave." She rubbed her palms on her eyes until she saw tiny dots of light.

"Are you moving to Cherry Lake?"

Hell no. Her body seized at the thought. "That is none of your business."

"I know." The girl flicked a strand of dark hair off her face.

"But I wanna know anyway." She opened the magazine, flipped to a dog-eared page and shoved it at her. "Did you see this? They ranked all seven of your albums from worst to best and they screwed it all up. They said that *Watch Me Fall* was worse than *Sugar and Cyanide*."

Adelia snatched the magazine out of her hands. "That can't be ri—What the hell? That's stupid. *Sugar* was the worst album I ever put out."

"Right? They go on and on about 'I'm Not Sorry', which is an awesome song, but kinda overplayed, and they don't talk about 'Soldier Heart' or 'The Last Time I Believed'. That's my favorite, of like, all of them. That video of you playing it on an acoustic was soooo good. I totally cried."

Desperate to escape the reverence in the girl's eyes, she swallowed and focused on the wall. "I, uh, thanks for saying that. But you need to go."

"But maybe we could talk more about the article if you took me home?" She squeaked out, her chin quivering. "I live in Ribbon Rail Park."

"Look, kid—"

"Jo," she said. "And I'm not a kid. I'm almost *fourteen*."

"Fine. Jo." She pushed the magazine back into the girl's hands. "I'm not taking you anywhere. You got out here on your own and that's how you're leaving."

Jo worked her facial expression like a radio knob, dialing the tragedy to eleven, channeling orphans and kicked puppies. "Will you sign my magazine?"

"No. Now please leave." She steered her toward the doorway. "Don't worship me. Or anyone."

The artificial sadness dropped from Jo's delicate features. Her expression hardened and her bruised raccoon eyes scanned the room. "Did you know that fans are like, looking for you? On social media?"

"Point?"

"I bet a lot of people would like to know that you're here."

Her throat burned with bile. "You're not a kid at all. You're a —a tiny gangster." The minute it hit social media the press would show up, nosing around. How could she be so stupid to think that she'd sneak under the radar? God, she never thought anything through. Just crashed blindly into the nearest china shop and worried about the damage later.

Too late now. She met Jo's glare with one of her own. "Take your threat and get out."

The girl marched out the door, her skinny body shaking with outrage. She threw the magazine at Adelia's feet. "It's *raining*," she said. "And you know what? I thought you'd be cool but you're not! You're a…an asshole!"

Adelia leaned out of the doorway. "It takes one to know one."

"Jo!"

The kid spun toward the parking lot. Adelia leaned further out, squinting into darkness. A man cut through the rain, rushing toward them. He clasped his hands on Jo's thin shoulders and gave her a tired smile. "You just couldn't resist, could you?"

Jo sniffled. "I—she—"

"She called me an asshole," she cut in, hoping the kid's dad would ground her forever.

"She called me one back!" Jo yelled.

"That's not…exactly what happened."

The guy stared at Adelia until she shrank back into the doorway. He tore his gaze away and leaned toward the kid. "Your mom's worried. Why don't you get in the truck and text her?"

The girl nodded and clomped toward a blurry blue truck, but she spun back toward them. "I lied," she hollered over the rain. "'The Last Time I Believed' sucks!" She climbed in and slammed the door behind her.

The man brushed a hand through his wet hair. Wow, he was gorgeous in a down-home-country kind of way; all jaw-scruff and pretty lips. His drenched shirt pulled tight across his chest, forcing her eye to follow every line of muscle beneath it. He tilted his head, studying her back. "Takes one to know one?" He coughed a laugh. "Jesus, you haven't changed at all, Winters."

Her breath huffed out like motor exhaust. Only one person ever called her that. She stepped out, looking closer at the man's green eyes and the light freckles across the bridge of his nose.

Eight. There used to be eight there. She'd counted them the night she ran away.

There were more now.

She blinked, unable to adjust her eyes. The Conor she'd known was a painfully shy, sweet boy with a face rounder than a cantaloupe. He'd been so overweight that he walked sideways up the aisle of the school bus. This man, with his cheekbones and his muscles and his slippery-gravel voice, could not be *her* Conor.

"I look different, I know." He shoved his hands deep into his pockets and shifted from foot to foot, giving her a tight smile that made her heart ache. How many times had she watched him do that? Hide his hands and sway, whenever he wanted to say something, and couldn't.

"I don't even know where to begin," he said.

She raised her chin. "Say what you want to say."

"You first."

Her knees wobbled under the weight of his gaze and the silence stretched between them until it nearly snapped. "I..." She stared at the tops of his boots and shook her head. Sorry didn't begin to cover what she'd done and too many years of silence had gone by for her to grovel for forgiveness now.

The boots were still for a moment. Maybe two, before spinning away. Then there was nothing but the bang of a truck door, the sputter of a V6 engine and the shrill grind of tires on wet concrete.

"I missed you," she whispered to the empty air.

CONOR USED to dream that Adelia would return.

That she'd show up on his doorstep with combat boots on her feet and regret spilling from her lips. Fourteen years of silence had destroyed that fantasy, along with the lovesick fat kid who'd invented it. Or at least, he thought it had.

The steel band tightening around his chest left him short of breath. Nothing had prepared him for seeing her in the flesh. She was still all swagger. Five ten-ish, long legs in snug jeans, brown hair tumbling down her back, dark eyes rich as a slice of chocolate cake.

His body had a very different reaction than his brain.

He squeezed the steering wheel. Dammit. She had no right to make him feel anything.

Jo sniffled, and he blew out a breath. "Did you text your mom?"

"Yeah."

"You okay?"

"No."

After years of Jo's babbling, her silence was unsettling. She stared out of the window, rubbing her nose with the back of her hand. He reached beneath the seat and pulled out a zippered bag, tossing it her way. "You know the drill. Tissues and hand sanitizer. My truck is a snot-free zone."

"You're so weird." She rubbed the clear gel on her hands, filling the cab with lemony scent. "You and mom never talk about her," she said as she zipped the bag up and tucked it beneath the seat. "I thought she'd be... different."

The rain beat down so hard, his windshield wipers couldn't keep up. He pulled off to the side of the road. It was too dangerous to drive and talk with Jo when he couldn't see more than an inch in front of his face. "I don't know her now, but nobody could ever live up to what you created in your head."

Jo twisted her hands together. "What was she like? When you were kids?"

A half-tamed bobcat. A fierce wild thing with unkempt hair, baggy clothing, and eyes too wise for a seven-year-old. He brushed a mote of dust off the dashboard and considered his words. "She was rough around the edges and hated people prying into her business. Which is why I told you to leave her alone." He didn't want to chastise Jo when she was hurting, but at the same time, she'd courted the pain. "Her dad just died. Tracking her down was not okay."

Jo puffed up, the way she did when she was about to lay it on thick for Shannon, but she caught his look and slumped in her seat. "I'm sorry."

"You're only sorry because it didn't go your way. Better crank out some tears for your mom, because she's the one who's going to ground your butt until you're my age."

She chewed on her fingernail and stared out the window. "Are you gonna tell her that I swore?"

"I seem to have developed amnesia." He leaned close and bumped his shoulder against hers. "I don't remember any swearing at all."

"Thanks," she said. "You're the best dad I never had."

"No problem. Don't forget this when I'm old."

"You're already old. You're like, thirty."

"My memory is coming back."

The rain slowed, and he was able to get back on the road. Jo flicked on the radio and hummed along for the rest of the ride. He parked between their trailers. "Your destination, madam."

"Wanna come in? I can nuke dinner. Mom made scalloped potatoes and meatloaf and there's a big barftastic salad full of all that crap you eat."

"You mean vegetables?"

"Yeah. Those."

He wanted to take a run and burn off all his confusing emotions, so he could get back to pretending Adelia didn't exist. But Jo stared at her hands and he felt his own heart crack to match hers.

"I'm in," he said. "But I'm not watching *Jurassic Park* again."

Jo's face lit up. "*Avengers?*"

He sighed heavily. "Can I make fun of Thor's hair?"

"Duh."

"Avengers it is, then."

CEILINGS WEREN'T THAT INTERESTING. Adelia stared at the one above her for hours. It was stucco. There was a dark stain above the bed that seemed to grow bigger the longer she watched it. If she squinted, it looked like a hawk-nosed demon doing a handstand and singing show tunes.

Her pillow was less comfortable than a sack full of river rocks. She yanked it out from beneath her head. No, that was worse. She shoved the pillow back into place and groaned. Even the bed was mad at her.

The girl had no right to barge in and ask those questions. So why did she feel like she'd done the wrong thing by throwing her out? And Conor. Was that his daughter? She mashed the pillow over her face and growled obscenities into it.

Almost one in the morning and she couldn't find her brain's off switch. She turned the television on and searched for something to focus on. Nothing. Her blinking phone demanded attention, so she took her time sifting through emails, deleting requests for interviews, and discarding a strange message from a woman asking to produce a song with her. Then she listened to and deleted angry voicemails and texts from EJ.

She itched to get her guitar out of the trunk of her car, but people were sleeping all around her and despite what EJ said, she had some manners.

1:05. 1:06.

She peeled open a candy bar, but it tasted like pencil lead. She searched for the waste basket and banged her toes on the pink camo backpack sitting at the foot of the bed. She hoisted it up. Lia buttons decorated the front pocket along with one that said, *Music is Life*.

It was probably full of homework and makeup and secret love notes to regrettable boys. Sucked for the kid to lose it, but that wasn't Adelia's problem. She heaved the backpack into the corner, harder than she intended. It smacked the wall and landed with a meaty thump on the floor, spilling books and magazines and pens everywhere.

"Oh, for fuck's sake." She got on her knees and scooped it all up. A skull-covered makeup purse. Freezer baggy full of chocolate chip cookies. An issue of *Power Chord* magazine, Lia Frost's digitally flawless face glaring out from the shiny cover.

Why did they do that? Her face was fine the way it was. Ordinary. A little crooked. She had a cool, faded scar on her cheekbone from a well-deserved lesson in gravity when she'd ridden Conor's bicycle up Adams Hill and come back down face-first.

Needing a distraction, she dropped to the floor and flipped through the magazine, shaking her head. It was nothing but dumb celebrity gossip. Which famous people were hooking up? Which rock singers were enemies and why? And right in the middle, "Breaking Down Lia Frost: *Power Chord* tries and fails to pry answers from rock's most mysterious woman."

"Ugh, gross." She did so many bullshit interviews she barely remembered this one. Lia is gruff and defiantly uninterested in the trappings of fame—blah blah blah—Known for her ratty jeans and refusal to play dress-up at the Grammys— Ratty? Her jeans were expensive as hell. Lia gave nothing but infuriated silence when I mentioned her number-two spot on AxGrinder's list of the hottest chicks in rock—She skimmed to the end of the article. Despite our best efforts, all we learned is that calling the baddest bitch in rock a hot chick pisses her off. Sadly, Lia remains chilly and untouchable as ever to the fans who want to know her.

She chewed on her thumbnail. Why did they have to dig? Everything you'd want to know about Lia Frost, you could find in her songs. That was where she existed. Why wasn't that ever enough?

What was it that girl had said? I know, but I wanna know anyway.

She hated reporters trying to crowbar their way into her emotional vaults. But Jo wasn't a reporter. She was a kid—an annoying one, but still—a kid with smudgy, cheap eyeliner and a backpack full of hope that she could reach through the pages and touch someone untouchable.

Adelia had been like that once, and she knew the frantic desire for connection through song. When every word and melody felt as if they were written just for her. She couldn't remember a night of her youth when she wasn't wearing a half-broken set of headphones, holding them into place as she listened to the same songs over and over again until she fell asleep. Like Jo, she'd dreamed of meeting her idols, so certain—as only a teenager could be—that they would understand her as much as she thought she understood them.

And having met them, Adelia knew better than anyone that nothing wrecked a dream faster than waking up. Most of her musical heroes turned out to be nothing but damaged, self-involved assholes.

Heat churned in her gut. Even for a cynic like her, that lesson had been painful.

The kid wasn't a cynic. Yet. And she hadn't deserved that.

She fished a marker out of the bag. In jagged letters, she scribbled her signature across the front of the magazine. Slipping it into the backpack, she sat the heavy thing on her lap and stared up at the ceiling.

Fuck.

WAITING until daylight wasn't an option. Running into Conor once had been enough. In the dark she could dump the damned backpack at the door and be done with it.

Maybe then she'd be able to sleep.

If you wanted to find someone in a small town—say, an annoying teenager with memorably awful hair—it wasn't hard to track them down. Even at one-thirty in the morning. The sleepy night clerk at the Dive Inn knew exactly who she was talking about and where she lived. The clerk yawned and sat back in her chair. "Can't miss it. Whistle Stop Lane. Pink trailer. Lots of flamingos."

"Whistle Stop," she mumbled as she typed it into her phone. "Wait, what did you say about flamin—"

The woman cut her off with an impressive snore. She poked at the clerk's shoulder and got a surly glare. "Also, I'm in room three and I think there's a leak in the ceiling."

"Didya put a garbage can under it?"

"No. There's no water coming in. It's a dark spot on the ceiling above my bed. I think it's getting bigger."

The woman shrugged and closed her eyes again. "I'll call maintenance in the morning."

"Thanks." Adelia hunched her shoulders and headed into the storm.

6

JESUS, it was almost 2 a.m. Conor had to be up in three hours. Why did he let Jo convince him to watch a second movie?

Because he hadn't wanted to be alone with his thoughts.

He shook her awake. "Go to bed, Flash."

She buried her face in the couch cushions. "Nooooo. I didn't see the part where Vision lifted Thor's hammer."

"You've seen it thirty times. Go to bed." He yanked the throw off her and switched the ceiling fan on full blast. She squealed and stumbled from the couch to her room. He followed behind her, catching the door before it slammed shut and woke her mother.

He cleaned the living room, neatly draping fuzzy throws on worn floral armrests. He washed all the dishes, packed away leftovers, wiped the counters and the folding tables. He distracted himself until there were no distractions left to keep Adelia out of his mind.

God, she'd looked good. She was never beautiful, not in the way movies measured beauty. But everything about her still called to him. The strong line of her nose ending at a broad tip, the full upper lip that bent into a perfect cupid's bow, and those sleepy, dark eyes, the color of bitter lager. Most people thought of brown eyes as innocent. Bambi and Labrador puppies. But she'd never looked innocent. Hers always hinted at something more sensuous than that.

He yanked his jacket on and pulled the door open. He was going to go home and get some rest and cease thinking about—

Adelia.

He froze, muscles seizing painfully. She stood on the other side of the screen. Eyes wide. Lips parted. A backpack clutched in her arms.

They stared at each other wordlessly for seconds that felt like minutes.

"What are you—why are—" He said, breaking the silence. "What are you doing here?"

Shadows played on the sharp planes of her face. Without a word, she spun and headed down the steps.

He threw open the door and followed. "Winters, stop."

She spun to face him. "What do you want?"

"Answers," he said.

"Don't have any."

"Then make some up."

Her gaze shifted sideways. "I know that it was—it just—it didn't have anything to do with you."

"Right." He wiped the rain from his eyes. "After we..." He took a breath. "You were my best friend since second grade and you just vanished. No texts. No phone calls. Gone. Tell me why."

"I—I wish that—I should've—" She looked at the ground. "I didn't mean—" Thunder boomed over their heads, her words lost in the rumble.

She shook her head and shoved past him and into her car. It sputtered. She turned the key again and again. Finally, the engine revved, roaring like a wounded animal. She hit the gas and the car jerked forward, then stopped, the roar fading to a meow and then silence.

After a few more tries with the key, she punched the steering wheel and let loose a string of violent obscenities that the storm couldn't muffle. She jumped out and kicked the car. "Mother-fucking-cocksucking-vintage-piece-of-shit!"

As far as tantrums went, it was perversely entertaining.

Stalking to the hood, she opened it and disappeared behind it, more invective punctuating her movements. She slammed it closed. "Son of a bitch," she yelled, giving it another kick.

He leaned against her car. "Winters, cars can't do any of the things you accused this one of. It doesn't even have a mother."

She slid into the driver's seat, grabbed her cell and jabbed at the screen. Then, she jabbed harder. Screeching in frustration she threw the phone across the car.

He leaned in. "No bars?"

She pressed her forehead to the steering wheel and shock flared within him. Was she crying? He couldn't remember a time he'd ever seen her cry. Not even when she fell face first down Adam's Hill. She'd stood, blood dripping from her forehead, dry-eyed and laughing.

He pulled out his phone. "Here, I've got two bars." He pushed it toward her. "You can call Paulie's for a tow."

Adelia squinted at him with dry, desolate eyes. Of course, she wasn't crying. She was made of steel wrapped in barbed wire.

"No thank you." The words squeezed out from behind gritted teeth. She bent and grabbed her phone, shoving it in her pocket, along with her keys. Her chest rose and fell rapidly, her jaw pulling so tight he could see the muscle twitch. She slammed the car door, pushed her hands into the pockets of her sodden hoodie and headed up the sidewalk without a backward glance.

"Winters!" He called out. "Adelia!"

She marched to the end of the street, rounded the corner and disappeared.

Screw it. Her obstinate ass could walk back to town. He locked Shannon's place and crossed the yard between their trailers. Glaring at her car, he swiped at the rain cascading over his face. The storm was worsening. It was over six miles to town, on a street with no sidewalks. In the best of circumstances, it would take her a couple hours to walk there. In a storm like the one crashing over their heads, it would be closer to three hours and that was only if she didn't slip in the mud, slide down the embankment, and drown in Hopeful Creek.

He clenched his fist, the rough edges of his keys digging into his palm. "Dammit," he ground out, as he threw himself into his truck. "Why couldn't you stay gone?"

After a long trek out of the park and onto the dimly lit road, his headlights finally lit onto her back. She was making pretty good time with those long legs of hers. He pulled over and rolled down his window, letting the rain rush in. "Get in. I'll drive you to the motel," he shouted.

She shook her head and kept on going. Stubborn woman.

He pulled over and shot out of the truck. "Stop being a martyr and get inside!"

Adelia spun and stalked toward him. "Go. Home. I don't want your help and I don't need your goddamn pity!"

"I can't believe you still haven't grown out of your suffer-in-silence bullshit." He threw his hands in the air. "You'd rather choke to death on your pride than accept help from anyone."

"Oh, perfect Conor Ross is judging me?" She pressed a finger into his chest. "Fuck. You."

"Oh, fuck me?" He leaned closer. "You already did that, Winters."

She shoved him.

His knees buckled before he realized what happened, and he fell backward, sliding down the hill, landing in mud so thick, he sank into it like a soft bed.

Adelia appeared above him, breathing heavy. She dropped to

her knees in the mud. "Shit. Are you okay? Did you hit your head?"

She held his head in her hands, gently squeezing his skull, as if she were checking a melon for ripeness. The sodden tendrils of his rage whipped away, caught in the same wind that lifted her wet hair and slapped it against her shoulders.

He flinched from her hands and gave an agonized groan.

"Oh, god. I'll call an ambulance." She reached for her phone. As soon as she turned her head, he shot forward, grabbing her around the waist, and rolled her onto her back in the mud, pinning her beneath him.

Her eyes narrowed, and he smirked, feeling victorious.

"You fucker," she said. "I can't believe I fell for that."

"I can't believe you did either."

She pushed onto her elbows. "So, you're fine?"

"No thanks to you. But I'll survive."

"Good." She slapped a wad of cold mud against his face and raised a challenging eyebrow. Energy crackled through him.

"That was childish." He grabbed her wrists and shoved her back down, rubbing his muddy face on her cheek. Her rusty laugh cracked the infuriatingly cold mask she'd been wearing, as she squirmed to buck him off.

"Give up," he said.

Her eyes flashed hotter and brighter than the lightning slashing the sky. Wrapping her legs around him, she gave a heave and flipped him flat onto his back, settling all of her weight onto his pelvis. "I win."

Intent on pushing her off, his fingers dug into the wet, tight denim clinging to her hips. Hips she never had as a gangly teenager.

She shifted to keep herself upright and suddenly the rise and fall of their bodies, matched to the rhythm of their heavy breaths, no longer felt combative.

He raised his hands in capitulation. "Fine. Victory is yours. Now, get off me."

She climbed off and he hoped the rain drowned out his groan at the sudden loss of her wriggling body. He cleared his throat. "Ugh, I need a shower. Maybe three," he said.

"I forgot about your dirt thing."

"Not wanting my underwear full of dirt isn't a *thing*."

"It's really a shame," she said. "I tried so hard to make you rugged and manly. Clearly, I failed."

"Really?" He stood, trying not to gag as mud sluiced down his body. "All you ever did was punch me in the arm and yell, 'Hit me back, you big baby, who cares if I'm a girl?'"

"See, a rugged manly man wouldn't have admitted that."

"I own a goose down comforter," he said. "And a salad spinner. Pretty sure rugged missed me by a mile."

She snickered and the tight band around his chest loosened. "Let me drive you into town."

"Thanks, but no."

He gave up.

The mud worked to suck the shoes off his feet as they climbed out of the ditch. Adelia crossed her arms and resumed her walk. If she didn't irritate him so much, he would have been impressed with her tenacity.

He pulled a tarp from his emergency kit and spread it across the bench seat of his truck and hoisted himself inside. He watched her go, until she disappeared, out of the range of his headlights.

Sighing, he pulled onto the road and followed behind her.

LIGHTS LIT THE ROAD AHEAD. Adelia growled as Conor's truck crept beside her, matching her pace.

She smacked on his door until he rolled down the window. "No means no."

"It does," he said. "And I respect your right to walk in a torrential downpour like a jackass. But I'm not going to spend all night worrying or feeling guilty because you got hurt out here. So, for the next five and a half miles, I'll follow your stubborn behind."

"Well, enjoy the view." She marched on, ignoring him.

After three miles she regretted her choice. She was exhausted. Her feet burned in the mud-filled prison of her combat boots and her tight, filthy jeans were chafing her thighs.

"Suck it up, Buttercup," she muttered, limping onward. She could fight like a man, swear like a biker with a busted thumb and make crowds of thousands scream her name. She'd be damned if blisters were going to defeat her.

The sign for the Dive Inn broke through the rain. If she could have, she would have cried with relief. Instead, she hobbled faster, eager to put a door between herself and Conor's concern.

The flashing lights in the parking lot stopped her. Two fire trucks blocked the front of the Dive Inn. The Cherry Lake Volunteer Fire Brigade and Brightwell Fire Department.

He passed her, pulling alongside the curb and raced out of the truck. Unsure what to do, she followed him.

"It's not safe!" a firefighter hollered at the gawkers gathered around. "You need to get back!" He swung his arm out. "Hey, I told y—oh, hey, Conor," he said with a grim smile.

"What the hell happened?" Conor asked.

"Roof leak. Ceiling busted open and destroyed a room. All the rest were flooded. Down-staters were practically dog-paddling out of the motel."

Adelia pushed past them and walked toward her room.

The firefighter grabbed her arm. "Sorry, ma'am, no one can go in."

She dipped her head low and held up her key card. "I need to get my stuff."

"Room three? Oh, thank god!" The man's shoulders dropped. "You're the only person unaccounted for. We thought...well, I'm glad you're all right." He cleared his throat. "I'm sorry, but you're not going to find much stuff to get. This room took the worst damage." He adjusted his helmet and popped the door open. Water sloshed out toward her feet. "There was about three feet of water in here."

What remained of the ceiling sagged around an enormous hole. Water gushed through it, dangling wires dancing in the torrent. Heavy chunks of plaster and thick, wet piles of insulation covered her bed entirely.

She ran her hands over her skull. "Jesus."

"Yeah," the fire fighter said. "The mayor has town hall set up for people to sleep on the floor for the night until they make other accommodations. They've got coffee and hot chocolate and snacks over there."

She mumbled her thanks and staggered to the curb, Conor following behind her.

"You going to the hall?" he asked.

"No."

"I can drive you into June Lake or Brightwell. You can get a hotel room there."

She tucked her hair behind her ears. "June Lake, Brightwell, and Hope Falls all scheduled their late spring festivals for the same week. Everywhere is full. That's why I stayed here. Even the rental houses were booked solid."

Not that she could use her credit cards anyhow. Fucking EJ.

"What are you going to do?" he asked.

She stared at her filthy boots. "I'm going to...whatever. Don't worry. I'll figure something out. I always do." She tried for a smile, but her mouth felt rusted shut.

"If you need a place to stay tonight—"

"No. No thanks. I'm good."

His eyebrows scrunched together, but he finally gave up, and headed back to his truck.

She could handle this. Absolutely. She was only covered in muddy water, her vehicle was dead, and nearly everything she had with her, except for her guitar, was floating in her murderous hotel room. Panic replaced her confidence.

Maybe she couldn't handle this.

Digging her phone out of her jeans, she wiped the mud off the screen and dialed.

"Just a min," EJ hollered. Music pulsed in the background. Another late-night party full of groupies and drugs. The music drifted away, and a door clicked shut. "Miss me already?"

"Hey," she said. She couldn't dredge up any of her usual bile for him.

"Are you—are you all right, duck?" She must've sounded awful if EJ wasn't being a dick.

"I'm fine."

"You don't sound fine. Whatever it is you need, I'll take care of it."

She didn't know what she needed. But EJ was good at fixing all the parts of her life she insisted on breaking, even if he was an asshole about it and would lord it over her forever.

Across the parking lot, the headlights of a car flashed on the aqua blue Ford still parked by the curb. Conor.

Through the rain she couldn't make out his face, but she could see his arm draped over the back of the seat. Comfortable. Relaxed. Waiting.

Everything frantic stilled inside her.

"Lia?" EJ said.

"Uh, I've got to go." She hung up. Conor's head swiveled slowly, following her path to his door. She raised her fist to the window and froze.

He had every right to spit in her eye. She was toxic sludge

and she'd oozed all over his life once and here she was doing it
again. It wasn't fair to him.

Wasn't that true? It felt sort of true. But there was something
else holding her back.

Fear.

No, that was bullshit. She dropped her fist, pride squawking
like a noisy bird. Lia Frost wasn't scared of anything. She was
tough, and she didn't need anyone. Not their pity, not their help.

The truck shifted and he tilted his head as though he could
read her every thought, his eyes stripping away everything.

That was what scared her the most.

She banged on the window anyway.

He rolled it down slowly—so slowly—a smile tugging at the
corners of his lips. "Yes, Winters?"

"I think—" She swallowed the disgust she felt for herself. "I
think I need your help."

7

DREAD CRAWLED over Adelia like army ants. She hunched down on the tarp-covered seat. Conor drove quietly, passing all the hiking paths the two of them discovered while they tramped through the woods, claiming the town, one meadow and snowmobile trail at a time. She could almost smell the sticky green citrus scent of the firs and pines, taste the cheap beer, hear his voice crack, yelling at her to get down as she climbed trees higher and higher, the rough bark cutting into her palms while she shimmied from branch to branch as if she were immortal.

She pressed her hands together, rubbing away sap that no longer stained them.

He slid his phone into a dash holder and clicked on the screen, filling the silence with melodic, crunchy riffs. Who was the band? Head Bash? Punch Face? They opened for her a few years back, but she couldn't remember their names or what they looked like. She never did more than say hello and wish them a good show before locking herself into yet another dingy auditorium green room to warm up alone.

"You want me to change the station?" he asked. "You're making that face."

She slouched deeper into the seat. "What face?"

"The one you make when you hate a song and you're disgusted with me for playing it in your presence."

"I don't do that."

"I watched you make that face for…" He stopped to count on his fingers. "Nine years."

"No such face."

He gave her a look and jabbed at his phone, until the music switched to a particularly awful nu metal song. He flipped the sun visor down and pointed at the mirror. Her face, smudged with crumbling mud, looked pretty rock n' roll, but her nose was all scrunched, along with her mouth.

"That's the face. Like you swallowed a stink bug."

She pushed the visor closed. "I always look like that."

He snorted and let her suffer through half of the album. Her head was throbbing by the time he pulled his truck in front of her car.

"It's so weird that you live in a trailer," she said.

He slammed his door closed and rounded the truck. "Seemed the best way to keep my mother from visiting."

"Smart. Does it work?"

"Best five grand I ever spent." He gave her a half-smile and pointed at the grey trailer with an enclosed pine porch. "Come on."

"I thought that was your trailer," she said pointing to the pink one he'd come out of earlier.

"Jo lives there," he said. "I live next door."

"So you've got like, visitation or something?"

His brows drew together. "She's not my daughter. I don't have kids." He gestured to the steps. "Come on."

Why did relief fall on her shoulders like raindrops? She rubbed at her arms and looked around the porch. It smelled like fresh pine and looked gleamingly new. "Wow, this is nice."

"Thanks. I built it from a kit. Not quite finished." He pointed to a white screen door and windows leaning against the wall waiting to be installed.

She ran her hands over the smooth pine. "You did a really nice job. How long did it take to build?"

He gave a dry laugh. "You don't care about that. You just don't want to go inside." He rubbed at the mud caked on his hands. "I'm dirty, and not the good kind of dirty. I need a shower. So, get those boots off and shed all the clothes you can. I don't want mud everywhere."

"Do you hear yourself when you talk?" She dropped her sodden, filthy hoodie and pulled her boots off, nearly crying with relief. She flipped a boot over and mud poured out of it. "You know what a lost cause this is, right?"

He chucked his shoes and jacket. "Okay, screw it. I'll shampoo the rugs tomorrow."

She pulled her socks off and draped them over her boots before grabbing her hair, twisting it into a disgusting bun so she'd drip and shed as little as possible.

He unlocked the door. "I should warn you that I—"

Something large and sleek shot out as soon as the door cracked open. It headed straight for her. She leaned backward as the squashed-faced creature pressed paws against her thighs, barked, spun in a circle, ran in and back out of the house and then leapt on Conor, pinning him to the door and licking his face with all the passion of a lover. A lover who really wanted to taste the inside of his nostrils.

He turned his head to escape but the dog managed to soak every inch of his face and collar. Then the slobbery thing veered for her again. She pressed her back against the wall, and he grabbed its collar.

"We both failed obedience school. Sorry." The dog sat on its wriggling rump, tongue lolling out of its mouth and looking much less like a raging monster beast.

Still, Adelia edged further away. "Does it bite?"

"It's a she, and not unless you're made of rawhide."

The dog raised and lowered her rear end, stub of a tail thumping on the wood floor as it inched closer.

"Put your hand out. She won't hurt you."

Her brain screamed for her to go sleep in her car, but she held her hand rigid as the dog rubbed a probing snout on her palm. "Oh, that's so gross."

"She's a boxer. They're...damp. You're acting like you've never touched a dog before."

She rubbed her hand on her sweater as heat engulfed her face. "I haven't."

He stilled and seemed to be waiting for her to say more, but she just shrugged.

Sighing, he shooed the dog into the trailer. "Come on."

"Thanks for letting me stay. This is beyond anything you needed to do."

"If it makes you feel better, I'm taking the first shower because I'm not *that* nice," he said. "I'll try to be quick. But, you're not allowed on the furniture until you're clean."

She sat on the tan kitchen linoleum and pulled her knees to her chest. "As soon as you leave the room, I'm rolling around on your couch."

"Then you and Cupcake already have something in common," he said as he shooed the dog down the hallway.

SOMETHING WET SMACKED against Adelia's ear. She dragged her heavy eyes open and pushed at the beast that was furiously licking the side of her face. The boxer pushed back, shoving her to the linoleum, and since it weighed roughly the same as a mid-size sedan, she was a helpless victim as it coated her in spit.

"Cupcake!" Conor pulled her off. "Stop that."

"I don't think I like dogs," she said, sitting up.

"Well, this one likes you."

"Yay." Her face smelled like dog breath and it was coated in sticky residue. She wrinkled her nose. "You're gross, Cupcake." The shameless thing wagged its tail.

"Come on." He led her to a sparkly clean bathroom and patted a pile of clothing on the counter. "I found something for you to wear." He slid a fluffy towel her way and left her alone.

She scrubbed herself until the water ran clear and her skin squeaked. Even then, she stood beneath the rapidly cooling water, letting it cascade over her. No matter how many years passed, every shower still felt like a gift from heaven.

Running water and warm beds were the most underrated of luxuries.

When the water turned icy, she forced herself out, shivering as the cool air kissed her wet skin. She took a shaky breath. The day had been a disaster. It wasn't the first time she had nothing but the dirty clothes on her back. Or the first time she'd swallowed her pride—and other things—for a warm place to stay. Of course, it was easier when it was a stranger and not Conor. He filled her with the most hated and persistent of all her emotions. Guilt.

Thinking about *that* was a well with no bottom.

She shook out the sweatpants he'd left her. They were far too big. She pulled them on and cinched the waist as far as she could, but they slid right off her hips. Dammit. She knotted the tie to keep them from falling off and she slid the baggy sweatshirt on, whistling at herself in the mirror. Second hottest chick in rock? Damn right.

She padded to the living room. Conor was making the couch into a bed, crisply tucking black sheets into the cushions. He laid a fuzzy grey blanket on top, folding it back on one side. He did everything with such precision, dropping the pillow into place and adjusting it so it was perfectly straight.

When he looked her way, his gaze flicked toward the pants.

"Um, they don't really fit," she said.

"Sorry. I don't have anything smaller." He picked up the remaining blanket. "Here, in case the couch isn't warm enough." She reached for it and he pulled it back, his brow furrowed. "A gentleman would give you the bed and take the couch himself."

"Lucky for you, I'm no lady," she said, snatching the blanket from him. "Anyway, letting me stay is gentlemanly enough."

"All right." He yawned and looked at his watch. "Shit, it's quarter to six. I've got to take Cupcake for a quick run and then I'm headed to work."

"But you haven't slept."

"It'll be fine." He rubbed at his eyes before leashing the dog.

Guilt gnawed a hole in her stomach. He was going to have a miserable day because of her.

"Feel free to raid the fridge. Oh, and call Paulie's for a tow. Your car is conspicuous. Especially here," he said. "If it's ready, I can take you to get it when I get out of work, but that won't be until after seven."

"Thank you again."

He nodded. "If you make other arrangements and take off early, it's okay to leave the door unlocked."

"If you give me your number I can let you know." She was never any good at reading people's emotions but he gave her nothing at all. Just cool, distant green.

"Don't worry about that." He headed out the door. "Let's leave it a surprise. Like last time."

Adelia flinched as the door slammed shut behind him.

8

CONOR'S TRUCK rumbled away and Adelia burrowed into the cushions, listening to her thudding heart. Then the rain. The whines of the dog that kept sticking its damp nose into her ear. Conor's voice reminding her what an epic asshole she was.

Sleep wasn't happening, so she got up and milled around the trailer. It was as spotless as his mother's house, but a lot less gaudy. The grey couch blended perfectly with the black wing-back chair and pale grey rug. Everything was in the same palette of grey, black, and white. Framed photographs were the only pops of color, all perfectly spaced, lining the walls like an art gallery.

She had no doubt that he took them. So many faces. Wrinkled smiles and crooked teeth. A familiar little girl with big grey eyes, ice cream smeared on her face, offering the cone to the photographer. Old Curtis grinning at the camera, his dentures popping out as he laughed. All of them caught in a moment of thought or laughter or joyful surprise. Each one had a tenderness, a naked flash of vulnerability that filled her with fluttering emotions she couldn't name but didn't particularly like.

She crossed her arms over her chest and looked elsewhere.

The sole bit of clutter was a stack of camera catalogues beneath some dog-eared fantasy novels. She picked up a book with a surly man in chainmail fighting a three-headed monster on the cover. He still read books about dragons and damsels in distress. She flipped through but got bored and closed the cover. Reading books was never her strong suit. She couldn't concentrate. When they were kids, she'd lay stretched on the bed beside him while he read her all the required books. *The Count of Monte Cristo, The Hobbit, Cold Sassy Tree, Romeo and Juliet.* He'd do silly voices to hold her interest and then quiz her on the themes. Thanks to him, she aced every English class.

Despite its roomy minimalism, the trailer was suddenly too small. She dropped the book back onto the stack and went out onto the porch. Still raining, the glow of the sunrise fought to shine through the cracks of the dark, rolling clouds.

In the almost-light, the Pepto-pink trailer caught her eye. The weedy remains of a garden lined the home. In the front, just like the motel lady had said, in place of flowers was a riot of pink flamingos, all jumbled into a festive bird orgy.

Cheerful pop music thumped from the trailer. Was it normal to be awake so early? The only time she was up at six in the morning was if she hadn't gone to bed yet.

The pop singer yowled out an overly-emotional chorus that made her ears itch. If Jo was awake, it was clear that she'd put her off rock music for a while.

Oh hell. She'd been in such a hurry to get out of there earlier, she'd forgotten to drop off the damned backpack. Hoping to get one thing right, she folded the legs of the sweatpants up to her knees, and retrieved the bag from her car. Thankful for the rain and music drowning everything out, she climbed the creaky steps and opened the screen door just wide enough to squeeze the bag into the dry doorway.

The inside door swung open and Jo stood there in a pink

raincoat. She gave a squawk of surprise and dropped the garbage bag she was holding.

She groaned. Busted. "Hey, kid."

The start of a smile collapsed in on itself and Jo frowned. "What are you doing here?"

"I have your backpack." She waved it at her.

"Who are you talking to?" A woman appeared over Jo's shoulder. The light behind her made a halo that perfectly framed a storm of wild curls. The woman's blinky-doll eyes went flat.

Her stomach sank to her bare feet. If she could have melted like sugar in the rain, she would have. But no one had ever accused her of being sweet. Certainly not Shannon Cooper.

Maybe the sky would swallow her whole. She looked up. The clouds cracked open and it rained harder. That was *it.* Mother Nature was now officially on her long list of things that could go fuck themselves.

Shannon looked her over, from ratty hair bun to sopping, oversized clothes. She crossed her arms. "What are you doing here?"

"Um, the hotel sort of...caved in. The ceiling did. So Conor —he...I'm staying for the...night."

"How the hell did he even—" Shannon waved the thought away. "You know what? I don't care." She pushed Jo aside and stepped out onto the porch. "But since you're here, I hope you're going to apologize."

"You and everyone else." She sat the bag at her feet.

"Mom, stop it!" Jo grabbed Shannon's arm.

Shannon shook her off. "Shut the door," she barked.

Jo's eyes widened, and she slowly closed the front door.

Shannon pushed the bag aside with the toe of a fuzzy slipper and stalked down the steps, an icy-eyed baby doll in Sponge Bob pajamas.

Though she was nearly a foot shorter than Adelia, Shannon

forced her backward onto the sidewalk. "You owe my daughter an apology and you will give it," she said. "I put up with a lot of years of your bullcrap, but I'll be damned if you'll make her feel the way you made me feel."

Her stomach turned sour. "Your kid is the one who barged in on me, okay?"

Shannon's eyes narrowed and she pointed at the door. "Get in. The house. Now."

If it were anyone else in the world, she would have told them to fuck off. But Conor wasn't the only one she'd bailed on.

Despite them being the same age, Shannon had been as close to a mother as Adelia ever had. Whether it was bringing her leftovers or clothes from the thrift store to replace the ones she'd clearly outgrown, all Shannon ever wanted was to care for her. But that kindness had always chafed, feeling a bit too much like pity. She hadn't been kind in return.

Another foot of water in the well of her guilt.

"Jesus." She wrapped her arms around her middle. "I've met pimps less scary than you."

"Don't you forget it," Shannon said, stomping into the trailer.

She followed and tried to quell the anxiety threatening to burst out of her chest *Alien*-style.

Shannon dropped the abused backpack next to Jo. She ran a hand through her wet curls. One small tilt of her head and Adelia already knew what she was going to say. "I'm sorry about your—"

"Don't be. We weren't close."

"Still, though."

Shannon's sincerity grated her nerves. "Seriously, it's fine."

Jo's gaze ping-ponged between them.

"How about this then?" Shannon said. "What the hell are you wearing? You look like you escaped from a nineties hip-hop video. Aren't you rich? Can't you afford pajamas?"

She tugged the baggy sweatpants. "What part of 'the hotel caved in' aren't you getting?"

Worry etched itself between Jo's brows. "The Dive? Was anyone hurt? Mr. Slaski? Mrs. Amadori?"

"No, kid. The fireman said everyone ran when they heard the ceiling collapse in my—on my—room." She forced away a shudder. "At least two pairs of eight-hundred-dollar leather pants didn't survive, though."

Shannon snorted. "So sorry for your loss."

"Yeah, I'll take that one."

Jo grabbed her wrist. "We're making breakfast. Want some breakfast?"

"Um, no. I'm good."

Shannon pursed her lips. "Jo, please finish taking out the trash. It's stinking up the house."

"But I—"

"It's the dumpster, not Antarctica. I'm sure Adelia will wait a couple minutes for you to get back."

Jo growled and grabbed the garbage bag. "Please don't go. I'll run."

"Don't run. You'll break your ankle in one of those potholes." Shannon flicked her gaze Adelia's way. "She'll wait."

Racing outside, Jo slammed the screen door shut behind her.

"Don't run!"

"Can't hear you!"

Shaking her head, Shannon crossed her arms. "I'd really like it if you stayed for Sunday breakfast."

"If you said that without clenching your teeth, I'd believe you."

"Look—"

"Nothing polite ever started with 'look.'"

"I've knew you too long to bother with politeness." She scooped a bunch of chopped potatoes off a cutting board and into a frying pan. "You always made it perfectly clear how you felt about me, no matter how much it hurt my feelings. Allow me to return that favor." She dropped the pan onto the stovetop and laid strips of bacon in another pan. "I don't like you. I won't say hate because I don't hate. But if I did…you'd deserve it."

She'd probably barf if she tried to speak, so Adelia nodded instead. Until middle school, their friendship had been lopsided but existent. Then Shannon sprouted perfect cartoon curves to match her perfect grades. Of course, Conor had noticed. Why wouldn't he? So, she went out of her way to make Little-Miss-Perky miserable. She rejected every sincere smile with sarcasm and every gesture of friendship with disdain. She couldn't let up on her, even for a second, because that was all the time it would have taken for him to see how perfect Shannon was for him. It was a greedy, cruel thing to do to both of them. He'd deserved the girl with the softness, not the one who was all sharp edges.

She stared at the flowers poking out of an old spaghetti sauce jar on the table. She owed a million apologies and they were all too late to matter.

"I'm not saying this to be petty," Shannon said. "The things we did when we were young and dumb? That's done. Can't take 'em back. But what happened with Jo is not okay. I know how she can be, but you made her cry." She turned and the cold fire in her eyes made Adelia shrivel like burned paper.

"That wasn't—"

"Oh, shut it," Shannon said. "I don't care what you have to say. Save it for Jo because she does care, and in the interest of not making me angrier than I am right now you will sit down, you will eat, and you will treat her like a person."

They were silent for a few moments.

"Milk or juice?" Shannon asked, prodding the potatoes.

She suspected that *neither* was an incorrect answer. "Milk is fine."

Shannon plunked a cup down and poured milk into it. "Jo

has a giant poster of your stupid face in her room. I never had the heart to tell her what a jerk you are."

"Now she knows." She poked at the flower jar and did some math. "Were you pregnant when I...left?"

"Yup, a couple months along. In the proud tradition of all the Cooper women that came before me, I got knocked up at sixteen. Our family crest should be a condom with a red X through it."

The screen door slammed against the wall and Jo half-fell into the entryway. "I'm back!" she yelled, as though anyone could have missed that entrance.

Shannon spun, stirring the potatoes and flipping the bacon. "Okay, clean up and get to work. This stuff is almost done."

Jo washed her hands and began doing whatever mysterious thing it was that turned bread into French toast. Mother and daughter bustled around the kitchen, like a dance they'd done a thousand times, never once bumping into each other. The shitty synth pop song jounced from the stereo speakers and Shannon atonally sang along, prompting groans from Jo.

She stroked the stems of the flowers in the jar. Lady's Mantle. Allium. Hosta leaves. Late spring in a jar. Was this life for other people? French toast and laughter and flowers on the table? She stared into the living room, where the gauzy tan curtains matched the worn throw rug and complemented the soft sea foam green on the walls. How did that happen? Since leaving Cherry Lake she'd never lived anywhere permanent. Not that she'd wanted to. There was no need to make beds, mow lawns, or cook dinner in hotel rooms. But now she felt as though she were learning about a new species. It was all so far removed from what she knew. How did you shop for curtains or rugs? How did you know what would look nice together?

Jo handed her a plate. Two slices of French toast and a mound of fried potatoes and bacon. It smelled like heaven.

Jo sat a pile of napkins on the table. "Can I change the radio station?"

"No," Shannon said. "You already used your veto on my country music. So now you will suffer through pop. Next Sunday you can play music that gives me indigestion." Shannon gave her a side-eye. "No offense."

"None taken. My mission statement is to rock so hard I give people diarrhea. All I feel is victory."

Jo pulled her chair closer. She shoveled a huge chunk of French toast in her mouth. "Why'dyoupunchthatguy?"

This was why she didn't talk to people. "It's uh... there's a lot of stuff that...and music is..." She sat back. "It's complicated."

"People always say that. What's that mean?"

"It means it's not easy to talk about," Shannon said.

"Hmm." Jo stabbed a forkful of potatoes. "I read that you were dating Matt and your record label tried to make you break up."

"Matt, my guitarist? Ugh, no."

"Why not? He's so hot. Everyone thinks you guys were hooking up."

"Why?"

"'Cuz he's got muscles and tattoos and dimples. And when you're singing on stage he looks at you like..." She took a drink of juice. "Like he likes you."

She stifled a laugh. Matt liked groupies. Lots of groupies. Often at the same time. She wasn't sure that was the kind of thing you tossed at a thirteen-year-old. "Trust me when I say he's in love with music and not with me."

Jo's smile drooped and disappeared. Another fantasy smashed by Lia Frost.

She thought a moment. "Anyway, it's hard to find someone hot when you've lived on a smelly tour bus with them." She cut into the drippy French toast. "Also, he farts."

"No!" Jo jerked upright. "He doesn't fart!"

"He does."

The rest of the meal was punctuated by Jo grilling her about the bodily functions of all the rock musicians she knew.

Shannon cleared the table, shaking off Adelia's offer to help. "Okay, daughter o' mine," she said to Jo. "It's seven. Chore time. If we get everything done by seven-thirty, we'll have time to watch a movie before I go to work."

"Mom I know how important our quality time is to you, but Lia is here. At our house."

"You've got twenty seconds to get the laundry started before I drag out your naked baby pictures."

Jo glared. "I hid them."

Shannon glared back. "I scanned them."

"You're a dream-squasher!" Jo slapped her fork on the table. She shuffled out of the kitchen, mumbling what sounded suspiciously like every swear word ever invented.

"Care to repeat that, Josephine?"

"I said, I'm going!"

Shannon shook her head. "She's usually better behav—no that's a lie. This is just how she is."

She wasn't sure what to say to that. "Um, you sure you don't want help with the dishes or anything?"

"No, I've got it. This is our routine." She stretched. "Speaking of…"

Adelia shot out of the chair, grabbing the dismissal like a lifeline. "Oh yeah. Thanks for food and stuff."

"Laundry's in," Jo said, running down the hall. "You're not leaving, are you?"

"Sorry. I need some sleep."

Jo bit her lip. "Oh, okay."

For fuck's sake. She breathed slowly through her nose. "I signed your magazines."

Jo's eyes widened. "For real?" She scrambled for her backpack and dumped it on the floor. The magazines were damp but not too much worse for wear, because Jo flipped through one easily enough. She ran a finger over the page, reading what she'd written. "'This article sucks—'"

She coughed and shook her head to stop Jo from reading it out loud.

"Baloney," Jo freestyled. "That's what it says."

Her mother snatched the magazine away. "'This article sucks balls. You're rad for noticing.'" She lifted her eyes toward the ceiling. "Really?"

"Well, I crossed out ba— that word. See?" She pointed to where she'd slashed through it. "It's not like I had white-out laying around."

"Could you autograph something that she can actually show to people?"

No good deed blah blah blah. "Fine. Go get something, kid. Make it quick though. I'm not autographing everything you own."

"Yes!" Jo ran out of the room like ground wasps were chasing her. She returned a minute later, out of breath with her arms full. "I couldn't decide."

She rifled through the pile. Magazines. T-shirts. A dusty poster with ragged edges that had probably been hanging on the wall forty seconds earlier. "You have no shame."

Jo failed to hide her grin as she held out a marker. "No risk, no reward."

Adelia signed it all. Every signature forced a higher squeak of joy from Jo. She rolled the signed poster and shoved it at her. "If I find this stuff on eBay later, I'm going to be mad at you." Jo nodded. "Also, I need you to keep this to yourself. Me being here, I mean. I'm trying to fly under the radar, so don't show any of this to your friends until I leave. Okay?"

Jo raised her hand as if she was giving an oath. "I won't. I was bluffing about telling people anyway." She eyed her mother. "I, um, I'm sorry for being rude yesterday." She took a step toward her and Adelia jerked backward. She wasn't a hugger. Jo's arms hung in the air for second before she dropped them.

Goodbyes were the worst. Even the tiny ones. She widened her mouth into something resembling a smile and Jo returned it. "Later."

Her legs grew heavy and every step back to Conor's was exhausting. At the door, she looked at her muddy feet. Shannon hadn't said anything, but she must have left dirty footprints all over her carpet. When she got back to L.A. she'd send her some cash to steam them.

She used the last of her energy to wipe the mud off her feet and legs before crawling into the couch bedding with a moan. Her belly was full and for the first time in a long time, her brain wasn't racing to keep her from sleep, bouncing thoughts around that she couldn't quite catch. Beyond the rain, everything felt quiet and warm and safe.

Weird.

9

"A NO-SHOW AND TWO CANCELLATIONS," Keith said for the fifth time.

Conor stared out the window at the crushing downpour. "Yup."

"And where the hell is Slaski?"

"Called in." He leaned against the window frame, his tired thoughts occupied with the leggy rock singer sleeping on his couch.

Keith sucked on his veneers. "Who the hell is gonna do the makeup today? I'm gonna fire that kid. He thinks he's such hot shit that he's—"

"Come on, man. Andrew's family has bigger problems than worrying about putting lipstick on tourists." Like the hole in the roof of their motel and the water that was still sluicing through it.

Keith smoothed his salt and pepper hair. "I don't see nobody caring about *my* business." He threw himself into a rolling chair and flicked on the studio monitor.

Oh, hell.

He sifted through the photos Conor had taken the day

before. "You should have talked them into the high-def airbrushing filter. Old ladies are sensitive about wrinkles."

"Those two are the most confident women I've ever photographed. They didn't need that level of airbrushing and they wouldn't have wanted it if I'd offered."

"Eh, women are women. You flash them that nice-looking smile and tell them how much better the pictures would be, and they'd buy everything you're selling."

He was too tired to deal with Keith. "My job is to help them *feel* as beautiful as they are. That's how you advertise it."

"Spare me the touchy-feely bullshit. I don't pay you to build their self-esteem. Your job is to flirt and make them self-conscious. Gotta make those wildebeests want to look like swans."

"Don't you ever get tired of being a jerk?"

"Sure. But whenever I get sad about it, I dry my tears with the money you make me." Keith squinted at one of the final proofs. "You should have pointed out those wrinkles and used a different color gel." For twenty minutes, he critiqued everything from Conor's sales to his lighting choices and aperture settings.

He tuned Keith out and reached into his pocket, finding the advertisement for a photo studio he'd torn out of a real estate catalog. As soon as his business plan was done, he'd be out of there. And he'd take Andrew with him.

The bell above the door jingled, interrupting his fantasy.

"Maureen!" Keith arranged his face into an expression Shannon had dubbed, *Prince Smarming.* "You look beautiful as ever."

"Thank you." Her frosty expression didn't warm a single degree. Keith was a good-looking guy but being handsome was not enough to capture his mother's interest. Ever since his dad ditched them to make a whole new family with the nanny, she was only impressed by upward mobility. "I sent out text messages, but I'm going shop to shop to tell everyone that the town council and I have decided to start a fundraiser for the Slaski family." She reached into her purse and pulled out an iPad with a credit card scanner on it. "They're without a motel *and* a home, since they live there. They have had to issue refunds to all the guests and that amounted to..." She checked the screen. "Around eleven thousand dollars."

She held the iPad out to Keith with both hands. "They'd appreciate anything you can donate."

Keith's face twisted. Losing a dollar was enough to give him palpitations, let alone giving dollars away.

"Don't forget that no hotel means less business for you and everyone else in this town," she said.

"Did Penny donate?" Keith's ex-wife, Penny was the owner of the Sudz N' Dudz, the town's one-stop laundromat, dry-cleaner, and video store.

"Yes," she said. "Dudz gave $500."

Keith rubbed the edge of his scalp. "How the hell did you get her to agree to that?"

"Persuasion," she said.

Conor swallowed a laugh. More like blackmail and arm-twisting. His mother kept tabs on everyone's sins, not just his.

As if she knew what he was thinking, she pushed past Keith and gave him a kiss that brushed right past his cheek. "I heard you were kind enough to take in one of the tourists," she whispered. "How gallant."

"Don't know what you're talking about," he whispered back.

"Michiko saw a woman get in your truck. We're in a crisis and you're busy thinking with your *genitals*."

Man, he sure missed last week when she was complaining that he never dated.

She pulled back and patted his cheek. "Don't worry about donating. I already donated on your behalf." The rest of the sentence was unspoken. *So you won't embarrass me.*

Keith donated $510 dollars, earning a warm-ish smile from her before she left.

"Mmph." Keith said, his gaze lingered on her legs, threatening Conor's gag reflex. "Christ," Keith said. "What I wouldn't give to—"

"Going to stop you right there." Conor rubbed at his throbbing forehead.

"Oh right. Sorry." Keith grinned. "But seriously, that woman. Oof," He slapped a hand on his shoulder. "I'll make an excellent step-father, don't you think?"

"I swear to Christ, I will quit if you don't stop talking."

"Nah, you won't." Keith took a swig of coffee and swung back toward the studio screen, jabbing a finger at it. "What the hell were you thinking, using that filter?"

CONOR COULDN'T WAIT to escape the studio at lunchtime. He headed for the town hall to check on Andrew and his family. He found Mr. and Mrs. Slaski beneath the back awning of the building, glassy-eyed and sharing a cigarette. They greeted him with hugs, like always.

Andrew tugged at the sleeve of the ratty plaid shirt he was wearing. Very different from his usual button downs and skinny jeans. "Our clothes got ruined. I'm rocking the lumberjack look now." He tried to smile, but it wavered.

"You look great." Conor gave his shoulder a squeeze. "This isn't forever."

"I know. But it feels like it."

"What do you guys need?" Conor asked.

"More money than even *your* mother can round up," Mr. Slaski said. "I'd tell you the number, but I'd cry."

"We're going to be fine," Mrs. Slaski said, rubbing the back of her husband's neck. "No one took any major injuries and our insurance will cover it in a few weeks. We just have to wait it out."

Conor's phone rang. His brother's name flashed across the screen. His thumb hovered over the *decline* button as usual. Talking to Liam was exactly what his ego didn't need.

Fuck it. The day was already miserable. He stepped inside the hall and answered.

"Conor?" Liam sounded stunned to get hold of him. "How are you?"

"Great," he said, forcing his teeth to unclench. Talking to Mr. Perfection made his jaw ache.

Liam paused. "I'm sorry to bother you during the workday, but mom called me this morning about the Dive. I've been thinking about how I can help but I wanted to talk to you about it."

"She knows more about what's needed than I do. Talk to her."

"I'd rather talk to you."

He preferred speaking to his brother as little as possible, so he let the silence carry his half of the conversation.

"What do they need?" Liam asked.

Conor pulled the phone away from his ear and closed his eyes. Money meant little to Liam, but it would mean the world to the Slaskis. To Andrew. But it also meant his brother swooping in to be the hero and their mother gloating about her favorite son.

He peered out the back door, where he could make out Andrew's tousled hair as he huddled with his family beneath an awning, the smoke from Mr. Slaski's cigarette curling around them.

"The Slaskis don't have the money to do more than cover the hole in their roof with a tarp," he said. "Before the insurance company gets around to it, they need money. To survive and to at least patch it."

"I'll make some calls. I'm sure I can convince a contractor to do some expedited work for them. As far as money goes, do you think $15,000 will help?"

Conor wanted to laugh and barf. Would $15,000 help? Fuck. "That's incredibly generous of you. More than enough and I know they'll really appreciate it."

"I'm not being too...well, I don't want to act like money will heal all."

"In this case, it might." He blew out a breath. "Thanks."

"Do me a favor, though. Let's keep this anonymous. Don't tell Mom. I'll transfer the money to you and you can disseminate it however you see fit."

Just like that, whatever warmth he felt dissipated. "I don't need to play dress-up with your money, Liam."

"That's not what I..." Liam sighed. "I didn't mean it like that. Could you give me the benefit of the doubt for once?"

Conor rubbed his eyes. He was tired and stressed about Adelia and being unfair. Talking to Liam hit all his sore spots. His brother wasn't a bad guy. Just...smarter. Richer. Perfect.

Everything he wasn't.

"I'm sorry. Let me put you on the phone with Mrs. Slaski so you can discuss it directly with her."

"Sounds good," Liam said. "But are you all right? I know we're not..." He trailed off and then cleared his throat. "You seem on edge. With me. More than usual."

"I'm fine. Just tired. One sec." He relaxed his tight jaw and headed back to the Slaskis, handing the phone to Andrew's mother. They could use some good news.

CONOR ONLY HAD fifteen minutes left for lunch, so he ran to the Railway for a salad. Shannon hurriedly put it together and gestured for him to follow her through the kitchen, to the back office.

She sat the to-go box on the desk and gave him a look over her shoulder. "Thanks for letting me know that you have freakin' Adelia staying at your place."

His jaw tightened, and he breathed out to relax it. "I didn't see any reason to wake you at 4 a.m. to tell you about it. Also, it's not a big deal."

The old office chair creaked as she tossed herself into it, sitting across the desk from him like an angry school principal. "*Not a big deal*? Are you serious right now?"

"It's fine. She's leaving tonight."

She crossed her arms and gave him that assessing look that annoyed him to no end, even when he wasn't exhausted. "You're worrying me," she said after a moment.

"Nothing to worry about." He tapped his fingers on the Formica desk. "Now is when you argue with me, I refuse to discuss it, and then you threaten to eventually find out whatever it is you think I'm hiding."

"I could threaten you now and argue later, if you want me to change things up."

"That'd be nice." He stood and wandered the room, stopping to rub at the thick layer of greasy dust on a bookshelf. "Ugh."

She reached into the desk drawer and tossed a kitchen towel at him. "Get it out of your system."

He wiped down the shelves, exposing the whorls of the wood pattern on the veneer. "How did you find out she was there?"

"She tried to drop off Jo's backpack and got busted. I made her come in and eat with us."

He folded the rag over and started on the outside of the shelf. "Why the hell would you do that?"

"Because she owed my daughter an apology."

He snorted. "What'd she say?"

"She admitted that her hostility was always a thinly veiled attempt to mask her throbbing sexual attraction to me. Then we scissored in the living room until we got all chafe-y."

He stopped dusting. "I hate you for that visual."

"I'm so sure." She rounded the desk and put her hand on his shoulder. Her expression turned serious. "Conor, I know you. Guilt was pouring off her like flop sweat, but, if you think you're going to pry answers out of her, give it up. I don't care how bad she feels, she's still the most closed-off person I've ever met. No one is cracking that shell. Not even you."

He folded the rag into a neat square and handed it to her. "Okay, I've only got a few minutes to get back to work, and I'm starving."

She made a face and grabbed the salad off the desk, holding it away from him "We're not done."

"Yes, we are." He held out his hand and raised an eyebrow. "Your concerns are noted."

She sighed and handed the Styrofoam box over. "And dismissed?"

"Bookmarked for later review." he gave her a one-armed hug and headed for the door. "After food. And a nap."

10

THE DAY HAD BEEN NEVER-ENDING. Keith finally gave in and closed the studio early, since no one wanted their pictures taken during a flash flood.

When Conor got home, he wasn't sure if he was relieved that Adelia hadn't taken off, or annoyed that she was still there.

She stared out the window that faced the back of the park, one of his notepads on her lap. She tapped a pen against the window frame. Click. Click. Click.

"Is Ribbon Rail Mobile Estates inspiring a new Lia song?" he asked.

She dropped the pen onto the notepad, her far-away gaze disappearing. "Don't know how that would go. 'Life in a tin can, working for the man.'" She screwed up her eyebrows. "Um..."

"'Always eating *Spam?*'"

"Grammys, here I come."

"Jo told me that you already won one."

"Yup. I've got a fancy paperweight for a shitty song."

He sat down. "Above all that, are you?"

"Nah, I'm not above anything. I make commercial music. But

it's all a bunch of nothing. It doesn't really matter." It was the most she'd said about anything. As if she realized that herself, she cleared her throat. "Then again, the way shit is going right now, another Grammy couldn't hurt. Think I need to capitalize *Spam?*"

"I'd err on the side of not pissing off the people who produce potted meat."

She stood and wrapped her arms around herself, clutching her elbows. "Listen, uh, the car place hasn't returned my calls at all today. I've left a few messages."

"That's Paulie for you," he said. "He's a flake. Don't worry about it. He'll call."

"But if he doesn't—"

"Then you'll stay here again. It's fine."

It wasn't fine at all. He was so tired he didn't know what he was saying. But she bit her lip and nodded in acceptance and he couldn't take it back.

Cupcake scratched at his pants leg and gave him her most pitiful expression. "Run?" he said. She barked, spun in a circle three times and raced for the door.

Adelia was back to staring at her scribbles when he got in his running gear and left. Outside, Cupcake loped beside him, splashing through the muck like the dumb, happy dog she was.

Some people went to therapy. Conor ran. It cleared his mind and reconnected him to his body. To the earth. To the weather. It was a competition of one and that was a competition he could win.

But his mind wouldn't clear. His body wouldn't connect. Memories he'd avoided for years played like bad songs on repeat. Even the rain battering the hood of his coat couldn't drown them out.

The night Adelia left, she'd shown up at his house in the middle of the night, clutching two stolen four packs of wine-coolers. They watched a movie, drinking bottle after bottle, until he had enough alcohol in him to do what he'd talked himself out of so many times before—he'd kissed her. Surprise melted into breathy reciprocation and her watermelon-soaked kisses increased in urgency until their clothes fell to the floor. Then, she'd climbed on top, conquering him like the mountain he was.

It was over humiliatingly fast. Virginities gone in a haze of lust and cheap booze on the itchy basement rug. And before he could stop himself, he'd blurted out the words beating in his chest for so long he was nothing but bruises inside.

"I love you."

Nude and trembling, he waited for them to come back to him. For her to tell him that the way he looked didn't matter. That it was possible to see him and love him without condition.

The buzz of the action movie played in the background. Explosions. A cry of pain from the hero. Ticks from the grandfather clock. Silence from Adelia.

And then she was gone.

No letters or phone calls. His best friend since he was seven years old walked out the door, and with her went whatever scraps of self-worth he'd accumulated.

The thick mud of the flooded path forced him to run faster, taking shorter strides. His legs burned with the extra exertion, but nothing burned as fiercely as the pain of what he'd lost that night.

Shannon thought she understood but she didn't. This wasn't just about answers.

He'd missed her.

Through all the years of confusion and the insecurity, of avoiding mirrors, of near-celibacy, he'd never stopped missing his best friend. Her wry sense of humor. Her passion for music. Her hard-won smiles. She might have given him the worst memory of his life. But she'd also given him some of his best ones.

Enough. He accelerated, shutting out the burn to focus on the feel of his shoes squelching in the mud, the sound of the rain thudding through the trees. He concentrated until his mind did what he wanted and slipped deep into the run, where thought submitted to sensation and nothing mattered but the next mile.

THERE WAS a lyric in Adelia's head, a lullaby tangled in the thrum of the rain. *Crying shame. Burning shame. Bane. Rain. Water main.*

She laughed. It wasn't a song yet, but writing kept her mind busy, and playing filled the silence. It had been months since she'd written anything, lyrics or track. She'd been stuck, unable to focus. Now, at least the words were coming. Whether they were good or not was something she could worry about later.

She sat her guitar aside, stood and stretched. Her phone pinged, letting her know she had an email. She scanned the message. Another one from that woman, Emi Hara, who wanted to produce a song for her. *In the industry for ten years...*blah blah blah. *My recording studio has state of the art...Am currently working with...would love a chance to...I have some tracks if you're...*

The woman had sent a link to her website. She worked with some indie singers that Adelia actually liked. Huh.

Instead of deleting the email, she replied and thanked Emi for her interest, but declined. She was between studios and had no idea when she'd be needing a producer again.

That was depressing. Setting her phone down, Adelia wandered over to the bookshelf and poked around. An MP3 player sitting on a high shelf caught her eye. *Old school.*

Conor was still out running and she had no frame of reference for when he might come back, but curiosity propelled her to pick up the player. You could learn a lot about a person by their music collection. What was he listening to these days? She powered it up and scrolled through the album lists, rolling her eyes. He always had abominable taste in music. That hadn't changed. Much of her youth was spent in Solomon Records, smacking bad CDs out of his hands. Buying music was a luxury she couldn't afford, so the quality of his collection was important for mooching purposes. Of course, he never believed her wide-eyed declarations that she was policing his purchases for his own good. He'd smile and tell her that if she wanted him to buy her a CD, all she had to do was ask.

She flicked through the albums and groaned. "A little My Chemical Romance is understandable, but this shit is excessive." Her grumbles worsened as she passed one shitty rock album after another. "Ugh."

She sat the player aside and ran her fingers along the book spines beside it. At the far end of the shelf, she found a clear CD case squished between a fantasy novel and a guide to running small businesses. Good enough CD to keep but bad enough to hide? Mysterious. She yanked it off the shelf. "This better not be prog rock," she muttered. Turning it over, her heart squeezed tight. It was the Queens of the Stone Age album she'd given him for his fifteenth birthday, her jagged handwriting scrawled in marker across the clear jewel case. *I stole this for you because no one should spend money on it! Happy Birthday. Love, Winters.*

A soft breath rushed out of her.

The door creaked open. She dropped the CD onto the shelf with a clack and spun guiltily.

Cupcake marched in, gave a woof and then flopped over beside the chair. He shut the door behind him and gave her a grim smile. "What are you doing?"

"Checking out your music," she said.

His gaze traveled to the shelf behind her. He frowned and

crossed the room, grabbing the CD and easing it back between the books. "Don't read too much into it," he said, his voice rumbling near her ear. "It's a good album. Ready for dinner?"

"Nah."

"Winters, you need to eat. I can hear your stomach growling."

"That's not my stomach. It's just a noise I make now. Being thirty is weird."

"Well, turn down the volume," he said with a tight smile. "You sound like a wolf gargling mouthwash."

After rustling around in the kitchen, he handed her a bowl of what he swore was tofu and lentil salad. It was like surprisingly tasty yard waste. Afterward, he sat on the couch and turned on a news station. She sat on the other end and studied her notes.

"In entertainment news, there's still no statement from Lia Frost regarding her recent assault of Gyroscope president Rod Norris." Ugh. They flashed a picture of Rod. Balding. Middle-aged. His nose swollen and taped over, glaring at the photographer as he climbed in his Bugatti. She tried to squash down the satisfaction she felt looking at his busted face.

Conor glanced over at her and then back at the TV.

"Frost's manager, EJ Davies, has been unusually tight-lipped about the situation." EJ appeared on the screen, blue eyes like the sky reflecting on a lake in winter. Black blazer over a black silk t-shirt and artfully torn designer jeans. It was a look he'd spent years perfecting. Tailored and expensive enough to hold his own with executives, but edgy enough to sucker young, dumb musicians into giving him twenty-five percent instead of the standard eighteen.

"No comment," he said, in his clipped Cornwall accent.

Conor turned, his gaze trailing to the swollen, bruised knuckles of her right hand. "Jesus." Before she could react, he took her hand and studied it, his thumb stroking the faint purple edges of the bruise. "Is it broken?"

The heat from his body pressed in on her and she fought the desire to lean toward it like a plant starved from the sun. "It's fine." She pulled her hand away. "Just sore. It wasn't the neatest punch I've ever landed."

He got up and returned with a bottle of ibuprofen and an ice pack. "This'll help with the swelling and soreness."

"Dude, it's five days old. It's fine."

He shook the bottle at her until she snatched it from him. "You didn't used to be so bossy," she said. "When did you start ordering people around?"

"When they started listening. Now go get some water and take your damn medicine."

Her phone buzzed, and she nodded at him, taking the bottle as she headed for the bathroom.

"Do you want your career or not?" EJ growled when she answered.

She sighed and closed the door. She put the phone on speaker and filled a disposable cup with water. "Of course I fucking do," she said.

He breathed out. "Then listen to me. I need you here, now. With a little groveling we can fix this. And if we're smart about it, we can use the press to start buzz on the new album. But we need to do it now."

"I want a new label."

"You are out of your goddamned mind! It doesn't get better than Gyroscope."

"I want to scrap what we've been working on. I've got something new." She had mostly blank paper, but whatever.

"What? That shit you were nattering on about at the meeting? We've already discussed that." His voice dipped to the soothing one that used to melt her panties and scramble her brains. "I need you to trust me. I built your career. I can repair it. But I can't rebuild it from the bottom. Attention spans are short and you're not getting any younger. You're not that sweet little teenaged bit of flesh any longer."

She flexed her swollen hand. She also wasn't a teenager blinded by EJ's power. Or the size of his dick. "No, I'm not. What I am is done with Gyroscope. Find. Me. Another. Label."

"You will fix this," he snarled. "You think you're something special, and I'm here to tell you that you're not. There are dozens of younger, hotter, more amenable girls in L.A. right now who can warble well enough to take your place. So get your head out of your arse!" The phone went dead in her ear.

She slammed it onto the counter. He wasn't listening. No one fucking listened to her. They just wanted her to shut up and do as she was told. Her hands shook as she pushed the pills in her mouth and swallowed them, nearly choking in the process. Fuck that. She knew what her career needed, and it wasn't Gyroscope. And even if it did, Rod still didn't deserve an apology.

She stayed in the bathroom until she no longer felt like breaking things. Back in the living room, she found Conor curled up on the couch, using his shoulder as a pillow on the armrest, the silence punctuated by an occasional tiny snore.

Cupcake lurched toward him and she grabbed her by the collar. "No! Sit," she hissed.

The rhythm of Conor's chest rose and fell in time to the music of the rain. She bit her lip. When he was awake, she barely looked at him, afraid of what she'd see in his eyes. Now she stared, memorizing everything new. The cheekbones. The mussed hair. The five o'clock shadow. He'd always been beautiful, no matter what he weighed, but now he was sharpened and polished like the edge of a knife.

Even weirder, he was a man now. A man with khaki pants and beard scruff. All these years she'd kept him perfectly preserved, flattened in the folds of her past; her lone scrap of faith. Proof that someone loved her. Seeing him all grown up hurt. That boy who cupped her face in his big hands and told her that he loved her was gone.

He was the best person she'd ever known. Though they both knew she didn't deserve it, he'd offered his home, his food, and his peace for her. She couldn't wake him. Snatching away his sleep for even a moment felt like a crime.

She carefully lifted his head and slid a pillow beneath. Unable to stop herself, the tips of her fingers brushed through his hair and lingered there. It closed in on her, all the things she'd walked away from. She wasn't there when he graduated from high school. Or college. Wasn't there when he decided on a career. She wasn't around to celebrate with him when he conquered his weight. There was a whole life that he'd lived without her. She'd never know all the moments that made him laugh that bobbing Adam's apple laugh, and she wasn't there for those times when he'd needed someone to talk to.

What would her life be like, if she'd stayed, spilling secrets like droplets of watermelon liquor? What if she told him that her father threw her out, choosing a house full of garbage over his daughter? What if Conor hadn't said—

She yanked her hand away. That was not a road she wanted to go down. She made her choices.

Shoving her hair behind her ears, she grabbed the soft blanket, covering him up, and switched off the light, leaving the room dark except for the dim glow of the street lamps outside. Climbing into the chair, she stretched her legs out and rested them on the ottoman.

Cupcake padded to him and put her paws on the couch, whining. "Leave him be. Come here," she whispered, patting the space beside her. The beast ran and threw herself into the chair, squishing Adelia against the arm. "Oof." They tussled for chair supremacy. It ended with Cupcake stretched over her lap like an eighty-pound afghan.

She sighed and ran her hands over the dog's short, slick fur. "What do you think I should do, dog?" Cupcake lifted her head, yawned, and was back to snoring in seconds.

"Good plan." She shut her eyes and let the shush of the rain take care of her problems. For now.

11

CONOR STRETCHED out his stiff neck and groaned. He reached for his pillow, but it was rough and unfamiliar to the touch. He pried his eyes open. *Couch?* Across the room, Adelia slept curled in his chair, snoring along with Cupcake draped over her lap.

His brain was still foggy. Yawning, he ran his thumbs over the fluffy blanket that covered him. She must have put it there. She looked so soft in her sleep, it was easy to forget that despite what happened between them, she wasn't the steel-clad bitch she wanted people to believe she was.

As quick as the thought warmed him, he went cold. Strike that. She was exactly that. She'd demolished him and still didn't have the decency to let him off the rusty hook and tell him why.

Cupcake yawned and raised her head. She gave a woof and leapt off Adelia, launching herself straight at him, butt wagging.

Adelia's eyes shot open. "What? What's happening?"

The dog paused her effusive affection and ran back to her, barking. She shoved the dog away. "Ugh. Wake me at noon." She flopped back into the chair and closed her eyes again.

Noon? His brain finally emerged from the fog of sleep. "Shit, what time is it?" He grabbed his cell from the coffee table. 8 a.m. *Shitfuckdamnitalltohell.*

She opened one eye. "What's wrong?"

"I was supposed to be to work a half-hour ago!" Dread— walking into gym class dread— smothered him. He had to call his boss.

"Are you injured?" Keith barked, skipping all niceties.

"No, but I—"

"Amnesia?"

"No, sir."

"Then I cannot wait to hear your excuse for why The Pérezes were standing outside of a locked building in the rain."

"I—"

"I used to be able to count on you, but you've been phoning it in for months, and now this." The familiar clack of Keith's pen hitting the desk punctuated his words. "You're a salesman, not an artist. I hired you because ladies love you and when you put on a tight shirt and smile, you can sell water to a drowning man. But your sales numbers are dropping like boulders and to be honest, you're not talented enough to sneak by on your photography skills alone."

Anger bubbled over the humiliation. "You know wh—"

"I expect you here in the next half hour." The phone snicked in his ear.

"Shit." He rubbed at the heat on his cheeks and ran to his room. He threw on the first thing he grabbed in his closet and brushed his teeth while combing his hair. He'd never been late in his life. He splashed water on his face and rushed for the door.

Adelia stood blocking his way. "He's wrong," she said, her voice flat.

He stared at her for a moment, his brain not catching up. "What?"

"Your boss," she said slowly. "He's wrong."

Keith was so loud on the phone, it wasn't a surprise that she heard the call. "Thanks, but I've got to—"

Her dark eyes narrowed. "I don't know who that guy is, but he's stupid if he doesn't see how valuable you are."

"It's all right. I'm used to it."

"That doesn't make it better. He shouldn't talk to you like that."

"No, he probably shouldn't. But complaining about it won't get me to work any faster."

Her tight, pinched expression didn't disappear. Instead, she stood aside, and shoved an old grocery bag at him. "Here."

The seconds were ticking away. "Thanks." He took it and raced out the door. "See you later."

It wasn't until he was in the truck, halfway to work, that he realized he probably wouldn't.

CONOR MADE it to work just under the wire. When he arrived, Keith was taking horrible pictures of a family dressed like train conductors. Andrew gave him a tired smile. "He's on a rampage, man."

"He's pissed at me. I'm sorry if he took it out on you."

Keith peered out from the studio and gave him a glare. "Will you help the Dubose family with their package options?"

Conor gave Andrew a pat on the shoulder and sat down at the computer. Afterward, Keith punished him by filling every second that wasn't in the studio with a pointless task. When lunch came around, he'd already finished purging the old sweaty costumes from the racks, and was now sorting all the old paper filings stacked in the back office. A job that would take the rest of the afternoon. A perfect end to a perfect Monday.

With a throbbing head and a growling stomach, he reached

for his wallet. Maybe Andrew could run over to Keys and get him some trail mix or something.

No wallet. Son of a bitch. It was sitting at home on his nightstand.

He hated to ask it, but Shan could probably comp him a meal and he could pay her back later. Grumbling, he reached for his phone and noticed the plastic bag Adelia had shoved at him. He shook out the contents. An apple. Powerbars. Yogurt and a spoon.

The stagnant room felt smaller than it had before.

The old casement window took some force to crank it open enough to let fresh air roll in, but when it did, he gulped at it. Her outrage over Keith's behavior made sense. She always had a streak of cold justice in her, never suffering bullies lightly, especially when it came to him. Apparently, that hadn't changed.

Every morning after she moved to town at age seven, she'd stalk to the back of the bus and sit with the high schoolers. And every day, he cowered behind the bus driver, marveling at her guts. He'd wanted to talk to her, but he'd been bullied to the point of muteness and barely spoke to anyone. One day, the Malinski brothers dragged him off the bus for a beating. The hiss of the doors told him no one was coming to help,

But they hissed again and Adelia barreled off in a blur of ragged clothing and fury. Punching, kicking, and cursing at his attackers, using words he'd never heard. As they scrambled to escape her wrath, she'd stood over him like a warrior queen claiming territory. "Touch him again and I'll beat you some more!"

The shock of the violence untied his usually knotted tongue. "How—how did you do that?"

"I'm from Flint," she'd said with a shrug.

The next morning, she'd walked him onto the bus. With a surly glare at the bruised and sullen Malinski brothers, she crammed into the seat beside him, making it clear that he belonged to her. And he had.

When it felt like he could breathe again, he shut the office door, blunting the sound of Keith stomping around, and flicked on some music. Rolling his shirt sleeves, he reached for the yogurt and sat it back down, choosing the apple instead.

He stroked the smooth, mottled red skin. Did this mean she still cared? Did it matter if she did?

His teeth broke the crisp flesh and juice dribbled down his chin.

It was sweeter than it had any right to be.

———

THE SUN WAS SETTING behind the rain when he got home from work. Adelia was still there. Frantically scribbling in a notebook, her guitar on the couch beside her.

"Hey."

She jerked in surprise. "Hey." She blinked as if coming out of a trance and grabbed her phone. "8:30? Seriously?"

"Yeah. You okay?"

"I had some song ideas and I started writing and lost track of..." She shook her head. "I wrote all day. I haven't done that in years."

"Sounds like you had a better day than I did." He grabbed the leash from the closet. "I'll let you get back to it. I'm going to take Cupcake out."

He didn't feel like running, so it was a short walk. The dog seemed as over the rain as he felt and rushed to get back into the house, groaning in misery when he slowed her down to clean the mud off before opening the door. She rushed to the couch, which was now unoccupied, and spun around confused.

Adelia was in his kitchen with her hands on her hips, eyebrows scrunched together. "Where's your food?" she asked.

He took off his coat. "The fridge is full of food, Winters."

A rosy pink crept along her cheekbones. "I mean like quick meals. Frozen. I was going to make you something."

He tried to squash the warmth he felt. "I don't eat frozen meals. Those things are loaded with salt and there's nothing in them but spongy meat and regret."

"Like my twenties," she said.

He laughed and ignored the smoke curl of jealousy inside him. Of course she'd been with other people. He'd had a couple of drunken hookups with the lights off in college. It wasn't like he'd been a monk.

Throwing open the fridge door, he removed a dish of marinated chicken. "I'll cook this chicken if you'll make the salad."

She bit her lip. "I don't um, cook."

"It's a salad."

The pink in her cheeks deepened. "I don't want to mess up your routine or whatever." She wrapped her arms around her middle.

He grabbed the salad fixings and sat them on the counter. "You've never made a salad in your life, have you?"

Her face pinched up. It was kind of adorable, not that he'd tell her that.

"Come on, grab a knife." He pulled out the cutting board. "We need cherry tomatoes and diced onions."

She stared at the knife. "I'm probably going to lose a finger."

He rolled a cherry tomato onto the board and with a smooth easy motion, sliced it in two. "Cut them like that and try not to hold anything with your middle finger. You don't want to cut off the one you use the most."

"Ha."

He went to work on the chicken and pineapple slices. It only took a few minutes in the broiler, since the chicken was already marinated and boiled. He pulled them out and sat the pan on a trivet. "How're you doing over there?"

She hunched over the cutting board, her face tight with concentration, as she pressed too hard on a tomato and squashed it before the knife could get through the skin. A pile of similarly mangled tomatoes and jagged onion chunks were shoved to the side of the board. "I think I'm more of a pizza delivery kind of woman."

"You're doing fine." He was already in motion before he could stop himself, grabbing the crushed remains of a cherry tomato and slipping it between her lush lips, his fingers lingering for a moment. Her face burned as red as his felt, and he cleared his throat, popping another one into his own mouth. "Great thing about fresh vegetables is that it's really hard to screw them up," he said hoarsely.

He scooped the veggies onto a mound of wilted greens, diced chicken, and pineapple, and sat a plate in front of her. In silence, she made short work of the meal and licked the back of her fork. "This is so good."

"Praise the hot sauce and lime juice. They did the hard work." He cut the pineapple with the edge of his fork and speared a chunk.

She dipped the last bit of chicken in the vinaigrette. "I didn't know rabbit food could taste good."

"Sometimes it doesn't. You happened to come here while I'm experimenting with flavor. You can only eat boiled chicken and quinoa for so long before you start to go nuts."

"Weird that it doesn't work in reverse. Like, there is literally no limit to the amount of Doritos I can eat."

"They engineer them that way," he said. "I read a fascinating article on the science they use to make junk food. It's a rigged game."

She pointed her fork at him. "Do not ruin Doritos for me. I've killed men for less."

"I said nothing." He put his hands in the air. "Your Doritos remain exalted. And terrible for you."

After dinner, he set to work on the dishes. She stared down at the cutting board for a long moment, before sliding it into the sink. "Can I ask you something?"

"Go for it," he said.

"All this stuff. The running and the rabbit food and the no Doritos." She looked up at him. "Are you happy?"

He stopped scraping the broiler tray. No one had ever asked that. They congratulated him. They offered unhelpful advice. But they never asked if any of it made him happy. He'd never really stopped to ask himself that either. To buy some time, he finished scrubbing the tray and then rinsed it off.

"I'm a Ross. We're not supposed to be happy. We're supposed to be perfect," he said finally. "Anyway, weight loss isn't magic."

"So why do it?" The question was straightforward. No judgment in it, no sarcasm.

"I run because I love it. Everything else…I guess I don't want to go back to feeling like food owns me." He laughed and scratched at the back of his neck. "How about you? You happy?"

She blinked at him, looking shocked that he'd lobbed the question back to her. After a few seconds, she shrugged.

No surprise. That was her answer for everything.

"I'll help dry," she said, parking herself beside him. And she did. At a rate of one dish per hour. Or at least it felt that way as she methodically dried and re-dried the same plate.

It was strangely intimate, standing hip to hip, her rough fingers brushing his as she took the silverware. He was relieved when she dropped the damp towel in a heap on the counter. "Cool. I helped."

He waited until she left the kitchen to wring out the towel and hang it to dry. Then he cleaned and disinfected the counters, the table, and the stove top, and swept the floor. Feeling a little more in control of his life, he headed to the living room.

Cupcake padded over to the couch and put her head on Adelia's knees. She sighed and patted the top of the dog's head with the ends of her fingers. Her teeth scraped over her bottom lip. "I—I should have woken you up last night," she said.

"No, I should have gone to bed and set my alarm like an adult. It was my own fault."

"Your boss is a prick," she said, her eyes darkening.

"That he is," he said. "Thank you for packing me some food."

She looked at the wall. "No problem."

Her phone buzzed and she grabbed it. "Hey. Is it—what?— You are out of your mind. I don't want that kind of work. Just get it road-ready." She stood and paced in front of his coffee table.

His stomach dropped.

"Are you a mechanic or not...yes, I know it's an old car, but you—fine. How long before you can get the parts?" She wrapped an arm around herself. "Four to five days?" Her mouth curved into silent curse words. "Look I'll pay whatever if you can overnight the parts. Uh-huh. Wait, what does your cousin have to do with any—" She opened her mouth and gave a silent scream into the phone. "So when will he be able to get here?— Tell him I'll pay triple if he can get here in the next couple days...That's fine. Thanks."

Hell. There was no way he could have her there for two or three more days, let alone five.

"Don't worry," she said, staring at him over the thumbnail she was now chewing. "I'll find someplace else to go."

There wasn't a thing he could say. His body was cold then hot then cold again. Like the flu.

She broke the silence, making hotel call after hotel call, her pacing turning into a march and then a sprint as she asked over and over if they took cash.

She stabbed the end-call button, hissing at the phone as she tossed it onto the coffee table and scrubbed her hands over her face, snarling into them.

"What'd Paulie say?"

"Apparently, the drive shaft is the least of my problems. The transmission is failing, the brakes are shot, and my rear drums fell off when he raised the car up. No matter where I send it, I've got to wait for parts to be special ordered. But even if they get here early, he called around and found that no one knows how to work on a car that old."

"Except for his cousin?"

She nodded. "He's coming in from Hope Falls in a few days. Sooner if he likes money."

"Christ."

"Yup." She closed her eyes and took slow breaths. "Fuck it," she said. Her face was hard and drawn. "Can you drive me to Port Agnes? Fuck the car, Paulie can have it." She didn't wait for an answer. Before he could think, she was folding the bedding on the couch into sloppy squares. She grabbed the notebook she'd been scribbling in and her guitar case and sat them by the front door. "I swear I'll pay you back for everything."

"Why are you here, Adelia?"

She stopped moving. "What?"

"You're here for a reason. What's the reason?"

"I—" A lock of dark hair brushed her cheek and she swatted it away. "My dad kicked the bucket, remember?"

"I remember. But you could have flown out here, gotten a rental car in Port Agnes, and driven out here and been back home by yesterday. But you didn't."

She raised her still-bruised fist. "I need to get away from the press. And my manager. He can and will check my credit card charges, so that's out unless I want him showing up to drag me back to California. Airbnbs and rental car companies want credit cards and ID. The Dive took cash."

"I don't buy it. What else?"

She went back to chewing on her thumbnail and looked at the wall. "Look, I just...I need a few days. To get my shit together. I fucked up and I have to figure out what to do."

That was probably true, but there was more to it. He could see it in the tension in her jaw and her clenched hands. Shannon was right. She was a lost cause. The smartest thing to do was to drive her to the airport. He grabbed his keys. Once she was gone, life would get back to normal.

He put his hand on the doorknob and thought about that apple, round and beautiful in his hand. The sweetness of it. The way it reminded him of all the things that were good about her. She was most definitely a lost cause, but the girl he knew was still in there and that counted for something, didn't it?

He turned and hung his keys back up. "You can stay here. Until your car is done."

She twisted the sleeve of his baggy sweatshirt. "No. No. You don't have to do that."

"I know I don't." He closed his eyes tight for a moment. "But we're already past the point of maximum discomfort. It can't get weirder. So just…stay. Until your car is done."

She stared at him for a moment. It was amazing how many mysteries could live in one person's eyes. She looked away and stared at the wall. "Shit can get so much weirder."

He carried her guitar case back to the side of the couch. "Well, what's life without a little weirdness?"

THE NEXT MORNING, Conor poured himself a cup of black coffee and flipped open the book on business loans he'd been meaning to read. The upside to his job—the only one—was that he worked a four-day week, Friday through Monday. Knowing that he didn't have to step into Razzle Dazzle for three glorious days, he woke up feeling relief so profound he'd checked the sheets to make sure he hadn't had one of *those* dreams.

Across the room, Cupcake flopped on top of a still-sleeping Adelia.

She shoved at the dog. "No! I don't like you. Go away."

He set his book aside and grabbed Cupcake by the collar, gently pulling her off the couch. He scratched her head. "Come on, baby. Adelia is crabby."

"I'm crabby because I spent half the night wrestling that beast off of me."

Cupcake looked at him with tragic brown eyes.

"Be nice to my dog, Winters. Or I'll feed her your breakfast and you'll be eating kibble."

Adelia sat up and half-heartedly patted the dog on her broad noggin. Cupcake groaned, mollified.

"Thank you." He pointed to the plastic bag on the table. "I went to the store after my run and got you a few things."

She reached inside the bag and raised an eyebrow. "I was fine using soap."

"I know. But you're going to be here for a few days and I wanted you to be comfortable."

Flipping the cap of the body wash, she breathed in and sighed contentedly. "Strawberries. I love the smell of strawberries."

"I know you're probably used to more expensive stuff, but—"

"No this is awesome. It smells like that perfume from Cherry Moon."

"It does." As soon as he'd smelled it in the store, he'd been transported back to Adelia's fourteenth birthday. He'd been so nervous about the gift, unsure if she'd think it was too girly. But she'd opened it with careful fingers, and when she pulled out the strawberry shaped glass bottle, her serious expression broke into a smile so beautiful it had nearly stopped his heart.

She sat the body wash aside and dug through the bag. "Shampoo, conditioner, brush…" She pulled out a box and barked a laugh. "Seriously?"

His face warmed but he refused to be childish about it. "What? Women get periods. I tried to think ahead."

She sat the multipack of tampons aside. "You're right. I just wasn't expecting that. This is really thoughtful—" The bag rustled as she pulled out a razor and shaving cream pack. "Do you expect me to shave my legs?"

"Again, I winged it. Your hair, or lack thereof, is your business."

"Damn straight it is," she said as she put everything back in the bag. "You wouldn't shave your legs, would you?"

"If I were trying to get laid and thought that would work I probably would. Men really aren't that complicated, Winters."

She rolled her eyes and headed for the bathroom. "I'm gonna go comb my leg hair."

"Whatever you want. Just don't use my comb."

The shower started a moment later and he tried to go back to his book and the chapter on sales projections, but he couldn't concentrate. He'd finally finished the chapter when the scent of strawberries pulled him from boring stats. He peered over the top of his book as Adelia sauntered into the living room.

"Sorry, but those pants were driving me nuts. Too big." Enveloped in another of his oversized sweatshirts, her bare legs peeked out from beneath it as she tossed herself onto the couch. He dragged his gaze from her legs and gripped his book tight, squashing the pages. Her wet hair was pulled into a braid and droplets of water trailed lazily down the long length of her neck. Her teeth scraped along her bottom lip as she read something on her phone.

Like a match in a drafty room, a spark of heat flashed and dissipated inside of him.

Even though they were across the room from each other, the space felt too small. "I'm gonna try to get some work done," he said. "Breakfast is on the stove."

He retreated to the office and shut the door, breathing deeply. The smell of strawberries lingered in the air.

Needing to burn away his discomfiting awareness, he bypassed his beefy computer setup for post-processing photographs and went straight to his home gym.

He did warm-ups and then dumbbell rows, bench presses and leg curls. Reverse crunches. Decline pushups. He worked himself to the point of exhaustion and muscle ache, but it didn't matter. An hour. Two hours. No amount of time was enough to release the hold Adelia had on his mind.

From the living room, a sweet and melancholy tune flowed from the strings of her guitar. She hummed along softly, stopping every now and again to switch keys or backtrack. The

sultry rasp of her voice, at turns delicate and powerful, filled
him with longing to know something—anything—about her.

He toweled off, wiped down the bench and weights, and
then typed her stage name into his computer. It didn't take long
to realize that much like in real life, she was taciturn and impossible to question. After pages of nothing, the only thing he
learned was that she lied and said she grew up in Flint,
Michigan. And that she was rumored to be dating a lot of guys
—and a few girls—and not one rumor was ever confirmed.

And that she really liked taco trucks.

Even fame couldn't pry her secrets from her. Frustration
sizzled inside of him. How the hell did she become Lia Frost?
Sure, she'd always had a great singing voice, belting metal songs
in the woods, but whenever he told her that she should become
a professional singer, she'd roll her eyes and change the subject.
So how did she end up in California, writing songs and playing
guitar? It wasn't a shock that he didn't fully know the woman
sleeping on his couch, but it hurt so much more to realize how
little he knew about the girl who'd been his best friend.

He put in his earbuds and watched concert footage. Her
voice was spectacularly soulful but easily slid into growls that
sent chills through him. She bounded from one end of the stage
to the other, animated in a way he'd never seen or imagined.
She worked the crowd like a second guitar, her serious expression giving way to dazzling smiles. He clicked on another video.
An unplugged session where she played a piano—a piano?—and
sang smoky, soaring vocals, pressing emotion into a word like
regret with a weariness that twisted his guts.

He ran a hand through his hair, wrestling with emotions he
hadn't let himself feel for a long time. Longing. Awe. Confusion.

A knock at the door jarred him.

He clicked off the video and pulled out his earbuds. "Come
in," he said, his voice gruff.

"Sorry to bother you, but I can't figure out your remote

controls," Adelia said. "You've got like three of them and I don't know what the hell I'm doing. I think I might have released a nuclear warhead."

It took him an uncomfortably long time to make words while she looked at him with those sleepy brown eyes that gave away nothing. "I'll be out in a second."

She hesitated. "You okay?"

"Can I ask you something?"

It was fascinating to watch her fold up like a lawn chair. Her body went rigid and she crossed her arms, gripping her elbows.

"How'd you learn to play the piano?"

She glanced at the computer and back at him. "That's… random," she said, dragging out each syllable.

"Just curious."

She squeezed her elbows so tight he feared it would leave bruises. After what felt like a millennium, she looked away and shrugged.

He should have known.

"You know what? Never mind." Disgusted with her and disgusted with himself, he brushed past her.

"Conor." She followed him. "I—"

He shook his head and threw open the front door, letting the damp chill of the air carry away the hurt that lingered beneath his anger. "Keep your damn secrets," he said. "It's not like it matters."

ADELIA STARED at the closed door, twisting the end of her braid. What the hell was wrong with her? Why couldn't she open her mouth and say things like other people? Why did she stockpile all the broken pieces of her life and lock the door behind them? What did it get her?

This. It got her this.

Not sure what she was doing, she grabbed hold of the door-knob and pushed past the screen door. It still sounded like monsoon season as the rain beat on the roof of the covered porch. He had his back to her, playing with the edge of the outdoor blinds that helped keep the space dry and private.

He turned and his mouth tightened as she walked toward him, his eyes shadowed with frustration. She didn't blame him. EJ once said getting her to talk was like wrestling a porcupine.

She ran her hand along the other side of the blind he was holding, and rain droplets splashed like balls of lead on her fingers. Looking at him felt overwhelming so she focused on the water as it drizzled down her hand and soaked the cuff of her sweatshirt.

"My mom played the piano."

He didn't say anything. It wasn't enough. She owed him some honesty. "She was a prodigy or something and she went to a fancy music academy but I don't remember the name." Droplets of rain made their way under the cuff of the shirt, trickling along her arm and making her shiver. "She played for the church we used to go to when I was a kid. St. Michaels. Even though it was the sin of pride, she always had to open the weekly program and find her name."

Lightning lit the dark edges of the porch. "What did she like to play?" he asked.

She took a breath. The grey shadows of her memories felt delicate. Breakable. She turned them over gently before speaking. "Everything. She liked Catholic music. 'Ave Maria.' 'Gloria.' She loved acoustic pop and folk, and she liked musicals, too. *Candide. Jesus Christ Superstar. My Fair Lady.* You name it." She plucked at the damp edges of her sleeves. "She also taught music lessons at the YMCA. I was playing as soon as I could sit upright."

"You've never talked about your mom."

"I…" She rolled her eyes toward the roof. "It makes me feel

sad. I don't like to think too hard about it because then I get all... I don't know."

"All what?" His steely expression was gone, replaced by soft meadow green, and she wished she deserved his concern.

Why was this so hard? She could sing to stadiums of people about her feelings but talking about them face to face made her want to crawl into a hole. "I—I start wondering what my life would have been like if that drunk driver had stayed home. If my mom hadn't gone out for cigarettes. If my dad hadn't..." No. She reigned in the words ready to spill off her tongue. Angry words. Pathetic words. She wrapped her arms around herself. "Basically, if I talk about it, I get all whiny because I didn't get the life that I should have had." She shook her head. "It makes me feel gross and... ungrateful. Because my life ended up taking me somewhere pretty good and a lot of kids like me, they didn't get that."

It was such a meager thing for her to share but he looked at her like she'd given him something important. An uncomfortable pressure built behind her eyes and she had the crazy desire to curl against his chest, wrapping her arms around him and holding on. Instead she twisted the end of her sleeve, working it into tighter and tighter spirals until it pinched her skin.

"Thank you for telling me." He pulled the sleeve from her fingers, and smoothed the fabric out, running his hand over it and brushed her skin with his. She closed her eyes, wanting him to keep touching her. Needing his warmth to seep into all of her coldness.

Needing him.

She crossed her arms over her chest. She didn't need him, she reminded herself.

She didn't need anyone.

13

"How can you hate movies with chainsaw killers?" Adelia shifted beside Conor on the couch.

"Because I don't enjoy watching people get diced in two." He changed the channel. "No chainsaw killers. No zombies. Nothing with power tools unless they're being used appropriately."

Since coming in from the porch, they'd spent hours battling over the TV. Once the weekday game shows and dramatized court programs ended, they'd started and stopped a half dozen movies, and he was ready to give up.

"You never used to be this squeamish. You were the one who made me watch *The Birds*." She shuddered. "I had nightmares for weeks. So much pecking."

"I forgot that you're scared of birds."

She gave him a serious blink. "Birds are freaky and they have dead, beady eyes."

"You need therapy." He flipped the channel again. "Here. *Stardust* is on. That's a good movie. It's action-y. And there are plenty of surprisingly gruesome deaths."

She groaned. "It's a fairytale. I hate fairytales."

"It's fantasy. And who hates fairytales?"

"They always have stupid perfect happy endings. I hate that."

"Why?"

"Because they don't exist. Same reason you don't like horror movies. I roll my eyes the whole time."

"You're a cynical woman."

She nodded and leaned out of the armchair, snatching the remote from his hand and changing the channel. "Ooooh, let's watch this." She pointed at the screen where two men were strumming banjos and happily singing about hanging a lady.

"What the hell is this?"

"It's *Cat Ballou*. That's Nat 'King' Cole. You've never seen this? There isn't a single chainsaw death, I promise."

"Are you seriously trying to make me watch a musical...western?"

"It's really good."

An hour and a half later, she was singing along with the closing lines of the movie.

"You are so full of shit," he said. "That movie had a seriously happy ending. Also, that whole thing was about people who think they're cynical but they really aren't."

"No," she said. "The story is that the only way to survive in a crappy world is harden the fuck up."

"Yeah, okay. Harden up, face your bullshit, and then still get a happy ending. You're not nearly as cynical as you think you are. You *like* happy endings, as long as everyone is extra miserable before they get them."

"Oh, shut up." She tossed a throw pillow at him. He caught it and tossed it back.

Something had changed between them. He'd spent nine years of his childhood with Adelia by his side. He knew a lot about her. She ate almost anything you put in front of her except asparagus. She said *warshcloth* and *melk* instead of *wash-cloth* and *milk*. Her favorite color was purple and she thought Metallica was a better band than the Beatles.

He would bet a million dollars that none of that stuff had changed. But when she'd stood there baring that tiny piece of herself and mangling his sweatshirt, he felt like he'd never met her until today.

She biffed him upside the head with the pillow and Cupcake, wanting in on the fun, crouched down, her butt in the air, stump of a tail wagging, and barked at Adelia. No response. So she crawled across the floor and groaned. Nothing. Refusing to be ignored, she trotted halfway out of the room before turning and barreling straight at her.

She squealed as the dog took her down to the seat of the couch, furiously licking her ears.

"Noooo," she shrieked, legs flailing. "I'm not ready for a relationship!"

He pulled the snorting dog off of her. "Sorry, Cupcake. She doesn't appreciate your love."

"Gah." She rubbed her neck with the sleeve of her sweater. "Gaaaaah."

"Oh, don't be a baby."

She gave him the stink-eye and reached for her glass of ice water, chugging half of it, and sat it on his coffee table.

"Please use the coaster," he said.

Her fingers stroked the rough edge of the slate coaster but she made no move to put the glass on it.

"You're going to leave a ring on the table."

"You turned into your mother," she said.

He put his hands on the table and leaned close to her. "You will take that back."

"I can't do that, *Maureen*."

"I'm three seconds from dumping that ice water on your head." She gave him a dubious look, so he picked up her glass and stood over her. "Take it back, Winters." She shook her head no, so he tilted the glass further.

Cold water splashed on her nose and she gave a shriek. "Gah, fine! Sorry. You aren't *exactly* like Maureen."

He slid the cup back into her hand and rested his hands on the table, leaning toward her. "Now. Use. The. Damn. Coaster."

She bent closer and without taking her eyes from his she sat the cup on it with a clank. "You do love to order a woman around," she said, her voice huskier than it had been.

He smirked. "Oh, you have no idea."

The easy flirtation he'd honed over the years poured off his tongue like sugar water, but a stinging heat crept up his neck. They had way too much baggage to ever...

Her eyes narrowed and heat flashed in her gaze, a glint of sunlight on water, and he lost the thought. Her lips parted and her tongue skirted along the inner edge of her lush mouth, exactly where he suddenly wanted to be.

Her stillness had a crackling energy to it and her head tilted ever so slightly upward—

A bang at the door startled them both and he shoved himself away from the table.

"A little help?" Shannon backed into the room carrying a Crock-Pot. He shot up to grab it out of her hands and she spun with a smile that dropped off her face when she saw Adelia sitting there. "Oh! Uh. I didn't know you were still—" She turned to him with question marks in her eyes.

Adelia's impassive face somehow managed to become cooler. "It's a long story."

Shannon gave him *the look*. He'd seen it a hundred times. Her expression said she'd ferret out the details and then some. But as soon as it appeared, it was gone, vanished into the blandly cheerful smile she used on her diner customers. "Okay. Good thing I made enough food to feed the entire park."

He sat the Crock-Pot on the counter, his brain preoccupied with thoughts of Adelia's lips.

Jo clambered into the doorway carrying a stack of containers. She squealed with such shrillness it made his ears ring. Cupcake jumped like a whistle had gone off in her ear.

"Lia! You're still here!" She dropped the containers in her rush to get to her. They tumbled to the floor and the top one flopped onto its side, spilling cornbread onto the carpet. Cupcake shot across the room and snuffed up half the bread before anyone could stop her. He dove for the container and managed to save the rest.

Oblivious, Jo threw herself onto the couch and began blathering about songwriting. Adelia nodded along and grazed him with a look of helpless bemusement.

He sat the containers on the counter. "I'm sorry, Shan," he whispered. "I forgot about movie night."

"I mean, why would you remember? We've only done it every Tuesday at 8 p.m. for ten years," she whispered back. "We can go if you'd rather be alone. With Adelia. At your house. Without her pants on."

"It's not like that." It wasn't the whole truth, but he needed some time to digest what had almost happened. "Circumstances changed and she's going to stay for a few more days. I'm being a good Samaritan."

Shannon tore the lids off the containers, her motions smooth, but there was tension around her eyes and mouth. "That is the stupidest thing you've ever said."

"I know." He rubbed the back of his neck. "But it's just until her car is repaired." He plugged the Crock-Pot in and set it to *warm*. "What'd you make?"

"Chili. Something to warm us all up. Though you don't seem to be need—"

"Shan," he held up a hand. "Let it go, please."

She grumbled something and rifled through his silverware drawer.

Adelia shook her head at Jo and grabbed the pen and paper from the table. She wrote something and stabbed at it with the pen. Wisps of long hair that escaped her braid floated like feathers, skimming the nape of her neck as she spoke animatedly, and the pads of his fingers twitched as though he could feel the hair tickling them.

She glanced at him and looked away. He couldn't read her expression Was it embarrassment? Excitement? Whatever it was, it burned him more than the heat rushing in his veins.

Shannon coughed dramatically. Reluctant to pull his eyes from Adelia, he slowly swung his head toward her. "Yes?"

She handed him a bowl of steaming chili, her eyes narrowed. "Stupid. Stupid. Stupid."

"WE ARE NOT WATCHING *Super Troopers* again," Conor said.

Shannon pouted, looking more kewpie doll than woman. "You don't appreciate good cinema." She pulled at her curls. "We've watched all my movies."

"That's because you only own six of them."

"Well, sending Jo to college is more important than owning the deluxe edition of *The Princess Bride*."

Jo scooted closer to Adelia and glared at her mother. "I don't need to go to college. I'm gonna be a musician."

"You'll still need a college education to navigate the world of unwashed rock singers," Shannon said.

"Rock singers take baths like everyone else, Mom" Jo looked toward the resident expert on the subject. "Right?"

Adelia shrugged. "Sorry. The road to rock and roll is littered with smelly musicians."

"You know, I'm a child. I'm allowed to, like, live in ignorance."

A shadow moved through her expression. "Living in ignorance isn't a right. A lot of kids don't get that privilege."

She said it lightly but there was something grim in her words. What the hell happened to her? He'd never pressed it, but he'd known something was wrong at home. She'd always been too thin. Her clothes had been worn out and he knew she stole most of them from the second-hand store. When they were little kids, his mother would purse her lips while Adelia devoured whatever food was put in front of her, eating with her hands like a bony animal.

He always told himself that it was because she was poor, but he knew that couldn't be the whole truth. It was too late to speculate now. It was a miracle she'd shared anything at all with him and it was likely all she was capable of.

"So, I told him to take a shower and he said he couldn't because of the boa constrictor," Adelia said.

He'd lost the thread of the conversation.

Shannon hooted with laughter. "Was he serious?"

"Totally serious. He didn't shower the entire tour, just scrubbed his junk in the hotel sinks so the damn boa constrictor wouldn't be uncomfortable."

"I'm taking down all my Flowers from a Wound posters when I get home," Jo said. "And burning all my fanfic. I hope you're happy. Now I have nothing left."

Adelia didn't look the least bit sorry. "You'll always have...no, no you're right. You've got nothing."

Jo giggled and bit her lip. "Did you and Tristan date?"

She hesitated. "Sort of." He nearly choked. For once he *could* read her expression and it screamed that she was done answering questions.

"Winters, care to help me clean up?"

"Sure thing, boss." She gathered all the bowls from the table and piled them in the sink in front of him. "Thank you," she said softly.

"You're welcome. It's not easy to explain fuck-buddies to a thirteen-year-old."

He followed her gaze as it flicked toward Shannon. "I imagine not."

He let that go. He'd long ago given up trying to convince people that he and Shannon were not a thing. Years ago, before he left for college, there was a humid summer night where too much beer and loneliness collided, and they'd kissed. They gave it a good try, turning their heads this way and that, trying to find some fire, some spark of heat, and finally gave up, both gulping beer to erase the taste. That kiss was an awkward promise that they'd never be more than friends, which suited them both fine.

"Conor, I'm freezing, can I turn up the heat?" Shannon wrapped his throw around her shoulders and looked pathetic.

"It's perfectly comfortable in here," he said. "But go ahead, you big whiner. Let's all suffer so Queen Shan won't have cold toes."

"I have poor circulation!"

"You're too cheap to run your heat at your place so you come over here and jack up my bill. I'm onto you."

"It's boiling in here," Adelia said as they made their way to the living room.

"The price we pay for getting a home-cooked meal from Shannon is we have to bake like overcooked pot roast," he said. "You get used to it."

After a few minutes, Shannon stretched out in the chair, groaning happily at the warmth.

Jo slipped her hoodie off and smoothed her Spoon Monkeys shirt. "Mom, it's too hot."

"Go home and change into shorts, then."

"You know," Jo said. "I'd probably be more comfortable if I were wearing a belly shirt. And since my birthday is coming up—"

"No. No belly shirts, Josephine."

Jo stamped her foot. "Mom, everyone is wearing them. I'll look like a total freak if I don't have one. Like people will think there's something wrong with my stomach."

"No one needs to see your belly button yet. Save that for marriage."

"You're crazy," Jo grumbled as she slid her hoodie back on. "Don't start the movie without me."

As soon as the door shut, Shannon sat upright. "We need to talk about Jo's birthday." She passed her phone to Adelia who passed it to him.

He studied the document on the Brightwell High app and grinned. "All As?"

"Unless she chokes on the final exams, she's acing every class." She beamed. "Even though she's grounded, I promised the little snot a birthday bash if she did better than last semester and she did."

"She's been working hard, she deserves a party."

"She does. But it's going to be expensive. She'd never say it, but she doesn't want some rinky-dink little homemade snacks affair. Most of her friends are lakesiders these days. They have money. She's been talking a lot about DeeDee Higgins's birthday party. All the girls got gift bags and *manicures*." Her nose crinkled up. "How the hell am I supposed to keep up with that? I can't afford to get her the new shoes she wants, let alone get a professional manicurist and a catered dinner."

"You know Jo doesn't care about that stuff."

"I think maybe she does."

Adelia's long, bare legs were right in front of him before she headed to the kitchen and returned with a glass of water. They looked so soft. Everything about her looked soft.

"What do you think?" Shannon asked.

"That could work," he said, without a clue of what she'd said.

The door slammed against the wall, jolting everyone. Jo barreled inside. "You guys done talking about my birthday?" She dropped to the floor in a smiling heap. "I know why you sent me home."

"You know no such thing."

"You're not slick, Mom."

Jo pushed her hair off her shoulders and tossed a bulging duffel bag at Adelia. "You said all your clothes drowned in the flood. So, I brought you some stuff."

She gave Jo a smile. "Thanks."

Jo's calculating eyes twinkled. "My birthday's in two weeks. I dunno how long you're staying but if you're still here you should totally come. Mom makes the best fudge cupcakes with cherry chip frosting. You don't have to come as Lia. You could like, be my aunt no one's ever met. You can wear sunglasses and a hat and I'll tell people you're a spy."

Adelia's expression hovering somewhere between terror and amusement. "I don't think I'll still be here, kid."

"Oh." Jo deflated, slumping against her mother's chair. "That's okay."

Shannon brushed Jo's hair behind her ears. "It's all right, baby. We can find another grumpy, washed-up celebrity to go to your party."

Adelia snorted. "If you don't mind boa constrictors, I can make a call."

As the easy tide of the conversation flowed around him, Conor went to the kitchen. In the bottom drawer of his refrigerator, he pulled out his treat bag for movie night. He unscrewed the cap and handed Jo a glass bottle of pop and sat the four-pack of light beer on the table for everyone else.

Shannon took a long drink from hers. "You missed it. Adelia picked the movie."

He groaned. "We're watching *Super Troopers,* aren't we?"

"Yup," Shannon said. "You were outvoted." She dimmed the lights.

"Go ahead and start without me." Adelia said, tugging at his sweatshirt. "I'm going to go change. It's hot as ball—" She backtracked. "Er, hell. Heck. In here."

The movie began and he took a swig of beer. The opening credits screeched to a close, and in the silence, the floor creaked.

Adelia bent to push Cupcake out of her spot and his entire body tightened. The enveloping sweatshirt was gone, replaced by a thin tank top with an angry skull nestled between the high curves of her braless breasts. The shirt left an expanse of soft, inviting skin between the hem and the matching pajama pants. All that would be enough to heat him up, but it didn't compete with the black lace tattoo that curved over her left shoulder and down her arm. It was a delicate filigree of netting, flowers and henna paisley that whorled to a dizzying stop at the junction between her thumb and forefinger.

It was indecent.

It was lingerie on flesh.

It was the sexiest thing he'd ever seen.

He couldn't take his eyes off it as she nestled into the couch. Tattoos weren't that uncommon anymore. He'd seen a few women with ink he'd classify as cute. But this wasn't cute. He'd never seen anything so intricate or so beautiful. He wanted to take pictures of it. To know the story of it. He wanted to trace the pattern with his fingers and feel...

"Want some beer?" The words croaked out of him.

She nodded and he sat the bottle on a coaster and slid it toward her. She took it, the soft scrape of her calloused fingers brushing against his, sparking like electricity against his skin.

She took a drink and grimaced. "Gah. Light beer?" Her

tongue darted out and brushed along the edge of her lip. "It's like being punished for having taste buds."

He stared at her mouth, transfixed by the soft, wide expanse.

"Shh, some of us are trying to watch the movie." Shannon said. "Close your eyes, Josephine. This scene is too dirty for you to be watching."

"It's only sex, Mom."

"Yes. Sex you don't need to see."

"You realize the internet exists, right? And it's pretty much cat videos and sex?"

He wished everyone would stop saying sex. He tried to concentrate on the movie, but Adelia stretched her neck and the troopers ceased to exist.

That tattoo went over her shoulder and disappeared beneath her tank top. He closed his eyes. He was *not* imagining what the rest of it looked like. He certainly wasn't thinking about how she'd look stretched out on his bed in only her decorated skin.

He opened them and found her staring at him, her brow furrowed. "You okay?" she whispered.

"No. Yeah. Your tattoo. I— I didn't see it until now."

"Isn't it cool? Got it a couple months ago." She stroked her fingers over her forearm and gave him a small smile and turned back to the movie.

Her laugh drew his eyes back to her over and over. For the first time, her shoulders were relaxed and loose and here he was, tense as hell and ogling her like a horny eighth grader.

Pull it together. The lust he was feeling wasn't real. Wanting her was just a habit he never broke.

He sat his now empty beer bottle on the end table as the lust pickling his brain drained away. He'd been here before, and it had ended in devastation. She thundered into everything like a hurricane and all she left behind was destruction. He couldn't go through that again. The beer sat like sludge in his gut. Soon enough she'd be leaving Cherry Lake, but this time, she wasn't taking his dignity with her when she left.

Never again.

He almost had himself convinced. Then she laughed that husky, sexy laugh and a jolt of sizzling electric current shot through him, leaving his pulse jackhammering in his neck.

Shannon was right. Having her there was a stupid, stupid, stupid idea.

14

CUPCAKE WHINED AND ADELIA SIGHED, opening one crusted eye to look at the time on her phone. Five-thirty. She could hear Conor bustling around in the bedroom. Five-thirty on a Wednesday. Why did these people insist on waking before the sun?

The gremlin-faced dog prodded her with a heavy paw, glossy back end swaying like a metronome.

"Why do you hate me?" Cupcake gave no reply so Adelia patted the couch. The dog clambered over and plunked onto her legs. "Feel better?" The only response was a satisfied woof she barely heard over the rain pounding on the tin roof of the trailer.

"Dumb dog," she said as she rubbed the slick fur behind Cupcake's ear.

"Morning, Winters." Conor yawned and rubbed a hand through his sleep-mussed hair.

Her heart pounded out a tuneless song. What the hell had she been thinking last night? One second, they were joking around and the next the room filled with electricity powerful enough to raise the hairs on her arms. He'd leaned toward her and every muscle in her body strained to meet him. If Shannon hadn't shown up...

She'd been celibate too long. That's all it was. It had been months since she kicked EJ out of her bed; or rather, walked away from his. This lust wasn't specific to Conor.

He dropped heavily into the chair, leaning his elbows on his knees and yawning. "Coffee's brewing."

Even rumpled, with the shadow of a scruffy beard and sleepy eyes, he looked better than a sunny day, not that she remembered what those looked like. He rolled his shoulders and she followed the motion greedily, wishing he wore short sleeves instead of the endless parade of long-sleeved Henleys.

Maybe it was him. A little.

"So," he said. "About last night."

"Nope." She shifted her legs and Cupcake gave a disapproving sigh. "I have to brush my teeth."

"Winters—"

She headed to the bathroom and shut the door, locking it behind her. She'd rather get kicked in the ovaries than talk about how close they'd come to kissing. There was a limit to how much she could talk about feelings and she'd bypassed it the minute she opened her mouth yesterday. Taking her time, she brushed her teeth and then her hair, yanking the brush through the snarls and leaving it a static mess. She pulled it into a ponytail and rifled through Jo's clothing. Everything was snug and too short, but whatever.

Once she was dressed, she turned to leave and noticed a glob of toothpaste in the sink. Did she always leave toothpaste like that? At hotels, EJ told her not to clean up, so she never really paid attention to that stuff. *That's what they hire staff for, duck,* he'd murmur before stripping off whatever garment kept him from her body.

It was always spectacular with him. And it never meant anything.

Last night, she'd jealously watched Shannon and Conor bustle around, their movie night ritual down to a science. While she'd been on the road, her life an endless blur of tour busses, aggressive fans, and empty sex, they'd been living. Really living. Movie nights and laughter and tidying the house together. Even if they were only friends—and that was up for debate—the intimacy of it was almost unbearable.

She grabbed a piece of tissue and wiped away the toothpaste.

Wrangling her nerves, she made her way down the hall. The familiar screech of what was turning into her least favorite song blared out from the living room. Conor grabbed her phone and held it out to her. Cupcake, who seemed to find the music distressing, barked and jumped at the phone, knocking it out of her hand.

"Oh, crap." He caught it before it landed screen down on the coffee table. He fumbled it as Cupcake gave it a head-butt. They both jumped for it and he raised a victorious arm, the phone clenched in his fist, Cupcake licking his face.

He looked so proud of himself. Laughter, the free easy kind she hadn't had in years, came rushing out of her. "You're an idiot."

He shook the phone at her, his smile cheerful, and nodded.

Warmth crept up her jaw and across her face. What the fuck was that? She didn't blush. She never fucking blushed. Snatching the phone up, she turned away from him. In all the scrabbling the answer button had been hit.

It was her own fault. She'd thought of EJ and conjured him like *Beetlejuice*. "What?"

"Who the fuck was that?" EJ asked, the lilt of his voice sharper than a blade.

"What do you want?"

"I'm not going to ask again."

"Good, because I'm not going to answer. What I do is my business."

His silence was heavy with expectation. Sucked to be him. She could out-mute a mute if necessary. After a full forty seconds of dead air, he sucked in his breath. "I miss you, duck."

"Oh my god, you don't seriously think that's going to work on me, do you?"

"Things have been...strained between us since France, but I love you and can't stand to see you throw away your career."

"No. You don't. You don't care about anyone or anything except yourself. And you're not worried about my career. You're worried about yours."

He abandoned that tactic and went back to blunt force. "Where the fuck are you?"

She hung up the phone and turned the volume off. It vibrated almost immediately as he called back. She sat it face down on the carpet beside the couch. Conor played with Cupcake on the floor, almost managing to look like someone who wasn't eavesdropping.

"Go ahead and ask."

"Nope," he said. "If you want to tell me, you will. If not..." He shrugged as he stood. "I need to take Cupcake for our run."

The word 'run' spurred Cupcake into action and she leaped toward the front door, nearly knocking her head on it as she twirled with joy. He slid on his gear and gave Adelia a nod before leaving.

She picked up her guitar and played a few chords, refusing to give EJ any space in her brain. The melody lurking in her head emerged and soon she was playing the bridge of something new. No words yet, but sometimes the track came first. She recorded it with her phone and then sat the guitar aside, her stomach rumbling. It was too early for her to be hungry, but Conor's damn grown-up schedule was ruining her.

She pulled leftover oatmeal out of the fridge. It was thick and dropped into the bowl like a spoonful of cement. She tossed the bowl in the microwave for five minutes. Maybe it would thin out when it was hot.

After three minutes, it started smoking. When she yanked the bowl out, she nearly burned her hands off. "Fuckity fuck." She tossed it on the counter. The edges of the oatmeal were dark and hard, and the center bubbled angrily.

She was incapable of the simplest household tasks.

All it took was a Google search to tell her what she'd done wrong. She tried it again, dribbling some almond milk into it and starting at two minutes.

When the door opened and Cupcake galloped into the trailer, she was at the table eating a bowl of warm oatmeal with bananas and some honey she'd found hiding in the back of the cupboard. Conor hung up his coat and used the towel hanging by the door to wipe down his hair and pants.

"Here." She pushed a second bowl his way. "I made that. I mean, I didn't make it-make it, but you usually want to eat as soon as you run and—"

He tilted his head and the words dried up. He had a way of listening that was equal parts endearing and terrifying.

"Thanks. I appreciate it," he said with a smile.

They ate in silence. She licked the honey off the back of her spoon and sat it in the empty bowl. "I feel like I'm going crazy without sunlight. Why won't the rain stop?"

"Late spring in Michigan is cruel." He pushed away from the table. "But I feel your pain. Want to play UNO?"

"That's not a good idea. I'd kick your ass and you'd be sad because I'm so awesome." In the living room, she pushed Cupcake away from her guitar. The dog was curled around it like the top half of a question mark. She opened one eye and groaned.

"I'd be sad because you don't know the joy of winning without cheating your skinny ass off," he said.

She gave him a withering look over her shoulder. "Um,

excuse me. The rest of me may be scrawny but this ass is fantastic."

His eyes trailed her body, grazing her bottom like a caress. "I know." His lip quirked. "I've seen it, remember?"

Blood rushed from her brain and headed south so fast she saw spots. Before she figured out how to respond to that, he disappeared down the hallway.

She leaned her elbows on the kitchen counter and took a breath. This had to stop. She could blame her woozy breathlessness on lust alone, but she knew it would be a lie. In the frantic beat of her heart and the throb behind her eyes, what she wanted more than anything was to talk to him. Really talk. To give into the mad hope she'd buried for so many years, that someday he would forgive her for breaking his heart. For not being capable of the kind of love he deserved.

It was way more dangerous than lust.

"Get out here, Winters," he called from the living room.

She pushed some strands of loose hair behind her ear. She could do this. She could put distance between them. They needed to get back to barely wanting to be in the same space. It was easier. She craned her neck until it cracked and came around the bar into the living room, "I'm not really—"

He was sitting on the floor, surrounded by an oasis of pillows and a soft, fluffy blanket with a pile of board games in the middle of the floor. Cupcake snored beside him and he patted the dog's side fondly before looking at her. "Ready to play some games?"

No, she wasn't. She didn't want any of this. No joking and sharing secrets and falling into the pit of shame that was sure to swallow her whole if she told him about her father's house. He was too easy to trust. She'd already ripped him apart once, hurting him before he could hurt her. And it ended up hurting anyhow. There was no way this would end any differently.

His long fingers ran through the sleep-mess of his hair and he watched her with patient eyes.

She shook her head, meaning it.

But not really.

Plunking down beside him, she smiled even as fear curled inside of her like campfire smoke." All right. Let's play."

15

"YAHTZEE, MOTHERFUCKER!" Adelia threw her arms up in victory, grinning at Conor like a lunatic.

He grabbed the score pad. "You cheated. You cheated at UNO, Checkers, Cribbage, Go Fish, and now Yahtzee."

She gathered the dice and dropped them into the shaker. "Believe what you want."

"Winters, I know that smirk. How the hell did you cheat?"

She widened her eyes and gave him an angelic smile. He shook his head. "I'm pretty sure that innocent act has never once worked for you."

"I can't help that my face always looks guilty."

He grabbed hold of her outstretched leg and she gave a squeal of shock as he yanked her toward him. "I'm going to pull on your toe hairs until I get an answer."

"I do not have toe hair!" She yanked her foot from his grip and searched it. After a thorough investigation she flopped back onto a pillow. "Oh my god, I have toe hair."

"Almost everyone does. It's not weird." He stroked his fingers along the side of her foot and felt her body relax. He knew an advantage when he saw one. He gripped her foot with both hands and kneaded below the ball. "Now tell me how you cheated."

She groaned. "This is not fair."

"Says the cheater."

She arched her back to get more comfortable, one leg bent and the other in his lap. His thoughts were no longer on finding out how she cheated at board games. Instead his mouth dried, and his hands drifted to her ankles.

"So, then he taught me how to cheat at cards and dice games."

He shook his head. "What? Sorry. I was listening to the… song…on the…player."

She sat up on her elbows. "Yeah, this is a good one." She turned over, giving him a glorious look at her backside before she got up and cranked the speaker volume.

"Anyway, it wasn't that interesting. I knew a guy with a gambling problem. Among other things. He taught me to cheat. I'm pretty sure there are a few casinos in California that would break my kneecaps if I ever stepped inside them again."

"You've lived a colorful life."

"More than you know." She sat back down, leaning against his couch. On shuffle, his old MP3 player found a musty pop song he didn't remember purchasing. She sang over the chorus —something about inner strength—her smoky voice giving the song a darker edge.

"I find it hard to believe that you've ever listened to this song, let alone learned the words."

"What? I have layers."

"Not when it comes to music."

"Well, not yours." She grinned. "That stuff is terrible."

His body came alive, tingling and throbbing, when she smiled. He cleared his throat, needing to change the direction of the conversation. "I'm all out of games. What do you want to do?"

She played with the edge of a pillow. "Got any illegitimate babies?"

"Twenty questions now?" He shook his head. "No. Not that I'm aware of."

"Are you into any of the following?" She raised three fingers in the air. "BDSM, clown fetishism, or toe shrimping?"

"I'm not sure what two of those things are, but I'm going to say no." He leaned his back against the couch, matching her pose. "It's unbelievable to me that journalists rarely mention what a charming conversationalist you are."

"I know, right? I've got shitloads of charm." She tilted her head and her expression turned serious. "Tell me about your job."

Ugh. Now that was a much-needed mood killer. "I work for..." He blinked several times. "A pro studio."

"That sounds shady. Are you taking porn pictures?"

"That would actually be a step up. I work for Razzle Dazzle Glamour and Costume Photography."

"Like senior pictures and stuff?"

"We do a little of everything, but it's mostly down-staters pretending to be train conductors, cowboys, and saloon girls, and a lot of older women who want to put on a corset and boa and get *sexy* pictures taken." He crooked his fingers over the word *sexy*.

"Hey, older women are sexy."

"Yes, they are, but not with what we take. The only thing those pictures are good for is giving grandsons permanent erectile dysfunction." His skin burned. "It's a stupid job."

"It doesn't sound stupid, but it sounds like you hate it."

She leaned her head back on the couch and turned to face him. She looked so lovely, her long neck stretched taut, delicate nerves exposed and begging to be touched and kissed until she went crazy for more. He pressed his hands firmly to the carpet keep from touching her and tried to remember what she'd said.

"Uh, that's why I don't usually talk about my job. It's fucking depressing," he said. "I love helping people see how themselves in a new way. But that's not what I'm doing."

She pointed at the pictures lining his living room wall. "So, you didn't take those for work?"

"No. Those are just for fun."

"Do you have more?"

It took him a moment to register her words. "What, seriously?"

"If you don't want to show me you don't have to."

"It's not that," he said. "I've just...never shown my portfolio to anyone." He cleared his suddenly dry throat. "Give me a second." He stood and jogged to his office, returning with the zippered book. She reached for it and he hesitated before pressing it into her hand.

He sat down beside her and she placed the book on her lap, tracing the leather cover with her fingers. "Nice."

He held his breath when she unzipped it and watched intently as she examined the first photograph. Sue Barryton's 70th birthday bash. In the foreground, a dozen senior citizens gathered around a bonfire at dusk, arthritic hands wrapped around bottles of beer and half-assembled s'mores. "It's not the best," he said. "I couldn't decide if I wanted to put the best picture up front or at the back. They have pros and cons. You could turn someone off right at the first page, but if you put the best picture on the first page, then they'd be disapp—"

She pressed her hand to his lips. "Dude. This picture is awesome." She pointed at the old woman, far in the background, leaning over a cooler and grinning as she flipped someone off outside the frame. "It's like those old Rockwell paintings, but twisted."

She slowly flipped through each page, pausing to run her fingers over the lines of trees or and faces and shadows, pointing out the things that caught her eye. He watched her, trying to interpret every twitch of her brow and every ghost of a smile. She stopped on a picture taken at the Railway. In a rare moment of stillness, Shannon stared out of the window, her hands buried in her hair, pulling it off her neck.

She studied the picture far longer than the rest and he rubbed the back of his own neck, failing to ease the tension in his shoulders. Why wasn't she saying anything?

She traced her fingers over the shadows that decorated Shannon's face. "This is how you see her, isn't it? A warrior?" Her eyes never left the photograph.

"Yes."

She didn't speak for a few seconds. Finally, she looked up, her dark eyes burning like a star at midnight, and he wasn't sure he'd ever breathe again. "Conor, I've met—and hated—a lot of talented photographers and I can't think of a single one who takes pictures like you. The way you capture people, it's like…" She hesitated. "You see inside of them."

He exhaled softly, his shoulders releasing their tension. "That's nice of you to say."

"When the fuck have I ever said something to be nice?" She pressed her palm to the photo. "This is *art*. Why aren't you doing this for a living?"

Heat burned the back of his neck and he could feel it rising in his cheeks. "I'm going to. I mean I will. Eventually. It's not the right time."

"When's the right time?"

"There's a lot of factors. Money and time and business plans. Finding the right location. Advertising…" He rubbed his neck again. "I'm not Liam. I have to—"

"Who gives a shit about Prince Liam?" She knew all about the one-sided rivalry that dominated his childhood.

"He's King Liam now. Businessman. Entrepreneur. Millionaire."

She scratched the end of her nose. "To be fair, they let any asshole be a millionaire these days."

His laugh made Cupcake's head shoot up from her nap spot. She settled back down with a woof.

Adelia closed the portfolio. "Forget Liam. What's your dream?"

He stared at his wall of photographs and ran a hand through his hair. He suddenly understood her nervous twisting of her sweatshirt the day before. Sharing something so personal—so close to your heart—was harder than it looked.

"I want my own studio," he said.

She tipped her face toward him, a lock of hair falling into her eyes. "Tell me about it."

It took an act of will to stop himself from tucking her hair behind her ear. Instead, he leaned over and grabbed his camera bag, pulling the crumpled real estate ad out of the front pocket and handing it to her.

"It's perfect," he said. Even his mother would be impressed by the high ceilings and the gleaming waiting area. "The location is great. Right off the highway. I mean, it seems perfect. I haven't seen it yet."

She studied it with the same intensity as she did his photographs. "What time is it?" she asked, finally.

He glanced at his phone. "Noon."

"Are you hungry?"

"If you're hinting for food, I can make lunch."

She climbed off the floor. "Let's go."

"What? Where?" He stood and reached for the ad but she held it out of reach and waggled it at him.

"To the studio."

"Why? I can't afford it anyway. It's just a dumb dream."

Her eyes narrowed. "Your dreams are not dumb. Come on."

"I'd like to remind you that I'm a grownup and you can't boss me around like you did when we were kids."

"I never bossed. Shannon bossed. I just offered... encouragement." She pressed the ad to his chest, the warmth of her hand radiating through paper and cloth and skin. "Let's go see your dream."

CONOR WRENCHED open the door to the truck and rushed Adelia in before they both got soaked from the rain. She was almost unrecognizable in a baggy black hoodie and squeezed into a pair of Jo's leggings, printed to look like pink and blue nebulas.

"You know this isn't necessary, right?" he said for the fifth time.

"It's necessary," she said. "Also, it's been days since I've eaten something deep fried and I don't want my body to go into shock."

He shut her door and headed for his side of the truck.

"Hey! Where ya going?" Jo flew down the front steps of her trailer and ran toward him, her soggy shoes squelching in the mud and a big canvas bag in her hands. "Mom told me to bring this over to you guys." She held the bag open, a stack of Tupperware containers piled inside. "For dinner."

Shannon occasionally made extra food and sent it his way but that looked like several meals. "Wow, what's the occasion?"

"Um, I think she's afraid you're starving Lia."

He sighed. "I'm sure Adelia will appreciate the sentiment. Your mom is awesome."

Jo shrugged. "She's all right."

Her gaze slid sideways until it connected with Adelia, who gave her a salute from inside the truck. "Hey, kid."

"Why aren't you at school, Flash?" he asked.

"I'm sick."

"Of school?"

"Well, yeah. Wednesdays are the worst. Anyway, Mom says I

can have two mental health days a semester. I haven't used any and the year's almost over so I stayed home," Jo said. "Can I come with you guys?"

"You don't even know where we're going."

"But I know it's gotta be more interesting than homework." She grinned her big bunny-rabbit overbite smile and he sighed.

"Touché. Get in the truck. I'll go put this away."

When he came back out of the house, Jo was in the center of the bench seat, putting some much-needed breathing room between himself and Adelia. He silently thanked her for that.

Almost as though she'd read his mind, Adelia gave him an amused smile. He couldn't help the foolish one he gave her back as he turned the key. "Let's take the long way."

He took them on a scenic tour of Cherry Lake, albeit through the mist of never-ending rain. Adelia rolled down the window and let the rain spatter everyone. She put an arm out and sighed as the wind flung it around. "It's so quiet."

"Country living has its perks," he said.

She snorted.

"See, I'd expect that kind of derision from a big city gal, not a fellow bumpkin like yourself."

"Gal? Did you say *gal*?"

"Yes, ma'am."

"Ma'am." She shook her head. "I oughta hit you for that."

They passed the silhouette of June Lake's Ferris wheel, otherwise hidden behind the gloom. Jo groaned. "Spring Fling Festival is gonna be underwater this year."

"That's a bummer," she said. "Where else will Conor take a purdy little gal to keep her safe from the big, bad gravity?"

"I'm afraid you have a very skewed view of my love life," he said.

She smirked. "What's it like?"

"My mom says the word to use is 'nonexistent,'" Jo said.

Adelia's laugh spilled out like a bucket of rusty nails.

"Your mom is judgmental and I take back all the nice things I say about her."

"Yeah, but sometimes she's right."

Still quaking, Adelia turned her body away from them.

"Get it all out of your system, Winters."

Since it was all back roads, they drove for almost an hour. Finally, he pulled into the driveway of what used to be BT Studios. He squinted through the rivulets of rain drenching his windshield. "There it is."

"What is it?" Jo asked.

"A dream," Adelia said. Then she threw open the door and climbed out of the truck, with Jo scrambling behind.

"What are you doing?" he hollered.

"I want to see it up close." She studied the sign in the front as he caught up, his camera bag smacking him painfully in the shoulder.

The steps leading to the wrap-around porch were so quiet that Adelia stopped to test them with her big boots.

"It's new," he said. "The ad said she tore out the original porch and added a more 'charming' one."

"Hm." She crossed the porch and ran her fingers along the faux chipped paint on the front window. What was she looking for?

Jo wandered toward the back yard and he and Adelia sat on a creaky porch swing. He held onto one of the chains and she held onto the other as she peppered him with dozens of questions about the space and what he planned to do with it. When she was finally out of questions, she kicked her legs out and rocked the swing in time to the rain hitting the roof.

"Sorry for being so nosy," she said.

"You're not being nosy." He pushed his feet off the porch, making the swing go faster. "This reminds me of old times."

"You mean back when I dragged you all over Cherry Lake looking for skinned knees and adventure?"

"No. Back when it was hard for me to talk, and you still treated everything I said like it mattered."

"Oh." Her hidden dimples made an appearance and she looked away. "Because it did. It does."

"You say things like that and you make it really damned hard not to hug you."

"I hate hugs," she said.

"Liar. You'd hiss like an angry housecat when I hugged you, but as soon as I had my arms around you, you'd go limp as a noodle. You only complained about it afterward, but you never once pulled away."

"An angry housecat? Really?"

"I don't know how else to describe it. Feral wolverine? Do they hiss?"

She laughed and leaned back, pressing her shoulder to his. It wasn't a hug, but it felt warm and right.

Sweetly oblivious to everything, Jo ran up the steps. "I'm bored."

"And I'm starving," Adelia said, pulling away from him, leaving a void where her warmth had been. "Do you want to take some pictures or anything?"

He shook his head. "No, I'm all set. Let's go get food."

He wouldn't tell them where they were going. Instead, he wound his way down back roads and muddy swamp streets until he pulled up to Uncle Jared's Cider Mill.

"Oooh," Jo said. "Doughnuts!"

"Let's start with actual food first," he said.

The enormous white barn sported an outdoor covered patio where down-staters usually loitered. With the Dive closed, there weren't as many tourists around and it was pretty quiet.

"I don't remember this place," she said.

"It was Sheppard Orchard when we were kids. Just a farm. But Jared, the Sheppards' oldest, bought the place out and turned it into an attraction." He gestured to a table, "You sit. I'll go get us some food."

"But I don't know what they have."

"I do. You won't be disappointed."

She gave him a smile that turned his insides upside down. "I'm trusting you."

He had to make two trips from the lunch counter to their table. Jo's eyes got wider and wider as he sat things down. "Damn, that's a lot of food," she said.

"Excuse me?" he said.

"I said dang."

"That's what I thought." He handed Adelia a drink.

She eyed the cloudy amber slush with suspicion, but took a sip. "Oh, that's good."

"Cider slushies. They're a specialty here. I've never had one, but the tourists love them." He spread out the food. Cheeseburgers and fries and an order of onion rings for them. A plain turkey sandwich and side salad for himself. And two mystery bags that Adelia kept eyeing while she ate.

"Did I steer you wrong?" he said, when she pushed her empty fry basket aside.

"Nope. That was really good." She poked at the bags. "What's that?"

"Dessert."

"Man, I feel bad eating stuff you can't eat."

"If I wanted to eat it, I could. I choose not to."

After Adelia and Jo decimated a cider maple doughnut each, they cleaned up the table.

"I like this place," Adelia said.

"I should bring you back here on Friday," he said. "They have a weekend Elvis impersonator who serenades you while you eat."

Her laugh echoed around the otherwise empty patio. "No fucking way," she said.

"Yes fucking way."

"Excuse me?" Jo said, her grey eyes sparkling.

"I said dang." He wrapped an arm around Jo's shoulder and kissed the top of her head. "Shut your trap about that and I'll send you home with some of these doughnuts."

"No, but seriously, an Elvis impersonator?" Adelia said, as they made their way to the parking lot.

They piled into the truck and Jo cranked the volume on a rock station playing Metallica.

Adelia sat higher and growled out an oddly melodic take on "Master of Puppets," the smoky rasp of her voice turning the song into the vocal equivalent of angry sex.

He never could carry a tune, but he gave it his best shot, growling along. Her serious expression softened as she nodded along, encouraging him to get louder as they hit the chorus together.

"Are you going to hire me to be a backup singer?" he asked.

"Sorry, but I'm going in a different direction."

He turned the radio down. "You mean the one with talent?"

"You have talent," she said. "Just not with singing."

"Chopping vegetables isn't actually a talent," he said.

"You're an amazing photographer."

That ache in his chest, the one he thought he'd left back at the trailer, came racing back. "Thanks. Maybe I should take your picture."

"Nah." She laughed and pointed at her chest. "There's nothing interesting here. It's all leather and barbed wire inside."

It wasn't true. He wished that it were because it would be easier to hate her. But he was finding his anger fading away with every moment he spent with her. Hiding beneath the leather and barbed wire was an animal, trembling and afraid.

As a kid, he thought Adelia was invincible. He envied her tough hide. It shamed him to think of how long it took him to wonder what that tough hide had cost her. And why it was there in the first place. He cut her a sideways glance and she looked away. A few seconds of silence passed between them.

"Don't forget about all the Doritos in there," he finally said.

"Those too." Relief tinged her scratchy voice like color.

"Wait," Jo said. "Do you have Doritos?"

He shook his head. "Sorry, but no."

When he pulled in front of his trailer, he invited Jo in but she begged off, climbing over Adelia and out of the truck, shouting something about a *Godzilla* marathon and a text date.

"Wait, what? Like a *date* date?" he yelled after her.

Jo raced up the steps and shouted, "Sorry, can't hear you," before slamming her door shut.

He turned. "A *date* date?"

"Yeah, she has a crush on some kid at school."

A groan of despair ripped from him as he unlocked his door.

"She'll be fine," she said.

"Doesn't mean I'm not going to worry." He hung their coats and grabbed a couple of towels, handing her one.

"Of course, you're going to worry," she said, squeezing the rain from her hair. "You're basically her father."

He laughed. "I'm really not a father type."

"Whatever type you are, you're her dad in all the ways that matter." She handed him the towel and scratched Cupcake behind her ears. "Like this right here? There is no way that Conor Ross woke up one day and decided to get a dog. You got this dog for her."

"Why would I do that?"

"Because her mom works nonstop and she probably wanted a dog and you decided to take on a ton of responsibility so she could have a puppy to play with."

The world shifted beneath him. "And you think you're not good with people?"

"I'm not. I'm good with you. I mean—" She took a step back. "I mean I get you."

He folded the towels. "Well, don't tell Jo any of that dad stuff. She'll be grossed out."

"She might pretend to be grossed out. But she loves you as much as you love her."

"She tolerates me, Winters. As much as any teenager tolerates their uncle with weird food habits."

"Jo loves you," she said. "You're hard not to love."

Of all the people in the fucking world to say that. A burst of bitter laughter surged out of him. "You did a pretty good job of it."

She turned her face away. A flush tinged her cheek and crept down her neck.

The friendly mood evaporated and he felt like a complete jackass. "I'm sorry. That was shitty of me to say."

She cleared her throat, still turned away from him. "No. I deserve that. I..." She took a slow breath. "I deserve it."

He hated the small part of himself that sat up, waiting for her to apologize. To explain. But there was only the sound of the rain.

"It wasn't like that," she said finally. That was it. No other explanation.

"So you keep telling me." He rubbed his hands over his face and gave a mirthless laugh. Getting her to talk was like scaling a glacier. "I'm going to take Cupcake out. Need anything before I go out?"

She twisted her hands and her mouth opened and closed as if she wanted to say something but thought better of it. Avoiding his eyes, she shook her head. "Enjoy your run."

16

THEY WERE NEVER GOING BACK to being friends.

For a few hours, Adelia was swept up in the fantasy that they could be. That maybe she could call Conor when she was on the road touring and tell him funny stories to make him laugh. And maybe she could come back and visit him and go somewhere to eat wheatgrass or whatever it was that he liked to eat and to maybe get cider slushies after. But it was a fantasy. He wasn't her friend. He was just a kind man with a lot of pent-up anger at her who wanted answers she couldn't give.

Why was it getting harder to remember that?

She sat cross-legged on the couch, playing her guitar and making notes for each song she was drafting, but secretly, she watched him. After he returned from an extremely long run, he'd showered and returned to the living room in his sweats and a long-sleeved t-shirt, making himself comfortable in the wing-back chair. He read the business guide he'd been working on for a couple of days. When it looked like he didn't understand something, he'd stop and reread the line, forehead scrunched up, mouthing each word. Then he'd scribble on a sticky note and slap it in the book.

Eventually, he sat the book aside and groaned, rubbing his eyes. There were so many stickies lining the outer edges of the pages, the whole thing looked like a tropical bird ready for flight.

"Are you hungry?" she asked. "You didn't eat much at lunch."

He nodded. "How about you?"

"I could eat." She sat her guitar aside and followed him into the kitchen. He opened the fridge and pulled several containers out of the bag Shannon had sent, and lined them up neatly on the counter.

She reached for the plates and looked down at the crisp row. It was all so...perfect. Unable to resist a little destruction, she nudged one of the containers, leaving it askew. Without turning her direction, his hand shot out and scooched it back into place.

Always in control. Always precise.

Her body ached in places it had no business aching.

"Jesus, how many meals did Shannon give us?" He peered into the bag and plucked out a pink sticky note. He read it and snorted, passing it to her.

Blue container has Spicy Quinoa Chicken. That's for you, Conor. Do not feed that low-cal crap to Adelia. I made her spaghetti and meatballs. She needs the carbs.

She opened the container closest to her. The acidic-sweet smell of spaghetti sauce filled the kitchen.

They heated the food and ate in silence. His meal smelled heavenly too and he caught her eyeballing it. He scraped some chicken onto her plate. "Don't tell Shannon that I fed you anything healthy."

It was spicy and hearty and the heat was pleasant, like a gulp of whisky warming the throat. "This is good, too. She's amazing."

He picked a cucumber slice from his salad and ate it. "Yup. Don't know what I'd do without her."

Longing and jealousy tangled in her chest until she couldn't tell from the other. She prodded her spaghetti noodles with her fork, pulling them apart, as if that were the key to unraveling her feelings.

After dinner, he went to work on the dishes and she grabbed a towel to dry them. Her phone buzzed on the counter, and he took the towel, his fingers brushing hers. "You better answer that," he said.

She grabbed the phone and leaned her back against the front door.

"He's blacklisting you." EJ didn't even bother with *hello*.

And like that, all the warm shivers went away, replaced by cold ones. "What? Did you talk to Orion? They've been trying to lure me away for—"

"They said no."

"Gold Dream?"

"No."

"What about Cryptiq?"

"They all. Said. No. I've talked to every major label and then all the mid-levels and a great deal of nothing labels I wouldn't trust to sell a bowl of Weetabix, let alone honor a recording contract. The answer is no. No one will risk pissing off Gyro-scope for your middling talents. And, not that you care, but I'm hemorrhaging bands over this. The bloody Spoon Monkeys left me for Hal Knickerbocker! You have fucked us both. I hope you're happy." He was breathing so heavily, she had to pull the phone from her ear.

"Well, the Spoon Monkeys sucked anyway," she said.

"You are an insufferable music snob with nothing but stock riffs and by-the-numbers lyrics."

She gritted her teeth hard enough to hurt her jaw. "Fuck. You. You're fired."

"You're not firing me. You and I have an active contract. Not that it's worth much anymore. By the time Rod Norris is done with you, no one—and I mean absolutely no one—will put a contract into your grubby hands. Or mine. For fuck's sake, Lia, all you have to do is apologize and sign the goddamned paperwork and we can get back to work. Isn't that what you want? To get back on the road? Back on the stage so you can satisfy that delightful ego of yours with all the applause? We can get back to that. The contract he offered, before you banjaxed everything, was great, and you know it."

It had been a great contract, but it meant continuing to make the kind of rock music she'd outgrown. And it meant working with Rod. Bending and proving him right.

"No. I do my job. I write the melodies and the songs. I tour harder and longer than any other band on their roster. I'm done trying to prove that I'm a musician to people like him. I'll go back to slinging my ass on Figueroa before I tell that asshole I'm sorry."

"Christ," EJ shouted. "What could he have possibly done? Grabbed a tit? Put his hand in your knickers? You're not new at this, duck. When a music mogul sticks his hand down your pants, you say *thank you* and beg for him to go dee—"

She hung up. He'd hit maximum EJ in under three minutes. A new record.

Fluttering started in her stomach and it moved into her chest. She gripped the phone tighter to keep her hand from shaking.

All along, she'd convinced herself that EJ could fix this. But if even the small labels weren't biting, she was fucked.

She'd finally done it. Lord knows, she'd tried to do it in the past, but somehow, she'd finally managed to completely ruin the only thing that mattered in her life. The only thing she was worth.

She hurled the phone across the room. It slammed into the edge of the coffee table. Profanities broke like waves from her lips. She sat heavily on the ottoman, pressing her hands to her face. She vaguely heard Conor say something, but the world was dark and gurgle-y like she'd plunged underwater.

And started to drown.

"Want to talk about it?" he asked.

"No. I don't." The sound of her heartbeat slammed in her ears. "You wouldn't understand."

"I would if you explained it to me." He sat on the couch. "Maybe I can help."

"You can't."

He shook his head. "Probably not. Even if I could you wouldn't let me."

"Just—not now."

"Yes, now." Every word was mild, exhausted. "You don't want to tell me about why you left, that's...well, it's not fine, but I'm trying to accept it. But why are you hiding things in the here and now? What good is that doing? What's the point?"

Frustration ticked in her like a bomb set to go off. "Because I'm not one of the heroines in your bullshit books. You can't magic up a way to fix it. To fix me. You can't make it better."

"Sometimes it's not about fixing it or making it better. It's about letting someone be there for you." He tilted his head. "Would you, for once, trust me to do that? I'm not asking for a lot here, Winters."

He was asking for everything. He just didn't know it. The world blurred as if her eyes were full of tears, but they weren't. Tears never came. Nothing ever came. She'd spent all her tears the night she left.

"When I found out that my dad was dead, I thought finally, I could be—" Her jaw tightened. "Then I went to that stupid studio meeting and got into it with Rod about my new contract. All I wanted was more control. A chance to take my career in a new direction. It got nasty. I told him to go to hell. He threw EJ out of the room and laid into me. He told me to do what I was told. Called me an ungrateful whore." The words came from

deep inside of her, rushing up like water before she could stop
them. "And that everyone in the industry knew I was good for
two things. Singing and sucking dick, and if I wasn't doing the
one, I should get busy doing the other."

She stood and paced, trying to outrun the outrage. "I busted
his nose. Blood went everywhere. And then I took a cab straight
to the garage where I'd been storing that stupid GTO. And I
drove. Here." She clenched her hands into fists. "Now I'm back
in this bullshit town with my dad's bullshit house and I just—I
was so close and every time I get there, it keeps..." She growled
and rubbed her face with her angry hands.

"So close to what?"

She had to adjust her vision like she was walking in the sun.
"What?"

"You said you were so close. Close to what?"

She wrapped her arms around her midsection. "Happy," she
whispered.

He shook his head, confused.

"So-close-to-happy." She ground each word out, because it
was the only way to say it aloud. "I've been chasing it. Can't
catch it. Not even with music." She stalked to the wall and
rubbed her fingers over the texture of the paint covering the
paneling. "I never had a lot of it. But I used to have a little.
Mostly with..." The ragged edges of her nails bumped over the
surface. "I had a little. But after my dad threw me out, it's like I
went numb. Like my arm went to sleep and I keep shaking it
because it hurts, but I can't...get the feeling back."

His eyes were huge. "What do you mean he threw you out?
He told me you moved."

She snorted. "Of course he did."

"After—" he swallowed. "After you left my house and didn't
come to school the next day, or the day after that, I wanted to
see you. But I didn't know where you actually lived. As soon as I
saw your dad in town, I jumped in front of his truck and asked

him if you were sick. He rolled down the window and told me that you moved and that if you had wanted me to have your address, you would have given it to me. Then he told me to get out of his way and not to bother him again."

"Good ol' friendly Lester Winters."

He rested his arms on his thighs and pressed his hands together, interlocking his fingers. "He threw you out, so you up and left town?"

"I followed orders. He told me to go. I went."

"But you could have—" His eyes crinkled up. "Was that why you came to my house? Did you know you were leaving when we—"

She stared at the wall. How much truth could he handle? How much could she?

How could she possibly explain how she'd driven to his house, ready to curl beside him and cry. To tell him the secrets that buried her. To ask to stay with him. But then he'd kissed her and it felt like a life raft in choppy waters, and she'd wrapped her arms around his neck and let everything blur into skin and touch.

She hadn't expected him to say he loved her.

"No," she said. "I didn't know."

She could see the conflict in his eyes. He wanted to ask her why, then. But he was hesitating.

"Look, I didn't have a plan. I took one of his beater cars, and drove to your house. And after that, I drove the beater until it died."

"All this time I assumed you were with family." He ran a hand through his hair. "You were sixteen. Where'd you live? How did you eat?"

Her legs wobbled, and she sat at the far end of the couch. She tried to never think about that time in her life. "I slept in the car until it got towed in Nevada. Hitchhiked to L.A. Tried shelters for a while." She twisted her hands together, shuffling through her memories. "You could make them work if you followed the rules. But they were worse than living on the street sometimes. Show weakness and the kids stole everything you owned. Stand up for yourself and get your ass kicked. Then they'd steal your stuff anyway. Most of the employees, they saw hundreds of us with the same sob stories and didn't care anymore. Which I get." She rubbed at the pads of her fingers where the skin had toughened from years of playing guitar. "I bailed on those places pretty quick."

She didn't need to look up to feel the weight of his gaze.

"Bailed and did what?" he asked.

She pulled a pillow to her chest, needing something between her raw nerves and the stinging air. "I know this is Cherry Lake, but you're really not that naïve, are you? How the hell do you think street kids get by? I fucked for cash. I lived wherever I could find a roof."

His jaw tightened and he stared at the floor for a long time without speaking. When he looked at her, his brows were drawn together and his eyes were glassy. "But you were just a kid."

"I was never a kid." She squeezed the pillow tighter. "Anyway, it doesn't matter. I survived."

"It matters."

He reached for her arm. She flung the pillow at him and stood to escape his touch. She hated him in that moment. Hated the pity in his eyes. She took long slow breaths. But each one made her feel dizzier. More frantic. The pulse of all the feelings she couldn't touch seemed just under the surface of her skin, threatening to break through.

Too much. It was too much.

She dropped herself onto his lap. "Do you want the dirty details now?" Pressing herself against him she arched her hips. He sucked in his breath, his startled eyes so bright it hurt to look at them. "Or a sample? I was very good at what I did."

It wasn't fair. He didn't deserve it, but she was splitting apart at the seams. He couldn't keep tugging on her threads and expect all the stuffing to stay inside.

His emotions rolled like summer waves on Lake Michigan. Lust. Anger. Hurt. Worry. And she was drowning in those rough waters. Feelings were so confusing, so raw. They left her weak. Sex she understood. She ground herself against him.

"Don't do this," he said softly.

She leaned forward and took his earlobe between her teeth, giving it a nip. "Don't act like you don't want to fuck me," she whispered in his ear.

Conor groaned, snaking his arms around her waist. His hands dipped low to cup her ass and his hips arched to her heat. Pressing closer and tighter, she teased his lips with hers and waited for it. For the tilt. The crush. The end of his ceaseless need to know things.

"No," he said, taking a shuddering breath. "Stop punishing the both of us, Adelia."

She jerked away from him, but his arm was still around her. She shoved at his shoulders, her self-loathing heavy as wet sand. She needed to leave his stupid trailer and his stupid green eyes and his stupid, stupid way of making her feel things.

His arms were prison bars, keeping her from escape. She fought against the comfort he wanted to give her. It was comfort she didn't deserve. "Let go of me," she ground out.

"Not going to do that." He gripped her head in his hands and pressed his forehead to hers. "I'm sorry that you went through so much."

"Fuck you, Conor. Don't pity me."

"It's not pity, it's caring." He stroked her hair. "You just can't tell the difference."

She didn't have an ounce of energy left. Out of breath, out of everything, she collapsed against him, pressing her face to his shoulder.

The tink-tink-tink of the rain and her uneven breaths made a melody as she inhaled the warm scent of his skin; soapy lemongrass and grapefruit and sweat from his morning run.

If she were capable of crying, she would have.

If she were capable of apologizing, she would have done that too.

"I'm such an asshole," she whispered against his neck.

"No. You wish you were, but you're not." He rubbed his thumbs up and down her back, making a slow trek along the sides of her spine. "Sex is a great distraction, but it's...temporary pleasure." He spread his hands against her lower back, holding her steady. "Like Doritos."

She wasn't willing to move her head from the warmth of his shoulder, but she turned her face toward his. "I warned you about taking Doritos from me."

His chest rose and fell with a laugh. "I remember that they taste good. Salty. And a handful now and then probably wouldn't hurt. But you can't have a handful. The flavor is intense, but temporary, so you eat another and another and there's nothing there. No nutrition. Nothing to actually satisfy you."

She sighed. "Man, I wish you had Doritos here. Not metaphorical sex ones. The real ones." It was only half true. But still.

His laugh rumbled beneath her and she held onto his shoulders. He felt so warm and solid wrapped around her. The right thing to do was to climb off the poor man and leave him be for a while. But she didn't want to.

"Can we just..." Not entirely sure of herself, she wrapped her arms around his shoulders, feeling like a needy child.

He held her tight, giving her a cocoon that was terrifying and wonderful at the same time.

"I've never told anyone about that stuff," she said after a

million years of silence. "I'm not ashamed of it. I did what I had to."

"I get that."

"I met EJ when I was working. I had a few wealthy clients and some of them were in the music business."

"Was Rod one of your...clients?"

"No. But some of his buddies were and he's never let me forget it." She pressed her chin into his shoulder. "I want to be more than what I had to do back then."

He held her quietly until the dog snored at the base of the couch, and her legs ached from straddling him. Still, she couldn't let go. She ran her fingers along the edges of his hair, and his hands returned to making a path up and down her back. She moaned softly, her shoulders loosening.

She shifted to get comfortable and he groaned. "Not to be crass, but I seem to be, uh...having a Dorito craving." He tilted his hips away from her but not before she felt the hard ridge beneath her.

"Oh." She snorted and the snort turned to a cackling laugh.

"You're making it worse!" He pressed further into the couch, putting space between them. "Women don't usually, you know, just loiter in this area. My dick got confused."

"They're often confused. I'll get up." She peeled herself away from him, the sudden space between their bodies making her shiver.

He pulled her back. "No, let's uh, let's do this." He rolled her over onto her back on the couch.

"Um, I don't think this is going to help your craving."

"Just turn over, would you?"

"Heard that before." She rolled onto her side and he squeezed in behind her, spoon style. Then, shoved a pillow between them.

"Seriously?" she said. "Is this what Catholic school prom feels like? I bet it is."

He wrapped his arm around her and breathed into her hair. "Winters, this is quiet time. So, shut your face, okay?"

"You're not the boss of me," she said. But the warmth of his arms soothed her like a child's lullaby, and she shut up.

CONOR WOKE to dim light coming through the blinds. They'd slept the whole night.

He pulled Adelia's snoring carcass closer, so she wouldn't tumble off the couch. She'd been down for the count as soon as they got comfortable.

What the hell would he say when she woke up? His mind whirled with more questions than ever. What the hell broke her so badly that she chose living on the streets over staying in Cherry Lake? To reaching out to him? He wished he knew how to help fight her demons the way she'd fought his. Of course, the demons of a second-grader were much less complicated.

Beside him, she groaned. He sat up a little and she made a grumpy sound of discontent. Eyes closed, she flipped over, her face pressed against his chest. She scrabbled for the pillow between their bodies and chucked it behind her. Sighing, she pressed herself tight against him.

He stroked her tangled hair. She was the toughest, most resilient person he'd ever known, tougher than he could ever dream of being, but that didn't mean she had to fight every battle alone. And some part of her desperately longed for the things she'd shoved away.

Did that include him?

Now that was a dangerous thought.

The soft pillow of her mouth brushed his neck and sent his pulse soaring. Her breath was hot against his skin and he tried not to respond, which was like trying not to breathe. She shifted again and now her lips were firmly pressed to his neck. He couldn't stop the heated grunt that dragged from him. The soft heat parted, and he felt the sting of teeth nipping his skin.

"Dammit, you're awake, aren't you?"

She faked a loud snore, but her shoulders shook with laughter.

"Okay, on the floor you go." He loosened his grip on her and she shrieked, wrapping her arms and legs around him, flipping him over. He fell off the couch and pulled her with him. She landed on top of him with a thump.

"Oh, my god," she groaned. "You used to be a lot softer when we wrestled around. I miss that."

"Are you really complaining that I'm too...firm, now?"

"Shut it." Something cautious lurked in her eyes despite her light tone. She was afraid of what else he'd ask. There were a thousand questions rattling around inside of him, but he had pushed her as far as he dared.

He took Cupcake out for her morning run and when he came back, music pounded from his speakers and she was in the kitchen, mangling fruit on the cutting board, clearly wanting to be left alone. He went to his office to work out. After a while, she leaned in the office doorway, watching him as she ate a bowl of oatmeal.

"You never wear short-sleeved shirts," she said.

He sat up. "No."

She stirred the oatmeal. "Why do all that work on your arms if you aren't going to show them off?"

He tugged at the cuffs of his long-sleeved shirt. "I don't do it to show off."

She gave a grunt of disbelief and ate another spoonful of oatmeal.

He grabbed the container of wipes and cleaned off the bench and the bar.

"You ever have sex on that thing?"

He stopped cleaning the bench cover and raised his eyebrows at her. "No."

"Just your bed, huh? Boring."

The rain lightened up, the steady thunks on the roof dissipating for a moment before starting to thump again. "Is this an infantile response to sharing sensitive things with me last night?"

"No." She licked the back of her spoon. "Maybe."

"Points for honesty." He threw away the wet wipe. "And if I were currently involved, my sex life wouldn't be boring. If you do it right, you don't need to be all...showy."

"You don't need to be *showy*? Seriously?" She shoved the bowl into his hands and brushed past him. Straddling the weight bench, she leaned back and tested the bar, but couldn't budge it.

"Damn," she said.

Laughing, he sat the bowl down and replaced the weight with the lightest ones he had. "That's what you get for talking shit."

She tested it out and still struggled. He bent her elbows in the correct position and stood behind the bar, spotting her. "Don't worry, I won't let it fall on you."

Three lifts and she groaned as he helped her guide it back onto the barbell hooks.

"Jesus, I've never appreciated being naturally scrawny until now," she said.

"Skinny doesn't equal healthy. If I recall, you eat Doritos by the pound."

"Shut up." She tried to push herself up and flopped back down. "My arms are dead. My guitar playing days are over."

Standing, he straddled the bench and reached for her, to help her up, but he couldn't help brushing a lock of her hair off her neck, thrilling at the feel of her skin on his. She swallowed and arched her neck to his touch.

What was he doing? He knew he should stop. He'd been trying not to think about last night and how she'd felt on his lap. How difficult it'd been not to give in and lose himself inside of her. To ignore how fragile she was in that moment, so he could satiate the lust he shouldn't have in the first place.

He ran his hands along her arms, stroking her soft skin, feeling her goosebumps rise. How simple would it be to slip his hands beneath her sweatshirt and cup her breasts, feeling her nipples pebble beneath the pads of his fingers? He closed his eyes to end the imaginary sensations, but that only intensified them.

Distance. They needed distance.

He grabbed her wrists and pulled her up. She stood on wobbly legs and he wrapped an arm around her waist, so she wouldn't fall backward. His fingers spread against the soft heat of her back. "Got you."

She gripped his shoulders and swallowed. "A little lower and you might," she said, her voice husky.

His hand slid a fraction lower and she pulled him closer. His body ached for more. But that was *not* distance.

He forced himself to let her go and took a step back. "In your dreams, Winters."

Shrugging, she stepped over the bench. In the doorway she turned his way. Her gaze dropped low and then back to his eyes. She gave him a sly smile, "In *yours*, Conor."

She turned on her heel and walked back to the living room while he sank against the wall and sighed.

His dreams were getting more vivid by the day.

17

LATE IN THE AFTERNOON, Adelia played her guitar and tried not to think about anything. Especially not Conor. The warmth of his arms and the timbre of his laugh. The way he'd touched her and looked at her. Every part of her body was tight, nipples to knees, and the weight of wanting him was crushing her.

Sleeping beside him had been the best sleep she'd ever had. And waking was miserable, knowing there would be no sequel. Not because he didn't want her, too, because he did. Emotions were difficult for her to discern, but she knew lust. This wasn't just lust. He loved stories about white knights rescuing damsels, but she wasn't some princess forced into a tower. That was what he didn't understand. Every small secret was a stone she'd mortared into place, one after another until she was safe inside, and she knew he wouldn't be happy until he took a sledge-hammer to whole damn thing, burying her in the rubble.

Running a hand through her hair, she grabbed her phone and saw another email from Emi Hara.

Thank you for replying. I understand your position, but I'm going to be honest, because I think you are the type to appreciate honesty. You can do better than the producers you have been working with, and

I am better. I know this is presumptuous, bordering on arrogant, but I've attached a track I made. It would be a great fit for you. Ignore it if you want. Or play with it and see what you come up with. Let me know if you like it.

The banging on the door distracted her before she could listen to the track. There was no doubt whose knock it was. "Come on in."

"Hey!" Jo tumbled into the room, tripping over her feet. "Just got outta school. Can I hang out here for a while?"

She nodded and Jo plopped on the floor, dangling a chew toy in front of Cupcake. "I have stupid homework to do. You don't know anything about *The Odyssey*, do you?"

"Not that I remember. Conor probably does, though."

"Where's he at?"

"I think he said he was running errands for the Dive Inn people."

Jo ogled Adelia's guitar. "Are you writing a song?"

"Not really. But I got a track that I haven't listened to yet. Want to hear it?"

Jo pushed away Cupcake's amorous kisses. "Yes!"

She played it and nodded her head along to the music. It was good. Mid-tempo. Bluesy. Edgy. It was the kind of music that would frame her voice beautifully. And she had a song that might work. *That song.* The one she'd been working on for years but could never find the right track, the right sound. Excitement flared inside of her and she grabbed her notebook and scribbled lyrics as she remembered them. She sang, setting them into the music like jewels. Pulling each note from deep inside, and humming the parts where the lyrics didn't work. Jo sat there, her smudgy makeup creasing under her giant grey eyes, and swayed, while she played the track several times, finessing the lyrics in her notebook, stopping to consider the lilt of her voice. "Well, what do you think?"

Jo tilted her head. "It's different than your usual stuff. Can you play it again, but like, slow it down a little more?"

"Sure." She fiddled with the music software on her phone and slowed the tempo, singing it again. She snatched up her guitar and played the song as she sang, slowing the notes until they lingered, hovering like phantoms before settling into the strings and disappearing.

"That's a lot better," Jo said. "I like this song."

"I do, too. The studios won't." Her excitement drained away.

"I thought if you wrote the songs, then you could do whatever you wanted with them."

"No. I answer to a lot of people who have a lot of money riding on me. They don't like me to do anything that might screw with my branding."

"Your branding?" Jo scratched Cupcake behind the ears. "Like, Lia the bitch?"

"Yup."

"So, you made her up?"

She sat on the floor and made a note on the paper pad beside her. "Not exactly." She leaned back against the couch. "It's me. Or maybe it's not. I don't know." She sighed. "Either way, it's not all I want to be anymore."

"Who do you want to be instead?"

"I have no idea."

Jo pursed her lips. "That's probably okay. To not know. Sometimes I think I know who I am, and then I do or say something and I'm like, why did I do that? Is that weird?"

"I don't know. But it's cool to be weird. I'm weird."

"Which you?" Jo asked.

"Adelia me." She got on the floor and sat beside Jo. "When I'm in hotel rooms, I like to stare at the ceiling like it's the sky and find patterns. Like clouds."

Jo made a face. "I don't get it."

She flopped on the floor and pointed at a bumpy patch

above her. "See those swirls right there? With the four pointy things below them?"

Jo laid beside her and followed her pointed finger. "I guess."

"It's a unicorn. With bunny slippers on."

Jo's laughter pealed out. "I *so* don't see that."

She went to the kitchen and returned with a step stool, climbing it to trace the unicorn with her fingers.

Jo tilted her head. "Huh. That's a unicorn with bunny slippers on."

"And it's next to Harrison Ford playing cribbage."

"Wow, that is super weird," Jo said. "No offense."

"None taken."

Jo bit her lip and sat up. "Did anyone ever make you feel bad for being weird?"

"Sure."

"What'd you do about it?"

"Punched them." Adelia thought for a moment. "Um, you probably shouldn't do that, though. Who's being a jerk to you?"

Jo shrugged and got up, grabbed the stepstool and clomped into the kitchen. "Want some chocolate?"

If Jo didn't want to talk about it, she wasn't going to push. "Always. But you're not going to find any chocolate in this house."

Jo climbed onto the counter. She stood and reached into the back of the cupboard.

"What are you doing?"

Jo's hand emerged, holding two chocolate bars. "I hid a whole box back there." She handed one over. "Here."

"Oh, you are my favorite person."

Jo's smile was bright enough to light the night sky.

"Why do you keep chocolate bars here and not at your house?" Adelia asked as she wadded up the wrapper.

"Cuz chocolate is better when you're not supposed to have it," Jo said, licking her fingers.

She and Jo massacred two more candy bars, while watching a terrible end-of-the-world flick about a family running from a killer storm.

"Oh, man, those people were stupid," Adelia said as a tinny, nondescript pop song blared over the credits.

Jo nodded. "Yeah. That science was not sound. But that's what I do for fun. What about you?"

Adelia wrapped her arms around her knees. "Um, I don't know. Sing?"

"That's borrrrrring. You don't, like, go out and get drunk and party? Or read? Or watch makeup tutorials? Nothing?"

"No. I tour nine months out of the year, every year. And I'm not much of a people person," she said. "You're not getting drunk and partying, are you?"

"No," Jo said, rolling her eyes. "My mom would end me. She only has a couple of rules. The main one is I'm not allowed to do anything that'll get me pregnant before I graduate high school." She pushed her ratted hair from her face. "So, what's the point of being rich and famous if you don't do fun stuff?"

"I mean, sometimes I do something fun."

Jo sat up. "You mean when you aren't ceiling watching?"

"Yes, smartass. In hotels. I blast Metallica and dance around in trashy clothes, doing my best James Hetfield impression."

Jo didn't say anything for a minute. Just sat there blinking slowly at her. "Let's do that," she whispered.

METALLICA BLARED from his trailer when Conor came home. His neighbor, Mrs. Nash, stood on her porch, white hair askew and nostrils flaring. "It sounds like the devil's orgy in there. Been blaring for forty-five minutes."

He shifted his grocery bags to one arm. "I'm sorry about that. I'll turn it off right now."

"You better. I was about to call the police."

He nodded and unlocked the door. The music was deafening, and his living room was in chaos. Throw pillows everywhere. The dog was barking and jumping. Jo was headbanging. Adelia stood on his couch, bent over as she gargled out the lyrics to "Leper Messiah."

She grinned at him, and he nearly passed out from the sudden directional change in blood flow. She jumped off the couch and bounced to the stereo, twisting it down to less ear-splitting volume.

"We were having a Metallica Dance Party!" Jo shouted, as if the music were still playing.

"I saw that. And heard it. So did Mrs. Nash."

"Oh, sorry," Adelia said.

Jo dropped to the floor, not looking sorry, and gave Cupcake a vigorous belly-rub. The traitorous dog barely lifted her furry head to acknowledge him.

"That was some dance party," he said. "Did you guys get bored plotting world domination?"

"I've already plotted it," Jo said. "It's only a matter of putting plans into action, now."

Adelia spun toward Jo, words burbling. Something about "Leper Messiah," and rhythm and cadence and other music lingo he didn't understand. He tried to focus on what she was saying, he really did, but the muscle shirt she wore left absolutely nothing to the imagination when she turned to the side. And the tiny jean shorts barely skimmed the bottom of her ass, leaving her incredible legs exposed.

Perfect legs.

Legs he needed to stop looking at.

He dragged his eyes upward.

"Obviously *Master of Puppets* is their best album and I...Conor?"

His face was burning. Dammit. "Sorry, I wasn't paying attention."

She nodded. "Nope. My fault. You don't even have your coat off yet." She pointed at the grocery bags hanging from his hand. "Want me to put those away?" She grabbed both bags. "Your fridge is so organized, I've been afraid to touch anything, but I think I know where everything goes now. It's a miracle."

"Mom says he's a neat freak and..." Jo paused. "Anal-retentive. I dunno know what that means."

She pulled a package of chicken thighs from one of the bags. "I think it means he likes things neat and exactly where he wants them to be. Stuff like that helps some people feel like they're in control."

He scowled in her direction, but she dodged eye contact, busying herself with putting the chicken away.

"Why didn't she just say that?" Jo asked. "What do butts have to do with it?"

Adelia made a choking sound.

"Ask your mother," he said.

Jo held her phone aloft, her expression mulish. "Or I could Google 'anal-retentive' and probably end up scarred for life."

"The great thing about not having kids is that your psychological damage isn't my problem," he told Jo.

She shook her phone at him again.

Sighing, he grabbed it from her hand and did a search. "You can read it while you let Cupcake out." He handed it back with the Wikipedia entry loaded up. "Here. Knowledge with minimal scarring."

Jo leashed the dog and shut the door behind her. Adelia dug into the other grocery bag and pulled out a bag of grapes. Her eyes snapped to his.

"They're yours," he said.

She dug her hand into the bag and paused. "Thank you."

He nodded. "You're welcome. But you need to wash them fir—"

"Sorrywhat'dyousay?" she said around a mouthful of grapes.

He snatched the bag and set it back on the counter. "Wash them, Winters."

"Yeeees, Dad."

She cranked the water and grabbed the sprayer, pressing hard on the button. Water surged out at high-speed velocity, surely bruising the grapes as it bounced off them and shot her in the face. She jerked backward and looked at him, face dripping, and brown eyes wide and confused.

He really didn't want to laugh at her, but laughter geysered out. The more he tried to control it, the harder he laughed.

She crossed her arms, over her water spattered shirt. "Really?"

"I'm sorry—" He swallowed another laugh. "But you looked...like Cupcake when I pretend to throw a stick." This sent him over the edge and his body shook with laughter.

The water that hit him in the face was freezing. He put up his hands, but she had it on full blast, soaking him.

He reached for the sprayer. "Give it."

She held it out of his reach. "No! You compared my face to your dog's face."

"It's a compliment. My dog's cute."

She sprayed him again. It took some tussling, but he managed to get her pinned against the counter, with one of his legs between hers, her wrists held above her head.

"Let go."

She loosened her grip and he pulled the sprayer away, twisting to drop it into the sink. He turned off the water with one hand, and kept her pinned with his body, in case she got any ideas.

"I let you win," she said.

"Whatever helps you sleep at night." Beads of water drizzled down his temples and he shook his head to escape them. She pressed her hands to his face and wiped the water away. His lingering laughter evaporated in the heat of her gaze.

Her fingers scraped past his cheeks and to his mouth. The rough pad of her thumb brushed a droplet from his lower lip. She lingered there, her gaze fixated on him. His heart thumped a warning the rest of him didn't want to hear and he pressed himself closer.

Her chest rose and fell hard against his, her breaths coming in tiny puffs. She stood on her tiptoes, tantalizingly close. Her breath, indefinably sweet, teased his lips. She lowered her lashes and his body tightened.

"Jo will be back soon," she said softly.

He stepped back, breathing heavily. "Yeah, she will."

Right on time, the clunk of Jo's heavy tread hit the porch. Adelia rushed out of the kitchen and returned with her sweater on, hiding those lithe, delicious curves. His disappointment was tempered by the oxygen and blood getting back to his brain.

Jo tossed the door open, slamming it against the wall. Cupcake galloped in ahead of her. "That Freud guy was weird," she announced.

"You aren't the first person to say that," he said.

"Also, Mom texted. She got Dany to cover the rest of her shift, so she's coming home. She says you're in charge of dinner." She looked at her phone. "Also, you guys are invited over for dinner."

Thank god. Maybe if they were surrounded by people, he'd be more likely to keep his hands off of Adelia. He glanced over at her and she gave him a small, tight smile, as if she'd been thinking the same thing.

"Sounds good," he said, finding his voice. "But I don't feel like cooking. We're getting takeout. Everyone pack it up, I'm not driving all the way back to town by myself."

Once they were all in the truck, Jo began texting, tuning

everyone out. A sure sign she was getting used to having Adelia around.

He parked the truck in front of Wong's Pizza and typed out a quick text.

Jo's phone pinged and her eyes spun heavenward. "Really?"

"Seemed the best way to get your attention. I texted you what to get. It's your responsibility to order it and bring it out." He handed her his bank card. "And don't go off script and get a double cheese and pineapple pizza like last time. Your mom said it was unacceptable both in flavor and texture."

"It was good!" she said as she climbed over Adelia and got out.

"Doubtful. Go. We'll be back to pick you up."

She slammed the door shut and raced into Wong's.

"Ooh, where are we going?" Adelia's eyes sparkled in the dim interior light. "Cider slushies?"

He checked his watch. "It's already seven. The mill closed at six. I was thinking we'd go to Keys and find something for an after-dinner treat."

"Maaaaan," she said, doing a pretty good impression of Jo.

"Sorry. How about pie? My buddy Jack is a baker and he's stocking some of his pies at Keys. Shannon is over the moon for them. We could pick one up."

She shrugged. "That'll work."

"Great." He reached behind the seat and grabbed a baseball cap. He pushed the hoodie off her head and slapped the cap on, then pulled the hoodie back over it. "There. Now you can go in with me."

In the market, she went straight to a display and frowned. "Damn. The dilly beans are sold out."

"There's more in the next aisle," Old Curtis hollered from his perch at the cash register.

Conor grabbed a cherry pie and went looking for Adelia. She was bent over, shuffling through the jars of pickled vegetables. It was a pleasant view. And he wasn't the only one who'd noticed. Shannon's boss, Dennis Littlewood, was pretending to look at a can of corn but had his eyes firmly on her backside. A couple of local women standing close to him wore pinched expressions as they eyed her as well.

"Down-staters," one woman hissed. "This country is going straight to H-E-double-hockey-sticks."

He sidled in front of her, blocking everyone's view. She turned around, holding a jar of dilly beans aloft. "Found them."

"You've got an audience," he said softly.

"I know," she said. "You should hear what they said about you. Gossipy bitches."

She threw her arms around his neck and bumped her nose with his, startling him. "Let's go back to your place," she purred, her voice carrying throughout the back half of the market. This was a game they'd played one hundred times before, though it was usually Adelia shouting inappropriate things about rashes or penis size.

"You sure you want to play the game this way?" he murmured near her ear.

She nodded, and he didn't need any other encouragement. He pulled her closer, his hands roaming over the rounded curve of her ass. "What was your name again?" he asked, making sure he could be heard halfway across the room.

She didn't hesitate. "Annie," she said. "But you can call me whatever you want."

The women huffed and their footsteps retreated, but he didn't let go of her. "They were properly scandalized," he whispered. "I'm sure my mother will be calling to yell at me about being uncouth."

"Just like old times," she said, laughing in his ear. She pulled away, but kept one of his hands in hers as she made her way to the front of the shop.

Old Curtis shook his head at them. "Conor Ross, you better

learn to behave yourself," he said. He swung a knobby finger at Adelia. "You too, young lady. This is a family place."

They dropped their heads and mumbled apologies. It really was like old times. Except for groping her. That was new.

"I swear, you kids today," Old Curtis said.

Kids. Conor supposed everyone was a kid when you were three thousand years old. He fished his wallet out of his back pocket. "I'm thirty."

"Couldn't tell by the way you were acting." The old man reached beneath the counter and grabbed something, shoving it in the bag without explanation. "Twenty-eight dollars and sixty-seven cents."

Before he could hand over his credit card, Adelia dropped some cash on the counter. "Keep the change." She grabbed the bags and hightailed it out the door.

He followed and climbed in the truck after her. "You gave him forty bucks."

"It's cool." She rooted around in the bag and froze. "Oh. My. God."

"What?"

She handed him a shiny black three-pack of extra-large condoms. He stared at them blankly. "He didn't."

"He did!"

Her crazed laughter bounced around the cab and landed like music and he sang the same tune, laughing until his cheeks ached.

"Honestly," he said, wiping wetness from his eye. "I don't know whether to be flattered by the size, or depressed that these things are going to fall off of me like baggy pants with no belt."

That sent her into another laughing fit. She was still snickering to herself when they pulled up to Wong's. He climbed out and walked around to her side of the truck, throwing open the door. "You done?"

Despite her nod, the wink of her dimples gave away her mirth. He gripped the sides of her shorts and pulled her to the edge of the bench seat. "Get over here." He meant to sound playful but it came out as a growl.

Her hands skated down the back of his neck to settle on the shoulders of his rain-soaked shirt. Using him for balance, she slid out, her body slithering against his, making him shiver. The breathy remainder of her laughter evaporated.

He breathed in her strawberry scent and pulled her tight against him. Her heated little exhalation set his nerve endings on fire.

The look she gave him nearly melted the zipper off of his jeans and everything in it dared him to make a move, and he wanted to. More than he'd ever wanted to touch anyone. The sweater over her muscle shirt was in his way, so he pushed it aside and pressed a knuckle to the soft exposed skin of her side, and brushed it upward, tracing her ribs with the back of his hand, skimming the side of her breast.

Her nipples hardened beneath her wet shirt. She shuddered and everything disappeared. Wherever they were, whatever time it was, gone. He cupped her jaw, and she arched up, straining toward him, her mouth so sweet and close to his.

"Pizza's ready!" Jo hollered from the restaurant. "I need more hands!"

She pulled back and gave him a rueful smile. "Be there in a second," she hollered.

He pressed his hands on the top of the truck. "It's not okay to kill her, right?"

Another dimple appeared beneath her rosy cheek and he wanted to kiss it. "Shannon would be upset if you did."

Brushing his hair back to keep his hands off her, he stepped back, willing his body to cool down.

Adelia wrapped her arms around herself and shook her head. "Conor, this is Doritos."

"Uh, what?"

"This." She gestured between them. "You said you gave them up for a reason. They're empty. They don't offer you anything. *I'm* Doritos."

His brain a few seconds to catch up. "You're not."

"I'm probably worse for you."

He took a step toward her. "Maybe I can handle a taste."

"Why are you guys always talkin' about Doritos?" Jo asked, as she came around the door.

"We have a…philosophical disagreement about them," he said.

"Hmph. That sounds made up," Jo said. "Come on. You wanted mushrooms and that's disgusting, so I went off script. I ordered three pizzas and breadsticks and a big salad." She grabbed Adelia's arm and dragged her toward the restaurant. A few seconds later, they emerged with arms full of greasy carbs he couldn't have.

Jo pulled out his credit card and played with it. "You know, I could do a lot of birthday shopping with this thing."

"Give me my card, you little ingrate," he said. "I bought you a treat from Keys, but I don't know if I should reward your bad behavior. We didn't need three pizzas."

Jo's handed the card over. "I'll be good. Now."

"Doubtful."

The brat took the window seat and piled the food beside her, leaving Adelia pressed against him. He couldn't say he minded all that much. Adelia opened one of the pizza boxes and studied it before picking a mushroom off. Warmth settled inside of him. Some things were fixed truths. The sun always rose. The sun always set. Adelia always loved mushrooms on her pizza.

He reached beneath his seat and pulled out the baggie full of tissues. "No eating in here. You'll get grease on my seats." He handed her a tissue. "Behave yourself, young lady."

Her smile flickered. "I don't know if I can."

Her words were soft. Uneven. They stared at each other.

Want throbbed within him, blunting everything, until he could barely remember all the reasons why he should stop this before it went any further.

He threw the truck into gear and gave her a tight smile. "I don't know if I can, either."

CONOR COULDN'T CONCENTRATE on anything. Not conversation. Not his cardboard pizza. Not the movie. Somewhere in the middle of the film Adelia removed her damp sweater, the thin muscle shirt leaving her as close to naked as she could be, while sitting next to him on a couch, with Shannon and Jo in the room.

He fiddled with the edge of his shirt. Scratched his nose and rubbed his eyes. Anything to distract himself. After finally having his hands on her, stroking her velvety soft skin, seeing her body respond to him, he wanted more. Being so close and not being able to touch her was torture.

Unable to stand it any longer, he stretched his arm out over the back of the couch and surreptitiously stroked his fingers beneath her hair and along the curve of her neck. She closed her eyes, leaning into his hand, and pressed her thigh against his, the heat of their bodies entwining until the end of the movie.

While Jo declared the film about rampaging crocodiles a masterpiece, they sat up, giving each other guilty glances. She grabbed their plates off the folding table and took them to the kitchen. He followed her as she tossed them in the garbage and flipped open the huge pizza box, the top obscuring them from view.

He stepped behind her and brushed the hair off her neck, making her shiver. She arched her back, brushing her ass against the front of his jeans and he growled, pulling her closer.

She cleared her throat and picked a mushroom off the pizza. "I forgot how good Wong's is." Her tongue darted out to lick the grease off her finger and his body hummed.

"It's only good because it has an inch of cheese on it," he said.

"Don't fat shame my food." She gave him a side eye and leaned over the pizza. "You're beautiful just as you are," she whispered.

"Pie!" Shannon yelled from the living room. "I was promised cherry pie!"

"I'm on it," Adelia yelled back. She moved out of the range of his hands to grab the pie and start slicing it up. He helped her carry the plates out to the living room and sit them on the tables.

Shannon stopped folding her afghan and stared at Adelia's shirt. "Sweet Mary Mother of God, are you charging by the hour?"

"Not recently."

He choked and Adelia smacked him on the back.

"You need more shirt with that shirt," Shannon said.

Much to his disappointment, she draped the sweater over her chest without putting it back on. "There. You can go back to silently judging me."

"I prefer to judge aloud," Shannon said. "Don't they make bras in California?"

"We aren't all as blessed as you. Have you seen me?" She pulled off the sweater and stuck out her chest. "The only upside of being small is I don't have to wear bras."

He went a bit lightheaded as her breasts jiggled beneath the shirt.

Shannon pulled at the neck of her sweatshirt and looked inside. "They're not really that great. I have to wear industrial-strength minimizers. Brutal in the summer. And when I was pregnant, I practically had to cart these things around with a wheelbarrow." She let go of her shirt. "Plus, you know, gravity is going to kick my ass one day."

"It's not kicking your ass today. You should focus on that." She scraped at her plate and licked the tines of her fork. He wanted to throw the fucking fork on the floor and kiss the taste of cherry pie off of her lips. Sex didn't burn as many calories as people thought it did, but maybe most people weren't trying hard enough. He pictured himself and Adelia making use of his weight bench in the most athletic way possible. He got harder by the second. When she slid her thumb in her mouth and sucked the sticky filling from it, he shot off the couch, nearly running to the bathroom.

What was he doing? He'd been horny before, but he'd never felt like this in his whole life. He was a resistance band stretched to the breaking point. It wasn't simple lust. He thought about the pie filling. Okay, lust was a part of it. But it was more than that. He didn't just want her. He wanted to claim her like a caveman in front of everyone; pull her onto his lap and kiss her like she'd never been kissed before. He closed his eyes, but behind his eyelids were visions of a very naked Adelia moaning his name.

He was making it worse. Conor adjusted himself and yanked on his shirt, wishing it were longer. Maybe no one would notice. But he saw himself in the full-length mirror on the back of the bathroom door. It was a *touch* noticeable. Fuck. He washed his face in ice-cold water and thought gross thoughts.

Grandma Margaret in her underwear. Scabs. Cockroaches. Old Curtis eating a Popsicle.

He looked down. Rock hard.

She *was* Doritos. The feeling in his gut, the need to touch her knowing it was going to make his life worse, was familiar. Every plate of French fries, every sticky sweet slice of cake. He'd never been content with a single bite.

But unlike French fries and cake, she wouldn't be everywhere he turned. She said it herself, she was...leaving.

And he couldn't binge on what wasn't there.

Maybe that's what they needed. A few nights of play and touch and heat in the dark. They could get out of each other's systems. Fuck like bunnies and then part ways and he could have some small sense of an ending to whatever it was they used to be.

He could manage that.

Feeling in control, he left the bathroom.

"Everything all right?" Shannon asked.

"I'm, uh, not feeling well," he said. "I think I'll head home. Go to bed." He held his breath and caught Adelia's eye, willing her to go with him.

She shot off the couch and grabbed her sweater. "I'm pretty beat, I'll go too."

He let out his breath.

"Aww," Jo said.

Shannon marched into the kitchen, her slippers clomping on the linoleum. "At least take some pie with you." She scooped a couple of pieces into a container and shoved it at Adelia. Her mouth was pinched tight and her eyes narrowed. "Get good *sleep.*"

The rain had slowed and it didn't feel so much like monsoon season as they headed to his house. She trailed after him, walking slower than usual, chin lifted toward the sky. The dim streetlight obscured her expression in shifting shadows.

New worry gnawed at him. He hadn't misread her desire, but maybe she was having second thoughts. He froze.

She'd seen him back when he...his jaw clenched. She might want his new body, but maybe her memory of what he'd been before would end this thing before it began, just like last time.

As soon as they entered the trailer, Cupcake whined pitifully and danced from side to side.

"Better walk her or you'll be shampooing the carpet all night," she said as she headed for the kitchen to put the food away.

He leashed the dog for a quick walk. When he came back, Adelia had her sweater on and zipped up. How depressing.

She scratched at her mane of hair. "I forgot that I had a dye kit in the stuff I pulled out of my car. I'm going to fix this mop," she said. "Remember when we used to get drunk and dye my hair with food coloring?"

"Yeah, I also recall the night you talked me into dying *my* hair."

"What? It was electric blue. You looked awesome."

"My mother had a coronary."

"That was the best part," she said with a grin. "It's not going to be as much fun without booze."

He reached into one of the cupboards. From the back he pulled out a hinged wooden box and sat it on the counter. She peered around his shoulder as he flipped the lid open. He pulled a gorgeous bottle of golden amber liquid from a bed of straw and sat it on the counter.

Adelia whistled and ran a finger over the midnight blue foil seal. "*The Macallan Whisky?* Scottish *and* fancy."

"I got it as a gift years ago. Never opened it."

She stared at the label. "This is thirty years old. You had a bottle of thirty-year-old whisky and you didn't drink it?" She shook her head sadly. "Thought I taught you better."

"Apparently not." He searched the cupboard for the novelty tumblers he'd stashed away and slapped them on the counter. "There we are."

She eyed the pink hearts and the words, *Love is all you need*, etched in loopy pastel letters.

"Gross," she declared.

"I know. Got those from Liam's wedding. Well, one of his weddings." He rinsed the dust out of the glasses and dried them.

"How many weddings?"

"Let's see. Engaged but it fell through. Then married and divorced a year later. Married again. Divorced again. Liam's learning curve is a circle." He pulled a corkscrew out from his kitchen drawer and sat it on the counter. "Turns out, love is temporary, but novelty glasses are forever."

He grabbed the edge of the foil around the bottleneck and she pressed her hand onto his. "Are you sure? This bottle is probably worth over two thousand dollars."

"You're kidding me. Liam sent it when I graduated from college." He tilted the bottle to get a better look at the label. "I should have guessed. He does love expensive whisky." The light shone through the liquid. "Seriously, two grand?"

"At least."

"Have you ever tasted two-thousand-dollar whisky?" he asked.

"I haven't had whisky in years, and when I did, it was Jim Beam and Coke. This is a completely different level of boozing." She stroked the bottle, her fingers skating over the curve at the neck.

He shrugged. "Let's live a little."

She took the corkscrew from him. With an expert hand, she flipped open a little compartment along the side of it, unfolding a small knife.

"I didn't know that was there," he said.

She ran the blade under the lip of the bottle, pressing with her thumb. Peeling the foil away, she gripped the stopper and pulled it out with a pop.

"That was…hot."

She bit her lower lip and looked down. God, he was jealous. He wanted to bite that lip, too.

"Thanks. A sommelier taught me how to open bottles because he got turned on by watching me do it naked. Weird guy."

He leaned against the counter. "Does it bother you to talk about that stuff?"

She played with the foil. "It's new for me to talk about it. But, no." She poured a finger of whisky into each glass. "Does it bother you?" Her expression was bland, but he had a suspicion that his answer mattered.

"Not really," he said slowly. "I'm not bothered that you did it. I'm sad that it felt like your only option. And I'm furious at the people who took advantage of you."

"Save your rage. I was pretty good at taking care of myself."

He swirled the glass on the counter, whisky spinning like a vortex inside. "Just because you could, didn't mean you should have had to."

"Fair enough." She picked up her tumbler, and stared into the golden liquid reverently. She swished it under her nose and breathed in the scent.

He took a sip. It tasted like oranges burning in a summer campfire. It was buttery rich and barely burned on the way down.

She followed suit, swishing it around in her mouth and fanning herself after she swallowed. "Whoo! That is nothing like Jack and Coke."

"Thank god for that." He took another drink and slammed the glass on the counter. "All right, Winters. Let's get drunk and dye your hair."

ADELIA WAS *HAMMERED*.

Of course, Conor wasn't faring much better. The warm haze of alcohol made everything shimmer prettily. He sat on the living room floor with his camera and took another swig from the bottle. They'd given up the tumblers a while ago.

He took some more pictures. Her vivid hair swayed as she danced around his living room, wearing his leather jacket for reasons he couldn't remember. The night was getting fuzzy around the edges and his head was floating toward the ceiling. He remembered dyeing her hair. After it was rinsed and dried, she declared that it still looked like crap, so she grabbed a pair of scissors and began snipping. Even drunk, she did a good job. She now had bangs, and her shoulder-length wavy hair was the same vibrant color as red velvet cake.

The music throbbed and she grinned at him as she spun in a circle, her breasts bouncing in a most hypnotizing way. She stopped spinning and dropped to her knees to take another swig of whisky. He followed the sweat droplets trickling down her throat, disappearing into her shirt.

Adelia wiped the sweat off and smacked his cheek with her

damp hand. "Don't be pervy." She tossed open her guitar case and ran her fingers along the soft fabric in the lid, sliding them into a hidden pocket and pulled out a handful of somethings. Pictures? Then she bounced her way into the kitchen, and nearly fell over, trying to hoist herself onto the counter.

He stumbled in and stared through bleary eyes. "What are you doing?"

"I want a candy bar."

"I don't have any candy bars. I don't eat that stuff."

Adelia gave up her scrambling. "But Jo does."

That made zero sense, but he grabbed her by the waist and lifted her onto the counter. She got on her knees, searching the cupboard and he kept hold of her hips.

For safety.

She clumsily pushed aside dishes, grumbling about his organization systems. With a cry of victory, she held a chocolate bar aloft as she crawled around on her knees and sat on the counter, her long legs dangling off the edge as she tore open the silvery wrapper and popped a chunk of chocolate into her mouth. "Mmm." Her eyes rolled back. "Oh, that's good."

She tore off another piece and then stared at it. "Don't you miss candy?" she asked.

"No. I miss French fries, sometimes."

She bobbed her head. "It would be sad to live without those."

She decimated half the candy bar, licked her fingers and then wiped them on her shirt. It should have grossed him out, but such was the power of Adelia. And whisky.

She handed him the pictures.

The first picture was her with a famous country singer he vaguely recognized. "Who took this picture? It's blurry."

She took it from him and stared at it. "No, it's...oh yeah."

The next one was of her with her band, and a smarmy looking guy in a suit. He would have known it was EJ even if he hadn't seen the guy's face on television. One arm was wrapped tightly around her, his hand gripping her shoulder, while he held her other arm immobile between their bodies. "Man," he said. "That is the body language of someone who wants to control you."

She stared at it and her lip curled. "He wants me to be a dancing monkey." She shoved that picture at the bottom of the pile and handed him the rest.

He flipped through the photos. Picture of her making devil horns alongside a bald man.

"Lead singer of Disturbed," she said

Another that had her giving an exaggerated side eye to a large group of guys in frightening masks. "Slipknot," she said. "Those guys are committed to their mission statement."

He laughed. She looked so fresh faced and happy.

He came to the last picture and stared at it, in awe. "Adelia, is that Metallica?"

She nodded, her expression impassive.

"You hung out with Metallica?"

"I sang with Metallica. It was for some charity benefit."

He raised his eyebrows high.

"It's not a big deal," she said.

"How can you say it's not a big deal?" He held the picture up to her face and stared at her.

Her lips twitched and then she gave up the fight to be cool, smiling wide. "Okay it was amazing. It's fucking Metallica!"

She reached for the picture and he stepped between her knees as she leaned forward and pointed to herself. "That was the best day of my life. See how I look surprised? Someone goosed me! I think it was Lars, though," she said, sounding disappointed.

"Bummer. James Hetfield was your dream guy."

"Was? No, is. He is so... sexy. Kind of quiet though. And married." She made a face. "Bah."

"*Lars* may have goosed you and James is married? Life really kicked you in the teeth."

"I know," she said. "Nothing ever goes my way."

"Except the money and the fame and all that," he said.

"I mean, if you want to count those things, life treated me pretty well."

He smiled and pressed his forehead against her. "I missed you," he said, the thud of his heart competing with the rushed beat of the music from the stereo.

She nodded, bumping their craniums together. "I missed you, too," she whispered. After a few seconds, she pulled away. "Whisky was a very bad idea."

"One of many," he said, pushing a tendril of hair away from her cheek.

Over the music, and the sound of his heart, another thumping intruded. He pulled away and listened. "What is that?"

"The door," she said.

"Well. Fuck."

He threw the door open. A Greene County officer, in his tan and brown uniform stood there, smoothing a porno mustache straight out of the seventies.

"Good evening, sir," the officer said loudly in clipped tones. "We received a complaint about the noise. Could you turn your music down?"

Conor stared at him. "Oh." He made careful I'm-not-drunk steps as he went to the stereo and turned it off. "Sorry about that."

"How you doing, tonight? Having a good time?"

"Uh, yeah."

"How many people you got in there?"

"Just me." There was a thunk, and Adelia rounded the counter, all bare legs and sexy jiggle, short circuiting his brain. *He really did like that outfit on her.*

The officer must have had the same thought. He straightened his already erect posture and cleared his throat, his fingers smoothing the wayward hairs of his vintage mustache. "How are you this evening, ma'am?" he asked, his icy tone considerably warmer than it had been.

She murmured that she was fine, and agitation prickled his skin.

"Mind if I come in, take a look around?" Without waiting for an answer, the guy entered the trailer. He made a show of looking around the room, but his eyes kept returning to her. He placed his hand on his belt buckle. "I'm Officer Bennett." He jerked his head sideways. "And you are…"

She lowered her lashes. Was she flirting? "Anne," she said. "Smith."

"Pleasure to meet you. Are you having a good time tonight?" His voice dropped low, and the officer gave her a hot lingering look. Conor's knuckles itched to connect to the guy's nose.

"Yeah. Visiting my friend. Didn't mean to cause any trouble." Her husky voice took on a silky quality that was phony as hell. But Officer Bennett didn't know any better, and he was shifting his stance wider, and adjusting his belt buckle. Preening like a peacock, for her attention.

He glanced at Conor, and his gaze dismissed him. "A friend?"

"A close friend." He stepped nearer to her. She gave him a death stare, and his surge of testosterone dissipated.

Officer Bennett grunted a nothing response, as he jotted a note down. "Listen," he said, gruffer than before. "You gotta keep the volume down. I got two calls about it. You're violating noise ordinances, not to mention the rules of this park, and I could give you a citation."

"Please don't," she said, stepping forward and placing her hand on the officer's arm. "It was my fault." She peered through her eyelashes and nailed the officer with a look that should have been accompanied by a naughty schoolgirl uniform and the phrase, *I've been a very bad girl.* "I'll keep it down."

"I suppose I could let it go. This time. If you behave your-self." Officer Bennett's voice dropped to match hers.

Conor ground his teeth. Adelia may not have been model-beautiful but she wore sex like a second skin, and he could practically hear the officer panting.

She blinked her languid eyes, and graced the officer with smile, her teeth skimming her bottom lip. "Thank you, Officer Bennett." Her voice rolled over the cop's name like a caress as she walked him to the door.

The guy had a dazed look, like he'd taken a punch to the head, which Conor wished he had. Churning in a second tsunami of angry testosterone, he missed whatever it was the officer murmured to Adelia, but he didn't miss him slipping a card into her hand, before leaving.

She shut the door and leaned against it, her nose scrunching up. "Blech." She chucked the card onto the counter.

"Oh, Officer Mustache," he said in a falsetto voice, batting his eyelashes. "How big your muscles look!"

"Shut up. I panicked. Once they get inside, they start looking for shit to bust you on."

"Officer, put your porno 'stache anywhere you want on me," he continued as if she hadn't spoken. "I'm soooo naughty."

"Cops freak me out. It was a reflex!"

"Reflexive flirting? That's what you're going with?"

"Cops *love* a bad girl. Most of them fantasize about some hot thing jumping on their nightstick. So it works."

He closed his eyes. "I don't want to know how you know that, do I?"

"You probably don't," she said with a shrug. "Let's say, I've been caught, but I've never been arrested." She cocked her hips to one side and rested her hands on them. "The only way to win an unfair fight is to use everything you've got."

"Weird that you've never bothered to use any of that sexy charm on me," he said.

"That's because you'd know I was full of shit." She smacked his arm and graced him with a genuine smile, one that turned his thoughts upside-down and erased any jealousy he felt toward Officer Mustache. "Oh, and by the way." She lowered her chin and graced him with a scowl. "I'm her friend," she said in a deep voice. "Her close friend."

Heat seared his cheeks. "I was concerned for your well-being. He was...lascivious."

She barked a laugh. "You don't get to act like a caveman and then use a ten-dollar word like that. Pick a way to be, man."

"Fine." He grabbed her around the waist and hoisted her onto his shoulder.

"Put me down," she shrieked through her laughter.

"Me Conor. You Adelia." He grunted in a suitably Neanderthal kind of way as he carried her, smacking her ass for good measure.

She was still giggling when he squatted to grab the bottle, stumbled down the hall, and deposited her on his bed with a thump.

He fell in beside her, and laid on his back, his hands resting on his chest, waiting for the head spin to stop.

She leaned over him and grabbed the bottle and took another drink. "Best. Whisky. Ever."

"Jesus, we drank most of the bottle," he said. "That's going to hurt tomorrow."

"Fuck yeah, it will!" She raised the bottle like it was a trophy.

She was such a big ball of energy and profanity and fire, he couldn't help but to smile. "You say 'fuck' more than any other person I've ever met."

"I'm colorful. Sue me."

They lay there silently for a while. The energy died down and she stared at his ceiling.

A question at the back of his mind, rose to the surface. "Why has the press never found out about the prostitution?"

She shrugged. "I was a minor. Anyone who blabs is admitting to being an accessory. Though, I've been waiting for that shoe to drop for a long time." She sighed. "I don't want to go back to California."

A tingling spread from his chest to all his limbs. "Because of that?"

"No. Because I hate it," she said. "And I don't have anything."

"Other than a mountain of money, you mean."

"Yeah, no. I mean, I have that. But I don't have something that means something, you know?" Her lips pursed petulantly, and he wanted to roll her onto her back and kiss her until she passed out.

He leaned close to her, mimicking her pouty expression. "Is Winters having a pity party?"

She ran her fingers along the edge of his collar. "Tread carefully," she said, her voice dry. "Winters is pretty sure she can take you in a fair fight."

He leaned over her, drawn in, danger bells clanged in his head. He ignored them and threw a knee between hers, then the other, and slowly pushed her legs apart. He ran his hands up her arms, until they were extended above her head, and brushed the tip of his nose with hers. She didn't try to escape, just watched.

He tilted his head slightly and brushed her lips, barely touching them.

"You think you can take me?" He shook his head. "I don't know." He arched his hips, making hot contact between their bodies. "I'm pretty sure I could take you now."

He felt the shudder that surged through her.

"What do you think?" he murmured.

Her eyes were sleepy and dangerous. "This isn't a fair fight."

His tongue grazed her lower lip, the delicate dance of touch and not touch, tilting ever so slightly. "You said the only way to win an unfair fight is to use everything you've got. Remember?"

Sliding her arms from his grip, she grabbed hold of his

shoulders. Her legs tightened against his hips. Before he could react, she flipped him flat onto his back and sat up. The heat of her center pressed against him. She arched and he grunted at the delicious friction. It was her turn to slide her arms up his, capturing his wrists, pressing them to the bed. Her breath was hot in his ear as she took his earlobe between her teeth, biting it gently. She snaked a hand between their bodies and stroked him until he moaned.

Unable to stand it any longer, he pulled his wrist from her grip and shoved his hands into her hair, pressing toward her lush mouth.

She pulled back, just out of his reach and smirked. "Conor, if I use everything I've got on you, you won't be able to move for a week."

Time slowed like maple syrup. Nothing could stop this. It was as inevitable as the earth spinning around the sun. He pulled her toward him. "Prove it," he said.

———

SHE TASTED like chocolate and whisky.

They'd been kissing for ages. Years, maybe. He ran his hand over her tattoo, stroking her soft, painted flesh. She held his face, kissing him feverishly while his hands slipped into the easily accessible sides of her muscle shirt. His thumbs brushed the hot points of her breasts and she exhaled, a sharp little pleasure sound that made him woozy.

Conor's focus narrowed to sensation and observation. His hand on her smooth breast. The swift rise and fall of her chest with each breath. His body demanded more touch, more contact, more her or he wouldn't survive. He sucked on the space between her neck and collarbone, licking and pulling while she whimpered encouragement. He said her name, wanting to taste it on his lips. To taste her.

The air between them thickened and he grabbed the belt loop of her shorts and pulled her close, tight against him, and then pushed her hips back, the friction making them both shudder. He jerked her hips again and watched her moan. They rocked back and forth, her hips grinding on him. He shoved aside the shirt and wrapped his mouth around one of her breasts. She dug her hands into his hair and rocked harder, her breathing shallow and uneven. He sucked, tugging on her nipple, scraping his teeth against her sensitive skin and marveling at all the stark contrasts of Adelia. Fair skin, dark nipples. Tiny breasts, cushioned bottom. Caustic disposition, sweet rescuer. She was everything at once, and he was dizzy at all the possibilities of her.

He grabbed her ass and pressed her harder against him. Her hips rolled in ever tighter spirals as she made pleading sounds, hot little *yeses* that he met with grunts of agreement. Her moans took on a frantic tone and whatever pain the future brought seemed like a small price to pay for this. Until she raised her hands and cupped his jaw, locking eyes on his. Jittery panic rushed through him. He arched his hips, crashing them against hers, bringing his heat and her heat together and even through clothing, it was enough to set the house on fire. Her eyes fluttered closed and her arms tightened around him as she panted his name, tremors of pleasure undulating through her body as she came.

It was beautiful.

He reached for her zipper, ready to end the ache that pulsated inside of him. Ready to slide into her and damn the consequences. But as she quivered over him, her mouth wet and parted, he was transported. Suddenly, they weren't in a mobile home in Ribbon Rail Estates. Instead he was on his back in his mother's basement, round belly quivering as she rode him, her eyes tightly closed, and her lips parted.

Reality came back like freezing water. "No."

Her eyes slowly opened, heavy with desire.

"Why did you leave?" He hadn't meant to ask it. He knew it was a landmine.

Looking as if she'd received her own bucket of icy water, she scrambled off his lap and retreated to the far end of the bed.

"Please don't ask me that," she said breathlessly.

He wanted to take the words back and tumble her onto the mattress like he'd been about to do, but he couldn't leave it alone. The question burned inside of him for fourteen years and now that it was out in the atmosphere, the fire could extinguish, if she'd just tell the truth.

"Was it me?" he asked. "Did you leave because of..." He gestured to his stomach. "Was it because of me?"

Her guarded expression softened as she crawled back to him and took his jaw in her calloused hands. He consumed her with his eyes, needing to believe what he read on her face. "No. That wasn't—no. Why would you ever think that?"

He was raw skin exposed to steam. Too much. He'd already said too much. He grabbed her and kissed her furiously. When she pulled away to take a breath, he breathed out the words that he'd held in since the day she came back to Cherry Lake. "Because you fucked me and then you left town for fourteen years. What was I supposed to think?"

She pressed her hand to the shirt covering his stomach. "I liked this part of you. I liked all the parts of you, mind and body. It wasn't that. It's hard to explain. I just..." She looked down. "I wish that saying sorry would make it better."

"The truth would make it better."

"What if it doesn't?" she whispered.

"What if it does?"

She shook her head, her beet-red waves bouncing. "Tomorrow. I'll tell you tomorrow."

"No, you won't," he said. "Tomorrow you'll be sober and bristly and cold."

She flinched, the hurt on her face more naked than he'd ever seen.

Whatever tact he normally possessed was gone, as whisky flowed toward his brain and his blood flowed in the opposite direction. "You shut everyone out."

She closed her eyes and opened them, deep dark water that he wanted drown in. "You would have looked at me differently and it would have hurt to see you—" She rubbed at her mouth. "I'd rather you hate me than pity me."

He had no idea what she was talking about, but he pressed his head against hers. "As much as I've wanted to, I could never hate you. And I've never pitied you."

Her hot mouth on his obliterated him. Then she pushed away, sitting back on her calves. "We need to go to my dad's house."

"Right now?" he asked.

"Right now."

"That's very *carpe diem* of you."

She reached past him and grabbed his cell off the end stand. "What's Shannon's number?" she asked, her tongue between her teeth.

"She's 2 on the speed dial."

"Of course, she is." She rolled her eyes and pressed the button

A few minutes later, they were stumbling into Shannon's yellow jalopy, as she eyed them with something close to malice. "My bed was the kind of comfy that some people kill for. And I still might. So, this had better be good."

He dumped flashlights into the backseat.

Shannon sighed. "Now, what the hell is going on?"

"No idea," he said. All he had were throbbing balls and the beginnings of a headache. "She said to bring flashlights."

Adelia emerged from the house, tugging on one of his

battery powered speed lights. "I don't want to be cold," she said as she sat it in the backseat.

"Then put a jacket on," Shannon said. "And maybe a bra."

"No, that's not...I can't make sense right now. I had a lot of whisky." She gestured to the road. "I'll tell you where to go and it'll all make sense when we get there, I think. But I might have a nervous breakdown though. If I do, don't say anything, because...don't."

Shannon looked to him for some sort of explanation. He shrugged. "A *lot* of whisky Shan. A lot of it."

They were on the road for a few minutes, with nothing but silence for company. Adelia slouched in the front seat, playing with the end of her hair. "I used to call you Cherry Pie," she said.

"How could I forget?" Shannon said, her voice as dry as his mouth.

"I didn't call you that because I thought you were a virgin. I mean, I did think you were a virgin, but I was one too. It's just... cherry pie was Conor's favorite."

"Oh," Shannon said. "I nev—that's crazy. You were his favorite. He walked around behind you with cartoon hearts and bluebirds circling his head."

He cleared his throat from the back seat. "I like to think I was a bit more subtle than that."

Shannon gave him a look in the rearview mirror. "You weren't."

Chewing on her thumbnail, Adelia sighed. "It doesn't matter now. I just wanted to tell you that. It wasn't that I didn't like you." She laid her head back on the seat and tugged on a bit of Shannon's long, sleep mussed curls. "Your hair is so pretty."

"Good baby Jesus, I didn't know they made whisky this strong," Shannon said. "How long is this going to take?"

"Not long." Adelia looked back at him for a long moment. "It's time to carpe some fucking diems."

19

SHANNON'S VW RABBIT felt like a raft carried along the mud river that used to be Big Dirt Road. Conor traced the fat droplets of rain thwacking against the window.

"Where the heck are we going?" Shannon asked. "I've never driven out this way. Is this still Cherry Lake?" She squinted through the windshield.

"Yeah." Adelia's self-assured swagger was gone. With every mile she curled further into herself.

He reached between the seats and pressed his hand on her shoulder. "We don't have to do this," he said, feeling the first stir of sobriety.

"Yes, we do."

"Here?" Shannon asked, as they reached the end of the road, which turned into a gated driveway.

Nodding, Adelia got out and fiddled with the heavy combination lock. She half-fell back inside the vehicle. "Drive straight ahead." Her voice wobbled, and he wished he'd never opened his mouth to ask why she'd left. They could be under a blanket, warm in the afterglow of bad decisions. Instead they were trudging through a storm, into something that had to be awful, because she looked like a victim of war, her face pale and her eyes clouded with fear.

The driveway was a stew of mud and gravel and the Rabbit's tires worked overtime to keep the vehicle moving. "How frigging long is this driveway?" Shannon asked.

"About a half-mile," Adelia creaked out.

On either side of the drive, several cars in various states of decay were haphazardly parked. They finally pulled up to a squat mobile home on a slab in the middle of the yard.

Adelia climbed out of the car, her breaths coming sharp and shaky. "Gimme a minute," she said.

In the wash of the headlights, she climbed to the top of the steps. She pulled a set of keys from her jacket pocket and stared at them and back at the door. Shaking her head, she stomped to the bottom step and sat heavily on it, her head in her hands.

He jumped out and made his way to the porch. Her expression was as flat as a pane of glass. "I can't," she said.

"Then don't."

"It was never about you, Conor."

"I'm starting to get that," he said. "Come on, let's go."

She stood on wobbly legs and looked back at the trailer. "If I don't do it now, I never will," she said softly. Then she turned and climbed the steps. She fought with the door a moment. "You might want to stand back a ways. And keep the headlights on."

Shannon gave him a frightened expression as they backed up until they were behind her car. "Um, her dad's not still in there, right?"

"God, I hope not," he said.

Adelia put both hands on the door and shoved it a couple of times, until it opened partway. A ghastly odor erupted from the house, carried on the wind right into their faces. It smelled like a dozen sweaty, un-deodorized chain-smokers sitting in a moldy landfill on a hot damp day. Shannon wretched and he threw his hand over his face, trying to hold onto the whisky that was threatening to make a reappearance.

"It'll go away in a minute. Well, the worst of it will." Her voice was lifeless as she walked toward them and grabbed the flashlights from the backseat of the car. She gave one to each of them, then trudged toward the trailer. They followed behind, covering their noses.

She was right, the odor dissipated somewhat after a minute. It was still the most disgusting thing he'd ever smelled, but he was pretty sure he could hold onto his lunch. She flicked the switch on the flashlight and gestured. "Single file, and only step where I step."

Unseen things crunched beneath his shoes as he squeezed past the partially opened door, Shannon close behind him. She swung the flashlight around, illuminating the space. He blinked, unable to make sense of what he was seeing.

"Here," she said in that terrible, dead voice.

"Oh my God," Shannon breathed beside him. "This is like, it's…" She trailed off, her head swiveling left and right.

He understood her stuttering. There were no words. He could only absorb it in increments. The floor hidden by a knee-high, rolling sea of unidentifiable stuff. Shadowed piles surrounded them, some of them at least five feet high. The space he assumed to be the kitchen was so full of stuff that the only thing he could make out was the small yellow sliver that may have been a refrigerator.

"This is…" Shannon stammered. "I don't know what this is." She crossed her arms. "This was your house? You lived like this?"

"More or less."

He pressed on his angry stomach and tried not to breathe through his nose. "Why didn't you tell me?" he asked.

"I couldn't tell anyone." Her voice was so small and fragile, it tore at his heart.

Shannon took dainty steps, creeping toward the kitchen area. "Where did you cook food?"

"Didn't."

Shannon gawked at him. The woman lived for feeding people and the thought of someone not having home-cooked meals appeared to traumatize her.

"Why?" she finally choked out.

"Electricity went off when I was twelve. So no stove or fridge. No heat. Plumbing broke down a little while after that, so there was no running water."

Horror gnawed at him. This was too much. "How did you... Jesus Christ, I don't understand." He knew his childhood, though unhappy, had been a privileged one compared to hers, but he never imagined she'd lived like this. How could he? She'd never told him *where* she lived, let alone what her home was like.

She curled tighter into herself, as small and vulnerable as he'd ever seen her. "No one normal can understand."

Shannon poked at a pile with her index finger. It wobbled precariously before tumbling down and raining debris everywhere.

"Sorry," she whispered.

Adelia didn't flinch, her expression blank as she stared past them out the front door, lost in some aching void they couldn't reach.

"How did you eat? Or bathe?" he asked.

She blinked slowly, as if she'd just woken up. "I washed in the sink at Keys. Sometimes at school. Stole food when I needed to or stuffed my face at your house."

Suddenly that bony, hungry girl of his childhood made sense.

"Your dad didn't feed you?" Shannon asked.

Adelia's haunted eyes swung around the room before she answered. "No."

His stomach turned over and he was pretty sure he was going to puke. He squeezed out of the door, the thick, muggy air a welcome relief from the airless stink of the trailer. With his hands on his knees, he leaned over and wretched.

Adelia lived like this. No electricity or water. Walking miles every day, summer and winter. Starving. Scrounging for survival. And he never knew.

He wrestled for control of his twisting guts and won. After a minute, the urge to throw up subsided. Still, he walked in a circle around the trailer, taking in huge swallows of damp air. When he had control of himself, he went back inside.

Shannon looked a little green in the flashlight's beam. Adelia sat on a slippery pile of magazines and fabric. Sheets, maybe? Her eyes huge and bleak, her knees pulled up to her chin and her arms wrapped around her legs. He'd seen her do that so many times, but now he recognized it for what it was.

Safety.

His confusion gave way to rage. He wished he could resurrect her father just to beat the man back into the grave for putting that look in Adelia's eyes. This was unconscionable. She'd deserved so much better than this.

He stumbled over the junk beneath his shoes. "Adelia." He said her name softly and reached to hold her, needing to make contact, as though he could absorb some of her pain with his touch.

She snatched a magazine from the pile and held it out like a shield. "Don't do that." Her voice broke. "Please." She ducked her head like she wanted to hide. "I'm not drunk enough to deal with pity."

He stepped back and she lowered her arm but didn't meet his eyes.

"I didn't show you so you'd feel sorry for me. There are lots of people who had it worse. He didn't beat me or touch my bad places. He just... ignored me."

"That's just as bad," he said. Indifference was a special kind of hell that he knew well. When someone punched you in the face, you took it and it hurt and you put ice on it. But when someone acted as though you weren't there, that you didn't matter, there was no relief, no place to go to heal. How could you heal what didn't exist?

"You wanted answers, here they are," she said.

Shannon stomped her foot. "Hon, this was abuse whether he hit you or not. You don't have to downplay it."

Adelia fiddled with the curled edges of the magazine. "He hated me." She said it so casually. *I like chicken. My dad hated me. Pass the carrots.*

He shook his head. "He didn't hate you."

Shannon squeezed around him and gave him a dark look. "Shush, Conor."

She curled her hands over the top of the magazine Adelia was holding. "Parents suck, sometimes. If you say he hated you, I believe that it felt like that. And maybe he did. But you have to know, this is absolutely bonkers." She shook the magazine. "How he felt was not a reflection of you. That was all him."

"It doesn't matter," she said. "But this is why I left." She glanced at him and then quickly away. With surprising deftness, she shot off the pile of junk and snaked her way toward the door. He followed along, a dark anxiety beating wings in his chest.

She wasn't telling the whole truth.

Outside, they gulped the relatively fresh air. Adelia's eyes were glassy and desolate.

"Give us a minute, Shan," he said.

She nodded and headed for the car, and he tugged Adelia off to the side of the trailer, out of view. She didn't pull away, so he slid his hands over her shoulders and down her arms, pulling her close to him. She melted against him, her face on his shoulder.

"I'm sorry," he said softly. "I'm sorry I didn't help you."

Rain trickled down their faces. Adelia wrapped her arms around him. Her soft mouth found his and he lost himself in the sweetness of her.

"You did," she said against his lips.

SHANNON PULLED into the driveway and got out of her car. She had her *let's talk* face on.

He handed Adelia his keys. "You look like you're going to fall over. Go inside."

As soon as the door closed behind her, Shannon grabbed his arm. "I know you're a grown man and all, but you need to slow this down."

"What the hell are you talking about?"

"Adelia has a hickey the size of Rhode Island." Shannon pressed her fingers to the spot between her neck and collarbone. "Right there."

Freezing droplets of reality trickled down his back. "Oh," was all he could think to say.

"She's going to leave. And it's going to hurt you."

He rubbed his hands across his lips, remembering the feel of Adelia's mouth of his. "I know what I'm doing. It's temporary and we both know it."

She threw her hands up in surrender. "Do what you want. But don't be surprised when this goes straight to hell."

He ignored her. He didn't want warnings and reality. He wanted Adelia in his arms.

Inside, he found her snoring in his chair with her neck stretched uncomfortably over one arm. He shook her shoulder, but she was out cold.

He tried to lift her but she was dead weight and he was woozy and the bedroom was a million miles away. Grabbing the blankets and pillows off the couch, he spread them on the floor, then tugged her off the chair and onto the blankets, rolling her onto her side. She didn't move so much as an eyelash as he curled up behind her, wrapping an arm around her so she wouldn't roll onto her back.

He closed his eyes and kissed her neck. Shannon's worried face flashed like a strobe behind his eyes, but he squeezed them tighter until he banished the image. "I know what I'm doing," he muttered as the whisky in his blood lulled him to sleep.

20

ADELIA WILLED the phone to stop ringing.

It rang again.

She groaned. Hips ached. Head throbbed. Mouth tasted like rusted steel coated in Windex. She smacked her tongue behind her teeth. *Whisky. Bad.*

Ring. Ring. Ring.

A heavy weight pressed against her chest. And something warm was against her back. Her eyes were gummed shut so she reached down to push the thing off her chest. Her hands skated over it and her brain tried to place it. *Furry bowling ball?*

She pried her eyes open. Conor was beside her, one arm around her waist, his face burrowed between her breasts.

Adelia batted at him. "Phone."

He mumbled something nonsensical, and nuzzled her right breast, sighing with contentment.

The relentless ringing continued, each shrill trill piercing her skull, like it was drilling for oil. "Get off, man." She shoved him over, and got up, stumbling over him to grab his phone.

"What?" she snarled into the speaker.

"Put Conor on the fucking phone!" The guy on the other end

breathed like a moose after a race, and nearly put a dent in her eardrum with the volume of his voice.

She sat the phone down and kicked at him. He rolled over and cuddled her foot.

"Get. Up." She slathered spit on one of her fingers and shoved it in his ear.

His bleary green eyes shot open and he jerked away from her hand, rubbing at his damp ear hole. "Gah! What?"

She shook the phone at him.

He rubbed at his eyes and took it from her. "Hello?"

"Rise and shine, jerkoff. It's 10 a.m.," the man yelled.

"What?" He rubbed at his face. "10 a.m.?" He looked at his phone. "No. No. Oh fuck." He shot up and looked around in a panic. "I'll uh, I'll be there soon."

"Don't bother," the guy growled. "If your mother weren't the mayor—and a vindictive bitch— I'd fire your ass right now." His voice dropped lower and she strained to hear him. "You're suspended for the next two weeks. Off the payroll. Let's see what missing an entire paycheck does for your attitude."

He closed his eyes. "Keith, I'm—"

"Don't care. Two weeks from now, if I don't see you here at 7:30 a.m., I will fire you, no matter who your mother is."

He blinked slowly at the abruptly silent phone.

Late again. And again, it was her fault. Despite the absolute misery of her headache, she reached for his shoulder and gave it a squeeze.

"Two weeks without pay." He coughed out a weary laugh. "Fuck my life."

"You know," she said. "I was gonna pay the motel to stay there. Hotel Du Ross is superior. Definitely cleaner. And you feed me. I could—"

"No," he shook his head and moaned, dropping it into his hands and squeezing his skull. "I have some savings. I'll be all right."

"Your boss is a dick."

He gave her a tired smile. "Keith *is* a dick. But he's a dick with a business to run. I can't blame him for being pissed." He sat silently for a moment, groaning and digging his fingers into his scalp. "The upside is I don't have to go to that stupid job for two weeks. No feather boas. No steam car backdrops. No Keith." His bloodshot eyes rolled skyward. "And let's not forget. Half-fired is slightly still-employed."

"I never realized you were such an optimist," she said.

"Neither did I." His voice faded away, and he gave the rumpled pile of bedding and pillows a baffled look. "Why'd we sleep on the floor?"

Her memory was fuzzy, which was to be expected. The real fun of liquor was your memory's slow reveal of all the stupid things you'd done. And from the looks of it, they broke the record for stupid last night. She raised up the fancy bottle that sat on the table and sloshed around the teaspoon of booze left in it.

"Whisky," she said. "Whisky is why."

"First and last time with that stuff." Sweat trickled down his temples and he fanned at himself.

"You okay?"

"I'm fine. My stomach hurts a little. It's really hot in here."

"It's really not."

"Oh." He covered his mouth with his hand, and hiccupped a loud, lingering burp, his face slowly draining of whatever color it had when he woke up.

"Oh, hell." She grabbed his hand. "Let's go this way."

He rose, wobbling on his feet, and she tugged him toward the bathroom. "What are we doing?" he asked.

"Nothing," she said, pushing him into the doorway and toward the toilet. She grabbed a towel off the hook and folded it, dropping it at the base of the toilet. "Kneel here."

"Winters, what are you—?" He clutched his stomach and groaned. "Oh god."

She pointed at the towel.

His Adam's apple worked overtime, probably trying to push back the metal taste in his mouth. "Am I going to..."

"Oh, yeah."

He dropped to his knees and she lifted the lid of the toilet bowl.

"Take your shirt off," she said.

"No, no. I'm good." He tried to give her a smile, but the first dry heave stole it. He gripped the sides of the toilet. "I don't think I'm going to throw up. I'm not." He groaned. "I'm not."

No, he definitely was going to. But she nodded and grabbed a washcloth, running cold water over it and placing it on the back of his neck.

"You're a much nicer person than the magazines say you are," he said.

"Yeah, well, don't go blowing my cover."

"I would ne—" He swung his head nearer to the toilet and just in time. His stomach let loose with a barrage of regret. Which is what happened when you had...she tried to sort the math out. Ten shots? Twelve? A fucking lot.

She sat on the floor, beside him, feeling queasy herself, but holding it together. She rubbed the back of his neck and applied cold washcloths to it. She got him to sip little paper cups full of water between episodes. He tried to get her to leave the room several times, but she ignored him. She'd prayed to the porcelain god a lot in her early twenties and it was much more miserable when you did it by yourself. Sharing the agony halved the awfulness.

Once he was down to empty heaves, she wiped his face off with the cold washcloth. "You're gonna make it."

"Are you sure I didn't die twenty minutes ago?" His deep voice cracked, and he pressed his head into her hands.

"How can anyone ever be sure?"

"I don't...brain...philosophy right now."

She laughed and rinsed out the washcloth, holding in a few wretches of her own. She grabbed another one and wiped the sweat off his head.

"Think you're going to barf again?"

"No. The tank is empty. But I might lose it if I don't take a shower right now."

"Okay, I'll be right back." She went to his bedroom, hesitating before entering. It was an absolute mess. The bed was rumpled. One of the pale grey pillow covers was smeared with red dye. "That's not good," she said. Ignoring the evidence of bad deeds done, she found a pair of neatly folded pajamas in the bottom drawer of his dresser and grabbed them.

He took them gratefully, and then kicked her out of the bathroom.

While he showered, she gathered all the bedding in the living room, folding it into Conor-approved, neat squares, and sat beside the pile. She rubbed at a tender spot on her chest and picked up his phone to looked at herself in the camera app. There was a livid hickey above her clavicle.

She searched the photos on his phone but found no evidence about the events of the night before. All she knew was she awoke clothed, but also had a vague memory of Conor's mouth on hers. His teeth on her nipples. Of riding him through her clothes until she came. Whatever happened afterward was a blur, but no matter how it ended, the line had been crossed.

In some ways she was relieved. It was done. They got it out of their systems.

The water turned off at the other end of the trailer. Good, her turn.

She pulled her sweater off and recoiled from the stench that puffed up from it. What was that? She sniffed again. It smelled like garbage and mildew. Aftershave and...cigarettes. Nausea rolled through her like waves in a storm. She threw the sweater onto the floor and stared at it.

Only one thing smelled like that. One place.

Oh, god.

She pushed through the fog of her memories and shapes emerged. Shadowy memories of being in a car. Of opening the door of the trailer. Of him holding her.

Her body shook, and her breaths came in short bursts. Numbness spread to her hands and she shook it away. The pounding of her heart rattled her teeth, so she clenched her jaw tight and wrapped her arms around herself. There wasn't enough whisky in the world for her to show anyone that place, was there?

Coming back to Cherry Lake was stupid. She knew it was stupid and she did it anyway. Words that would be etched on her tombstone.

And now he knew about that thing, stinking and rotting to the ground, and inside of her. That fucking thing that existed as reminder that some things couldn't be cleaned up.

She ran her hands through her hair and squeezed her skull. There were times in her life when the noise in her head, the beat-beat-beat of regrets and bad choices and hurt threatened to drive her straight to her knees, but she was an expert at cranking the volume to drown it out. She pushed up and up, until nothing but static remained.

By the time he sat across from her, dressed and clean, she had herself together. Except for her shaking hands. She crossed her arms to hide them. She searched his eyes for some sign of his thoughts.

"What's wrong, Winters? I'm not going to barf again if that's what you're wondering."

"No. Uh, I need a shower." She headed for the bathroom, but he grabbed her arm. She clenched her teeth together, waiting for the worst.

"Thank you for taking care of me," he said.

The soft look in his eyes threatened to undo all the work she'd done to get her emotions in check. "No problem," she said. She pulled her arm from his hand and raced to the bathroom, locking herself in.

Stripping everything off, she showered with the water extra-hot, and scrubbed herself so raw that the pink dye flowing out of her hair matched her flesh. After her shower, she stood at the mirror brushing her hair. The color had faded dramatically. Instead of her dark auburn, or the punky bright red she'd chosen, it was light auburn. Oh well. At least it didn't smell anymore.

The bathroom was a mess when she was done dressing, so she took a few minutes to clean it up. She rinsed out the tub and threw the towels into the neatly labeled hamper.

"Hey, I think I ruined some of your towels," she said when she got back to the living room. "They're pink now."

"That's what bleach is for," he said as he poured a cup of black coffee. He slid a napkin across the counter toward her, with a couple of pain relievers on it. She stuck them in her mouth and reached for a water glass.

"Are we gonna talk about it?" he asked.

She froze, the pills melting to bitterness on her tongue. "Talk about what?"

"Last night."

She filled the glass with water and chugged it. "What's there to talk about?"

"I don't know. I thought, maybe we could piece together what happened. Because clearly—" he gestured to the hickey peeking out from her t-shirt. "Something happened."

Relief nearly knocked her to her knees. He didn't remember anything. Otherwise making out would be the least of his confusion. It wouldn't last, but it was a reprieve at least.

"We danced. Then we sucked face—and neck. That's it."

The same knee-knocking relief seemed to have hit him. Which was a touch insulting.

"Okay, so we...didn't."

"Nope. You passed out, you stud."

"Clothes stayed on?"

"Dude, we've seen each other naked before."

"That was...different."

"Okay. Well, you stayed clothed. I stayed mostly clothed."

His eyes flicked down and back up and she wondered if any of it was coming back to him and if the memory was making him ache the way it made her ache.

She turned away, afraid that her desire—or worse, her lie—would be visible. "Anyway, that's all that happened. We got drunk and we reverted to high school. It happens. Let's not make it weird."

"You think it was just the alcohol?"

She washed her glass slowly, rinsing it and putting it in the drying rack. "I think the best cure for a hangover is food. Want to go get some breakfast?"

"Smooth," he said. "But food doesn't sound good."

"You'll feel better, I swear."

He wanted to argue. She could see it in the pinch between his brows and the way he rolled on the balls of his feet. But he blew out a breath and nodded. "Fine. But you're buying."

THE SUN KEPT PEEKING through the grey, drizzling clouds, and into the diner windows, each bright little dart of light jabbing Adelia in the eyes before disappearing, only to do it again. She adjusted her baseball cap to block out the light.

The Railway was blissfully empty, as he'd assured her it would be. No motel meant no tourists. The downside being that she had too much quiet time to think about last night. She sipped a soft drink and stared at the cheesy train photos dotting the walls.

"Yours are better. They should be here," she said, pointing at a picture.

He slumped in his seat and rubbed his eyes with the palm of his hand. "God willing, one day I'll be good enough for Dennis Littlewood's walls. For now, it's Razzle Dazzle or nothing."

"What about the studio?"

"It's a nice dream," he said. "But my business plan isn't ready."

"Have you talked to anyone at the bank?"

Conor's brows slammed together. "No. Because my business plan *isn't* ready."

"Man, you're cranky. I think you should go to the bank and talk to somebody. Maybe it is ready and you just don't know it."

"Okay, so say I get a loan and the studio is still available. Then what?" He threw his hands up. "It turns out that I suck at running a business and the whole thing tanks? I need to do some more research before I go trying to be mini-Liam."

The waitress sat a plate of fries in front of her and a wilted, over-dressed salad in front of him. He poked at it and pushed it aside.

She squirted a mound of ketchup on her plate and swirled a fry into it. "When I was seventeen, I got onstage for the first time. Hitchhiked to a little dive bar with a karaoke contest. Real rough place." She bit into the fry and chewed for a moment. "Got some idiot to buy me whisky shots and slammed two of them, ate a bowl of beer nuts and got onstage. No experience. No brains at all, really."

He sighed. "And you won, right? Is that the point of this?"

"No, it's not the fucking point," she said. "The point is, I froze. Forgot the tune. Never sang a note. The real victory was that I made it off the stage before I barfed, like, everywhere."

He shoved his gloppy salad further away. "Mm, the only

thing better than discussing my job while I'm hungover is talking about vomiting right now. If this is your idea of a pep talk, you may want to stick to music."

She flung a fry at him. It bounced off his head and landed in his glass of water. He rubbed the greasy smear off his forehead, giving her a death stare.

"You're being such a baby right now." She grabbed the bowl of salad and flagged down the waitress. "Hey, Karen, this is the wrong dressing. Can he get another salad with balsamic dressing, but on the side?" At the waitress's nod, she continued. "Great. While we're at it, can I have this?" She pointed at the early bird special sign. "The blackened green tomato, cucumber sandwich? Pesto mayo on the side?"

After Karen departed, he pulled the sign toward him. "You ordered from the menu for old people, Winters."

"I know. But I was reading the other day that it's usually full of healthier stuff." She waved off his questioning look. "Look. Forget Liam and your business plan. I barfed my way through six different contests before I made it through a single song onstage. But I kept going. Because what I wanted was worth failing for. Over and over. So, take a chance. If it goes ass up, so what? Everyone fails."

By the time the waitress dropped off a new salad, a cup of vinaigrette and the sandwich, he didn't look any more convinced. That was okay. Conor always had to be pushed to take chances.

She took a bite of the sandwich. It was heavenly. Maybe better than her French fries. Which was the worst kind of blasphemy. She cut it in half and slid the plate toward him. "Here. It's healthy-ish."

He shook his head. "I'll pass."

She narrowed her eyes and jiggled the plate at him.

Exasperated, he snatched it up, and took a bite. After a

moment, his scowl softened, and he quit chewing like he was eating a leather belt.

"See? It's good." She pushed a tomato back into the bread, reached across the table and dipped the end of the sandwich into his balsamic dressing.

He looked at the sandwich for a moment before submerging the corner of it into the balsamic as well. He rolled his head back like he'd just discovered food and devoured the rest of it, stopping short of biting off his fingers, and then ordered another one and ate the whole thing.

She finished her fries and pushed the plate away. "I told you that food would make you feel better," she said.

He leaned his head back and sighed. "And you were right."

"You should go to the bank."

"Jesus, you're not going to let this go, are you?"

"Nope. Keith didn't give you a punishment, he gave you a fucking opportunity. Take it."

"Fine." He stood and gestured for her to slide out of the booth. "But you're going with me."

Tendrils of warmth, as skittish and jarring as the sunrays coming through the window, prodded at her. Demanding she soak them in before they retreated.

"I'm in," she said.

IT NEVER OCCURRED to Adelia how much work was involved in getting people to give you money for your dream. The cheerful loan specialist gave Conor a lot of advice along with some worksheets and a warning that getting business loans was difficult. She told him that he needed to create a visual presentation for his business plan.

He hadn't said much since they'd left the bank. Just stared

straight ahead, his mouth a stressed slash, eyes gathering clouds like the drippy sky above the truck.

They drove aimlessly down muck-filled back roads, without even music to dull the discomfort. His phone kept buzzing, and every time it did, her heart slammed into her ribs, wondering if it was Shannon calling to remind him of last night's disaster.

Lucky for her, he wasn't in the mood to chat and ignored the calls.

Guilt gnawed at her. She scooted closer and pressed her hand to the back of his neck. He arched it and leaned into her hand. "It's worse than I thought," he said.

"No shit," she said. "I've never appreciated EJ more than I do right now. He handles all my contracts and banking and bullshit."

"Then maybe you should stop telling him to go fuck himself every time he calls."

She tried to imagine what that would look like and snorted. "Nah, he pounces on weakness like an alley cat on a rodent."

His phone buzzed for the fifth time and he growled, pulling the truck off to the side of the road. Throwing it into park, he snatched it up, his lips parted in whatever grumpy salutation he was going to use, but he paused and closed his eyes. "And hello to you too, Mom."

Relief that it wasn't Shannon came and went, leaving her gut twisted. He never walked away from a conversation with Maureen unscathed. This was not the best time for her bullshit.

He flicked the stereo on low, effectively drowning out his mom's end of the call. "I'm not fired," he said. "I'm on...sabbatical." His expression darkened. "Excuse me?" He gripped the steering wheel and continued giving clipped responses to whatever his mother was lobbing at him. "You can rest easy. I'm not handing money out to anyone. I went to talk about getting a loan to...to start my own studio..." He grunted non-answers for a moment, then flinched. "Yes, I'm aware that I'm not Liam.

Thanks for your concern." He tossed the phone on the seat and pressed his head against the steering wheel.

The phone buzzed again. Adelia grabbed it, declined the call and set it to mute.

"Why is it that no matter how long it's been going on, it never gets easier?" he asked.

"Because she's the worst. What'd she say?"

"The whole town knows about Razzle, and she's humiliated to have a son who is so incapable of being an adult." He turned to look at her. "Then she told me that everyone knows I have a woman staying at my house and wants to know who."

"Wow, that's Puritan, even for her. She does remember that you're a thirty-year-old man, right?"

"Apparently I'm not acting like one. Between the police being called because of loud music and my sudden 'shack up,' she's concerned."

"I can't possibly be the first woman to stay at your place. You've had girlfriends."

"I uh, I don't really do relationships."

"Why? Don't want a wedding and a bunch of roly-poly babies?"

His face contorted in horror. "God, no."

"But I mean, you've had hookups."

He stared at the steering wheel. "A couple in college, but..." He tapped his fingers on the dash. "Anyhow, Juanita Foster told Alicia Biggins that Caroline and Dale Gillesby saw me at the bank, talking to a loan specialist, with a woman in tow. My mother is extremely concerned that I've met a floozy and am taking out loans for her."

"She's half right."

"She thinks I shouldn't be taking any major steps without Liam's input. She wants me to be ambitious, but says I'm regressing and maybe I should focus on why I'm barely holding onto a job that's only a step up from minimum wage, before I go off chasing my dreams."

Adelia clenched her jaw to stop all the nasty words she wanted to use about his mother. "Don't listen to her."

"But she's right. I'm already over my head."

"No."

"Winters—"

"Conor, fucking no," she said. "Stop hiding behind your mom and your brother. This isn't about them. You've been fucking up, but it's not because *you're* a fuck up. It's because that job isn't what you're meant to do. Your brain says you need it, but your heart is rebelling, because it goddamn knows better."

"I'm not hiding behind them." It was clear he'd quit listening after she'd said that. His voice crackled with a warning for her to back off.

She never listened to those kinds of warnings.

"You sure as fuck are. You're scared, and making it about those two is easier than facing the fact that you're the one holding yourself back. Not her or him. You."

"Do you really want to do this, Adelia?" The warning was darker and more dire.

"Yeah, I do. Because you need to get out of your own way."

"That's beyond rich coming from you," he said. "For one thing, you don't have a stake in this. When you're done licking your wounds here, you'll fuck right back off to California, like you did before, and I'll be here, trying to keep the lights on. So, your faith in me isn't the motivator you think it is. Second, you, of all people, have no business lecturing me about hiding."

Dammit, she'd screwed up the whole conversation. Her hands knotted in her lap and she bit the inside of her lip. "This isn't about me. I was making a poin—"

"I understand your point. I need to get over my mommy issues and upend my whole life for a joke of a dream that I'm not qualified to actually have, meanwhile—"

"It's not—"

"Meanwhile," he repeated. "You're still hiding inside that fucking trailer, so you can blame daddy for every shitty thing you do." He glared. "Is that about right?"

Clouds moved in front of the sun and the glass of the window suddenly cooled. It used to be that she was always cold inside. And she never let herself miss the sun. But now that she'd felt what it was like to be warm again, it hurt to lose the light.

She shivered and kept her eyes straight ahead. She'd known this was coming all day. "I thought you said you didn't remember anything."

"I didn't know if we had sex." His voice lost its hard edge. "I remembered the trailer. I just didn't know how to bring it up."

A laugh bubbled like battery acid in her throat. "Well, it sure was worth the wait."

"I'm so…"

The seat creaked. He slid closer, the heat of his body mingling with hers, and her caustic laughter dried up. She didn't look at him. Didn't need to. Instead she squeezed closer to the door and shook her head. "Just fucking drive, Conor."

21

THE MOMENT CONOR pulled into the driveway, Adelia jumped out of the truck, needing an escape. He let her in the trailer, and then, without a word, he loped down the porch and took off in his truck.

Paulie's Towing still went to voicemail. She left a message letting him know how much she needed her car and offered him triple the money to rush the repair, then she went to the stereo and found a decent rock station to pace to. It couldn't be too much longer before her beastly car was road-ready. All she had to do was keep her mouth shut and get through the next couple nights and she could finally put Cherry Lake in the rearview. No more talking. Joking. Making out. Painful conversations.

You're still hiding inside that fucking trailer, so you can blame daddy for every shitty thing you do.

She bit her thumbnail. Her father set her on a path of self-destruction that swallowed her life, no matter how much she achieved. She wasn't delusional. She just preferred not to think too hard about all the things she couldn't change. This was who she was. Toxic waste, spilling along, destroying all the good stuff. Hurting anyone who dared to love her.

She was a coward. It always hurt enough to know that about herself. It hurt more to have Conor know it, too.

Ugh. She needed a distraction and the music wasn't cutting it. Cupcake whined and put her paws on Adelia's thighs.

That would do.

She leashed her and took her around to the back of the trailer and into the woods. The dog ran until the strap ran out and turned to give her sad eyes.

There was a button somewhere on the dumb leash. She found it and pressed it. Cupcake ran happily ahead of her. She followed along for a few minutes, but her feet were heavier with every step. She stopped to lean against a tree. Cupcake tugged at the leash and she pulled back on it. "No." Cupcake loped toward her, barked her indignation, turned and took off at a dead run, yanking the leash out of her hand.

"Oh, come on!"

The dog was gone, chasing who knew what. She tried to follow, but there was no sign of her.

After a half-hour of calling and searching, Adelia was exhausted and completely turned around. Fucking great. What was next after lying, yelling at Conor and basically calling him a pansy, and then losing his dog? Slashing his tires? Setting his house on fire?

Not her best day.

It took her a while to find her way back to the trailer. Rounding the corner, Cupcake greeted her at the steps, leash handle twenty feet behind her, nubbin wagging. Covered top to bottom in mud.

Relief was quickly squashed. "You're not making my life easy, dog." She made her way around the trailer, looking for a hose, but if Conor had one, it wasn't outside. She checked Shannon's place and found a hose-less spigot too short to fit a dog under.

The hard way, then. Was there any other? She took the dog to the back yard and tied the leash to the railing of the backdoor steps. Going in through the front door, she opened kitchen drawers until she found the garbage bags, and lined the hallway with them. In the linen closet, she refused to let herself linger on his neat handwriting at the front of each basket: *Rags, Washcloths, Extra Kitchen Towels.* She tugged out a handful of rags and tossed them beside the tub.

She opened the back door to a mud-soaked, but ecstatic dog. "How are you so happy all the time?" she asked. "Aren't you exhausted by it?"

Cupcake shook her wobbly back end and didn't answer.

"You're really bad at small talk." Adelia pulled the dog into the house and led her to the bathroom. But no amount of talking or gestures would get Cupcake into the tub. She tried everything, including middle fingers. Out of options and patience, she hoisted the heavy beast up, grunting in misery, and climbed into the tub with her, clothes and all.

Scratching the dog with one hand, she cranked the shower water with the other. By the time Cupcake realized what was happening, she was already being washed.

"Sorry, dog. I'm sneaky."

Cupcake gave her a disappointed look and groaned.

"I think your dad has first dibs on being disgusted with me, so get in line."

The boxer gave a mournful woof of understanding. She sat with a thump and submitted herself with a certain amount of doggy dignity, only broken when she tried to drink the dirty bath water.

She used Conor's shampoo on the dog, filling the air with the scent of grapefruit and lemongrass. The smell made her melancholy. Well, more melancholy.

After the third wash, the water ran clear off Cupcake, though Adelia was soaked from top to bottom in filthy water and covered in shampoo suds.

"You're a very good dog," she said, pressing a kiss on the white patch on the dog's head. "I wonder if he has treats hidden somewhere in this house."

Cupcake went ballistic at the word, "treats," and scrabbled to escape the tub. Adelia grabbed for her, but the sodden animal slipped right through her arms. She heard an *oomph* from the hallway and leaned out of the tub to see Conor, pinned against the wall by the lick-happy dog.

"Hey," she said as she scrambled out, dripping water everywhere. She pulled Cupcake back into the bathroom. "I took her for a walk and she was all covered in mud and..."

His mouth quirked at the corner and she realized how silly she looked, draining like a leaky radiator all over his bathroom floor, with the last of her pink hair dye drizzling onto his sparkling linoleum, as she wrestled with the eighty-pound dog.

Cupcake broke free and lunged for freedom, knocking him aside as she tore toward the living room, sounding like a Clydesdale on a Slip 'n Slide as she raced over the plastic bags lining the hallway.

"Oops," she said.

He closed his eyes as the dog thumped around the living room, probably rubbing her wet butt on every available surface. Sighing, he opened them. "Thanks for washing her."

"Not a problem." She looked back at the mud smeared on the floor and across the side of the tub. "Uh, I should probably, you know, clean and stuff."

He nodded slowly. "I'll help."

She cleaned the bathtub, while he mopped the floor. The air was so sticky-thick with all the things they weren't saying that it hurt to breathe.

He gathered all the towels and put them in the hamper and

turned around with a small stack of neatly folded clothes. "Here," he said. "I washed your pajamas last night, so you can change. And I'll get Cupcake that treat you promised her." He shut the bathroom door quietly behind him.

Taking a long, deep breath, she put on Jo's skull pajamas and padded into the living room.

He was on the floor, holding a toy, and losing a game of Tug-of-War with Cupcake. "Sorry to say, she got her revenge. Your bedding and the couch are soaked through." He didn't take his eyes off the dog as he spoke.

"I've slept on worse," she said.

"Are you hungry?" He shook the toy and Cupcake growled with mock ferocity. "I didn't much feel like cooking, so I raided Shannon's fridge. Food's on the counter."

So, they were playing avoid-the-fight. She could handle that. Just a couple more nights. And then gone.

There were several aluminum pans on the counter. One had slices of stuff she'd heard of but had never eaten in her life. "Is that meatloaf?"

"Yeah." He washed his hands. "Meatloaf, leftover chili and cornbread. I put out some salad, too."

Her stomach was too twisty for a lot of anything, so she took a small slice of meatloaf and a bit of salad. He sat a bowl of chili and a plate of salad on the table and joined her.

The meatloaf was good, but the salad tasted better. She scooped up a big forkful and a drop of dressing escaped, landing in the center of the skull on her pajama top. He silently handed her a napkin and she dabbed at it. Something wriggled its way to her brain's surface. "Did you say you did laundry last night?"

"Yeah."

"Last night?"

"Yes, Winters."

"We got drunk last night, and you did laundry?"

He grabbed the wadded napkin from her and took it to the

garbage can. "Well, you were drying your hair. And I needed clean socks."

She stared at him for a long moment, trying to process that logic.

His brows drew together. "Drunk or not, no one likes wearing sweaty socks."

Laughter brayed out of her. Every time she thought she had it together, the idea of a wobbly, drunk Conor folding laundry started her off again. And at some point, he caught her laughter like a cold.

Her eyes were watering by the time her belly laughs dried up. "Oh my god," she said, wiping her cheeks. "I needed that."

"You're welcome." His beautiful smile made all the lights in the room look dim. He grabbed his dishes. "You didn't eat much. Do you want something else?"

"Nah, I'm good." She took her dishes to the sink. Without much thought, they worked together. He washed and passed them to her to rinse and dry. He handed her a clean plate to rinse but he didn't let go when she grabbed for it.

"I'm sorry about earlier," he said.

"Nothing to be sorry about."

"Let me—"

"Don't bother." She kept her voice light. "Sorry doesn't fix anything. That's why I never say it." She slid the plate from his hand and dipped it in the cool rinse water.

"I disagree, but let's put that on the back burner." He turned toward her. "I drove for a long time and thought about what you said. It's not something I wanted to hear, and I didn't react well to it."

"I was being pushy." She made slow circles on a dish as she dried it. "You were right. I don't have any stake in this. It's not my business what you do."

"You said it because you care."

It was clear he wasn't going to let it go. That was fine. All she had to do was keep things short and sweet. She shook her head. "Why would I care? I said it so you wouldn't think too hard and remember the trailer. That's all."

"I don't believe that."

Say nothing. Say nothing. Say nothing. She dried a cup, jamming her hand into it. "Believe what you want."

"Maybe you were right. I don't like doing things unless they're…" He ran a hand through his hair.

"Perfect," she muttered.

"I'll admit it. Messy things, like taking chances make me hyperventilate." He pulled the plug from the sink, and the dingy water swirled down the drain. "That said, I didn't say it as sensitively as I could have, but I wasn't wrong either."

She shrugged and put the dishes away. She couldn't stand knowing what she might find in his eyes. Disgust? Or worse, pity. *Poor whiner-baby rock star and her issues.*

"I don't think you came back to Cherry Lake to bury your dad."

She gave him a bored look that hid the pulsing anxiety his words gave her. "Do tell."

"I think you came back to tear that thing down."

The writhing mass of anxiety surged past her mask of boredom. "What?"

"That pile of garbage is hurting you. And you told me that you've been chasing happy. I think it starts there."

Swallowing the horror she felt, she slammed the cupboard door shut. "Thanks for the analysis, Dr. Freud, but no." She reached into the lower cupboard and pulled out some aluminum foil to repack the leftovers.

"Come on, what's the alternative? Pay taxes on your dad's neglect forever?"

Her body shook so hard, she clenched her teeth to keep her brain from sloshing around in her skull. She crossed her arms. "I don't need you to rescue me."

"I know that. You need to rescue yourself."

"I did. I left. I moved on."

"Did you?"

She ripped a large shiny piece of aluminum foil away from the box and slammed it on top of the pan. "I knew you'd be like this."

"Like what?"

She shoved the pan aside and put her hands on the counter. "Like someone who looks at me and sees nothing but garbage." She turned to face him. "Like I'm something messy to be scrubbed up."

"No, you aren't—"

"My things are in there!" The words tore out of her, and she pressed her hands to her mouth.

He stilled. "What do you mean?"

She tried to get the static back, the dull roar that drowned out all these awful feelings, but it was gone. Leaving her with nothing but the silence in the dark. "I wasn't like you. I didn't have a house full of pretty, disposable things. All that crap belonged to my dad, but there are things..." She clenched her fist. "I don't remember what my mother looked like. And there might be pictures in there. Pictures of her holding me. Her sheet music. The ragdoll with yarn hair she made me." She looked at the floor. "It's all in there. Ruined. But it's in there. And I'm not letting strangers stomp through it, throwing that stuff away." She slapped her hand on the counter. "It belongs to me!"

He shrank back from her outrage. "I get it."

"No, you goddamn don't! My father loved garbage more than he loved me. But my mother, she loved me, and he can't take that away from me. I won't let him. Someone loved me, and as long as that trailer is there, I can prove it. I can..."

Every word ripped from inside of her, leaving gaping wounds behind. She felt wetness cling to her lashes. It was as close to crying as she'd been in years and she hated herself for her weakness. She turned and headed for the hallway. She needed space between, them. A door. A yard. A country, maybe.

"Adelia, stop."

She blinked, pushing back against the waves trying to break free.

"Look at me."

She turned. He stood in the middle of the living room, his eyes were bright and swimming with pain. "You're right. I don't get it. And I can't imagine what it did to you. But you don't have to prove anything. Maybe it hurts so much that you can't remember, but you were loved. Shannon loved you." He gave her a pained smile. "I loved you."

The eight feet that separated them felt too far and not far enough. Her ribs were so tight, she could hardly breathe. "It wasn't going to last. Eventually you wouldn't have."

"We'll never know. You didn't give me the chance to prove you wrong."

"Because I wasn't stupid enough to wait around to be proved right."

He stilled, and she swallowed. Knowing she'd said exactly the wrong thing.

"It wasn't the trailer, was it?"

She didn't answer, just stared at the wall.

"Did you leave because I told you that I loved you?"

If her ribs were tight before, now they were crushing in on her, piercing her lungs. Holding her heart prisoner in an ever-narrowing cage. *Say nothing. Say nothing. Say—*

"Yes," she said. She pressed her lips together and stared over his shoulder. The ragged edge of his breathing drew her gaze back to his.

"Did you love me?"

She could feel the weight of all the years that question sat on his shoulders. How much time he must have spent wondering and grieving and burning with pain. But she couldn't say the words. She never could. All those years ago, she'd been so starved. Her father denied her even a scrap of affection, so when she found it with Conor, she'd leapt on it like a hungry dog. But the truth, carved deep into her bones, was that there was something wrong with her. Some deficit and she couldn't have his love, or anyone else's.

"It doesn't matt—"

"It matters," he said softly. "Did you love me?"

Her heart throbbed as the cage around it grew smaller. "Yes," she said, her voice barely above a whisper.

He rubbed his hand over his mouth and took a shaky breath. She closed her eyes. When she opened them, he was crossing the room, compressing the space between them. He took her by the shoulders and drew her body to his. He wrapped his arms around her and held her. She breathed deep against his shoulder and put her arms around him, too. His hand slid up her neck and into her hair. He cupped the back of her head and kissed her temple, holding her like something precious.

The cage around her heart loosened, her ribs slipping back into place, giving her back her breath. She traced the lines of his face with her fingers. Cheekbones, nose, lips. She tilted her head and brushed her mouth against his. The curve of his upper lip called to her and she pressed a kiss there before taking his lower lip between hers to taste it. He didn't pull away, but he didn't press back either. He stood still as she touched him. Her cheeks burned, and she dropped her hand, her body leaden with regret. She pushed to get out from his arms. "I shouldn't have done that," she said.

He nodded, his eyes burning into hers. And then he kissed her.

This wasn't like the honeyed, drunken kisses they'd shared the night before. He consumed her, his teeth scraping her lips and then sucking away the tinge of pain. She moaned, giving into the deep dark she'd been drowning in. His hands held her jaw firm as he took everything from her with his kiss. Burning away her fear and regret and leaving nothing but need.

He pressed her against the wall and she whimpered when he broke his mouth away. His tongue traced a spot on her neck and he bit her there, not a nibble, but a sharp pain, hard enough to awaken every nerve in her body. He pulled the flimsy pajama top aside and wrapped his tongue around her nipple. As he drew her sensitive flesh in, she arched toward him, her body thrumming a steady beat only she could hear.

She tugged on his hair until he came back to her mouth and curled her arms around his neck. He cupped her ass and lifted her off the ground, groaning when she wrapped her legs tight around his hips. She bit his lip and traced it with her tongue while he ground against her. He breathed her name against her lips and carried her to the bedroom, kicking the door shut behind him, and tossed her onto the bed. She sank into the feathery mattress as he climbed on top of her. She wanted to make a joke about him being a control freak, even in the bedroom, but she was afraid to break the spell, to send them both back to reality where this was the worst possible idea anyone had ever had.

His fingers teased along her midriff. He pulled her pajama top over her head and gazed at her exposed flesh. Her nipples puckered with the friction of the fabric and he stroked them roughly with his thumbs before taking them in his mouth, one after the other. His breathing sped up as he kissed her stomach, licking along the edge of her pajama pants.

"Take them off," he ordered.

She scrambled to slide the pants off her hips, loving the harsh whip of his voice, loving the way he took control. He stared down at her naked body and the light in his eyes gleamed brighter. "I want you so fucking much," he said.

She wanted more skin. Running her hands over his shoulders, she tugged at his shirt, but he pulled away from her eager hands, and sat upright on the bed. He lifted one of her legs over his shoulder and bit her calf before kissing and licking his way to her thigh. An ache pulsed inside of her.

He scraped at her thigh with his teeth and she laughed. He paused.

"It tickled," she said.

"I'm going to do more than tickle you."

"Big talk. All men say it. So few deliver."

He held her gaze. "I'll deliver." He bit her again, making her squeal. She felt his laughter rumble against the sensitive flesh of her inner thigh and she wanted to cry with the joy of it. The absolute fucking joy of Conor being hers for even a moment. She didn't deserve it, but she was always selfish when it came to him. Tonight, she'd be selfish again, and deal with the fallout in the morning.

He found her pulsing center and her thoughts turned to steam. Like his kisses, he didn't bother teasing. He sucked and licked until she lost track of his movements, and simply melted like ice cream beneath his tongue, helpless against the beautiful ache building inside of her. It spread and throbbed until he clutched her hips, pulling her tighter against his hungry mouth and the ache swelled and arced, cresting into pleasure that left her empty and full at the same time.

He licked his lower lip and gave her a satisfied smirk from between her thighs.

"No one likes a show-off," she said.

"You do." He climbed over her and kissed her, a hot open kiss, sharing her salty taste as he tangled his tongue with hers.

She slid her hands under his shirt, digging her nails into his back, making him hiss. She wanted that shirt off. She pulled it up and he pulled it back down. Slipping sideways, he snapped off the light and they were plunged into darkness. She grunted in disappointment.

It was all sounds to unravel after that. The clunk of his belt hitting the floor. A drawer sliding open. The rustle of a condom wrapper.

They were really doing this.

She could see the barest outline of him in the dark as he stripped off his shirt. He lifted her hips and pressed a pillow beneath her. Then he was on top of her, the hair on his chest scraping her hypersensitive nipples. She ran her hands all over him, trying to memorize the planes of his back muscles and the hard curves of his shoulders.

His cock pressed against her abdomen, and her breath quickened. She pushed herself off the bed, trying to shove him onto his back so she could be on top, where she could control the pace. He pushed back, not giving her an inch. He used his knees to spread her legs, holding her firm against the bed.

The hot tip of him pressed into her, teasing. She longed for it, needed it. He held still as she bucked, trying to get it where it belonged. "Please," she moaned.

"One night won't be enough." His voice scraped against her nerve endings. He pressed further into her, an agonizing centimeter of promise. "Whatever this is, I'm going to want you again." He pressed a little deeper and she trembled. "And you're going to want me again." His lips took a taste of hers, a sharp bite of pleasure that left her desperate for more. "I'm not asking you to stay." He slid a little further. "Just promise me that you'll tell me when you decide to go."

The ping of pain she felt did little to dim the throb of need between her legs. *I'm not asking you to stay.* Want beat a powerful drum in her chest. She wanted him to stop talking, she wanted all of him buried inside of her, and she wanted the damn light on.

But mostly, she wanted him to want her to stay.

She dug a hole inside of herself and buried that away. Best to take the things she could get. "I promise," she said.

The ferocious kiss he gave made her woozy. Then he

slammed home, and she cried out, wrapping her legs behind his back, meeting him thrust for dizzying thrust. He set a bruising pace that sent her close to the edge. She dug her heels into his ass and her nails into his back, making him growl. Spots of color began to spark behind her eyelids. She bucked beneath him, murmuring "pleasepleaseplease" in an endless rhythm. In a prayer.

His breath scorched her ear. "I'm not stopping until you come again," he growled against her mouth. Shifting her legs over his shoulders, he drove deeper and faster, until the edge disappeared beneath her. Her body tightened painfully from the soles of her feet to her jaw, and she snapped and released like a broken guitar string, crying his name like a song.

22

LAZY CONTENTMENT FILLED Conor's bones as he awoke. Beneath the t-shirt he'd slipped back on last night, his back stung from Adelia's ragged fingernails and his abs were sore. Worth it. Nothing had ever felt as powerful or right as her trembling beneath him, moaning his name over and over again.

A lightness filled him. She had loved him. It shouldn't matter after all this time, but it did. He turned onto his side, eager to pull her into his arms and kiss her awake. Nothing but cool, empty space met him.

He opened his sleepy eyes and found himself alone. All of the oxygen in his body came out in one whoosh. *She didn't. She wouldn't.* He peeled back the covers and shot down the hall.

She lay curled in the couch cushions, fast asleep. Relief hit him hard enough to see spots. She hadn't left.

A strand of faded red hair stuck up at an odd angle and he tucked it behind her ear, finding it damp. She must have showered. She was probably afraid to wake him when she came back to bed.

Cupcake barked to let him know that she, too, was a pretty lady who needed attention. Sighing, he took her for a run.

Adelia was still sawing logs when he came back, so he took a shower.

The heat of the water and slick soap sent his mind back to her squirming and moaning, her long legs wrapped around his hips. He groaned, needing to think with the head on his shoulders and not the upright one demanding a soapy handshake it wasn't going to get.

No matter what was going on between them, Adelia was hurting about that trailer, and ignoring that was not an option for him. There *was* a way to help her, but it filled him with horror to think about it.

After his shower, he got on his computer to do some research. By the time she stirred, he was making a pot of coffee, feeling sufficiently educated.

She yawned wide and rubbed her eyes. The blanket slid down her naked breasts as she stretched, leaving him with a mouthful of melted resolve.

He crossed the room in four steps and kissed the painted lace on her shoulder and down her arm, stopping to nip the inside of her elbow and wrist, making his way across her stomach, and between her breasts. She laughed, and they jiggled merrily. "Morning," she said, gasping as he grazed her nipple. Kissing his way, he scraped the stubble on his chin against her chest, upward to her neck and jaw.

She turned her head slightly. "Let me go brush my teeth and—"

"Fuck that," he said, yanking her close and kissing her greedily. She gave a surprised squeak against his lips, and threw her arms around his neck, kissing him with just as much greed. He pulled back, nearly drowning in the dark eddies of her eyes. "Morning," he said, hauling her upright and leading her to the bedroom.

He shut the door. Hazy light filtered through his closed

blinds, so he pulled the room-darkening curtains closed, turning the room grey as the storming sky.

Though she was little more than a shadowy outline, his mouth went dry. "Come here."

She put her hands on her hips. "*You* come here," she said.

After a moment of stillness, he lunged at her and she shrieked with laughter as she ran. He tackled her to the bed and she turned to scramble away but he held her face down over his lap and gave her ass a smack.

She gasped, arching her back, and his blood shot south.

"Adelia, you naughty lady. Empowered woman. You like this?" He smacked harder and felt her breath change pattern from laughter to panting desire. "You do! Say 'please sir, may I have another.'"

She snorted. "Oh, please."

He smacked again. "'Please *sir*, may I have another.'"

She wriggled her bottom. "I don't beg."

That wasn't how he remembered it. So, he slapped her ass harder still and then slid his hand between her legs. "You will before I'm done with you," he said, lifting her hips until she was face down and ass up.

She arched against his fingers. Then his tongue. Then his cock. Until she was soaking his bedsheets and convulsing, tightening so hard around him that he nearly went blind as he came. Shuddering, he pressed his forehead between her shoulder blades and kissed her sweat-slicked back.

"I told you you'd beg," he said, out of breath.

She laughed and fell forward with a grunt, onto her stomach. "I didn't know about that little trick you were going to do with your—"

"I am full of surprises." He tossed the condom in the trash, slid on his underwear, and stretched beside her, pulling her close.

She rested her head on the shoulder of his shirt. "I'm glad we're going to keep doing that."

"Me, too." He kissed her forehead. "We both got really good at it."

She fell into silence, and played with his collar, her finger dipping beneath it to brush at his chest hair. After a few minutes, she raised herself up on her elbow. "I was thinking last night."

He turned to look at her, or as much as he could in the dingy light. "About what?"

"The trailer." She shook her hair off her face. "I did a search to find professional arsonists, but they don't advertise for some reason."

"Weird. I wouldn't trust an arsonist who doesn't allocate at least a small portion of his budget to marketing," he said. "Seems shortsighted."

She flopped onto her back. "I'm out of ideas."

He swung his leg over her and climbed on top, kissing the dip in her throat. "I have an idea," he said, breathing softly near her ear until she shivered. He kissed her, afraid it might be the last time, after he told her his plan.

"Tell me." she said.

"I think we should clean it out."

She stiffened and sat up, forcing him back onto his knees. "You're not serious."

"Hear me out," he said. "We'll look for your pictures and your sheet music and your doll. And *then* hire an arsonist, if you want."

"I...but the stuff is probably ruined anyway." She seemed more stunned than angry, which was better than he anticipated.

"It matters to you. Ruined or not."

She chewed on the edge of her thumbnail. "No one is getting that thing clean."

"Have you met me, Winters? There is *nothing* I can't clean."

"It would take a lifetime to go through everything. I don't know how much longer I can put off my manager." She was trembling, and her voice shifted in that way it did when she was shutting down, detaching to keep herself safe.

She was terrified, and he had to find a way to meet her where she was. Give her a reason to begin. "It's a small trailer. With a plan I think we can get it done in about ten days." He slid his hands into her hair and pulled her close, teasing her lips with his, until impatience won out and she gave a soft moan and kissed him, entwining her arms behind his neck. He ran his hands down her ribs and sighed against her pillowy mouth. "And I'll apply for the business loan."

She leaned back. "Seriously?"

It twisted his stomach into knots, but he nodded.

He needed a reason to begin, too.

CONOR PULLED UP TO KEYS. "I'm going to get some food and we'll be on our way, okay?"

Adelia nodded, her hands twisting in her lap. She was so skittish, he half-feared she'd jump out of the truck and walk back to California to avoid what they were doing.

At the hardware store earlier, she'd followed in silence while he grabbed supplies from his list. Heavy-duty garbage bags, boxes, industrial gloves, a camping toilet and sink, masks, goggles. Two pop up canopies. The cost was astronomical, and the only time she spoke was to tell him she was paying for it, before pulling out a wad of cash and handing it to him.

He left her slumped in the truck, his baseball cap pulled low to obscure her face, while he maneuvered around the slow, squinting tourists who had come out of their caves, like mole people, and into the first sunshine anyone had seen in weeks. He headed into Keys.

"Hello, young man," Old Curtis said.

There was something knowing on the old guy's face. Conor stopped and sighed. "Go ahead."

"I hear you have a girlfriend now! Is that so?"

"No. I have a...friend. Who is female. We are not dating. Pass it on."

His wrinkly face fell. "Oh, that's a shame. I told Miss Janice that it was about time you found that girl and settled down."

"I'm not into it. Relationships are a lot of hassle."

Miss Janice, Old Curtis's wife, shuffled up, holding some cans of vegetables. If Curtis's age was a local mystery, Janice's was even more so. She was somehow old and young at the same time, her smooth dark skin as tight as Curtis's fair skin was loose. The cotton fluff of her white hair rimmed her head like a halo as she sat the cans down with rough hands, gnarled with arthritis.

"Lord, life is hassle, Conor Ross. Grow up and find someone to go through it with you."

"Miss Janice, you were lucky to find that person. I don't see it happening for me." He aimed for his usual careless smile, the charming distraction.

She snorted and Old Curtis shook his head.

"Maybe it was luck that we met. Everything else was choices. Hard ones. You think it was luck that kept us together when our families disowned us for dating outside our races?" She shook her crooked finger at him. "No. You gotta fight for the things that matter."

Old Curtis raised a shaky hand and tugged on Janice's earlobe. "Love is worth the fuss."

She leaned into his hand and sighed. Then she pierced Conor with rheumy brown eyes. "Speaking of that, we wanted to talk to your cynical behind about taking pictures for our wedding anniversary this year."

"My cynical behind is listening," he said

"We've got a few months to go, but I wanted to get on your calendar. None of them Razzle kind of pictures. Some nice ones," she said. "We'll pay what they're worth."

"My contract doesn't allow me to charge for photography outside of Razzle. But I'll do as an anniversary gift." He entered the date into his phone. "Just promise to recommend me to friends when I get my own studio." He gave her a wink and handed Old Curtis his credit card.

When he climbed into the truck, Adelia pushed her sunglasses down her nose to look at the bags. "What'd you get?"

He smacked her hand. "Mind your business, nosy."

She pushed her sunglasses back up. "It took a long time for one little bag."

"Old Curtis and Miss Janice had some questions about my —" he crooked his fingers into quotation marks, "—girlfriend."

"The horror. Best way to put people off about stuff like that is to talk about sex. Did you tell him what a great lay I am? You should have amped up the details. Made me a gymnast."

"I don't need to make anything up." He started the truck. "You are a phenomenal lay."

"I know. I was being humble."

"Stop it. It doesn't suit you."

She tilted her hat down. "We've got an audience."

From the window of Keys, Miss Janice peeked out, pretending to reorganize the already flawless display of canned goods. Outside the shop, Dennis Littlewood barely hid his stare behind a copy of *Wheeler Dealer*. In her car, two spaces down, Grace Archibald met Conor's eye and began feverishly texting.

"Damned nosy people," he said. "We'd better get going. We're going to need all the sunlight we can get."

The smile fell away from Adelia's face.

Nodding, she lapsed into silence all the way to her father's trailer.

THE SUNLIGHT GLINTED off the bile-yellow trailer squatting in front of the river and beneath the canopy of white pines, as vile and out of place as a banana slug.

Adelia clenched her jaw to stop her quaking.

The screen in the storm door had broken free from the corner of the frame. It slapped back and forth like a flag, until a gust of wind caught the entire storm door, slamming it against the side of the trailer, making her jump.

It was one thing to drag Conor to the trailer when she was drunk off her ass, but coming here stone-cold sober was so much more painful. And humiliating.

"You ready to do this?" he asked.

She stared at the hated aluminum box. "No." She looked at him over her shoulder, giving him a sultry smile. "Wanna bone?"

He raised his eyebrows. "No. Yes. But no."

She turned and wrapped her arms around him, kissing him hungrily until they were both out of breath.

He blinked dazedly. "Dammit, I just got the blood back to my brain, woman."

She stroked the hard ridge in his jeans. "It's gone again.

Might as well enjoy it." She nipped at his ear. "I can do some things with my mouth that'll have you singing hallelujah."

He grabbed her and kissed her. She wrapped her arms around his neck and gave back everything he gave, lips for lips, tongue for tongue. She unbuttoned his pants and reached inside, eager to feel him in her hands for once.

He grabbed her wrists and pried them away from his underwear. "As much as I want to do this, that trailer will still be there, waiting for you afterward." He kissed her hands. "You can make me sing hallelujah later."

She flopped back onto the seat. "It's a one-time offer."

He gave her an exasperated look. "Then I'll live in regret. Now, get out of the truck and quit trying to steal my virtue." His smile melted her like a cider slushie on a summer day. "And if you're lucky, I'll make *you* sing hallelujah later."

Her nipples tightened, and she bit her lip. "My motives aren't pure, but I would sincerely like to have sex with you right now."

His eyes flashed with lust and for a moment it looked like he might give in, but she knew he wouldn't. Conor didn't lose one hundred and thirty pounds without iron-clad dedication to his goal, and right now, his goal was to start cleaning the trailer.

"Let's get four hours done," he said. "Then we'll go home, shower and I'll make you bow legged for a week."

Damn. She hated being right.

He unpacked the truck, setting up a makeshift bathroom with portable sink and toilet, near the woods for privacy. It was hard to decide whether to kill him or kiss him for forcing this on her. She helped him put together the two canopies. One long one for working beneath. One small square one with plastic walls to serve as the private bathroom. Then it was wood pallets, in case it rained again, with tarps draped over them, so they could sit and sort.

It took a while to set everything up, but she appreciated the time it gave her to avoid going inside. Eventually, they ran out

of set-up. He helped her into a disposable pair of hooded coveralls and sat her on the back of the truck to slip the covers over
the cheap steel toed boots he picked up for the both of them.
Then heavy gloves and a pair of goggles.

"Christ, is this necessary? I lived in that place for nine years.
I'm fine."

He pulled a mask out of a bag. "I did my homework. Yes, you
have to wear it." He slid the mask into place.

"I feel like an astronaut."

"You look like one." He kissed her forehead. "There, now
you're ready to conquer this planet."

He dressed and she slipped off a glove, to nibble at her
fingernail. "I, uh, I'd like to go in first."

He gave her a nod. With a deep breath, she hoisted herself
off the truck bed and stalked to the covered porch, stopping to
kick a corroded muffler off the steps and into the mud. She slid
the key into the lock, held her breath and twisted. It didn't
turn.

Sweat pooled at the small of her back. "Open, you piece of…"
She cracked her knuckles and shook the stiffness from her
hands. Then she gripped it again and wrenched the ever-loving
hell out of the key. It still didn't budge.

She could feel his eyes on her, and she pressed her palms
against the doorframe, and closed her eyes. This was a bad idea.
With every second she was shrinking, changing back into the
grubby kid she used to be. The one that dreaded coming home
from school and always hesitated at the door. She opened her
eyes. The kid who always forgot to pull on the doorknob as she
turned the key.

Maybe she hadn't wanted to remember.

She put one hand on the handle and the other on the key.
With a sharp exhale she turned them at the same time, and
shoved the door open as far as it would go. The familiar surge
of moldy, nicotine-tinged air rolled over her, blending into the

greasy stink of car parts and rancid body odor. She covered her
nose and gagged.

Like the passage of a hedge maze, a thin path ran through
the trailer. But instead of sculpted greenery walling her in, it
was junk. Piles and piles of boxes, bins and bags. Busted alternators and flea-market cast-offs. Broken radios. Wadded up clothing. Endless mountains of garbage. She inched along the path
until she came to a small curve that most people, disoriented by
the smell and the visual assault, would walk right past. She
followed it to the nubby green chair hiding behind the teetering
wall of boxes.

Her stomach heaved. The old battery-powered radio sat on
top of a stack of ancient encyclopedias, exactly where it'd been
fourteen years ago. A pack of cigarettes sat beside it. She picked
it up. Marlboro Reds.

Her father used to sit there, smoking cigarette after
cigarette, yelling at the baseball announcers on the radio.
Ignoring her. No matter how much she grew out of her clothes
or how loud her stomach growled, he ignored her. No matter
how much she needed him, he sat there, smoking his Reds,
pretending she didn't exist.

She sat the pack down and backed away. There were no
cherished memories to be found here. If she ever had any they
were long ago tainted by the rotting bags of garbage, oily
carburetors and heaps of broken antiques her father loved so
much.

Her breath skipped like an old record. The room was too
small. Too narrow. She spun and her elbow banged into a
plastic crate of exhaust pipes. It tumbled off a mountain of
lumpy bags and knocked into a box full of dishes sitting on a
stack of newspapers. A landslide of pipes, plates, and paper
came crashing toward her.

She stumbled out, slamming the door shut, and gripped the
porch rail. Heat spread in her guts. She tore off the goggles and

mask, and with no fanfare, she tossed her breakfast over the railing and into the overgrown grass.

Conor raced up the steps, tearing off his gloves, and pressed a warm hand on her back. He made small, slow circles as her stomach emptied.

"I'm good," she croaked. Her stomach already felt better.

He insisted she sit on the steps, while he ran to the truck. He came back with a napkin and a bottle of mouthwash.

"You...you actually anticipated this?"

"Of course," he said through the mask. "We were bound to find something gross in there that would have made me barf, so I came prepared. I brought a toothbrush too, if you need it."

She took the mouthwash, swigging and spitting several times until her mouth felt minty.

He slid his mask down and stroked her hair. "How do you feel?"

With more torque than necessary, she tightened the cap. "Exactly like I did when I left here. Hungry. Angry. Desperate to escape."

"Huh," he said. "That's sort of poetic."

"If the poet was an asshole." She shook her head. "I don't think I can do this."

"Why?"

"I'm afraid of what's going to happen after."

"What do you think will happen?"

"I don't know." The Little Brown Bat River whooshed behind them like the static from a dozen cheap guitar amps and she fought the impulse to turn and chuck the house key straight into water. Then there'd be nothing left to do but to hit the highway straight back to California. Book another tour. Keep dodging and weaving and running until her legs gave out, and they were halfway there already. How much longer could she keep doing that?

"I think the way I feel about my dad...it's what drives me."

She unscrewed the mouthwash cap and tightened it again. "It made me what I am. Kept me tough. I wanted to make music because I loved it, but I wanted to be successful to spit in his eye. Show him what he missed out on." She snorted. "I bought the Pontiac out of spite. The sixty-seven GTO was his favorite. He dreamed about owning one." She pressed her forehead to the bottle. "Who will I be once this is done?"

Conor tugged the mouthwash away. Setting it aside, he cupped her jaw, tilting her head until she looked at him. "Your dad was just a man with mental illness. Don't give him the credit for making you strong. You survived because you were strong. You were already driven. Maybe he's been the accelerant, but your fire was already burning."

"It all comes back to arson, doesn't it?" she said with a tired smile.

He turned, the ridiculous plastic coveralls crinkling. "Do you know what's weird about losing weight? I always thought—or maybe fantasized—that I'd become this fundamentally different person. Cooler. In control. That I'd look in the mirror and see... perfection." His jaw clenched, and he stared at his hands. "And maybe some of that stuff you can wear, like a mask. But who you are is who you are. And I think you'll still be you. Foul-mouthed. Tough. Sweet. Funny. Passionate. Loving." He pinned her with the intensity of his gaze. "You'll still be all those things, and maybe happy too."

Her heart twisted like an old dishrag. When had anyone ever described her like that? "I think you're the first person in the world to call me sweet or loving."

"You may not advertise those parts of yourself, but that doesn't make them any less real." He gave her a small smile. "You're more than this thing, Adelia."

She searched his eyes, looking for pity or lies. She found nothing but conviction.

Nodding, she slid her mask back into place. "Okay. Let's do this."

THE TARP CRUNCHED beneath them as they went through the mountain of junk they brought out of the trailer. Adelia glanced over at Conor. To his credit he showed no outward signs of disgust. Just a bulletproof cheerfulness that carried her through the day.

She'd given him her blessing to throw away anything that looked like garbage and to set aside questionable items for her to judge. He held up a VHS copy of Teenage Mutant Ninja Turtles. The tape was twisted and hanging out of the top like spilled intestines. "Did you guys even own a machine to play this?"

"Nope. Don't think too hard about it. None of it makes sense," she said.

He shoved it into the garbage. Reaching into the dwindling mass, he pulled out a stack of bundled real estate catalogues, yellowed and moldy with age.

Adelia's throat tightened and distress propelled her to yank the stack from his hands before he could throw it away.

"What is it?"

She shook her head, unable to speak. The cover boasted some lumpy hearts scribbled on the top cover in faded Crayola Indigo. Underneath them, in broad cursive ink were the words, *Page 6! The one!* She skimmed the letters with her gloved fingers over and over, entranced by the wobbly tail on the G and the exclamation point dotted with a crooked skinny heart. A hollow ache settled into her chest. She'd drawn the crayon hearts, sitting on her mother's lap in their tiny Flint apartment.

Her memory was hazy, her mother's features indistinct, except for the coppery red hair. But she remembered how much her mom longed for a home. She'd spent her life in tiny, low-income apartments and she'd dreamed of a place of her own. Every week she brought home a real estate catalogue and pored over it, pointing to the prettiest properties and asking Adelia to imagine what it would be like to live there. To have a happily-ever-after home.

The memory ached like a bruise.

"Are you okay?"

She blinked, the light suddenly too bright for her eyes.

"I—uh, yeah. I'm fine." Adelia sat the stack next to her hip. "What's next?" she asked, trying to infuse her voice with cheer-fulness.

His brow furrowed. "I'm kind of hungry. Want to take a break? We've been at this for pretty close to three hours."

She nodded, grateful for a chance to regain her footing so she could climb out of the pit of gloom she'd fallen into.

After stripping off their gloves, he insisted on hand washing and then using a massive amount of hand sanitizer before they could touch the food.

"It stings my cuticles," she grumped.

"Better that than some deadly hoarding disease. Now cheer up, I bought you all the stuff to make ants on a log."

That did perk her up. They sat quietly, piling low-fat peanut butter onto celery stalks. He ate his all healthy-like, but she poured handfuls of raisins onto the sticky stalk, patting them down and then devouring them. The conversation drifted away, and she leaned back on her elbows, listening to the shushing of the tree leaves in the wind and the gentle lap and rush of the river.

"You've got to admit, it's beautiful out here," he said.

She looked around, trying to see it through his eyes. The river wound its way along the western and southern edges of the property, the shoreline overgrown with bushy yellow and green grass, cat tails and unidentifiable leafy plants. On the other side, huge birch and pine trees dotted the hilly bank. The grassy yard where the trailer sat was small, but the lot actually extended into the forest in two different directions, almost an acre each way.

"I never really thought about it, but I guess it is." She stared at the river. "My mom picked it out." Like crests of rolling water, the words rushed out. "Those were her magazines. She was looking for our happily-ever-after home." Adelia rolled her eyes. "Like that even exists. But my mom loved that kind of romantic stuff. My dad and she used to get dressed up and go on dates. Sometimes he'd bring her lilacs. They were her favorite. And he'd—" She swallowed the bitter taste in her mouth. "He'd pick one out of the bunch for me."

Conor nodded, but didn't reach for her or touch her and she was grateful for it.

"She found this place in one of those magazines. My dad sold his car repair shop, took out a huge mortgage, and bought it for her."

She sat up, crossing her legs at the ankle and folding her knees under her chin. "The trailer was supposed to be temporary because he was going to build her dream house here. But she died before we moved. Never made it out of low-income housing. So much for happily-ever-after."

She'd been so young when her mother had died and barely understood the loss. One day she was there, all sweet smiles and nicotine-stained fingers, and the next she was gone. No more braying donkey laughs and late-night games of Sorry. Just a simple grave and a broken family.

"I never cried when she died. Not once. My dad said I had to be strong. But he fell apart. Moved us out to the middle of nowhere and gave up. It was like they both died."

She climbed out of the truck bed and stalked to the pile of garbage on the tarp. "He quit taking care of himself and quit taking care of me." She ran a hand through her hair. "Then he started bringing home all of this shit."

Every once in a great while he'd drag her to the flea market and she'd want to scream as he filled the truck bed with basement cast-offs, vintage car parts, and broken antiques, on the never-ending hunt for something valuable to fill the bottomless bucket where his heart had been.

One violent kick sent junk tumbling across the yard. "I hate him. And I hate that I hate him."

Conor didn't speak, but he sat his hand on his knee, palm up. Holding it there for her, just in case she needed it. She swallowed, afraid to reach for him. But the pull of his eyes, the warmth of his body reached out and peeled her back in layers. She wanted to cry. Not because of her mother or her father. It was because this man cared enough to sit with her in squalor and listen to her ramble on about her childhood without wanting to strangle himself. Because he obsessively washed things and vacuumed his dog. Because he knew when to touch her and when not to. Because he never forgot that she liked ants on a log. Because he was Conor and she had never stopped loving him.

She grabbed for his hand and held on tight.

24

CONOR WOKE to an empty bed again.

Four nights in a row they'd gone to bed together and he'd woken up alone. It stung. He wanted to kiss Adelia awake, to curl behind her and wrap his arm around her for five more minutes of sleep. But she was never there. He groaned and slapped the pillow.

When he got up, she was in the living room chair, staring into space and holding a dingy cardboard square in her hand.

"Hey," she said. Her voice sounded raspier than usual and there were shadows under her eyes. The cleaning wasn't getting any easier, and every day she seemed to fall deeper into melancholy.

"You all right?" he asked.

She didn't look up at him. "I'm fine."

"What is that?"

She flipped the thing in her hand around. It looked like it used to be black or maybe dark blue. Now it was faded, with a barely visible yellow circle on it.

"Record jacket," she said. "I found it at the trailer. I sprayed it with Lysol and stuff."

He sat on the ottoman and stroked her knee. "Tell me about it."

"Bonnie Raitt. *Streetlights*. It was a near perfect album. It had this song on it, 'Angel From Montgomery'. It was so beautiful."

"I didn't know you were a Bonnie Raitt fan."

"I told you I had layers." Her small smile slipped away as she ran her fingers over the faded image. "It was my mom's favorite. She played 'Angel From Montgomery' over and over on the record player. She loved all that stuff. Bonnie Raitt. Janice Joplin. Stevie Nicks. Annie Lennox. I haven't heard any of these songs since I was a kid."

"Where's the record?"

"It was broken. I threw it out." Standing suddenly, she crossed the room and ripped the ancient record jacket in two, stuffing it into his kitchen garbage can.

He could feel her sadness and rage pulsing like his own heart. She needed to do something with that anger.

"Want to go for a run with me?" he asked.

She shook her head. "I don't have running gear."

"I have some clothes you can wear. We can walk if you don't want to run. Focusing on something outside of your own head might be good for you."

She looked dubious. "It's not even daylight yet."

"Perfect. No one will see us." He gave her his most charming smile. "Please?"

After a moment, her shoulders slumped. "Sure," she said as she headed to the kitchen sink. "But only because of that thing you did last night."

"We made out and watched a *Daria* marathon last night."

"Exactly." She washed her hands. "Let's go for a run, Jane Lane."

"I see myself more like Tom. The charming, wealthy boy who fell for a cynical girl."

"I wasn't cynical. I was a realist."

He spun her around and kissed her until her body relaxed. "Keep telling yourself that, Daria."

They got dressed and wound their way along spongy dirt trails, the silence broken by the squelch of their shoes and the chickadees whistling a come-hither song. He pointed to a huge birch tree. "There's a hawk's nest up there. Some mornings, he swoops right over my head. Makes Cupcake nuts." He made a screeching noise and flapped his arms over her head, making Cupcake groan and Adelia laugh.

He loved hearing her laugh.

She yawned and rolled her neck. "I haven't gone outside and just walked in a long time. It's so quiet. California isn't quiet."

"Nope. It's loud and smoggy and full of jerks who want to make you into a dancing monkey," he said with a smile.

"Yeah. Maybe it's time for a change. After I get my career figured out, I could move to Vegas. I always thought that I would have made an excellent showgirl."

"Hmm, maybe." He tamped down the dread he felt. A whole country between them hadn't seemed far enough two weeks ago; now, it was an unbearable thought. Not seeing and touching her would make him insane. Not talking to her would break his heart.

Not break his heart. *Bother him. It would bother him.*

They walked until she groaned. "I'm sick of exercise." She hooked Cupcake's leash around a tree, letting it out to full length, so the dog could roam.

Adelia looked adorable swimming in his t-shirt and baggy sweats, with her hair pulled into a messy ponytail, hands on her hips. But telling her that would only earn him an eye-roll. So, he complimented her in the way he knew she'd accept. He pressed her against a tree and kissed her. She returned it with enthusiasm, sucking on his lower lip and taking the kiss from sweet to scorching. She rolled her hips against his and grabbed at his shirt.

He pulled back. "Let's go home."

"Let's do it right here." She gave him a sultry smile and whipped off her shirt. He could have died right there. Her skin gleamed in the barely-there glow of the sunrise, her tattoo more stark and erotic than ever before. Her fingers trailed over the ridges of her areolas and she pulled on her nipples. "Fuck me, Conor."

His mouth went dry. How difficult would it be to take off his shirt and make love to her in the daylight? To feel her nails scrape his stomach, her mouth on his cock.

It was impossible.

He walked toward her slowly, afraid to move too fast, to break his fragile thread of rationality. She stared at him as she untied her sweatpants. They pooled around her ankles and she kicked them aside, leaving her in nothing but a pair of muddy Converse.

God, he wished he had his camera. She was Botticelli's *Birth of Venus* without the false modesty. A goddess in filthy shoes, and faded Manic Panic hair, standing in a clamshell full of issues.

She was perfect.

He took his time, touching and worshipping every plane and valley of her body. He slid her arms above her head, pressing them into the bark of the birch tree.

She arched her pelvis toward him. He slid his fingers between her thighs, skimming over the red-brown hair to give her a few teasing strokes that made her breath catch.

"Keep your hands on the tree and I'll keep going," he said. "Take them off the tree and I'll stop."

"No, I want to touch you."

Those words arced through him and sparked. He wanted that, too. But he pushed his desire aside and clicked his tongue at her. "Behave yourself and I'll make it worth your while. Don't, and we'll go home and watch TV instead."

She bit her lip, mutiny in her expression.

He increased the friction of his strokes and leaned toward her ear. "Come on, Winters." He slid his fingers inside and crooked them. "Don't you want to sing hallelujah for me?"

Her whimpers turned to moans and then keening sobs of pleasure. She pressed her hands tight against the tree.

The victory was a hollow one.

Still, he did as he promised and dropped to his knees, parted her beautiful thighs, and spent the next twenty minutes making her sing.

***

ADELIA BARELY MADE the walk back to the trailer. Her legs were jelly. It wasn't natural for any man to be that good at what he did. Inside, he laid her down and made love to her in the cool darkness. Always in the dark. While she recovered her senses, he kissed her forehead and slid out of the bed to shower.

Her heart ached. Was it possible to love someone as much as she loved Conor? It lit her from the inside, a roman candle ready to explode, and in the end, it would be her blown to pieces.

The nights were the hardest. Laying there, listening to him fall asleep and wanting to snuggle beside him and fall asleep too. Instead, she went back to the couch, knowing that sleeping beside him was too much like...home.

It wasn't real and it wasn't meant to last.

He sauntered into the room, dressed and smelling like heaven. "I think we're going to have to skip the trailer today."

"Say it isn't so."

He leaned over her and kissed her softly. "It's so," he said. "I need to finish the loan presentation. I scheduled an appointment with the bank for Friday." He looked like he might get sick. "I've also got plans from five-thirty to seven. Then, Shan and Jo are coming over at eight for movie night."

"Plans? That's mysterious."

"It's Nerd Night at Crowley's Tavern. Trivia contest. I really feel like this is my big moment. Plus, I've got a hot date."

She knew he was messing with her, but the thought still twisted her insides up. Digging up a wry smile, she leaned back. "Tell me about this babe."

"Mmm, pretty little thing," he said. "Dark hair. Big blue eyes. Name is Jack."

"Pie Jack? I had no idea you were so adventurous. Bring him back here."

His eyes narrowed. "No."

"Oh-ho, papa doesn't share?"

He slid his hand into her hair, tugging her close, and kissed her. Hot and hungry, his tongue curling against hers, his teeth tugging on her bottom lip. She moaned and scrambled to get on her knees. Sinking into the soft bedding she fought to keep contact with him. He laughed against her mouth and leaned toward her ear, his warm breath tickling her flesh. "Papa does not," he growled.

Electricity surged up her spine. There was something both sweet and territorial in his gaze and it made her insides melt. No one had ever looked at her like that.

He stroked his fingers over her lips. "Let's explore that little kink later," he murmured. "Maybe after breakfast."

Sadly, they didn't go exploring. He decided to work on his loan presentation and holed himself in his office for hours, only coming out for lunch before going right back inside. Disappointing as that was, it gave her a chance to work.

Sunlight and a soft breeze streamed through the thin curtains of the open window. Everything smelled musty and woodsy and slightly damp from all the recent rain. She sat her notebook full of scribbles and song lyrics in front of her.

Searching her phone for the half-dozen potential songs she'd recorded into it, she found the track Emi had sent her. She converted it for guitar and changed the key to one that suited her voice a little better, dropping the tempo and nudging the lyrics around some more, slipping them into place like broken bones. This was the part of making music she loved.

She stood and walked from one end of the room to the other as if it were a stage. Closing her eyes, she listened; not to herself humming the words, but to the fans who would one day sing the song back to her. Outside of concerts, it was so hard to talk to people. Their questions and adoration made her equally uncomfortable. But onstage, after giving all those pieces of herself away, she'd point the microphone out and ask for a little bit back. And they gave it. She couldn't see them beneath the bright lights, but she could hear them singing every word back to her. Loud. Off-key. Each inflection different than her own. Taking her song, her story, and binding it with theirs until she couldn't tell one from the other. It was communion.

She could almost hear them. It was nearly there.

Too excited to be cool about it, she pulled Emi's phone number out of her email and texted her.

I have no fucking idea what I'm doing. I have no label and my manager usually handles everything. But I loved the track and I'm sending you a little of what I worked on.

Then she paced, waiting to hear back. After twenty painful minutes, Emi responded. *I've listened to it four times. It's beautiful. Give me a chance to shine it up. In the meantime, I have another track with which to seduce you into working with me. Want it?*

She did. Emi sent it and more excitement coursed through her. Mid-tempo, with a guitar line she could make her own. She started making notes.

The door to the office creaked open. Conor emerged, looking exhausted as he got on the floor and sat beside her. She grabbed a pillow from the couch, dropping it onto her crossed legs, and he flopped over, resting his head on it and sighed.

"This presentation is a nightmare," he said. "Razzle Dazzle is looking better and better."

She ran her fingers over the frown line between his eyebrows until he relaxed. "Razzle Dazzle is Keith. Keith is an epic dick who doesn't appreciate you."

"Keith never made me create slide shows, so I'm feeling forgiving." He leaned into her fingers. "How is this stuff easy for Liam?"

"No idea. All I know is that you can do this."

He gave her a tight smile. "Now who's an optimist?"

"I find that offensive."

He laughed, and the tension in his face melted away. He took her hand in his and kissed her palm and each of the divots in her fingertips from playing. "Do they hurt?"

"Nah, I don't feel it anymore."

He placed her hand on his chest and drummed his fingers over her knuckles. "Can I hear what you're working on? Or would that be weird for you?"

"Not weird at all." She grabbed her guitar.

He sprawled on the floor with his hands beneath his head. "I don't know anything about guitars, but that one is pretty."

She ran her fingers over the strings. "BC Rich custom. They wanted to do a signature model with me, but EJ thought it wasn't the right time." She strummed a quick chord and then reached to tune it. "Should have done it."

"Whatever that song was you've been playing all day, I love the melody. It's beautiful. Will you play it again?"

If anything had ever turned her insides to goo, it was Conor asking that. "Sure. It's not done yet." It *was* done, but she wasn't ready for him to hear those lyrics out loud.

She didn't close her eyes this time. Instead she hummed the words as she played and watched his tiny reactions. His feet moving to the beat. His head swaying and the small smile that widened when she hit the chorus. And when the chorus came a second time, he hummed along as best he could.

It was so much better than the faceless crowd singing it back.

It wasn't perfect, there were rough spots. The music rolled from her, delicate and vulnerable, mistakes lingering. That was all right. It was better with them. The mistakes made it real.

"Wow," he said, when she finished. "You're amazing. I can't wait to hear you sing it."

She bit her lip. "Want to hear another one?"

"Are you asking me if I want my own personal Lia Frost concert?"

"Ugh, never mind. You get nothing."

He laughed and pulled at her guitar. "I meant, yes. Please. I'd like that."

She played a few of the new songs that had come to her recently. Ones she didn't mind him hearing. His eyes went from gleaming to something darker, almost confused. She stopped strumming. "What's the matter?"

"How do you do it?"

"I pluck the strings and noise comes out."

"No, how do you just, hold so much in, but then put all that emotion into the music?"

"It's gotta go somewhere," she said. "Otherwise, my guts would get all...explode-y."

"A Grammy for writing? Really?"

"Shut up, man."

He lay there while she worked for a long time, before glancing at his phone. "Shit, I've gotta go. Nerd Night waits for no man."

He gathered his stuff and threw on his jacket. "Thank you for the concert."

"You're welcome. Kick ass and take names. Be the nerdiest nerd of them all. Don't make out with Jack unless you record it."

"No promises," he said with a warm smile that crinkled his eyes. He tilted her chin and gave her a sweet, lingering kiss before leaving.

She leaned against the door, long after he'd left, her hand on her chest as if she could feel the roman candle sparking inside.

Just waiting to go off.

25

"Taco night is the best night," Adelia said. She flopped back on the couch, squished between Shannon, Jo, and Cupcake. Conor didn't want Jo thinking they were involved, so they were playing pretend-we're-not-boning by sitting away from each other.

Jo picked at her barely-eaten food. She'd been silent all evening. It was strange, but Adelia missed the kid's endless chatter and contagious energy. She tried to pry a smile out of her, even offering to play her a new song, but Jo shook her head no.

"What's going on, Flash?" Conor asked from the kitchen. "You seem upset."

Jo shrugged. "Don't feel good. I'm gonna go home."

"I'll walk you," he said. "We can talk."

"Nah, I don't really wanna talk." She grabbed her backpack. "Thanks, though." Giving a half-hearted wave, she shut the door softly behind her.

"She's not okay," Adelia said.

Shannon chugged her beer. "She will be. She's having some issues with those damn Malinski twins. Little snots."

"Still with the Malinskis?" Adelia said. "That family is a menace."

"Yeah, Alan's girls. Maddison and Addison. They're nasty about Jo not having money, but it's worse now. I don't know what to do or tell her. I've said all the parent stuff. *Money doesn't make happiness. Being poor isn't a character flaw. Those girls might be put together, but their insides are ugly.*" She shook her head. "She rolls her eyes and shuts down."

Jo's questions about people making her feel weird suddenly made sense. Adelia shoved her hair behind her ears, needing to rough something up. Bullies were the worst. Especially the Malinskis, who'd made Conor's childhood so miserable.

"They have some nerve," Shannon said. "Their parents grew up in this park. Alan's mother picked up cans by the roadside for beer money. But he makes a fortune selling Ski-Doos and the next thing you know, they're lakesiders, looking down on us."

Conor returned to the living room, sitting more bottles of beer in front of everyone. He leaned against the wall with his own. "What's got the twins so frothed up anyhow?"

Shannon groaned. "A boy. Cody Hickman. Addison likes him. He likes Jo."

"He's a lakesider," he said with a frown. "They're the worst."

"Dude, *you* were a lakesider," Adelia said.

"They've been texting nonstop," Shannon continued. "She won't let me see her phone and I'm not going to violate her privacy, but god, it's like I'm reliving the months before I got pregnant." She slumped into the couch. "Please don't let her get pregnant. Especially not by a lakesider."

"Jo isn't getting pregnant." Conor's eyes were wide with horror. "That's not...a thing."

"She's not a baby anymore," Shannon said. "She's going to make out and drink and get her heart hurt."

"Ground her. Ground her forever."

Shannon gave a small smile. "Hitting puberty is not a groundable offense, Conor."

Conor's brows drew together. "But I don't want her to get a broken heart."

He looked so devastated by the idea, that Adelia had to force herself not go put her arms around him.

"That's not your choice." Shannon took a gulp of her beer. "Anyway, Jo isn't the type to stress about what we don't have. But last night she said she doesn't want a party. She's afraid to be humiliated in front of the entire town because we're broke and weird." She shoved a hand in her thick hair and pushed it away from her face. "It's only four days away. If I had time, I could maybe cobble together a party that wouldn't be a total disaster, but I can't afford anything beyond paper plates and cupcakes at the town hall, and I refuse to blow a dime of Jo's college money to impress the damned Malinskis."

"She'll have to learn that money doesn't matter," he said.

"It matters." Adelia leaned forward and put her forearms on her thighs, unable to stay quiet. "Conor, all of your birthday parties were catered at the June Lake Country Club. I'm pretty sure I never once saw you eat anything off a paper plate."

"What does that have to do with anything?"

"Jo started off a step behind everyone else. She's the teen mom's kid. A trailer park girl. She has to work twice as hard, do everything better, just to catch up to everyone else. And she does it. Bullies shouldn't take that from her." She crossed her arms. "I'll take care of her party. All of it."

"Absolutely not," Shannon said, shooting upright.

"I can—"

"No. My daughter is not just some way for you to stroke your ego or alleviate your guilt. It's easy to swan in with some money and think you can fix things for us little people. But Jo's got to live here after you and your money are gone."

That hurt. More than it should have.

"You don't trust me and that's fair, but you fucking know me better than that, Shannon."

"Maybe. But not enough to let you screw with my kid's heart."

"It won't help anyway," Conor cut in. "There is nothing you can do to impress a bully, no matter how much debt you go into."

"It's not about how they react. It's about how it makes Jo feel." She stood and faced Shannon. "I can't fix it. But I can make damn sure the kid knows how awesome she is. You know just like I know that being poor gets inside of you. You see other people with so much, and at first, you wonder *why* they get those things and you don't. But after a while, you start to think, maybe they *deserve* those things, and you don't. We shouldn't have ever had to feel like that, and Jo shouldn't either."

She turned and pressed her hand to Conor's chest. "And you know what it's like too; you've lived every day of your life like that, with Liam."

He cupped her chin with one hand and stared at her for a long moment. "Winters, I swear I just saw your heart grow three sizes."

Her face burned, and she turned away from him. "Whatever. Shut up. I'm taking care of it." She swung toward Shannon. "Okay?"

Shannon assessed her for a long moment and nodded. "Fine."

"Good." Needing to move, Adelia clomped into the kitchen and started angrily packing up the taco fixings. Fucking Malinskis.

Shannon wandered into the kitchen and pulled her thick hair into a bun. "Conor, why don't you take the food over to my house? You can check on Jo while you're at it."

Uh oh. That meant Shannon had things to say. Fun. Adelia

grabbed a bag and shoved the containers into it. Best to get this over with.

Conor took the bag. With his free hand, he pushed aside some of her hair and kissed her softly. "I'll be back."

Clearing her throat, Adelia nodded turned and began filling the sink with warm water.

Shannon scooched her out of the way. "I've got this." Rolling up her sleeves she started washing the plates, passing them to Adelia to dry. They worked quietly for a few minutes.

"So," Shannon said slowly, breaking the silence. "What's going on with you and Conor?"

Adelia shrugged. "What do you mean?"

"Oh, don't give me that."

"It's just sex," Adelia said. "Amazing sex. Actually, it's the best—"

"Don't talk to me about Conor-sex, please. I'll never stop gagging."

"Fine, I won't tell you what he did to me in the woods or where he put his tongu—"

Shannon wretched dramatically, and Adelia held up her hands. "Okay, I'm done. I swear."

"In the woods? Really?" Shannon's eyebrows bunched up. "I always assumed he'd only do it on plastic sheets with garbage bags taped to his hands so he wouldn't get dirty."

"You would be wrong."

"Ewww." Shannon made a face and shuddered. She leaned against the counter and crossed her arms and her expression turned serious. "Don't think I don't appreciate what you want to do for Jo. But I'm worried about all of this. I just don't want anyone to get their heart broken."

"I get it." Adelia stared intently at the plate she was drying. "But like I said, it's just sex. No hearts involved," she said, the lie burning her tongue.

The click of the doorknob put a merciful end to the conversation.

"Jo talk to you?" Shannon asked Conor as she drained the sink.

"Not a word."

"So what took you so long?"

He shrugged. "I organized your fridge."

"It was already organized!"

"No. It wasn't. Your system had no internal logic."

Shannon rolled her eyes and gave Adelia a pointed look as she left. "We'll talk more later. About the party."

Before the door latched, Conor had Adelia in his arms. He shoved his hands into her hair and decimated her with each bite of her lip and curl of his tongue. "I've been waiting to do that all night." His graveled voice scraped her nerve endings, firing them all off at once. If they were firing with pleasure, her neurons were all pain.

I just don't want anyone to get their heart broken.

His fingers brushed beneath her jaw and lifted her chin. "You okay?"

"Yeah, I'm fine."

He kissed her, this time with a gentleness that was worse than lust. "Did Shannon say something that upset you?" His eyes were a rush of green, like the first color change after spring storms.

"No." She dug up a smile. "My stomach hurts a little. I've eaten more in the last few weeks than I have in the last two years."

He slid his warm hand beneath her shirt and rubbed gently at her belly. "Do you need me to run to the store and get you something for it?"

Adelia's heart sputtered like an old engine.

It was involved. It was way too involved.

She wrapped her arms around his neck. "I'm fine." She kissed him until they both forgot to be worried. "Take me to bed."

LATER THAT NIGHT, Adelia curled against Conor's side like a contented cat, her hair tickling his shoulder.

"Is it me or is the sex actually getting better?" she asked. "That doesn't seem possible."

He dragged her toward him and found her lips in the darkness. "It's definitely getting better."

Her stomach growled between them. "See what you did with that little marathon? Burned off all my taco calories. Want something to eat?"

"No, I'm too tired. But go ahead. There's cereal and bananas."

"Ooh!" She ran naked from the room, throwing the door open and letting the light spill in. He grabbed for his shirt and slid it on, along with his pajama pants.

He was glad for a few minutes to catch his breath. If last night told him anything, it was that no matter how much had changed, she was still the same caring, kind, prickly-as-hell girl he'd loved so desperately as a kid.

And he was on much more dangerous ground than he thought he'd been.

She returned, sitting a cereal bowl on the nightstand before leaping back into bed. She didn't close the bedroom door, and the hall light glanced off the side of her nude body, casting a golden glow on her flesh.

She shoved a spoonful of cereal in her mouth, and then looked sideways at him, as he stared at her. "What?"

"You're gorgeous."

Her mouth tilted at the corners, but she scrunched her nose at him. "Dude, don't gross me out. I'm eating."

He snatched the bowl away from her and sat it down.

"Hey!" she cried.

He pushed her onto the bed and nipped her neck. "I said, 'You're gorgeous.' Now you say...What?"

She wriggled beneath him. "I say, give me back my cereal, you sex maniac."

"Wrong answer." He trailed his hand down her side. "If I remember correctly, you are very ticklish."

"And violent," she said, her voice rising in pitch.

His fingers grazed the back of her thigh and stopped at the crook of her knee.

"What do you say when I tell you that you're gorgeous?" He strummed his fingers across her sensitive skin.

Her body jerked as if she'd been electrocuted. "I will destroy you, Conor Ross."

He increased the thrum of his fingers. "No. No, that's not right."

She bucked for escape, but he locked one leg over hers and kept going until she shrieked. "Ahh! Thank you! Thank you, asshole!"

He stopped tickling and kissed her shoulder. "You're welcome. How difficult was that?"

"I don't like you," she said.

"Yes, you do," he said as he rolled her over and kissed her until she moaned. "Forgive me?"

"No."

He leaned over and grabbed the cereal bowl, handing it to her. "How about now?"

She grinned and snatched it from his hands.

"I want you to know," he said. "That it's a testament to how great the sex is that I'm allowing you to eat in my bed."

"Got it," she said, shoveling a heap of sliced bananas and cornflakes into her mouth.

His fingers trailed over the fine thread pattern of her tattoo. He followed it down her back and spread his hand over her side where the tail of the design curled into her rib cage. "Can I ask you a question?"

"You always do," she said, her eyes twinkling. "Go ahead."

"Why black lace? Of all the things I could imagine you putting on your body..."

"You mean, why no flaming skulls or spider webs?" Her smile melted away. "It's a long story."

"I've got nothing but time, Winters."

Her stormy eyes searched his for a long moment. Finally, she raked her teeth over her bottom lip and pushed the cereal bowl onto the nightstand. "My last tour was in Europe." She sat up, leaning against the headboard, and sighed. "I don't really like traveling anymore. It makes me feel more lost. I mean, I've never felt settled, but it was okay because I chose it. The stage *was* my home, but now..."

"It's not enough."

"Yeah." She brushed her knuckles over the stubble on his cheek. "When we got to Paris, I was coming out of my skin. I couldn't stand being cooped up in the hotel, so I went wandering." She raised her eyes to the ceiling, as if the memory hung there, just out of reach. "Paris isn't like anywhere I've ever been. I was wearing jeans and a t-shirt, and every woman looked like she was on her way to a photo shoot. The clothes were flawless. Classy. Even their hair was...done up? No, that's not the right word."

"Coiffed?"

"Oh, good word. Yeah, that," she said. "I got lost in the St. Germaine district, and found a little shop that didn't have a sign or a name. Just a pink door, and a display window with the most beautiful lingerie I've ever seen." She looked at her arm. "I never thought about wearing that shit. It seemed like a waste to pay for something that ends up on the floor thirty seconds after you put it on. But this stuff wasn't like that. Everything was silk and handmade lace. Bras and panties. Stockings with garters." Her hand skimmed over her thigh as though she could feel the stockings there.

"I'm sorry, but I need a minute to picture you in thigh-highs." He paused and kissed her ear. "Okay, I've filed that away for a lonely night."

She laughed. "The owner hand-knit all the lace herself. Can you believe that? She was about a thousand years old and coiffed as fuck," she said. "She didn't speak a word of English and I can only cuss in French. But she kind of pushed me into a dressing room and measured me. Then she handed me tons of stuff to try on." Her brows drew together. "It wasn't like the stuff you wear for sex. It was for me. For my pleasure. I've never felt so...so beautiful. Elegant." She shook her head. "That's stupid, right? I say fuck all the time and drink beer and listen to metal. I'm not classy."

"I'm not sure you have to be all one thing or the other," he said. "Whether you wear silk panties under your jeans, or pretty bras under your band t-shirts, or nothing at all, none of it changes who you are. Maybe you're never going to be some pinky-up with a teacup kind of woman, but you don't have to shove yourself into one narrow definition of what you think you're supposed to be. You have layers, Winters."

Her eyes lowered, and she crossed her arms over her chest, rubbing them, as if she was cold.

The silence dragged on until he couldn't stand it. "I'm sorry. Did I say the wrong thing?"

"No. It's just..." She cleared her throat. "Guy I was...with didn't agree with you."

"What idiot wouldn't want to see you in lingerie?" He shook his head. "Ah, EJ, right?"

She nodded and he fought to push his jealousy aside. The idea of her joking with that guy, kissing him, touching his bare skin with her rough hands...it burned. He pushed the feeling aside. This was a fling, and you didn't get jealous in a fling. That's the shit you did if you were in love. And he wasn't.

Something twisted in his chest, folding itself into sharp points and jabbing at everything soft. He rubbed his chest.

He wasn't.

"She made everything custom. I was there for hours and my order was a full page long. I didn't say anything to anyone about it. It was for me, you know? I had her ship it all to EJ's house. He got my mail there, anyway. When the tour ended, I went there to pick it up, but he'd already opened it."

Conor's hackles rose. "What did he do?"

"Threw them away." The words were as flat and lifeless as her expression.

"What the fuck? Why?"

She shook her head, and twisted her hands together, but he pried them apart and kissed her palms. "Tell me."

"I..." Her vacant eyes sharpened and fixed on him. "EJ wants me to be eighteen forever. Because eighteen-year-old me was an idiot who did what she was told." The fire in her gaze, burned into him. "The lingerie was just another fight about control. 'Who are these for, duck?'" she said, deepening her voice, affecting an English accent. "'This isn't who you are.'" Her fingers curled over his and gripped them tight. "'If you want to look sexy, get on your knees and—'" She pulled her hands away, and balled them into fists. "All I wanted were some fucking French lace panties."

Jesus. He'd never been a fighter, but he wished he were, so he could punch every single man who ever made her feel like less. "EJ wants to keep you where he found you," he said.

She rolled her eyes. "Yup. Stupid, easy, and in the gutter."

He stroked her tattoo. "So you got lingerie he couldn't take away from you."

She nodded, and sat up, crisscrossing her legs. "You can go ahead and ask me why I put up with him. Why don't I fire him?"

"I know why." He slid his hands into her hair and tugged her close for a kiss. "It's because the control is comforting. Your life is kind of...rudderless. He's a fixed point. You know what you're dealing with, even if you hate it."

She tilted her head away from him and stared. "Wow. I just thought I was dumb."

"That is not a word I'd use to describe you, ever."

"I hate to ask what word you'd use."

He kissed the tip of her nose. "They don't make words for a woman like you. But I can show you. Might take a few days, though." He rolled over to his side of the bed and pulled his camera from the bag. "May I?"

She eyed the camera warily. "I want it noted that I'm only saying yes because of how good the sex is."

"Noted," he said, with a smile.

ADELIA CROSSED her arms and sat back in the rigid bank lobby chairs, trying to stop her knee from nervously bouncing up and down.

They'd spent the last few days in a warm haze. Trailer cleaning. Prepping for Jo's party. Conor taking an obnoxious number of photographs of her. But today, the warm haze was gone. They were both nervous wrecks.

He emerged from the bank officer's meeting room, looking tired and gorgeous in a business suit he'd purchased in Port Agnes when they went there for party supplies. He shook the woman's hand and gave her a charming smile that didn't reach his eyes.

Her palms were sweating. She rubbed them on her pants and stood. "How'd it go?"

He didn't answer until they were out the doors and on the sidewalk. "I have no idea, but it's done. She asked a lot of questions and looked at my portfolio and said they'd call in a week after reviewing everything." He took a shuddering breath. "Hopefully they call before next Friday. It'd be nice to tell Keith I'm not coming back."

"I'd like to be there for that," she said.

He laughed. "Actually, I'd let you tell him. You'd say it more colorfully than I would." He dropped his laptop and portfolio onto the truck seat and climbed in. "I forgot to tell you that I scheduled to meet with a real estate agent for the studio. He's also going to show me another place he thinks might work, too. Next week. You want to come with me?"

She warmed at the invitation. "That'd be cool."

Driving through town, she leaned over to read the sign in front of the Dive Inn. "Grand re-opening, huh?"

"Yup, thanks to Liam, the Dive will be open soon. They're having a parking lot BBQ next week and I'm taking pictures for the town newsletter. Want to be my date?"

"Two dates in one week? This is getting serious," she said with a grin.

He glanced sideways at her, green eyes intense, and her grin trickled away. They stared at each other until he cleared his throat and looked back at the street. "You keep looking hot and I'll make it three."

She let out her breath. "I demand lobster for the third one."

"Would you settle for cider slushies and a Nirvana cover band? It's going to be a rockin' weekend at the orchard."

"Ooh, sold."

He reached over and stroked her hair. "You excited about tonight?"

She leaned into his hand. "I actually am. I hope Jo likes her present."

"She will," he said. "I forgot that I needed to make a stop. You want some ice cream?"

"Conor, you don't need to seduce me. I'm already there."

He pulled into the parking lot of the Cherry on Top ice cream parlor. For a Friday afternoon in Cherry Lake, it was fairly quiet. But still, there were a few groups of tourist families and some teenagers shivering in wet bathing suits and eating ice cream cones.

Inside, he made his way to the counter and she followed him in. It looked the same as it always had. Brightly colored tables and chairs. White walls. Not a single other piece of décor beyond the almost acrid sweetness in the air.

Georgie McIntosh was another relic of the town, like Old Curtis. Though he was a lot more bald than she remembered. The old man grinned at Conor. "Did ya bring my pictures?"

"I did." Conor handed him a folder. "I printed some larger ones in case you wanted to put them up."

The old man flipped through them. "These are so danged good. Are you sure you won't take no money for printin' them out?"

"Can't. Razzle doesn't allow it, Georgie."

The old man made a face. "What if I pay you in ice cream?"

"None for me, but I bet you she'd like some." he said, pointing to Adelia.

"Ah, so this is the young lady everyone's been talking about," he said.

Adelia rolled her eyes. "Gosh, I hope they're only saying bad things."

"Ha," Georgie said. "It's a small town. Ain't good or bad. Just news."

She raised an eyebrow.

He nodded, his little puff of hair bobbing. "Okay, some if it's bad. Well, most of it." He grinned. "What'll you have?"

After ordering the Black Raspberry Blast, they sat in one of the kitschy fifties-style tables. She had just finished her cone, when a hand dropped onto her shoulder. She looked up at a middle-aged white lady wearing a flower crown and...a dashiki?

Bold.

The lady smiled at her benignly. "I'm so sorry to bother you, but your aura was calling to me from the sidewalk."

"Uh, what?" She looked to Conor for help. But he was too busy staring out the window, a smile tugging at his mouth. She kicked him under the table.

"I'm Mags." The woman waved her hands around Adelia's head. "Yes, this is a beautiful aura. You've chosen well, Conor."

"Sure have. What's her aura say, Mags?" he asked, kicking Adelia back.

"That she's an extraordinary young woman. Kind and friendly. Not prone to foolish choices. Comes from a very fine family. Makes everyone feel at ease. It's rare to see an aura this vibrant." She wiggled her fingers in front of Adelia's throat. "Your chakras could use an alignment, though."

She pulled a business card from her pocket and held it out. When Adelia reached for it, Mags grabbed her hand and stared at it. "That's what I thought." she said. "Yes, we have a lot to talk about. Call me." She patted her hand and smiled, crinkling her nose in Conor's direction. "She's a delight!"

With that, Mags swept out of the parlor and all of the towns-folk pretended like they hadn't been listening to every word.

Adelia shook her head. "This town, man. When did we get a psychic anyway?"

He didn't answer, because he was busy slapping his hand on the table. "Friendly!" His shoulders shook with laughter. "Makes everyone feel at ease!" He laughed so hard he snorted.

She kicked him harder and stood to throw away her napkin. "Shut the fuck up," she whispered, with a grin. "Despite my chakras, I am a goddamned delight."

Conor laughed all the way to the car. He was still chuckling when he pulled up to the trailer and kissed her sweetly.

He ran his fingers along her jaw. "I'll stay gone until midnight. Have fun. Don't teach her anything bad."

"Good. I will. No promises." She got out of the truck and hefted all of her bags into the house. Once she set up the bath-room and put out the snacks, she ran over to Shannon's and banged on the door. Jo peeked her head out, looking exhausted.

"There's something wrong with Cupcake," Adelia said.

Jo ran out of the trailer and ahead of her, barely making it in the door before Cupcake shot awake from her nap. She barked merrily, rushing at Jo to give her all the wet kisses she had.

"What the hell?" Jo said, her eyebrows folded together.

"You fixed her. It's a miracle."

Jo rolled her eyes. "I knew she was fine."

"Liar." She lifted two heavy bags and shook them at Jo. "Birthday presents."

"Yeah?" *Now* she was interested. She reached for the bags, but Adelia held them out of her reach. "First, you need to know something."

"I already know that Mom didn't cancel my birthday party, if that's what you're gonna tell me."

"I wasn't going to say that."

"Liar," Jo said.

"Do you want your damn presents or not?"

Jo's eyes lit on the bags. "I want my damn presents."

"What's the magic word?"

"Adelia rocks?"

"Eh, close enough." She dropped one of the bags into the kid's arms.

Jo sat on the floor, freeing a pile of makeup products, numerous boxes of hair dye and color stripper. Towels, gloves. She grabbed the box of hot pink dye and grinned. "Tonight?"

"We're both going to dye our hair. Conor gave us permission and already has, like, a plan and two back-up plans for any dye stains."

"So, does that mean you're coming to my party?" Jo asked.

"I can swing by and wave at you through the door. It's way more likely I'd get recognized by a group of kids than adults."

"What would happen if they did?"

"It's like a forest fire," she said. "Within fifteen minutes, someone will have it on social media. Then it spreads. Then the press gets hold of it. They start calling everyone here, harassing everyone, trying to get information. Then they come here and it's a total clusterf—mess."

"So what?" Jo's brow furrowed. "I mean, it would suck 'cause of the phone calls, but it's not that big of a deal."

"First, I like my privacy. Second, if my manager knew where to find me, he'd show up to drag me back."

"So, you don't wanna go back to LA?"

The words in Adelia's mouth dried up. "Um, that's...not what I said."

"So you wanna go back?"

"I didn't say that either."

Jo stared at her, clearly hoping for more. She shook her head, and Jo sighed. "Why did you get all of this makeup?"

"Because I'm going to show you some tricks. There is a vast middle ground between church lady and Slipknot groupie and we're going to aim for that."

"But you never wear makeup," Jo said. "Not even in, like, pictures and stuff."

"Just because I'm lazy doesn't mean I don't know how to apply it, kid. Now come on, I have a vision for your hair, and it's going to take some time."

AFTER FIVE HOURS of hair snipping, color stripping, shampooing, conditioning and re-dyeing, Adelia was exhausted and Jo was ecstatic. Her hair, now five inches shorter, was glossy black on top, shifting into a vibrant hot pink toward the bottom.

"This is the coolest I've ever looked in my life," Jo said. "You used to do this all by yourself? No help?"

"Well, Conor used to help. But after I left, it was only me."

Jo looked her through the mirror. "Was leaving scary?"

She threw away the empty dye packaging. "Yeah, it was," she said. "But my philosophy is, be scared and do it anyway. Though, now that I say it out loud, that sounds like terrible advice."

"I asked my mom about your dad the other day," Jo said. "She said he wasn't nice. Was that why you left?"

"I left because he told me to. That's it." She stood over Jo and checked out her own hair, satisfied with the same deep, cherry red as before. As long as she didn't go giving the dog another bath, the color would keep.

In silence, they cleaned the bathroom, fist-bumping each other when they found no stains in the tub. She sat Jo in a chair in front of a mirror on the counter, so she could watch while she showed her how to properly apply eyeliner.

Jo played with a tube of mascara on the counter. "Thanks for doing this."

Adelia nodded as she stared at the various glosses she'd purchased. "No problem. I want you to feel kickass tomorrow."

"I'm kinda glad Mom didn't let me cancel it. Cody said he's gonna show," Jo said. "But someone told me that the twins plan to crash."

"What are you gonna do if they do?

"I don't know. Ignore them?"

"It's not what I'd do, so that's probably a good choice."

"They keep getting meaner. Maddison's started talking shit about my dad, or lack of dad." Her eyes narrowed, and she suddenly looked exactly like her mother. "I hate her."

Adelia tested the different eyeliners on the back of her hand, choosing the one that was the darkest, truest black. "She sounds pretty awful."

After a few minutes of silence, Jo sighed. "Can I ask you a question?"

"Ask away. Can't promise I'll answer."

"I was listening to, 'Where I Am' the other day. And, like, I've listened to it a million times. But I always thought it was about a broken heart."

"It is." She tilted Jo's head back to smudge some liner under her lower lashes.

"I thought it was, like, a girl sad about her boyfriend, but it's not about that, is it?"

Adelia picked up the mascara and focused on the slippery tube. "No, it's not."

"Is it about your dad?"

"I don't like this mascara," Adelia said. She rummaged through the pile of makeup and pulled out a different brand. She unscrewed the top and studied the brush. "This one's better." She gestured for Jo to lean toward her. Those big grey eyes drilled into hers, brimming with more than curiosity.

"Yes," Adelia said through gritted teeth. "It was about my dad."

Jo looked at her lap. "That day at the Dive. Conor told me not to bother you, 'cause of your dad's funeral. I did it anyway. I didn't...get it." She looked miserable. "I'm sorry."

"No need to be sorry," Adelia said. "It was a burial for someone I didn't even care about."

"But, it's just... you're not Lia. Lia's, like, made up. She doesn't have a mom or a dad. She just *is*." Jo sat up straighter. "But Adelia is—you're a person. And you care. If you didn't care, you wouldn't have written the song, right?"

Unable to speak, Adelia stared at the pink tube of mascara, tiny divots decorating the cap, like tire tracks.

"Because I say all the time that I don't care about my dad," Jo continued. "Talking about it makes my mom sad. She says he was a down-stater and she doesn't know who he is, but she's making it up. I can tell." She swallowed. "He doesn't want me. And she doesn't want to tell me that." She twisted her hands together in her lap. "I know it's not the same, but when I say that I don't care, I don't mean it. It's just easier to pretend not to. You know?"

Something fragile as an egg broke open inside of her. She leaned her head back and stared at the ceiling trying to seal it back up. Breathing out, she looked at Jo. The kid's expression was full of something raw and honest.

Fear.

Whatever porcelain emotion had fractured within her, it splintered further. She pressed her hand to her chest, as if she could put enough pressure on the wound to stop it from bleeding inside.

"I know," Adelia said. "I know."

ADELIA SNUGGLED WITH CUPCAKE, who was taking an excessive amount of space but was also delightfully warm. She wrapped an arm around the dog and heard the click of a camera.

"Murder," she said. "I'm going to murder you." After Jo left the night before, she and Conor spent an hour filling swag bags for the party and it felt like she hadn't slept at all.

But when he grinned at her, she forgot why she was annoyed.

"Come on, Winters, we can go decorate most of the hall before anyone is awake enough to snoop around."

She groaned. "But we have to blow up so many balloons."

"Hey, you could have picked a different theme."

"It was called *Rock Star Diva*. Jo needed it."

"No one needs any of this stuff. *You* wanted it for her."

She ignored that and ran to take a shower and get dressed. Along with the list of decorations and party supplies, she'd asked him to get her a pair of jeans and a couple of tops. As fun as it was wearing a thirteen-year-old's clothes, she was over it.

She smoothed the snug fabric of her new jeans. Amazing

how well-fitting clothing could make a person feel whole. Feeling good, she even threw on some eyeliner and mascara.

He had her guitar case in hand when she got out of the bathroom. "I've got your guitar and notebook. You're going to be cooped up in the boardroom for a couple of hou—" He stared at her. "Good god, Winters, are you trying to kill me?"

She flushed under the heat of his gaze. "It's only eyeliner." She grabbed her purple leather jacket and slid it on over the black tank top that dipped a touch too low. "Get a grip."

He crossed the room and kissed her, his hands roaming her body.

"You know that's not what I meant."

He kissed her ear. "Want to fool around in a broom closet during the party?"

She wrapped her arms around his neck and kissed him. "What are we? High schoolers?" she said. "No. Let's do it on the boardroom table like adults."

———

CONOR HAD DECREED the boardroom too musty for boning.

Adelia suspected it had more to do with the bright fluorescents than anything, since he'd dodged her every attempt at sex with the lights on.

So unboned, Adelia sat in the basement boardroom, recording all the early stages of songs she'd been working on. An actual album was forming, and it was better than the one she'd pitched to Gyroscope.

Excitement rippled through her as she sent them to Emi. It was a bad idea to send her work to a perfect stranger with no contract. EJ would lose his shit if he knew. But for once, people were listening to her. Encouraging her. She hadn't realized how starved she was for that.

It wasn't a huge thing to want.

Didn't she deserve that?

After a nail-biting twenty minutes, Emi called and her exuberance rushed through the phone like river water. "Bitch, you need ta' get your butt in my studio so we can make an album already. Screw Gyroscope, this is so good the other labels are gonna *beg* to sign you."

It had been years since Adelia felt this energized or reckless. "Screw all the labels. Just send me a contract."

"Yaasssssss!" Emi said. "That's the shit I'm talking about!"

After that call, Adelia was too wound up to sit still. She wanted to tell Conor about it, but decided against it. She still wasn't sure what any of it meant. She reached inside the lunch bag Conor had packed and pulled out apple slices and a jar of natural peanut butter. A sticky note on the jar said, *When you get bored, text me.*

Warmth spread through her and she messaged him. He was upstairs running a photo booth, but she caught him on a bathroom break. He met her at the top of the stairs, by the side door and pressed her against the wall, kissing her until she was dizzy.

"Having fun?" she asked.

"Jesus, no," he said. "Kids are awful. I didn't like them when I was a kid, and I still don't. It's shrill chaos in there, and I'm the only adult."

"The things you do for love, huh?" Adelia said.

"Yup." He brushed her hair aside and kissed her ear. "The automated photo booth is working, so I'm trying to stay out of the way as much as possible. You want to fool around in the board room now?"

"No. Maybe." She pulled away and went to the door that led into the hall. Pushing herself as far from view as possible, she peered inside the door's window. The entire center of the ceiling was full of magenta and black balloons, the curly ribbons hanging like falling confetti. The beams were wrapped in little white lights and the cement walls were decorated with big black poster board stars. She'd handwritten Jo's favorite song lyrics on them with a chalk pen.

"Did she like the decorations?"

"She loves them," Conor said.

"Did her boy show up yet?"

"That isn't what I want to talk about." He grasped her hips from behind and rested his chin on her shoulder. "But yes. Cody is here. So of course, the Malinskis have crashed. So far, they've been ignoring Jo, but that's not going to last."

The hall was swarming with teenagers, clustered into laughing groups. It wasn't hard to spot Jo with that magenta hair and a top that showed a sinful three inches of skin above her jeans, belly button wantonly on display. "She finally wore her mom down about the shirt, huh?"

"Shan said it wasn't a hill she wanted to die on."

A skinny boy with lanky black hair and dangerous dimples gestured toward Jo's hair. She laughed and shoved him playfully. "So that's Cody, huh?"

"Yes," he growled impatiently. "Stop talking." Conor's hands slid around her waist, and under her shirt.

She slapped at them. "You can grope me later, I'm here for Jo."

A pair of girls with matching faces crossed the room and walked past Jo, one on either side of her, banging into her. A few kids, smelling blood in the water, circled in closer.

"Uh-oh," he said, releasing her waist. "I'd better get in there."

"You can't. If you break it up, you'll embarrass her, and make her look weak to those barracudas-in-training. They'll wait until you're not around and start it all over again."

"You always jumped into it for me," he said. "And everyone else."

Thing One pointed at Jo and said something Adelia couldn't hear through the door. "It's different," she said. "We're not kids. We can't go in there throwing punches."

Jo rolled her eyes at Thing One and stepped closer to her. Whatever she was saying, she said it calmly, but Adelia knew a take-down when she saw one.

Wanting to hear better, she cracked the door.

"—welcome to leave," Jo said.

"Poor people are rude," Thing One said, raising her voice to make sure their audience heard every word. "All I asked was what dumpster you got those tacky cupcakes from."

"Same one you crawled out of," Jo said. The crowd of teenagers made varying sounds of shock and malicious laughter, but Jo's bored expression never changed. "And FYI, *you're* tacky to come here, snort up all the food, and then complain about it. No one invited you two jerks."

Thing Two stepped into Jo's personal space, and Adelia's hackles rose. "Uh, you can stop talking to us now, trailer trash."

"I actually prefer talking to people I like anyway, so…" Jo made a shooing motion with her hands. "Don't you have an overpriced shack by the lake? Go be the worst there."

"Hey, you know what I've got at my *shack*, besides money and better food and clothes?" Thing Two said. "A dad. Because my mom's not a slut like yours."

Conor lurched for the door. Adelia pushed him back and shook her head.

Jo flinched, but then put her emotions in her pocket, the same way her mom did, and smiled brightly. "My mom's not a slut. But if she was, so what? I'm a bad person because she had sex? Your parents had sex. Gross, sweaty sex. Without a condom. Or you two wouldn't be here."

"You're disgusting, you—"

Jo held up a hand and cut her off. "Yeah, yeah, I'm trailer trash, blah blah blah. I am. And I still have lots of friends. People like me. But nobody likes you two, you know that, right?" She straightened her shoulders. "You're popular because you have money. And it's lucky that you do, because if you were broke, no one would like you. You're not cool, or interesting at all."

Cody, perhaps realizing that his money was also being maligned, moved slightly away from Jo, and Adelia tried to stomp out the spark of anger inside herself.

Thing One blinked rapidly, clearly unsure how they'd lost this fight. Thing Two's mouth curled into a snarl. "Your party is lame, your hair is a pathetic attempt at attention, and you're boring and poor. Nobody cool cares what you think." She gripped her sister's hand, crossing the hall, and sat at a table, defiantly. A group of girls surrounded them, casting guilty looks at the birthday girl.

Cody mumbled something Adelia couldn't hear and pointed a thumb toward the door. Jo nodded, her shoulders slumping as he walked out. She stood straighter, and grabbed a cupcake off the food table, taking a big bite. There was no joy on her face, but she ate it.

Adelia flexed her hands to calm the rampaging thump of her heart. "I don't care who her dad is, that kid is one-hundred percent Shannon Cooper."

"And then some. I'm suddenly a lot less worried about boys." Conor stroked her arms. "You okay?"

"No. I'm so pissed off right now." She raised her shaking hand. "I don't know what the hell is wrong with me."

"You care about her. Some people burrow right under your skin as soon as you meet them. If anyone was going to get beneath that steely hide of yours, it was Jo. You two are a lot alike." He kissed her softly. "I'm not going to interfere, but I'd better get back in there."

After the door closed behind him, she took another look inside. Things One and Two eyed Conor and whispered something to their cronies, who laughed. Jo made herself a plate and sat beside a blonde girl who appeared to be consoling her, but Jo wasn't having it. She shook her head and stared at the wall of song lyrics, her chin raised.

They *were* a lot alike. But unlike Adelia, Jo was all exposed nerves, feeling and expressing everything deeply. The party was supposed to be a celebration of all the things that made her special. And it was ruined.

Adelia stomped back to the basement. She couldn't go out there swinging fists, but she could give the kid something better.

Jo deserved better.

28

CONOR RE-ADJUSTED the lights in the photo booth corner and tried to catch Jo's eye so she knew she was safe if those girls decided to get physical, but she avoided looking at him.

Things had calmed down. Jo sat with her best friend, Hannah, and a few other kids, chatting and pretending nothing had happened. But Adelia had been right. Every once in a while, Maddison and Addison would burst into loud laughter and watch Jo, looking for any signs of weakness.

Barracudas-in-training indeed.

Uninvited kids appeared, likely lured in by social media posts and eager to be part of the carnage. Jo greeted each of them and waved, smiling the same easy, bland smile her mother used on customers.

Another burst of laughter came from the Malinski girls as they stood. Maddison yawned. "We're bored. Anyone want to go to our house? The food is way better since it wasn't fished out of garbage cans." They headed for the exit, with a cadre of giggling girls following, and a handful of other kids leaving as well. The heavy front doors of the hall slammed behind them.

A second slam, like an echo, came from the side door.

He followed Jo's baffled gaze. Adelia strode to the dais, her guitar case in hand, her shoulders squared, her expression fierce. Jesus Christ, she looked amazing.

It took a minute. Kids stared as if she were a mirage. "OMG, is that Lia?" someone yelled. The broken hush gave way to a slurry of exhalations, exclamations, and phones snapping away. Without a word, Adelia leaned down, and unclipped the case, freeing her guitar.

What the hell was she doing? He rushed for his camera bag.

She flicked a lock of her cherry chip hair off the shoulder of her purple leather jacket and made a shushing sound. The room went silent. "We're here today to celebrate my friend, Josephine Cooper." The kids gasped and many of them typed feverishly on their screens. She raised an eyebrow and waited until it died back down. "She started off as a big fan of mine, and now I'm a big fan of her." Adelia strummed the guitar. "I'm going to play some songs that I know she loves." Her fingers rolled over the strings. "Happy birthday, Jo."

She launched into "I'm Not Lost," and he lowered the camera, entranced. Without the loud growling that accompanied the original, the song trembled with melancholy rather than defiance.

She played for over an hour. Kids that had left came rushing back into the hall. More people arrived. Not just kids, but adults, squeezing in, taking pictures. The Brightwell police showed up, unsurprisingly. No Cherry Lake party was too small to avoid someone calling the cops about the noise. Officer Mustache stood at the back of the room, staring at Adelia in disbelief.

After an upbeat rendition of "This Fire," Adelia raised her head from the guitar, looking ready to fall over from exhaustion. Her voice was scratchy and low. "I'm going to do one last song. This is a new one. Well, new to you. I started it a long time ago, and it's taken me a lot of years to get it right." Closing her eyes, her calloused fingers skated over the strings. When she opened her eyes, they locked with his and he felt her look down to his toes. Then, her soft rasp of a voice began.

Every word fell like rain in a spring storm, coming faster and faster as thunder crashed over his head. Her weary voice rose to the smoky, heartbreaking crescendo of the song and he nearly drowned in the downpour.

"Can't forgive myself... The apologies I never gave... wrote you a letter... burned it in shame... sorry for the words that never came..."

The lyrics were a rush of rusty pain as she hammered out the last chords and sang, *"I was just tryin' to survive."*

For a few moments, the only sound in the room were sniffles and whispered sighs.

"I love you, Lia!" someone shouted from the back of the room, breaking the hush. At that, everyone began shouting at once.

She sat back, her dark lashes lowered, hiding her thoughts. A deep breath rippled through her as she stood and gave the crowd a half-smile. "Thanks for listening. Go home. Be awesome. I'm going to eat a cupcake now."

The crowd didn't budge and the officers, waking from their fugue state, mobilized to move everyone out. Adelia grabbed her guitar and a cupcake off the table, then she slipped out the side door, likely back to the basement.

It took nearly forty-five minutes for the police to get the gawkers out. Jo, who hadn't said a single word since Adelia hit the stage, turned to him, her eyes wide and glistening. "Why?"

He scrubbed a hand over his jaw. "Some people have tough shells because they're protecting all the tenderness underneath. And underneath that shell, she cares about you. And when Adelia cares about someone, they're more important to her than things like privacy."

"Don't believe a word he says." Adelia suddenly appeared beside him, her arms crossed over her chest. "Doctor told me my heart is made of old beef jerky. And under my shell there are at *least* five more shells."

Jo lunged and wrapped her skinny arms around her. Adelia stiffened for a moment before relaxing and hugging her back.

"Thank you," Jo whispered.

"You're welcome," she whispered back.

There was that storm again, slamming down until he felt like he'd never breathe again.

"All right," Adelia said. "Enough of that. I'm allergic to emotional stuff."

Jo grinned. "Conor told your secret. You're a softie. I'm onto you now."

Adelia turned to him, her face twisted into mock horror. "See what you did? You gave her leverage."

"I'm pretty sure you did that with this little stunt," he said, unable to stop the smile that stole across his face.

Jo grabbed her friend and shoved her at Adelia. "This is my best friend, Hannah."

Hannah's brown eyes took up most of her face as she stared. "You're Lia," she whispered.

"I am."

"And you know Jo."

"I do."

"And she didn't tell me."

"I swore her to secrecy."

Hannah was out of things to say. She blinked rapidly.

"Breathe, kid. It's gonna be all right," Adelia said.

There was a banging at the locked front doors. Shannon was yelling at a police officer, one hand smacking on the glass door. Conor unlocked it and assured the officers that it was fine.

"What the hell is going on?" Shannon hollered. "It is crazy outside! I threatened a cop."

"Lia played a concert at my party!" Jo hollered back. "And Hannah's about to drop dead. And Adelia has allergies."

Shannon put her hands on her hips. "Allergies to what? Bras and sobriety?"

While Jo explained what happened, Adelia and Conor tore down the photo booth and packed up all the food.

"Girls, get all of those gifts into a bag," Shannon said. "And don't lose any of the cards. You still have to send thank-yous. Being broke is no excuse for bad manners."

"Shouldn't it be one of the perks?" Adelia whispered to him, making him snort, while she yanked a tablecloth off the table.

"Don't worry about that," Shannon said. "The rental includes clean up. They'll take care of the rest, as soon as the cops let them in." She pressed her hand to Adelia's. "Thank you for doing this for her."

"It's cool," Adelia said. "Everyone can stop thanking me now."

"Fine," Shannon said. "But at least take some pie home." She turned to Conor. "I gotta get back to work. Can you drive Jo and Hannah to Lindsey's for their sleepover?"

"Of course," he said.

"We should leave out the back door," Adelia said. "Most of the crowd is at the front." She slid on her sunglasses. "Keep your heads down, don't answer any questions if people start yelling stuff at you. Keep plowing forward. Crowds don't worry about hurting you, so you can't worry about hurting them. Make them get out of your way." She hoisted her guitar case. "I'll go last, so they'll swarm me and give you some room to get in the truck."

Conor wasn't sure what he expected. It wasn't a massive crowd at the back. But there was a sizable group of onlookers and a local news van parked in the back lot. Everyone audibly groaned with disappointment when they emerged.

A microphone was pushed into his face. "Staci Collins, Channel Seven News. Is Lia still in there?" He tried to keep moving, but she stood in his way. "What's your relationship to her? Do you know why she's here?"

Between the clacking phone cameras, the crowd, the police,

the reporter, he felt naked. Exposed. Anxiety crept through him like a slow-growing vine. He pushed on, like Adelia had instructed. As soon as the back door creaked opened and her boots hit the pavement, people gasped and turned.

"Lia, Staci Collins, Channel Seven News," the reporter yelled. "This was quite a special gift you gave to a fan. What brought you to Cherry Lake?"

Adelia ignored her and stomped through the crowd, taking huge strides, trouncing on toes and banging her guitar case into expensive camera equipment without concern. She crammed into the truck, beside the girls and covered her face with her hand.

He gingerly pulled out of the parking lot, for fear of running someone over. After a lot of horn beeps and shouting, he kept his foot on the brake and hit the gas, frightening the crowd, who finally leapt out of the way of the truck. Once he made it to the street, he gunned it, taking back roads, needing to put a million miles between himself and those cameras.

They dropped Jo and Hannah off with instructions not to answer their phones to any numbers they didn't recognize and to say nothing on social media. After they were gone, the silence was thick in the truck. He hoped the engine would drown out the violent thud of his heart.

"So," he said.

"So," she answered.

"That song was beautiful."

She stared out the window. "Thanks."

"Adelia, I—" Something in the rearview caught his eye. A white SUV, following close. "I think that SUV is following us."

She glanced into the rearview. "Yup."

He accelerated, and they accelerated. He slowed, and they did too. Without using his turn signal, at the next intersection, he veered off Ribbon Rail and onto a side street. They did the same, no signal in sight.

"What should I do?" he asked.

"It's probably a contract photographer working for one of the bigger rags," she said. "We have three options. Drive and hope we lose them, let them follow us home and hide inside, or give them a show so they get their damned pictures and go away."

"Let's start with option one." He drove past the heart of Cherry Lake, taking dirt and gravel roads, going deep into the boonies, where the woods were so dense that, day or night, it was always dusk beneath the canopy of trees. The occasional uninhabited farm broke up the monotony of the woods, though they were nothing but creaky houses, dilapidated outbuildings, and overgrown fields.

He checked the rear view. "We're not losing him."

"No money shot, no money. They're pretty persistent."

"Fuck it." He sped down the incline of a rolling, nameless road. "Remember when we used to joyride the back roads in Spoondrift?"

Nodding, her lips curved into the promise of a smile, but he wanted more than that meager response. "Bet you missed this." He hit the gas, and Adelia screamed as he gunned it up the slope. They sailed for a moment before hitting the dirt and zooming down the hill.

"I hate this," she shrieked, though she was laughing, and her eyes were bright with excitement.

"You always said that. I didn't buy it then." He peeled up the next hill. "And I don't buy it now."

They roller-coastered the hilly road, defying physics and their stomachs. "Here comes a big one," he yelled over his engine and Adelia's frantic laughter. They crested the steep rise. "Ready?"

She leaned toward the windshield. "No. But do it anyway."

They shot down the incline, flying and falling, helpless as gravity took control.

When the truck skidded to a stop, powdery dust blurred the road. The tires of the SUV squealed as they came to a stop behind them, puffing up more dust. He laughed over the pulse pounding in his ears. Adelia turned toward him. Rosy-cheeked and breathless, he'd never in his life seen a woman more beautiful. Not the kind of beautiful that was static, made of filters and perfection, but a living sort of beauty. River and lake beautiful. The kind of loveliness that rushed and moved and made your heart pound just to look at it.

"Option three?" she said.

"Option three," he said.

Her lips descended on his as a camera clacked away outside the window.

29

KISSING Conor was better than thousand-dollar whisky. Always. He cupped the back of her head, subtly controlling everything and making her body knot with pleasure.

She pulled away to take a breath and he ran his hands into her hair, the soft green of his eyes melting her like a snowflake in June.

The guy outside the truck moved from taking pictures through the windshield, to through the driver's side window.

"Let's go," she said softly.

He untangled his fingers from her hair and hit the gas. The photographer flew backward to avoid having his toes run over. Conor took a couple of sharp corners and hit the paved road. He drove for a few miles, doing eighty, while she clutched her seat belt.

Finally slowing, he pulled into the drive of an old farmhouse. The paint was peeling off the home in sheets. The fenced area that probably once held horses was overgrown with weeds and rain-mashed grass. The barn behind the house had a sizable hole in the roof. It looked like no one had lived there for twenty years. He drove around the barn and parked behind it.

"We should wait it out for a little bit." He grabbed his camera bag and slung the strap over his shoulder. "I've been out here before. Want to see something beautiful?"

He tugged her toward the woods, and up a narrow trail. The sun had done its job and dried most of the dirt, but occasional patches of muck squelched beneath their shoes. They turned and passed an arch of creaky old walnut trees. His hand was warm in hers as they made their way toward a rocky path.

At the top was a black cherry tree. The town was full of them, but they were usually spindly little thirty-foot affairs. This one was massive, all by itself on the hill. Gleaming green leaves and grey cracked bark gave way to at least sixty feet of tree, widespread limbs spilling a bouquet of white flowers, dotted with pale green berries that hung from the branches like Christmas ornaments. "Wow." She breathed out the word slowly. "That's gotta be a hundred years old." She approached it reverently, stroking the thick, coarse bark, and walked all the way around, taking in its beauty from all angles.

"I stopped one day to take some pictures of the farmhouse and found this tree. I love it." He held his camera aloft. "Mind if I take a few?"

"It's fine," she murmured, enraptured.

The camera clicked while she eyed the wide V where the trunk branched off in separate directions. She grabbed at the lowest branch and hoisted herself up, staying close to the trunk.

"What are you doing? You're going to kill yourself," he said.

She grunted while she stretched her leg over the cranny between the two enormous branches. She slid her other leg over and carefully stood.

"I'm good at climbing trees, remember?" She inched closer to a thick branch on her right, testing it with her arms before swinging onto it.

"Seriously. This is dangerous."

She straddled the crook of a branch and leaned against the trunk, her feet swaying. "Come up here."

"Not happening," he said. "Remember how this works? You climb the trees, I tell you you're crazy, you do it anyway, and I photograph the results. It's practically tradition."

"You couldn't climb trees when you were a kid. You can now. So do it."

"You're nuts. This camera cost as much as a used car."

She made chicken noises at him. Not the most creative way to get what she wanted, but whatever worked. "I'm not coming down until you come up," she said when she'd exhausted all the bawk-bawk noises she could make. "I might live here forever." She kept moving upward, branch by branch.

She stopped to take a breath and looked down. He twisted the lens onto his camera before sliding the strap over his shoulder and chest, messenger bag style, and climbed.

"I'm going to be so pissed at you if I die, Winters."

"That's fair. But you've got to see the view from here. Plus, we aren't that high up. It's only what, thirty or forty feet off the ground?"

He huffed out a string of curse words, but he kept climbing while she shouted directions.

When he was one branch below hers, she stopped him. "Okay, now stand. It's really solid where you are."

He laughed. "No goddamn way."

"Yes way."

"I'm going to fall and die," He said as he grabbed the trunk and stood on wobbly legs. "And I'm going to haunt you."

She moved her feet out of his way. "It's sturdy, I swear," she said. "Now turn around and look."

"Whoa," he said, releasing the word like a held breath. "That is—"

"Stunning."

From above, the mud-soaked fields of newly green grass

swayed like wheat. Hope River flowed along its lazy journey south, and if you turned your head the other way, you could see Cherry Lake, glistening in the distance.

"This town is so beautiful." She shifted above him and leaned into the breeze.

He poked at the branch Adelia was sitting on. "How sturdy is that thing?"

She shrugged. "Pretty sturdy."

"Well, scoot down a little." He hoisted himself onto the branch and it swayed a bit as he seated himself behind her. "If I'm going to die, I want it to be with a sexy woman between my legs."

"Romantic," she said.

He lifted his camera and snapped a picture. "My middle name is romance."

"Your middle name is James."

He sat the camera on top of her head. "Whatever you do, don't move."

She managed to stay relatively still while his camera clicked on her head. When he finished, he leaned against her back, warm and solid. "It's gorgeous. I'm glad you made me climb up, but I'd like my feet on the ground now."

She nodded, and he was already a branch below her and moving steadily toward the ground. She waited a few seconds and began a slow descent, feeling sadder with each branch. Up in the air, everything felt possible. The town she'd spent so many years hating was a beautiful, magical place, and longing for that beauty flowed inside of her. Heading back to earth, that feeling felt further and further away.

He released a shaky breath below her, letting her know he survived. Then his camera clicked.

"Now you're just taking pictures of my ass."

"Hey, remember all that mind-blowing sex? This is the cost."

She looked down at him. "I wouldn't say *mind-blowing*."

He raised an eyebrow. "Winters, I am excellent at three things. Grout cleaning, photography, and supplying you with knee-buckling orgasms. A little respect, please."

"Your grout *is* spotless."

"Yup. I make mold my bitch." He laughed as his hands encircled her waist, guiding her to the ground. As soon as her feet hit the grass, he pressed her against the tree and kissed her softly. There was no lust in it, or hurried desire. It was measured and sweet and decadent, his soft lips on hers. He pulled back and stroked her hair, and alarms went off inside her skull. There was a new light in his eyes, one that left her unsteady.

Her phone buzzed from inside of her pocket. Needing a lifeline, she grabbed it. Three missed calls from EJ, going on four. "I should take this. Sorry."

He opened his mouth, as if to say something. Instead, he nodded and stepped out of her way.

Heading down the steep path, she tried to calm her racing heart. Her phone stopped buzzing and started again. She took a deep breath and answered. "You've reached Lia Frost. She thinks you should be shot in the dick with a poisoned arrow. Don't leave a message."

"Very funny," EJ said.

"I'm known for my sense of humor."

He snorted. "Michigan, eh? Wouldn't have guessed that." She could hear his fingernails clacking on the phone screen. "You look fantastic by the way. Even if you're singing next to a...what is that? A bingo machine covered in a sheet?"

She let the silence dangle until he cleared his throat. "I have news." Not a surprise, with the smog of smug wafting through the speaker.

"Spit it out."

"Rod caved," he said.

"What?"

"I thought you were off having a strop." He chuckled.

"Instead you were laying low until the press were practically eating themselves to get a sound bite, and then turned up at some fan's birthday party? Fucking brilliant."

"What?" she repeated.

"It worked. Got a call from Rod and we had a long talk. This is going to be a media blitz. We'll get you into a mutual sit-down interview with Rod and Hardkor Rock News. You'll say you've worked through your differences, blah blah blah. No apologies necessary."

"We haven't. I still hate him."

"He hates you too. But he loves money, and right now whatever dreck you put out will go platinum. We need to get you in the studio as soon as possible. He agreed to let you have more control, *and* dangled a lovely little carrot for you. Mister Bobby. To produce."

She gasped. Mister Bobby was always on her list. This was big.

"Knew you'd like that." He laughed. "I spoke to the man myself and told him about the concept for your new album."

The tingling excitement faded. "What do you mean? You don't know the concept for my new album."

"I'm sure I do, love. Rod and I know. A heap of introspective shout-y ballads about how hard it is to be famous and unloved. And that's fine. Mister Bobby can take all that and mold it into something worthwhile."

Her stomach churned. That wasn't it at all.

"Actually, I've been talking to a producer that I'm interested in working with. She gets me and I think—"

"Who?" he interrupted.

"Emi Hara."

"That woman who worked with Demetria Varga?"

"Yeah, and Larch Street Blues. She's amazing and she's been sending me—"

"Lia." EJ's voice was sharp. "Listen to me, this is a huge

opportunity. Don't blow it out of some sisterly solidarity rubbish. I'm sure she's a nice girl, but she's not Mister Bobby." He gave a long-suffering sigh. "Rod's pacified for now, but burn him on this, and he'll make sure you never get a record contract again." He took on a pleading tone. "You've never been happy offstage. You need stadiums. Cheering fans. Music to drown the world out."

"I could do it on my own," she said, but it sounded more like a question than a statement to her own ears.

"You could try. But there's a reason why people dream of what you have. Managers and record deals and industry support. Don't think you're too good for it. Without all that, what will you have?" he said. "A sentimental temper tantrum of an indie album? Everyone, industry and fans, will write you off, no matter how prettily you warble and strum."

She gave very few fucks about what the industry thought of her, but what about her fans? Would she be a joke, a spoiled brat who got her way, only to find that her way was foolish? Would everyone laugh at her self-indulgence?

Would she be Metallica, making *St. Anger*?

She rubbed her burning stomach. "I'm not sure that I...I have to think about it."

"There's no time for thinking. If you're out, then you're out, and I need to know."

"Fine. Jesus. Give me two weeks."

"Five days, love. I'll give you five. We've got to get on this before the press loses interest."

"Five, then," she said.

EJ released a shaky breath. "You're making the right choice. I know you're still mad about the knickers and all that, and I'm truly sorry. When you get back, let's talk about us. I know I've been a prat, but I'm ready to—"

"No," she said. The thought of going back to EJ's bed, of loathing herself as he made her come, was repulsive. How could she go back to that, when she'd had something so beautiful with Conor? "I don't forgive you for that and I never will. You're my manager, and that's all you are. There's no us. There never was."

She hung up the phone and pressed it against her forehead. It buzzed and she looked at it. Email from Emi with the contract. Fuck. She scribbled a quick reply about needing to run it by a lawyer and then turned off her ringer and shoved the phone in her pocket. She used to know exactly what she wanted. It was simple. Make music. Now everything was complicated, and she hated it. A warm breeze caught her hair and wrapped around her like an embrace.

She shivered, feeling colder than ever.

At the top of the hill, Conor was rocking on his heels, his arms crossed over his chest, eyes following shadows of tree limbs on the ground. "Was it a gossip site asking for my name?"

"No, just EJ. Being EJ."

"EJ." He nodded and ran his hands through his hair. "So, I'm guessing that concert was because you're leaving. When?"

A thousand moths fluttered in her chest. "I don't know."

"The trailer's not done."

"It doesn't matter. There's nothing in there worth searching for." She wrapped her arms around herself, wishing they were his instead. "I'm glad we tried, but once something's in the garbage can, it's garbage."

A shadow passed through his eyes and she wished she was better at reading peoples' faces.

After a moment, he slid his hands in his pockets. "I'm pretty sure we shook that van. We can go now." He was already making his way down the path before her knees unlocked, and she followed behind him.

It was always more fun climbing up than it was climbing back down.

CONOR STARED AT THE ROAD, pain squeezing his heart and lungs tight.

Adelia was leaving. It wasn't as if he hadn't known it was coming to an end. But now he saw the foolishness of his justifications for getting involved with her. She wasn't some stranger he could bone and then say goodbye to. She was elemental. Wild, primitive energy that he needed like the blood pumping in his veins.

She was the missing part of him.

How could he say goodbye to that?

Adelia shifted and crossed her legs beside him, all her playfulness gone. She tensed even further when they came home to people already milling outside with cameras.

They hustled inside. He wanted to talk to her, to say...something. But her silence was a hand over his mouth, and he couldn't figure out how to talk around it.

"Want some dinner?" she asked.

"No. I'm not hungry." He pulled her close. "Talk to me."

"Got nothing to say." Her gaze drifted everywhere but his eyes, but there was bright color in her cheeks.

"Whatever it is, I can handle it."

She pulled away from him, her eyes hardening. "I know this is super hard for you to grasp, but not everything is about you."

He backed away from her, hoping his face didn't betray the hurt he felt. "I'm aware of that, Winters," he said softly. "But sometimes, it's not all about you, either." He leashed Cupcake silently, feeling the weight of her eyes on him, and knowing that it didn't matter. She'd apologized in her own way, but it changed nothing.

After a long walk, he avoided the photographers outside the trailer and went in through the back door. The house was silent and the only light came from the dim fluorescent one over the sink.

"Adelia?" Halfway through the living room, he stopped and stared.

Adelia was on his kitchen table.

Naked.

She was naked and eating pie out of the container.

Every bone in his body melted in lava heat.

"Damn, I thought I'd have time to finish this before you got back." She licked her sticky lips. "This is less sexy than I was shooting for."

He tried to say words but what came out instead was the gurgle of a man drowning in quicksand.

"Don't worry," she said. "I'm sitting on a kitchen towel. You can burn it later."

He found his voice. "Or frame it."

Her lips curved as she lifted the fork, cherries glistening on the end of it. "This pie is amazing. I would never want to derail your health, but I feel like life isn't worth living without a bite of pie every now and then."

He dropped his coat on the floor and crossed the room. "I'll watch you eat it naked," he said. "That'll make life worth living."

She shook her head and wiggled the fork at him. "Not the same thing."

"I don't want pie. I want you," he said.

She slid the fork into her mouth with slow, sensual precision. Then she turned the utensil around and rubbed the back of it on her lips until they glistened with cherry syrup.

He pulled the fork from her hand and dropped it into the bowl beside her. She ran her hands along his neck and jaw and leaned forward, brushing her lips over his and then pulling back before doing it again. His breath was unsteady as she skimmed her tongue along his lower lip, teasing until he couldn't take it anymore. He slid his hands into her hair and put an end to his torture.

He devoured her mouth. The overpowering saccharine melted into the tartness of fresh cherry juice as he sucked on her pink-stained tongue. *It was sin.* Bitter and sweet in perfect balance.

It was also a distraction.

He pulled away and shook his head. "You were kind of a jerk to me."

She caressed him through his jeans. "I know. I—" She bit her lip. "You didn't deserve that." Her brown eyes were melting into a sea of dark anxiety. "Let me make it up to you." With eager fingers, she unzipped his pants, sliding them low onto his hips, and reached inside his boxer briefs. Her hot hand grasped hold of him and he wanted to come right then as she stroked him without ever breaking her velvety dark gaze from his.

"Sit," she ordered in a raw voice.

"Look, we need to—"

Adelia pushed him into the chair, pushed down his briefs and climbed on top.

"Oh god," he groaned, as she arched her hips, teasing him with the promise of being inside.

She reached beside her and pulled a condom out from beneath the towel. She tore it open and slid it on.

It took more will than he knew he possessed to grip her wrist and hold it still. "Stop."

She stared at him, that deep well of anxiety still swirling in her gaze.

He stroked the long line of her neck and ran his thumbs over the edges of her jaw. "I didn't know it would feel like this."

Her lips parted as though she were going to make a joke, but she shook her head. "I knew."

He pushed a lock of hair from her temple and turned her chin until she was forced to look at him. "I know you're leaving. But...I don't want you to."

The swift rise and fall of her breasts against his chest came to a shuddering stop. "What?"

His heart was beating outside of his skin. They'd been here before. And he'd chased her out the door with his naked emotion. But he couldn't stop himself. "Stay."

She released a trembling breath. There was so much hidden in the tightness of her jaw. The shimmer in her eyes. The pulse pounding at the side of her neck. She swallowed and pressed her hand to his chest, until his heartbeat matched the throb of hers. The edge of her mouth curled into the specter of a smile. "I don't want to go, either," she said.

Before he could think about what that meant, she kissed him, her hot mouth blazing fire on his. He grabbed hold of her ass and with one jerk of his hips, lost himself inside of her slick heat. She gave a cry and arched to meet him. There was nothing smooth or controlled about it as they collided. She ground against him with every thrust, her moans pitching higher and higher, until she cried out, her body contracting, release shuddering through her.

He wrapped his arms around her and kept going. *She wanted*

to stay. She wanted to stay. She wanted to... The heat built inside of him until it pulsed like a beating heart and exploded.

For a moment, nothing existed in the universe except Adelia. She was everything and she was his.

THE BARELY-THERE PINK light of sunrise penetrated the grey cocoon of Conor's bedroom. Adelia's hair spilled like red paint across the pillow, and her body folded into his, the warmth of her back on his chest a switchblade snug in the grip.

Five nights, she'd slept in his bed. Five nights, they'd made love as though they were both about to die. Five nights, they hadn't spoken about what they'd said.

It was all so fragile. He couldn't bring himself to ask her what it all meant.

She wriggled her bottom against him and sighed.

He kissed her neck. "You awake?"

"I hate that the answer to that is yes," she grumbled.

He laughed softly near her ear, making her shudder, and let his fingers trail down her stomach to disappear between her thighs.

Cupcake scratched at the door and whined.

"She has no sense of timing," he growled. Adelia rolled onto her side and laughed.

He smacked her ass. "You stay right there. When I come

back, I'm going to get very naughty with you before we go work on the trailer."

"How naughty we talking? Handcuffs and grape jam?"

"Maybe." He stood and smoothed out his t-shirt. "But only if the jam is sugar-free."

"Impressive. Naughtiness and a healthy diet rarely go together."

"I'm an innovator." He leaned down to kiss her, and she wound her arms around his neck and kissed him first, pulling him back onto the bed.

"So, how tight do you want your handcuffs?" she asked. He kissed the laughter from her lips and left her naked while he went into the bathroom and dressed for his run.

WHILE CONOR TOOK the dog out, Adelia stared at the ceiling, minutes piling on top of minutes, looking for answers that weren't there. She was supposed to be gone today. But she hadn't booked a flight or even picked up her car from the repair shop.

When he told her he didn't want her to go, happiness, a kind she'd never experienced, bloomed inside of her like a single flower in the desert. It was what she'd dreamed of in all the secret chambers of her heart. Conor. Hers. And she'd slept in his bed like an idiot. And now she wanted to do it again and again.

And she hadn't told him that she was leaving.

He had to know that she was going, didn't he? She had a career to get back to. A stage to exist on. And it wasn't like she could ask him to leave his life. He loved Cherry Lake, but more importantly, he loved Jo. And that kid deserved to have a dad in her life.

No matter how much she wanted him, Adelia couldn't ask him to go.

The other option was to stay. Which wasn't an option at all. She couldn't have a home, Conor, and music too. She was barely able to manage one of those things, let alone all of them.

Anyway, what kind of life could they make when he still didn't trust her enough to turn the fucking lights on? Or take his shirt off? Or let her touch him? If she had more time, maybe they could get there, but she couldn't upend her career on a maybe. On a *for a while.*

She rolled out of bed, pushed aside the room-darkening curtain, and slid her fingers between the blades of the blinds. It was a gorgeous day. The sun peeked from the horizon, and light shimmered on the ground and around the trees. That was what her life was like with Conor in it. Shimmering. Warm. Everything growing green and new inside of her.

Was the heartache of *for a while* worth that feeling?

She closed the curtain, spilling darkness back into the room. Before she could talk herself out of it, she grabbed her phone and dialed EJ's number.

"It's three in the goddamn morning here," he grumbled through a yawn. "What time am I picking you up from the airport?"

"You're not."

Damning silence lingered on the other end of the phone. "What does that mean?"

She sat on the bed and picked up Conor's pillow, breathing in his scent. "I need a few more days."

"No, you bloody well do not!" he said, brutally awake. "I arranged that interview with Rod for tomorrow morning. I need you here today."

"Can't. Something came up."

"I'm sure it did," he snarled. "Came up every evening. I saw the pictures on KMZ. You mashing faces with some yokel."

"He's not a yokel."

"Yes, of course, he's special, is he? Some hack photographer who happened to get caught kissing a famous rock singer? I'm sure his motives are pure."

"They are," she said softly. "Hard as it is for you to believe, there are people in this world who care about me." She stared at the pillow. "People who love me."

"You're going to hang your career by the neck for *love?*" Disdain oozed from the word. "Love doesn't exist, duck. You, of all people, know that. You want love, eat a fucking chocolate bar, it's the same chemicals in your idiot brain."

"I will call you tomorrow—"

"You are not puttin' me on hold for one more bloody day while you shack up with junior Captain America. I'm warning you—"

"Tomorrow," she repeated, keeping her voice steady. "I will call you and let you know what I plan to do and when I'll be back. If you don't like that, you can rightfully terminate our contract and I'll sort out my career without you. Your choice." She took a long, cleansing breath and hung up the phone.

One day. She had one day to figure out if *for a while* could be something more.

Fuck.

"WE'RE ALMOST DONE," Conor said, tossing another rusted cookie sheet into the scrap pile. "One more day ought to do it. Sucks I have to go back to work tomorrow."

The kitchen, living room, and hallway were empty and they were nearly done with her old bedroom. There was an ever-growing pile of car parts to take to the scrapyard, and the huge dumpster was filling fast with broken antiques and a shocking number of busted wooden chairs.

But no photos or sheet music or dolls.

"Keep hope alive. The bank might still call," Adelia said through her mask.

"It's after five. They're closed."

"After five already?" She pulled her mask down and looked at him with wide eyes

"Yeah, it's almost five-thirty, now."

"Fuck. Can we call it a day?" She fumbled with the zipper on her moon-man coveralls, calling it a bunch of inappropriate names.

He stepped over the stuff between them to help her but she'd already torn the thing off.

Adelia had been antsy all day. Not that she was ever excited about cleaning out the trailer, but she'd required a lot more pushing than usual to get her there, and now she seemed to be in a low-level state of panic and he had no idea why.

Once they cleaned up and got in the truck she slid across the seat, stretching the seat belt so she could rest head on his shoulder while he drove. It felt cozy and wonderful, but also left him anxious. Unless they'd just had sex, Adelia wasn't much of a cuddler.

"You all right?" he asked.

"Yeah," she said softly. He could feel her eyes on him but she didn't say much of anything else.

Once home, they took showers and he went on a run with Cupcake. When he returned, Adelia was on the couch, picking at a handful of cherries and staring at nothing. Cupcake gamboled up to her and put her giant paws on her lap. Smiling sadly, Adelia scrubbed at the spot below Cupcake's ear, earning grunts of joy.

Something was definitely wrong, but he knew better than to ask again. If she didn't want to share, he surely wouldn't get anything out of her. Dammit. He'd been waiting all day to give her the gift he had stashed in his office, but now he wasn't sure if he should. Was now a bad time? Good time?

Only one way to find out.

"I have a present for you,"

She sat the cherries on a napkin and gave him small smile. "You do? Is it handcuffs?"

"No, and it's not grape jam either." He kissed her temple. "Don't move."

He went to his office and returned with the large black portfolio he'd picked up the day before. He put it on the coffee table and sat down beside her.

She gave him a baffled look and peeled the Velcro fasteners apart. With slow hands, she removed the first 11x14 photograph from the stack. In it, she sat on his floor cleaning her guitar strings, head dipped low, sunlight streaming through the window giving her an angelic glow.

Her breath caught. "I didn't hear you take that one."

"I turned the sound off. No clicks."

She studied each photo. Her playing and losing tug-of-war with Cupcake, smile so big it took up half her face. Her drunkenly dancing and holding that expensive-ass whisky bottle. Pictures of her flipping him off. Climbing the cherry tree and reaching a hand toward him. She and Jo assembling tacos in his kitchen. Her sitting at the town hall, eyes closed, body folding into itself as she played.

"You asked me how I'd describe you." He spread the pictures across the table. "I'd describe you like this."

In the last picture she was sitting up in bed, wrapped in his black sheets, one hand in her messy hair and her mouth curved into a soft smile.

She traced the folds of the bedsheet in the picture, her eyes unreadable.

Her silence was making him nervous, but he plowed on, reaching into the portfolio pocket and handing her the envelope he'd stashed there.

She blinked at him, her brows drawn together.

"It's permission to use the pictures. All of them. For whatever. I promised you could have them, remember?"

"I—" She swallowed. "This is..." She shook her head and blew out a breath. "When you go back to work tomorrow, Keith had better not say a single word about your skills. I'll break his fucking face. These are beautiful."

"Is that Adelia-speak for liking them?"

"I love them. I love..." She wrapped her arms around him. His body tightened up, waiting, aching, for her to finish that sentence.

Instead, she pushed him backward, climbed on top and

kissed him, her tongue curling against his. The disappointment would have dropped him to his knees if he hadn't been on his back already.

Her hand slid between them, heading for his jogging pants.

"I just ran," he said. "I'm sweaty."

"Who cares?" She massaged him until his hips ground of their own volition into her hand.

"I see your point," he grunted.

She worked her hand inside the waistband of his pants and gripped him tight.

He closed his eyes and moaned. Reaching behind him, he snapped off the living room light.

Adelia reached over him and snapped it back on, pushing it further back on the end stand. "I want to see you," she said.

He shook his head. "Let's go to the bedroom."

Instead of responding, she kissed him until he forgot everything but the stroke of her hand between them and the sweetness of her lips.

She pulled back, her eyes brimming with intensity. And then she shifted, taking her body heat away, and he felt cool air on his cock, and then her hot mouth warming him.

No. He needed to stop her. He didn't do that. It was too exposed. Too close to the things he didn't want anyone seeing or touching. Especially her. But then she took him all the way down and he lost that thought as he gripped her hair.

She wasn't kidding about making *him* sing hallelujah.

Heat gathered in his pelvis as she made slow, sensual work of him, stroking his balls and pulling him in with intense suction, nearly to the point of pain, before releasing and soothing him with her tongue. He moved his hips gently, wanting more. She gave a victorious moan and pumped her mouth faster, until his body was tight, and hot sparks popped behind his eyes. He was almost done for.

Until her hands crept beneath his shirt. Her rough fingers scraping over his scarred skin.

Panic replaced heat. He reached for the lamp but she'd pushed it too far away. Needing to escape, he pulled out of her warm mouth and yanked his pants up. "The couch is uncomfortable. Let's go to the bedroom," he said, mustering up a charming smile as he stood and reached for her hand.

She climbed off the couch and stood there, hands on her hips, hair sticking up, pursed lips red as cinnamon candies. "I don't want to make love to you in the dark like you're something to be ashamed of." She cupped his jaw and stared into his eyes. "You see me. You see me like no one else does. Why can't I see you?"

Her hands felt like fire, scorching him, burning away his protective layers. He stepped out of her reach. "You know what? I'm sweaty from my run and I'm going to go take a shower."

Defeat chased away the cooling heat in her gaze, and guilt boiled in his gut. He left her in the living room to take a shower he didn't actually need.

He stroked himself, trying to relieve the ache, but he couldn't come. The heat of the water and the slip of the soap were poor company when Adelia was down the hall, practically begging for him to come in her luscious mouth.

Frustrated, clean, and dressed in sweats and a t-shirt, he emerged and found Adelia on the couch, her arms crossed and her eyes distant. The photos were zipped back up in the portfolio.

"Want to go to bed?" he asked her.

"Nah," she said, her voice hollow. "I'm going to watch some TV. Go without me."

The chilly bed was poor company too.

33

"His Majesty returns," Keith said.

Conor hung up his coat and didn't engage. He hadn't slept for shit, and Adelia never came to bed. He'd found her asleep on the couch, holding Cupcake like a body pillow. When he tried to wake her she rolled over and didn't respond, not even when he'd kissed her goodbye. A miserable start to what was sure to be a miserable day.

Keith leaned on the counter and smirked. "I heard through the grapevine that you were trying to start your own studio. How'd that work out for you?"

"Don't know yet. I'll keep you posted."

"I'm not too worried about it," Keith said, tapping his fingers on the counter. "I saw the pictures of you with that singer. The guy who took them had a lot of talent. Maybe I should fire you and hire him, huh?"

So it began.

The schedule was jam-packed, but it turned out that nearly every single client was there for no other reason than to ask questions about Lia Frost. Conor half suspected a couple of them were reporters, which gave him a chill. The last thing he

wanted were his shitty Razzle Dazzle pictures strewn in magazines. But there was nothing he could do besides putting on his
most convincing smile and answering the questions with,
"Today is about you, not me. Let's focus on your pictures."

By lunchtime he was drained, and a whole lot more empa-
thetic to Adelia's hatred of questions.

"Sooooo," Andrew said, around his mouthful of burger.
"What's Lia like?"

Conor picked at his salad. "Not you too, man."

"Sorry."

After eating, he texted Adelia for the fifth time. She didn't
respond. When he called her it went straight to voicemail. He
rubbed the back of his neck and shoved the phone back in his
pocket.

Keith appeared in the doorway and scowled. "You're two
minutes late. Your next appointment will be here any second."

Conor got up. "Sorry, I—" His phone chimed. "Shit, I'll be
out in a minute."

"You'll be out there now."

"I have to take this," Conor said, blindly pressing the phone
to his hear. "Winters?"

"Hi Mr. Ross, This is Shelby Dewitt. I'm calling about your
application for a business loan, are you available to speak for a
moment?"

"Sure," he said, heart pounding in his ears. It had to be a
good sign if they called.

Keith cleared his throat and Conor turned away to look out
the window. Freedom in his grasp.

"Usually we send a letter, but I wanted to talk to you. Your
business plan was excellent."

"Thank you."

"But your loan application was denied."

Ice filled his belly and spread outward, cold tendrils snaking
in every direction. "May I ask why?"

"It's fairly common." Paper shuffled in the background. "In your case, it's an issue of long-term security for the loan. Your lack of collateral. Unfortunately, a mobile home and a fifteen-year-old truck are not sufficient, so you have nothing of value to put up in case you default."

"Nothing of value?"

"Not for our purposes. But I wanted to tell you that there are some other options to consider. If you can put up thirty-percent of the loan, which is, uh, seventy thousand dollars, we could do a—"

"Did you say seventy thousand?"

"Yes, but there are some other options. Have you considered..." Her voice disappeared as the ringing in his ears intensified.

"Er, are you there?"

He pressed his head against the wall. "Still here," he said.

"I can email you some information about the different loan options if you'd like."

"No, uh, thank you, though."

"Please don't let this discourage you. Getting denied for a loan is the first step to getting approved for one. Have a good day, Mr. Ross."

His throat was arid. He kept swallowing but couldn't make the feeling go away. He turned around and Keith raised his eyebrow. "Bad news?"

The front bell tinkled and Conor tried to move around him, but Keith blocked the office doorway, eyes gleaming. "Maybe now you'll get your shit together," he said. "The only reason you still have a job here is because your mother called and tore me a new one when she heard that I planned to fire you when you showed up today. You need to stop thinking you're too good to work for me. You're barely holding onto this, how the hell were you planning to run your own business?" He snorted and stepped aside. "Go take care of those customers."

ADELIA RUMMAGED through the cabinet beneath the sink and pulled out the bin of neatly labeled cleaning products, looking for furniture polish. She'd been scrubbing for hours, cleaning things that were already clean.

Her tears were still locked away, but she felt them pulsing behind her eyes. For so many years, she'd avoided hurt and now she remembered why. Emptiness was better than heartache.

She found the polish and read the back of the container. Reasonably sure she knew how to use it, she grabbed a towel and set to work on the coffee table.

It was her own fault. That much was clear. Fourteen years just wasn't enough time to erase the scars she'd left behind.

Her phone vibrated again. She shook her head and kept cleaning.

She couldn't do it. She couldn't fantasize that this thing could have a happy ending. Those pictures were overwhelming. Vulnerable. Terrifying. But no matter how much they meant to her, he still didn't trust her, and he'd made it pretty clear he wasn't going to.

So what did breaking his nonexistent trust matter?

She mopped and vacuumed. Cleaned and dusted his office. She changed the sheets on his bed and threw the old ones in the wash.

Finally, there was nothing to do but pack. She folded up Jo's clothing and sat it neatly on top of the washer, and crammed everything else into her duffel bag, including the portfolio of photos.

She sat in the chair in the living room, staring at the floor. Cupcake whined and padded over, dropping her big, heavy head onto her lap, peering up with sad eyes.

"Yeah, me too." She stroked her silky fur and smooched the top of her giant head. Cupcake licked her nose.

"I'll miss you, dog." Giving her a scratch behind the ear, Adelia stood.

She hauled her guitar case and duffel bag up and left, locking the door behind her. Cupcake whined on the other side, but it was too late. She didn't have a key.

Couldn't get back in, even if she wanted to.

The handful of reporters and fans that had been hovering around the trailer were gone for the moment. A lone teenaged girl was in the yard. "Ohmuhgod!" She fumbled for her phone. "Lia, I can't believe it's you!"

"Take a picture and you'll be fishing that phone out of Hopeful Creek."

The girl stilled. "I'm sorry," she whispered.

"It's all right. Put it back in your pocket." Adelia spotted a beat-up little Honda parked in front of Shannon's house. "What's your name?"

The girl's eyes widened. "Ellie."

"Is that your car, Ellie?"

"Uh, yeah."

"Can I bum a ride?"

"THANK YOU, MR. AND MRS. WALLACE," Conor said listlessly as his customers left. He'd been a zombie all afternoon, shuffling and grunting through the sessions. Thankfully, Keith left early and there was only one more session to get through. No clue if it was a family or a single session. Keith's notes weren't particularly helpful, but that wasn't unusual. He often forgot to write down phone numbers and names and even when he did, his handwriting was illegible.

He skimmed through the last terrible photos, sighing when the bell jangled. A man walked in, wearing sunglasses. He stopped in the doorway. Expensive black-on-black suit. No tie. Top button undone.

Conor disliked him immediately. "Hi, can I help you?"

The man smiled and shut the door behind him. "Yes, you can, mate. I've got an appointment." He slid off his sunglasses and pierced Conor with the most glacial blue eyes he'd ever seen.

"EJ Davies. Pleasure to meet you."

34

EJ sat on the couch in the waiting area and gestured for Conor to sit in the adjacent chair, as though he were a guest in EJ's home.

Conor debated standing, but decided it was a childish kind of power play and sat.

"I'll get straight to it," EJ said. "Lia said she was returning to LA, but she's been dragging her heels, and I suspect you're the reason."

The bottom fell out of his gut. "She...said she was going back?"

"Yes. She wanted a bit more time, but yes." EJ sat back and assessed him. "I take it she hasn't told you. Classic Lia. No apologies and no goodbyes. That's my girl."

Conor chafed at the words *my girl* for many reasons, but he ignored both the possessive caveman inside and the desire to point out that Adelia was no girl. Instead, he gestured for EJ to continue.

"I don't know what you think you're doing with someone like her," EJ said. "But I feel it necessary to help you understand what's happening here."

"And what's that?"

"I'm sure you know that Lia thoroughly fucked her career, and mine as well, with that little stunt in L.A. And I've spent the last few weeks trying to unfuck it."

"I know it's a big deal to punch your boss, but I don't get why you're acting like it's the end of the road for her."

"Because he's not some cheap-suit-wearing boss of Razzle bloody Dazzle," EJ snarled. "He's one of the most powerful men in the industry and he has shut her career *down*. I've talked to a hundred people trying to get her another contract and no one would work with her. If she doesn't get her ass back there to make nice with the Gyroscope, she's out." EJ smiled a shark's grin. "She didn't tell you that either?"

She had. Sort of. But she didn't say how dire the situation was. Conor ran a hand through his hair. "What's your point?"

"Lia comes alive when she's onstage. It's the only thing that truly makes her happy, and you're keeping her from that happiness."

"You only see who you want her to be. The stage doesn't make her happy. The music does."

EJ stood and adjusted his blazer. "Your two weeks of insight into Lia is impressive, but I've known her a bit longer than you have."

"I've known her since she was seven."

That dropped the smirk from EJ's face, but he recovered it quickly. "Then you should be well aware that you're not good enough for Lia to fuck, let alone throw her career away for." He leaned down and brushed a piece of invisible fuzz from Conor's shoulder. "You're a big fish in a very small pond. What do you have to offer her? A metal home? A rusted truck?" EJ scanned the pictures on the walls. "Photographs of corseted geriatrics?" He shook his head. "I can give her back her *career*. Rod is ready to give her another chance, and you're standing in the way of that."

The heat of humiliation roasted Conor from the inside. He pushed out of the chair, denying EJ any more time spent hovering over him. "This pitch is pretty self-serving. You're the one who needs her career back."

EJ shrugged. "My career matters to me and she's cocked it up proper. I won't lie about that." He smiled. "But I also want what's best for her."

"You really believe that. Whether it's her career or lingerie, EJ knows best. But she knows what she wants, and she's way smarter than you give her credit for."

"Told you about the knickers, eh?" EJ's eyes narrowed until the blue disappeared. "That's…unlike her."

"Maybe you don't know her like you think you do."

"We're whipping them out to measure, are we?" EJ looked him up and down and Conor's spine tingled with fury. "Let's say you're right, and this new-found streak of honesty and openness is the stuff *vomit* is made of," EJ said. "Do you believe she's going to stay here? In this dull, pile-of-dirt town with you? Because if there's one thing I know about Lia, it's that she never met a feeling she couldn't outrun." He poked a finger into Conor's chest. "She didn't tell you she was leaving, because she wasn't going to tell you." He slid his sunglasses back on. "You've had your fun, so don't feel too bad, mate. She's hard to resist. All those pent-up emotions. All that self-loathing. It makes her so damned fuckable." He grinned.

Conor would have loved the satisfaction of chipping a few of those perfect capped teeth, but he knew it wouldn't make anything better. Instead, he threw open the door and gestured EJ out.

EJ took his time, sauntering out and making a show of unlocking his sports car with his key fob. "I think you'll find this is for the…" He trailed off, staring across the street.

Conor followed his line of vision.

In front of Paulie's, Adelia stood beside a Honda, taking a

selfie with a teenage girl. She waved her off, turned, and froze. Her eyes narrowed in EJ's direction and she stormed across the street. "What the fuck are you doing here?"

Conor stared at the duffel bag in her hand. Guitar case in the other.

His stomach knotted until he thought he might throw up.

Here he was again. The kid on the carpet. Watching Adelia slide on her clothes and walk out the door, humiliating him.

And why would she stay? What did he have to offer her?

Nothing of value.

35

ADELIA'S WORLD went red and hazy. "You have no business being here."

"Yes, well, technically neither do you," EJ said.

"Go away."

He smirked and swiveled his head away from her. "It was nice meeting you."

No. No. No. Conor stood in the doorway of the building, face drawn, jaw twitching. "Can't say the same," he said, never breaking eye contact with her.

This was not how it was supposed to happen.

Instead of leaving, EJ sauntered closer and breathed deeply near her ear. "I'll be in the car, duck."

As soon as his car door snicked shut, she turned to Conor. "I'm sorry he came here."

Conor shrugged. "I'm glad. Someone had to tell the truth."

She stilled. "What does that mean?"

"He said you were leaving. And you weren't going to say goodbye." He tilted his chin toward her bag and guitar case. "Were you going to tell me?"

Shame ate her alive and spit out her bones. "I don't know."

"I am such an idiot." The acid in his laughter burned her. "Shannon warned me. She told me it was going to end like this. And I didn't believe her. I thought you felt the same way I did."

"I do," she said.

"Oh, come on. What was I? A living vibrator? A pity fuck?"

"I never made love to you out of pity. Don't you dare turn what we've shared into that."

"No, don't *you* dare romanticize this with your bags in your hands." He jabbed a finger in her direction. "It was fucking. Apparently that's all we've ever done."

She closed her eyes tight and reached for the numbing static that had protected her from pain for so long, but there was no amount of static that could drown out the devastation ringing in her ears like church bells. "Maybe that's what you've been doing," she said. "But that wasn't what I did with you." The sun, starting its downward descent, left little spots of light on the toes of her boots. "I don't know how to do this," she said, staring at the spots. "I don't know how to deal with my bullshit and yours at the same time. I don't know how we make this work."

"I don't have bullshit. I'm not the one who can't stop hiding and lying."

Her eyes shot to his and anger pulsed its way through her heartache. "Seriously? You're not hiding?" She dropped her stuff and stalked to the doorway, forcing him back into the studio. She wound her arms around his neck. His eyes widened and suddenly his arms were around her. His lips hovered over hers, a question to be answered.

She slid her hands into his hair and yanked on it, pulling him closer and answering.

He kissed her. A hot careless kiss, all lust and no precision. She scraped her teeth over his lower lip, making him shudder. He pushed her against the counter and demolished her with his mouth. She could taste his fury and it bled together with hers.

"Take me home," she said, against his lips. He pulled back

and stared at her. "Take me home. Make love to me with the lights on. And I'll stay."

He backed away, color rising fast in his cheeks and his eyes skimming the floor.

"See, Conor? You want *everything* from me. All my scars. But you don't want to give everything back." She slid her hands under his jaw and forced him to look at her. "You look at your-self and all you see are imperfections and failures. I don't see you that way. I see someone amazing and I always have."

He gripped her wrists and shoved her hands away from him. "So amazing you have to run out on me? Again?" He ran a hand through his hair, the strands parting like wheat in a windstorm. "Could you just be honest? For once in your life? Because you keep telling me that I'm worthwhile, that you care about me, then you treat me like a piece of junk you pulled out of your dad's trailer and can't wait to throw away."

She reared back from his bruising words. "You know, I spent most of my life thinking I was in love with you," she said. "And I was wrong."

He closed his eyes. "You can leave now."

Her thoughts were jumbled up. She tried to make sense of them. "What I mean is that I loved you like a kid loves a toy. You were my thing. My safe space. All mine. If it was love, it was a selfish kind of love." She bit her lip, needing the sting. "But we're not safe. Either of us. And I see who you are now. The man who isn't all mine. The one who's scared and moody and has body issues. The one who's stubborn and flawed and who hates taking chances." She locked her knees to keep herself from folding to the floor. "And I love that man. Because of it. In spite of it. Whatever." She took a breath. "I love you."

The only sound in the room was their breathing, denting the air. She could count the seconds by the clenching and unclenching of his jaw.

She pressed her tongue to the roof of her mouth. When she

was ten, on a dare from Conor she'd eaten an orange, rind and all. She still remembered the taste, and it wasn't half as bitter and indigestible as his silence.

When it was clear he wasn't going to speak, she swallowed. "I get it. You were never going to trust me and—It's fine. You don't have to love me back." Her voice shook. "I'm going to love you either way."

She turned and walked out the door. Without looking back, she grabbed her stuff and climbed into EJ's waiting car, leaving her heart behind, like a pile of broken glass on the dirty concrete.

ADELIA STARED straight ahead through the windshield, as drained as an empty jug.

A sign on the door of the Dive Inn screamed, "GRAND RE-OPENING!!!"

"I got us a room in this dump," EJ said. "The next flight isn't until tomorrow." She followed him listlessly as he pulled his key card and went straight to room three.

Of course.

The ceiling above the bed was smooth and white, no show-tune-singing demons anywhere. The room looked nice. It had a fresh coat of paint. New bedding. Everything was clean, except for the familiar painting on the wall. It was dirty, as if they'd forgotten to wipe it down, but it was the same one. A charmingly crooked house on the water, curtains floating on the breeze. Windows open. Warm. Inviting.

EJ stood behind her, his body brushing hers. "I'm sorry."

"No, you're not."

He chuckled. "You're right. I'm not."

"You had no right to come here and screw everything up."

"Oh, come now. You were the one with your bags packed."

"I told you I would contact you and let you know what I was going to do."

"And I told you I knew exactly what you were going to do before you did it. Because you aren't going to leave your career for emotions you're barely capable of feeling." He slid his hand around her waist. "Love is for sprogs and optimists, and you're neither. You're like me and you always have been." He pushed her hair aside and kissed her neck.

She felt nothing. Just an empty dullness as his hand crept beneath her shirt.

Maybe this was what she deserved.

The picture on the wall was so lovely. The home called to her, but it was out of reach and moving further and further away until it felt like she was looking at it from across a field.

She turned toward EJ. "I hate you."

"So you say." The cold in his eyes burned hers. "But all I've ever done is what you wanted. You wanted to work and never stop, and I gave you that. I've booked monster tours that consumed the rest of my career to keep you doing what *you* wanted, but you insist on blaming me for your damnable unhappiness. I'm a prick, I won't deny it, but maybe it's time you realize that you, not me, have created the misery you're wallowing in. The person you hate? It's you, duck."

He swung her around and his mouth trailed the back of her neck, his hands caressing her breasts. "Forget Mister Small-Town-America," he murmured. "Let's get you back in the studio. You can channel all that angst into something worth selling, and I'll get you back on the stage where you belong. You always fight me so hard, but it's time to admit how much you need what I give you." He unbuttoned the top button of her jeans. "You don't hate me when I make you come."

Bile rose in her throat. Was this all there was for her? Hate-fucking her manager, making boring albums and working endless tours until music was just another way to punish herself for her mistakes?

She turned and pushed him away. "You're fired."

"Of course, I am." He smirked and dove for her mouth.

"I mean it." She stepped out of his reach and re-buttoned her jeans. "I don't want you. Not as a manager, and not as...anything."

She grabbed his leather bag and shoved it at him. "I'm keeping the room, but you need to leave. There are hotels in Port Agnes, near the airport." She opened the door. "I'll pay what the contract stipulates to terminate our working relationship."

"You're not serious." He stared hard at her, waiting for the fight she always gave. He usually won those fights. Cajoling. Seducing. Knocking her arguments aside. This time, she didn't argue. She pressed her lips together and pointed out the door.

His eyes narrowed until they nearly disappeared. "You fucking ungrateful slag! After everything I've done for you, you're going to sack me so you can screw some hillbilly while your career disintegrates?" He vibrated with fury. "I'd like you to remember precisely where I found you. You were a whore giving out blowjobs at bachelor parties. You were nothing. And without me, you still are." He slapped the back of his hand against his palm. "I built your career, I made you a star. I got a record deal that cannot be rivaled, and I got Rod Norris to agree to give you a second chance. You owe me something for that."

She clenched her fists. The desire to knock him the fuck out was strong, but what was the point? He wouldn't learn one damned thing.

And she was tired of throwing punches, anyway.

"I have given you what I owe you," she said. "Which is eighteen percent of my take. And yeah, I was a whore. I did what I had to. But I wasn't nothing." She took a shuddering breath. "Maybe I wouldn't have a career without you. We'll never know.

But I'd like *you* to remember that I was the one that took *my* career from the one-note pop-rock bullshit you wanted it to be and turned it into gold. I was the one who wrote all the songs. I was the one who won a goddamn Grammy and I was the one the fans were cheering for. Not you, EJ."

"All that cheering has gone to your head," he sneered.

"No. It hasn't." She lifted her chin. "You're right. You're not the reason I'm unhappy, but you have no problem using my unhappiness to control me." The words came out without any thought, but the weight of their truth landed with a thud between them. "I've been ungrateful in a lot of ways and I'm genuinely sorry about that. You have worked your ass off to help build my career and it's not your fault that I don't want this anymore. But it doesn't change the fact that *I don't want this anymore*."

His mouth curled into a snarl. "You're destroying everything we've worked for. Once you realize that, you'll come crawling back."

"Hold your breath on that." She went to the door and opened it.

He fired a barrage of cruel expletives at her and marched out. "You're nothing without m—"

She shut the door.

Her breaths came in short bursts, increasing in speed and pitch. She'd finally destroyed everything she'd worked for.

Dropping onto the bed, she wrapped her arms around herself, wishing they were Conor's. Wishing he was kissing her and telling her it was going to be all right.

But she'd destroyed that too.

She was her father's daughter in every way.

Pain throbbed in her head and behind her eyes. Falling onto her back, she looked at the ceiling, and imagined that she could still see the scars from where everything had collapsed.

CONOR SNAPPED ANOTHER PICTURE. The pregnant sisters stood back to back, wearing shirts that said, "Humped and Bumped." What were their names? Jilly and Bev? Jess and Billy? *Didn't fucking matter.*

The night before, he'd gone home to the scents of disinfectant and regret. Adelia had cleaned everything. Even his weights. The only proof she'd been there were the smear marks on the mirrors, and he couldn't bring himself to wipe them away.

He didn't get a single second of sleep. The sheets, which had smelled so gloriously like her, now smelled like detergent and the fragrance burned his nose. When the sun finally rose, he'd forced himself to take a shower and nearly fell asleep standing up.

While toweling off, he'd stared at himself in the streaky mirror.

What would she have thought about his body, with all the remnants of his life as a fat man? The slight softness that never left his middle no matter how many crunches he did. The stretch marks that lined his upper arms, stomach, hips, and back, telling the story of afternoons spent binge-eating double bacon cheeseburgers, chili-cheese fries, and drippy slices of cherry pie?

Would she truly have stayed if he'd been able to show himself to her? Or was that an excuse? Was it his fault? Her fault? Or were they just too broken for something real?

"Hey." Jilly or Jess or whoever waved a hand near his face. "We wanna pose topless. You know, holding our boobs like celebrities do on magazine covers. Can we do that?"

"If that's what you want." He tried for a smile but couldn't remember what they felt like. Whatever his face did, it must have replicated human emotion because she didn't seem alarmed.

Andrew pushed his glasses up and gave him a once over. "You know, not many men can pull off that mountain man look with the beard. And you can't either. You should shave."

"I don't care how I look."

"Obviously."

Conor's phone vibrated for the twentieth time. He didn't answer. A group of down-staters had snuck some blurry photos of him and Adelia arguing outside the studio. Thanks to them, it was either a reporter looking for a story, or another well-meaning acquaintance offering condolences on the breakup. He could have turned his phone off, but the buzzing was the only thing keeping him awake.

The session was a blur. After showing them the options, they bought a pricey photo package with lots of airbrushing they didn't need, and he hoped he'd snapped the last picture he would ever take of topless pregnant sisters in matching knee-high socks.

After they left, Keith stared at the photos. "Pictures suck, but it was a good sale. About time you got your shit together."

It was the nicest thing he'd said in ages. But then, Keith

could afford to be gracious, since much of their sudden business was due to the implosion of Conor's love life.

"That's not actually a compliment. Do you mind if I run over to Keys?" He didn't actually need anything, other than an escape from that airless prison of a studio.

"Sure. Next client isn't for twenty minutes. Pick me up one of them iced coffees, a slice of pie, and some mints."

Keith didn't offer any money. Conor knew he wouldn't, but had no energy to cajole ten bucks out of the cheapskate.

At the market's backdoor, his phone pinged again. Voicemail from Liam. His thumb hovered over the trash can icon, but he clicked on it.

Hey brother, I know you're going to delete this without listening to it, but if you don't, give me a call.

Maybe it was the lack of sleep, or his bruised heart, but a tinge of guilt penetrated the pain he'd been wallowing in. He dialed his brother's number.

"You called," Liam said by way of answering.

"What's up?" he asked, already half-regretting his impulsiveness.

"I don't know much about what's going on with your life, but Mom has been blowing up my phone, blathering on about rock singers and business loans. She's a wreck."

"Guilt. My favorite."

"It's not my intention to guilt you. Mom said that you applied for a loan and didn't get it."

Humiliation burned its way through him. He'd reached peak failure in a single twenty-four hour period. "Yup," he said.

"She threatened to go to the bank and raise hell. I talked her down off of that particular ledge."

"Of course. She can't stand to see a Ross fail."

"She can't stand to see you unhappy," Liam said. "Mom isn't perfect, and I'm not going to say that she was even a particularly good parent. She can be—"

"Overbearing? Status-obsessed? Type-A perfectionist?"

"Yes. The latter of which is a trait you *both* share."

Conor itched to hang up the phone.

"I don't want to fight with you. I—" A sharp voice intruded on Liam's end, stepping on whatever he planned to say. "Jesus, Bree," he said. "Tell them I had something unexpected come up and I'll be late. If they want to reschedule, reschedule them. Yes, this is important." He sighed. "Sorry, Conor."

"Maybe you shouldn't have kept your ex-wife on as your business manager."

"It seemed like a good idea. Better than the marriage, anyway," Liam said. "Look, I know how much it sucks to get rejected for a loan."

"I'm sure you don't."

"Did you even read my fucking book?"

"You mean the one Mom not-so-subtly gave me for Christmas? No, I didn't read past the autograph."

Liam seemed to breathe in for a long time before speaking. "No one gets it right the first time. Some people *are* lucky, but most of us fail our way up. If you want to run your business plan by me, I'm happy to listen and offer some advice if I can. If you want to read my book so you don't have to listen to me, do it that way. But whatever you do, don't give up on it and don't be afraid to start small. Sometimes losing what you thought you wanted can set you on the path of what you actually need."

Conor closed his eyes, trying to block out the memory of Adelia walking away. This wasn't about that. Was it?

"Thanks, man. I'll uh, think about all of that."

"You probably won't," Liam said. "I'll talk to you later, brother."

Conor pushed the phone back into his pocket and ran a hand over his mouth. What did starting small look like? What if he couldn't get it right? What if he wrecked his life for a dumb dream?

Your dreams are not dumb.

He could see Adelia standing there, holding the real estate ad aloft, assuring him that his dreams mattered. Adelia in a tree, hand outstretched, daring him to climb up. Adelia in her purple hoodie and candy-colored hair, staring fiercely into his eyes. *You look at yourself and all you see are imperfections and failures. I don't see you that way. I see someone amazing and I always have.*

He turned and walked back to the studio. Keith sucked on his teeth and eyed Conor's empty hands. "Where's my stuff?"

"I didn't get it."

"Then what the hell were you doing?"

"Thinking."

"Heh, no wonder it was a short walk."

Conor grabbed the dust rag from under the counter and started wiping down surfaces, needing to keep his hands busy so he didn't strangle Keith. "Why do you act like I'm stupid? I'm not. I graduated salutatorian from Sutcliffe."

Keith's gaze followed the erratic jabs of Conor's hands. "So what? You think you're better than me cuz you've got a fancy piece of paper?"

"No, I don't. But I'm better than the way you talk to me."

"Aww, do I hurt your *feewings*?" Keith crossed his arms over his chest. "I thought this bullshit was over with when you didn't get your loan. You ain't better than me or this job."

"I'm not better than hard work, but we both know that I'm better than this job, Keith." He scrubbed harder at the already dust-free counter. A sickly euphoria came over him, like when a roller coaster readies to shoot upward. Click. Click.

"You ain't though, and everyone knows that. Why do you think your ma is up my ass about keeping you on?"

Click. Click.

"Cuz she knows as well as I do that you'll end up stocking shelves at Keys with the high schoolers. You're mediocre talent with a pretty face and you of all people ain't taking my business away from me."

Click.

"I'm done," Conor said, throwing down the dust rag. "I'm done listening to this. I'm done living down to your expectations. There's room for both of us in Cherry Lake."

"I ain't worried. One of us couldn't get a fucking loan."

"So I'll start small and build my way up."

Keith's face turned a violent shade of burgundy. "I won't be taking you back when you figure out how good you had it here and—"

The thudding between Conor's ears worked better than cotton to mute Keith's vitriolic rant. "I'm willing to give you two weeks' notice so you can hire someone else," he interrupted, when it was clear Keith wouldn't be shutting up anything soon.

Keith jammed a finger into Conor's chest. "You quit on me and you ain't getting two weeks of extra pay."

"Then consider this my notice." Conor walked past him and into the studio to pack his personal equipment with shaking hands.

Andrew peered from outside the makeup room, his faux-hawk bobbing in the air conditioning. "You didn't."

Conor cleared his throat. "I did."

"Dear god, take me with you."

"I don't even have a studio yet. I've got a lot to figure out. I can't take you away from a good job. What if—"

"I believe in you." Andrew pushed his blue glasses higher on his nose. "And anyway, I used to do all the bookkeeping for the Dive, so I can be way more useful than just applying makeup. And I'm excellent at implementing ideas."

"Your resume is outstanding. But I'm not sure I could pay you what—"

"It'll be worth a pay reduction. Thanks to you, my family is back to being slightly above the poverty line. It's fine."

He stared at Andrew, who looked back, his jaw set, his eyes bright with anticipation.

What fun was a rollercoaster if you were the only one in the car?

Conor nodded and pulled his camera bag over his shoulder. "Grab your stuff," he said. "And let's burn this bridge to ashes."

They walked past an apoplectic Keith and headed to the Railway. Over a couple of blackened green tomato cucumber sandwiches that tasted like heartache, they worked out some rough details.

Afterward, Conor stared at his phone, wishing he could call Adelia and knowing that he couldn't. Instead, he dialed another number.

Liam answered on the first ring. "Hello, brother."

"Hey, can I run something by you?"

Conor felt bruised all over, but the roller coaster feeling pushed past that. Higher and higher it went, and for once, instead of wanting to jump out, he buckled himself in and prepared for the ride.

ADELIA HAD no idea that grief could leach so much of a person's energy.

She moved like an automaton for three days, eating junk food from the vending machine, ignoring the knocks on her motel door, and staring at the ceiling, checking for cracks.

Then, the pain broke like a fever, and beneath it was blessed apathy. Nothing mattered so nothing could hurt her anymore.

That was comforting, in its own way.

After a much-needed shower, she ate a bag of chips, crunching mechanically. Sunlight streamed into the room through the tiny window and dust motes danced in the air. Her phone flashed notification of a new text from Emi asking if they could meet to discuss the contract that was still sitting in her inbox.

Why the fuck not? There was nothing else to do, was there? Just get her car and start screwing her life up all over again.

She slid on her sunglasses and walked to Paulie's Towing and Repair.

The door to the office was propped open. Classic rock blasted from the shop floor and a warm breeze swirled the scent of musty car interiors, tire rubber, and gasoline around the room.

She breathed deeply, and the scent crawled inside of her. For years, she was unable to recall a single happy memory of her youth. Now, there it was. Her mother taking her to visit her father at his repair shop in Flint. Smelling like Marlboros, motor oil, and exhaust, he'd lift her with grease-stained hands and pretend to be the kiss monster, smooching her until she squealed, while he growled that he loved his Dilly Bean. She'd wriggle out of his arms and race around the shop, swinging wrenches and hugging alternators, and her father would yank her mother onto his lap and they would share a cigarette and whisper grownup talk, her mother occasionally bursting into braying laughter as they played their own version of kiss monster.

"Can I help you?" The mechanic, wearing a badge that said Paulie, wiped his hands on a towel and gave her a grin. Unlike her father, who was so lean and tall he looked like a wraith, Paulie looked like a gnome and a beach ball jumbled together.

"I'm picking up the GTO," she said, blinking away the pressure behind her eyes.

"Oh, the goat!" Paulie said. "I love that car. Can I keep it?" He gave a wheezing laugh. "You know why they call them goats? It's because they eat everything. Roads. Oil. Money. Especially money." He stuck his head into the doorway separating the office and the shop floor. "Goat owner's here!"

A woman and a man in stained jumpsuits appeared. The guy looked a lot like Paulie. Short and balding with greasy, huge hands. Actually, the woman looked a lot like him too.

"This is my daughter Fran and my cousin Tony," Paulie said. "Tony drove out from Hope Falls. He knows his way around those vintage monsters."

"I don't know how you made it off whatever lot you got that car from," Tony said. "But If someone told you it was okay to drive it like that, you should sue 'em. You're damned lucky it died before it had a chance to kill you."

"The motel already gave it a good shot, why not the car, too?" she said.

Fran's eyes widened. "Oh no, were you one of the people stayin' there?"

"Yup."

"All that and then your car bein' here for so long?" She gave her father a look and he nodded, slipping the repair estimate onto the counter. "We'll give ya the Dive special." She started crossing things off the list. Adelia put her hand over the paper. "That's not necessary. I have money to pay for it."

Fran patted her hand and pushed it aside. "That ain't the point. Don't want you leaving Cherry Lake thinking that this is our best. We take care of our own and when you stay here, you're one of our own too."

Adelia handed her credit card over to Fran, who stared at it. "You're that singer, huh?"

Tony broke the stunned silence. "You know, with a little more time, I could have that car in pristine condition."

"And you'd do an awesome job," Adelia said, grabbing her keys. "But I'm not staying."

Outside, sunlight glinted off her freshly washed car. It started with a smooth growl that should have thrilled her, but didn't. She pulled out of the lot and her stomach growled louder than the car, reminding her that she'd eaten nothing but potato chips and Skittles for days.

She drove over to Keys and picked up a couple sandwiches from the fridge, a light beer, and a salad. Then she stocked up on dilly beans and cherry pie for the road, along with a Styrofoam cooler and a bag of ice.

"Hello, young lady," Old Curtis said, as he rang her up. His pale eyes shone with warmth. She held out a twenty-dollar bill and he shook his head. "It's on the house, Miss Winters. You overpaid the last two times. Threw my books outta whack."

She stared at him.

"Ha, thought you fooled me. I knew it was you weeks ago. Flirting with Conor Ross and throwing cash at me and running out the door."

She looked at the counter. "I owed you."

He slid her sandwiches into a bag. "Why? Because of the shoplifting?"

Her eyes snapped to his and shame coiled in her gut like a garden snake.

"You were such a skinny little thing, Pocketing everything that wasn't nailed down."

"But you—you never busted me."

"Why would I? I know good kids from lousy kids. You were just hungry," he said. "And not nearly as sneaky as you thought you were." He gave her a knowing smile. "Maybe it's wrong of me to bring up such painful things. Miss Janice would give me hell for it. But it's weighed on me for a long time. Wondering if I did enough."

"I don't understand."

His crooked fingers smoothed the already smooth wrapper of a candy bar. "You were so skinny and hungry. And you were taking baths in my restroom sink. Your daddy..." he shook his head. "I'm sorry to speak ill of the dead. He didn't come around much, but I spoke to him enough to know he wasn't well." He reached for her hand and gripped it shockingly tight. "I called social services more than once. I always worried that I made it worse, but I didn't know what else to do."

Her hand shook beneath his. "You didn't make it worse." A couple times she'd been pulled out of her middle school classes and forced to answer questions from breathless, worried strangers about her home life. Whether it was instinct or shame, she hadn't trusted them with the truth. The thought of people knowing that she lived in trash was a nightmare. The thought of being taken from Cherry Lake—from Conor—was worse. So she'd lied. Her home was great. Her dad was wonderful. She had plenty to eat.

His bony shoulders slumped further. "So, I didn't hurt anything, but I didn't help either. I should have done more."

"Not sure there was much you could do. You let me take food. Not starving was pretty helpful." She tried for a smile, but she didn't have it in her, and Old Curtis's serious expression never broke.

"For what it's worth, I'm real proud that you went and did something with yourself." He gave her hand another squeeze. "I went on the computer and listened to your rock and roller songs. Your voice is beautiful. Loud, but beautiful. You could probably do with a few less curse words, though."

He let go of her hand and slid the bag toward her.

She looked down at the last of her cash.

"Don't you dare mess up my books again," he said.

She shoved the cash back in her pocket. Walking around the counter, she wrapped her arms around him, hugging him tight. "Thank you," she said. "For trying."

He patted her cheek. "Behave yourself out there."

"No promises." She took a shaky breath, so many emotions tangling in her head like Christmas lights. Outside, a gentle breeze wafted by, carrying the smell of pine trees and lake water. Breathing in, she threw her car into gear. And then back to park. Through the window, she watched Old Curtis rearrange a candy display and wave to a group of kids who wandered into the market.

All this time, she never knew that someone actually saw past her bravado and secrets. Saw how hard she struggled. How much different would her life have been if she'd known that someone cared about her like that? Would she have given up on Cherry Lake? Given up on love?

She'd always told herself that she wasn't meant for happy endings. Maybe she was right. Maybe everything she did would end in bittersweet pain. But how would she know? She gave up before anything could end. Her life was a series of dangling threads she was too scared to snip.

She put the car into gear and drove to Buck's Hardware. She filled her backseat with supplies and headed back down Big Dirt Road.

It was time to cut a thread.

***

ADELIA SLID on a mask and gloves and tried not to think about Conor sliding the mask on her face, showing her how to seal it, and checking her outfit to make sure she was covered and safe. A twinge of something broke through the emptiness and she shoved it back down. Numbness was better.

They'd been so close to finishing. Except for the heavier car parts and a few assorted boxes, there was only the bathroom and her father's bedroom left. The bathroom didn't take too long. But her father's room was the worst one.

She was relentless, throwing things away in a frenzy and dragging garbage bags out to the container. It took most of the day, but by the time the sun started its slow path toward the horizon, she had only one box left to sort. The room was empty. She sat on the floor with the last garbage bag next to her and opened the box.

On top were bent antique picture frames without glass. Methodically she pulled them out and stuffed them in the garbage, not caring what they might be worth. She pulled out some broken figurines, and a stained copy of *A Tree Grows in Brooklyn*. Conor read that book to her years ago. She smoothed the folded pages and dimly wondered if the book belonged to her mother or if it was junk her father had picked up. He didn't really read, but there was no telling why he might decide to bring something home. She threw it in the garbage. It didn't matter.

She reached in the box again. Her gloved fingers caught on something and she squinted in the rapidly deteriorating light. A flash of dingy red made her heart race. She dug both arms in.

Crammed into the bottom, squashed beneath a rusty eggbeater and an ancient jar of peanut butter, she found her rag doll. Tossing the eggbeater aside, she pulled it out and traced the little round face and faded pink circles on its cheeks with her gloved fingers.

One of her few hazy memories of her mother was the day she'd handed Adelia the doll, telling her to treat it with care. She'd been five and had taken her mother seriously, tending to the doll like a sick baby. She finger-combed the yarn hair and wiped it with damp rags as though it were running temperatures. She tucked it in at night and whispered secrets to it.

Then her mother died, and they'd moved from Flint to the boonies of Cherry Lake. And somewhere along the way her father had crammed the beloved totem into a sticky box, piling rusted kitchen implements and rancid peanut butter on top of it.

Her hand shook, and she closed her eyes. *It's just a thing.*

Something fractured inside her. A sob erupted. Then another. And another. Her vision blurred, and breaths skipped. She ripped the mask off and tossed it aside. Gloves too.

She pressed her fingers to her cheeks, and tears rushed over her fingers like the cliff's edge of a waterfall. One sob turned to so many she lost track. She cried until she thought she was going to throw up. Her stomach hurt and her face was sore, but the tears kept coming. Fourteen years' worth. Tears for her father and tears for the broken girl who chose selling bits of herself over indifference and starvation.

Pressing the doll against her face, she smelled the stink of the trailer, the mildew and decay. Even if she scrubbed it every day, the doll would always smell like that. Anger bubbled to the surface. More than she'd ever allowed herself to feel. She set the doll aside and stared at the wooden doors of his closet. She hated doors. And secrets. And shadowy places where valuable things were lost.

She kicked the closet door. And kicked it again. She kicked until her leg ached and the wood splintered. She tore the hinges from the rotting wood paneling and tossed the door on the floor and stomped it until it was rubble.

Angry tears kept burning and boiling against her cheeks as she took every door down. Then, she grabbed an old exhaust pipe from one of the piles of leftover car parts. Going room to room, she smashed everything. Cupboards. Mirrors. Gagging on her tears, she demolished every window, then went outside and beat the side of the trailer until she could barely lift her arms.

When there was nothing left to hit, she walked back to her father's room, glass crunching beneath her boots. It was time to move on. She snatched up the doll and shoved it into the lumpy garbage bag.

But she couldn't let go of it. It was nothing but a tattered, ruined thing. It wasn't worth saving. It would always be damaged and stained.

She pulled it out and smoothed the dark red yarn hair. Maybe it was beyond repair, but she was tired of throwing away everything that meant something to her.

Adelia picked her way through the fresh debris and stopped in the broken doorway. She took a last look around. Her dad had been there. He'd lived there long after she left, listening to the radio and ranting about sports teams, collecting garbage, all alone with his endless grief that left no room for any other feelings.

"I'm sorry about your wife," she whispered, her voice raw.

"And I'm sorry that when you looked at me, all you saw was what you lost. But I'm going to stop being sorry for all of this." She kicked at the glass. "I wasn't garbage. I was your daughter and I deserved better."

She took the doll with her when she drove away.

39

AFTER MORE TEARS and a scalding shower, Adelia drove out to Ribbon Rail. There were more threads to cut.

Shannon answered the door with narrowed grey eyes.

"I came to say goodbye."

"That's refreshing," Shannon said, her voice arctic. "Bye." She started to shut the door.

"Can I say please say goodbye to Jo?"

"No."

"I know you're ang—"

"You don't know one thing about what I'm feeling."

"Mom, stop." Jo tugged at her mother.

"Josephine, stay inside." Shannon pulled away and threw the screen door open, forcing Adelia down the steps.

"I warned you," she hissed. "I warned him. This is déjà vu. How many more times are you going to screw this up?" Shannon ran a hand through her curls. "You know what kills me? You two idiots could have lit up Spoondrift at night with all the love you radiated. I only wish someone looked at me the way he looked at you."

"We had too much baggage," Adelia said softly.

"You think I don't know about his baggage? The man cleans his grout twice a week. He's a basket case. But his baggage *complements* yours. It always has."

"I don't need you lecturing me about what I'm losing!" Adelia pressed her palm to her mouth, wishing she could take back the tremble in her voice. "It's done. I came to say goodbye and to tell you thank you. For everything you've ever done for me. I'm not...I don't make it easy for people to..." Her hands tingled and she tried shaking the feeling into them, tightening into fists and releasing. But the sensation spread. "Just tell Jo she can text me if she wants. And tell her that I'll miss her."

The ground felt like it was breaking apart beneath her feet as she walked back to her car. Once inside, her tears nearly choked her. She couldn't stop them and didn't try. She covered her face with her hands and let them fill with all her regret.

The passenger door snapped open and the seat shifted beside her. "Hey," Jo said.

"Hey, kid." A sob garbled her words. She couldn't see her through her drowning eyeballs, but she felt Jo scoot closer and lay a hand on her arm. Which only made her cry harder.

Jo left the silence alone and stayed until her sobs turned to whimpers and then sniffles.

Something poked at Adelia's arm. A box of tissues.

"Oh god, I must look disgusting."

"I mean, kinda," Jo said. "That's a lot of snot."

Laughing, she grabbed a handful of tissues. "I haven't cried in fourteen years."

"That's...effed up."

"Right? So much for Lia the badass, huh?"

"Eh." Jo said. "Lia's cool. But I sorta love Adelia."

Her heart twisted, squeezed out like a dishrag. "You're the only one. I'm not even sure *I* like her."

"Then you're dumb. You should totally love her," Jo said. "Anyways, I'm not the only one. Mom loves you."

Adelia snorted and shook her head.

"She told me to bring you these." Jo sat the box on the seat between them. "She worries about you. Mom doesn't waste a lot of time worrying about people she doesn't like. She's really upset with you *and* Conor, but she can't yell at him because he's so sad. Pretty sure she thinks you're tougher than he is."

"He's tough. Just in a different way."

"I know." Jo looked at her hands. "You guys seemed so happy. I think whatever happened, he loves you too."

Adelia brushed fresh tears away. Any more crying and she'd hurl.

"Do you love him?"

She wadded up a tissue. "I don't think it's normal how much I love him. It's like being in pain, all the time."

"That's pretty dramatic," Jo said. "Maybe that's why things didn't work out. You need to, like, bring it down a notch. Start with, 'I like you.'"

Adelia laughed. "That was pure Shannon, kid."

"Ugh, I'll own it." Jo bit her lip. "So what now? Are you guys gonna make up?"

"No. I'm leaving."

"You can't leave!"

Adelia stared out the window. "What am I supposed to do?"

"Just…stay."

"I don't know *how* to stay," she said, her voice crackling over the words.

"Where are you going to go then?"

"Back to California. For now."

"I dunno why you think you gotta leave. There's nothing there that you can't find here."

"I'm not trying to find anything. I'm just trying to…I don't know. Start fresh."

"But Cherry Lake makes you happy. You're so much nicer than you were when you got here, and you smile a lot—'course, not now—but I think you're, like, alone too much. Cuz you don't like L.A. So why go back, when you like it here and it makes you smile?"

"It's not that simple. Conor and I imploded. It wasn't pretty."

"That sucks. But my mom always tells me not to do things for boys. She says that it's a recipe for misery. If I want to do anything, even wear lipstick, it should be for me," Jo said. "And I love Conor and I'm sad that he's sad, but he's a boy and that's means he's a dumb reason not to stay."

She stared into Jo's big grey eyes and for a moment all of her broken parts felt repairable. Then she just felt broken again. "I can't. I'm scared," she whispered.

Jo climbed onto her knees and wrapped her arms around her. "It's okay to be scared sometimes. Be scared and do it anyway."

"I regret teaching you that."

Jo gave her another squeeze. "I gotta go back in."

"What's the rush?"

"Cody wants to talk to me about something. There's a dumb spring-end dance thing and I think he's gonna tell me he asked out Maddison."

"Why would he do that?"

"Because he's stupid," Jo said, with no rancor. "She's all over him. I'm not. Anyway, I lost interest when he ditched me at the party. They deserve each other."

"You're pretty mature."

"One of us has to be," she said, rolling her big grey eyes.

"Wait." Adelia grabbed Jo's hand and searched her pixie face. "Will you hate me? For leaving?"

"No." Jo slid across the seat and opened the door. "That's not how love works."

ADELIA DROVE past the woods and trails and lakes that made the town so beautiful. She caught the mill right before close and bought a cider slushie for the road.

She passed townies on their porches, enjoying the warm evening and the last of the sunlight. Georgie McIntosh sat in a rocking chair in front of the parlor, gabbing with a few other old-timers and eating sundaes. The world's worst psychic, Mags, who apparently owned an endless supply of dashikis, stopped to wave at her while she locked up her shop. At the stop sign, swells of tourists crossed the road, carrying bags of marshmallows and folding chairs, all headed to the beach for bonfires, passing signs explicitly stating that beach bonfires were illegal.

Instead of going straight, she turned into the beach parking lot. Grabbing her bag and her drink, she wandered near the water and sat on an empty picnic table, planting her feet on the bench. The slushie burned sweet and tart in her throat.

For the second and last time she was leaving Cherry Lake in the middle of the night after doing as much damage as she could. Last time, she cried the whole way, but she knew in her gut that she had to leave. Whether her reasons were foolish or not, she was set on that path.

This time, she felt an invisible hand holding her there. Unwilling to let her go.

It would be easy to say that it was because of Conor. But if she were being honest with herself, and it was way past time for that, she didn't come to Cherry Lake for him.

She came there to grieve.

Not for all that she'd lost as a kid or even for her father himself, but for what she'd truly lost the day he died.

Hope.

She never acknowledged it, but it was always there. A single, brightly-colored balloon afloat inside of her. Hope that one day things could be fixed. Hope that she'd have the nerve to pull into her dad's driveway and present him with the car, and he he'd hug her, tears in his eyes and tell her how much he missed her, and how sorry he was. Hope that they could find a way to be whole, together. But that was gone.

What did she hope for now?

The lake lapped the shore gently and the breeze carried the smell of burning wood and melted chocolate. Her phone pinged a text from Jo. A selfie, with part of Jo's giant eyeball in the foreground and Shannon half-scowling, half-laughing in the background.

We'll miss u. Next time ur home, bring mom a hot guy.

A second later, she got a message from Shannon. *Do NOT bring me a hot guy. What would I do with one? Make him pancakes?* There was a pause and more text popped up. *Sorry I yelled at you. Come home soon, so I don't miss your stupid face.*

Laughing, Adelia texted back. *Aww, you like me.*

Despite your personality, you do grow on a person, Shannon typed. *Like mold.*

She snorted and reread the messages, her heart full and empty at the same time.

Come home.

What did home look like? That question had haunted Adelia her entire life, spoken like a soft whisper first in her mother's voice and then in her own.

She listened to the swoosh and hush of the lake, but the water didn't have an answer either. Sighing, she scrolled through her phone apps. Music didn't always have answers but sometimes it led her to them.

Humming a familiar melody, she found what she was looking for and purchased a few albums. Her mother's favorites. She set the new playlist to shuffle, and then dug into her duffel bag for a pen and paper. She bit her lip and wrote, *WHAT IS HOME?* at the top of the page. She stared at it for ages. Nothing came to her and after a few minutes she closed her eyes and focused on the music.

Many of those songs she hadn't heard in years. The slide guitars and earthy, bluesy voices transported her to the tiny apartment she'd lived in on Flushing Road in Flint. The walls were paper-thin and the hallways smelled like half-cooked meat and skunk weed. She could feel her mother's energy. The naked longing for something special. The streak of Irish melancholy. The chain-smoking nervousness. The whimsical dreams of romance and lilacs and happily-ever-after homes. The love of music.

She still couldn't remember her mother's face and maybe that didn't matter. So much of who her mother was and what she dreamed of lived inside of her.

By the time "Angel From Montgomery" played, Adelia was crying, but there was no grief in it, not for mothers or lost loves or sick fathers. Instead, all the things she'd longed for and denied herself ebbed and overflowed until her tears matched the rhythm of the waves.

On the paper in front of her, she scribbled out a crooked house with huge windows that let the light pour in, so there were no dark corners. Chimney. Old-fashioned porch. The more details she scribbled out, the more peaceful she felt. It would be somewhere isolated with lots of forest trails to walk and a rushing river to fish in. She'd never fished, but it always seemed like something she'd enjoy. She drew a familiar river behind it. Looming white pines above. Woods all around. She stared at it.

Fuck.

Jo was right. Whether Conor wanted her or not was irrelevant. What mattered was how much it hurt to think of leaving. She wanted what was there. Old-timer gossip, bad psychics, and endless tourists. Nirvana cover bands and cider slushies and picturesque hiking trails. Long, awful winters and glorious, too-short summers. Excellent pie. Questionable politics. Family.

She wanted to have Shannon and Jo and Old Curtis and Miss Janice over for dinner.

She wanted to learn to make dinner.

And she wanted a Christmas tree. She'd never had one of those.

By the time she'd packed everything up and made it to the edge of town, Adelia felt as though she'd gotten back that single balloon of hope and turned it into a thousand, drifting her toward the home she'd always wanted.

Cherry Lake.

Man, she really should have seen that coming.

40

HE MISSED TALKING TO HER.

For fourteen years, Conor managed just fine, but the last four months were torture. He ran into Adelia nearly every day at Keys or the Railway. They'd skim past one another with regretful eyes and it felt like he was being pulled apart each and every time.

Now he was reduced to eavesdropping on her conversation in Buck's Hardware to hear her voice.

She flicked a lock of hair over her shoulder as she and Jo gave serious consideration to the pumpkin carving kits hanging from an endcap display.

"I can't believe you've never carved a pumpkin," Jo said.

Adelia turned the kit over. "I've never done anything. No pumpkins. No Christmas trees. Nothing."

He picked up and sat down the same container of auto wipes, then picked it up again. Jo swiveled her head around, as though she could sense him. "Hey, Conor," she said, giving him a wave. "Best friends and you never carved pumpkins together? That's weird. Hannah and I always carve 'em."

Busted, he sat the container down, cleared his throat and

walked over. "My mother hired people to carve pumpkins for us."

Adelia bit her lip. "God forbid we make a memory."

"Ugh, who wants that?" he said.

She smiled nervously and he could hardly breathe. She looked amazing. A little extra weight filled out the sharp edges of her face, leaving her softer and more alluring. Her hair had gone through a couple permutations in the past few months. Now, one side was shaved and the other was a thick fall of auburn hair streaked with gold.

Jo tossed the pumpkin carving kit on the shelf and eyed them both. "Um, I need to use the bathroom. Be right back!" She disappeared down the aisle.

They both shuffled uncomfortably. She exhaled a little laugh and drummed the kit she held against her hand. "So, how's business?" she asked.

Grabbing the lifeline she offered, he smiled. "Good. Great. Lots of work. Don't have a studio yet, so I'm only doing location shoots. But I arranged with the Dive to rent a room that I can use for studio sessions. It's not as creepy as it sounds, though. There'll be a sign and stuff. Professional."

Her dark eyes warmed and she bit her lip. "That's awesome."

He grabbed Jo's discarded carving kit and tapped it lightly against the shelf. He hadn't stood this close to Adelia for more than a second in months. He leaned closer. "So," he said. "Your first real Halloween?"

She nodded. "I'm thinking about getting some decorations. Something scary and gross and guaranteed to give nightmares."

"A chainsaw maniac on the front lawn?" he said.

"Got to get one of those. Wouldn't want to waste all that yard on *nature*." She leaned in as well and the subtle trace of some new perfume laced with her strawberry shampoo made him weak.

"Oh, yeah, Shannon said you built a house on your dad's old property. I've got to admit that was a surprise."

"I like to think of it as my mom's property. It was her dream. And now it's mine," she said softly. "It's sort of a modern log cabin. Huge windows. Lots of sunlight. It's so pretty. It has hardwood floors and a fireplace. I'm chopping my own firewood. And it has a loft and a kitchen and I'm babbling." She flushed the prettiest pink and ran her fingers along the edge of the shelf.

"Anyway, my contractor was disappointed that I didn't want something more mansion-y. Had to break it to him that I'm way more Beverly Hillbilly than most people imagine." And then she smiled. Her lips parted into one of those rare, true Adelia smiles. The ones where her eyes softened and her face stretched extra wide to accommodate all those teeth. The ones where she looked like a falling star, blinding you as she descended.

That smile.

He swallowed. Months ago, she'd sent him a letter letting him know that she was moving to Cherry Lake, and he'd resented her for it. Now, he felt the rightness of her being there. She looked so happy and vibrant.

He reached for her hand on the shelf. "Adelia, I'm—"

"Miss Winters, here's your paint."

They jerked apart. The cashier lugged paint and supplies onto the counter. "Two cans of Punk Rock Pink. I got you brushes and brush cleaner and a pan and some plastic, too."

"Cool. Thanks, Jeremy." She handed him a credit card and turned back to Conor. "Jo didn't like the color of the guest bedroom, so..." She trailed off and looked into her big black leather purse as if searching for something.

"Yeah, she's...yeah," was his brilliant reply. How could they both run out of words when there was so much unsaid? "Uh, it was nice talking to you." He backed away and turned toward the auto aisle.

"Wait," she said. He looked back and found her inscrutable eyes on him. "Since you're here, I, uh, I've been meaning to...I was going to send Jo maybe to drop it off, but I wasn't sure if you'd even—" She dug around in her purse and pulled out a large heavy-duty manila envelope. "Here." She shook it at him.

Confused, he walked back and took it from her. She didn't explain anything though. Just grabbed her paint and supplies and walked away.

He stared at the heavy envelope, unable to recall why he'd come to the hardware store in the first place.

Jo sidled over and pressed the forgotten container of auto wipes into his free hand.

"You're a nosy, pushy kid," he whispered.

"I'm my mother's daughter," she said with a self-satisfied grin. "See ya."

"Bye," he said faintly as she followed Adelia out the door.

CONOR TOSSED the unopened envelope on his coffee table. He was intrigued and anxious at the same time.

Cupcake trudged out of the hallway and stared at him with mournful eyes. She'd been looking at him like that ever since Adelia left. Nothing made a home melancholier than a sad dog. She gave a half-hearted jump and licked his nose. Then, she curled into the center of the couch and looked at him in judgment. He didn't bother to push her down because the empty couch made him sad, too.

Sitting beside her, he took a breath and opened the envelope. A magazine slid out along with a piece of paper. Adelia's sharp handwriting slashed across the paper. *No one should have to pay for this magazine, so I stole it for you.*

A laugh huffed out of him and he traced her handwriting

with his fingers. Further down the page, in smaller print, she wrote, *Old Curtis caught me. Send bail money.*

Still laughing, he sat the note aside. Front and center on the cover of *Spinning Rock* magazine was Adelia, sitting sideways in his living room chair, his t-shirt slipping off her shoulder, exposing the lace of her tattoo. She looked directly at the camera, as if daring anyone to read further. "Our Lady of Perpetual Silence," the headline said. "Lia speaks for the first (and last) time about her painful past, present plans, and the punch heard 'round the world."

He flipped through the album reviews and ads until he found it. They weren't joking. She talked about *everything*. Her father's mental illness, her runaway years, the frustrations of working with labels, being blacklisted by Gyroscope, her new music producer and the indie album she was dropping at the end of the month. The article was punctuated by photographs he'd taken of her. They really were beautiful.

When asked why she was doing this now, after so many years of silence, she picked at the holes in the knees of her jeans and said, "I value my privacy and I don't like talking about my past. It's painful. But this last year has taught me that you can't run and hide forever. If you want to make good music, or have a life that fucking matters, you have to let people—" She hesitated. "You just have to show your scars." Lia then swung around and lifted her shirt to show off a new tattoo on her rib cage. It said, 'Be scared. Do it anyway.'

Conor took a shuddering breath and rubbed his hand over his stomach, through his shirt. Adelia had said something like that to him the day everything went to hell. *You want everything from me. All my scars. But you don't want to give everything back.*

There was a sharp knock on his door and Shannon popped her head in. "Hey, can you help me? I think the pilot went out on my furnace. You're the only one who get the damn thing lit again. It's freezing." She tilted her head. "Uh oh, you're wearing your brooding duck lips."

"My what?"

She pursed her lips and made sad eyes at him. "That's what you look like."

He pressed his hand to his mouth. He *was* making duck lips. "Shut up," he said, folding his lips together.

Shannon scooted Cupcake aside and sat down. She pulled the magazine closer to look at it and flipped the page. "Wow. She told me she was using your pictures. I knew you were great, but these are…" She looked up at him. "Are you all right?"

He scrubbed his hands over his jaw. "I love her."

"I know you do."

"I'm fucking miserable without her."

She smiled softly. "I knew that too."

"Has she said anything—"

"Nooope." She gave his shoulder a squeeze. "If you want to know how she feels, man up, get your head out of your butt, and ask her. I don't know what you've been waiting for." She picked up Adelia's note and laughed. "I will say, she loved you even knowing about your grout obsession and your awful, warm kale salads. Pretty sure that kind of love doesn't disappear in a few months."

"You like my kale salad," he said.

"Oh, sweetie. No one likes your kale salad. We lie to you." She stood and pursed her lips. "I'll leave you to your brooding."

"Funny. Give me a few minutes and I'll fix your furnace."

"You're the best," she said. Her eyes softened and she pointed at the magazine. "That picture is amazing."

As the door closed behind her, Conor stared at the photograph. Adelia, sitting high in the giant cherry tree with her feet dangling, staring down at him, her mouth curved into a half smile and her hand held toward him. In her eyes was a challenge. A dare. Climb up. Take chances. Show your scars.

Be scared. Do it anyway.

ADELIA TURNED to face Jo in the backseat. "That movie sucked."

Shannon nodded and rounded the corner on Big Dirt Road. "Agreed. We'll never get those hours of our lives back."

"Mom, you watch *My Boyfriend the Vampire*. You can't waste more minutes than that," Jo said.

"You like that show," Shannon said. "Quit pretending to be cool. Anyway, Ewan and Makayla are the only reason I still believe in romance."

"Ewan has bad hair. And he eats people."

"No love story is perfect, Josephine."

Jo picked at the popcorn in her teeth. "It had robots and explosions. How could it be bad?"

Shannon pulled alongside to the gate. "Sorry, but I agree with Adelia. The film suffered from implausibility."

"Is that what I said? I'm soooo smart." Adelia climbed out of the car and unlocked the gate, pausing to study the black thing hanging from it.

"What's that?" Shannon hollered.

"It's a plastic bat. Weird." She unlocked the gate and waved

Shannon through and then hung it back on the gate. "It's kind of cool."

They made the half-mile trek down her newly paved driveway.

"Where'd those come from?" Jo asked, pointing at the little lit-up pumpkins on stakes that lined the driveway every few feet.

Adelia leaned her head out the window. "What the fu—hell is going on?"

"Crazed fan?" Shannon said.

"With my gate code?"

"Whoa, creepy," Jo whispered.

A straw-stuffed body made of garbage bags hung from a tree.

Her stomach plummeted. "I'm officially freaked out." The house came into view and she gasped. Her front yard was filled with Halloween decorations. Ghosts saying *boo*, moaning zombies, and a bloody chainsaw-wielding guy made of plastic standing over another straw-stuffed bag dressed to look like a body. At least, she hoped it was straw-stuffed.

"Oh cool, a coffin!" Jo shouted.

A coffin with RIP spray-painted on the side, leaned against her porch, and a big red handprint marred her front door, with a sign dangling from it that read, "I wouldn't eat the candy if I were you."

"Maybe you should stay in here and call the police," Shannon said.

Adelia climbed out and stalked to her porch. "No one's scaring me away from my home."

Two uncarved pumpkins sat on either side of her door and between them was a large box wrapped in black paper.

"Don't open that!" Shannon shouted, racing out of the car. "You don't know what that is!"

"What the hell?" She lifted the box. It didn't weigh very much.

Beneath the din of moaning zombies, she heard grunting. She walked slowly around the side of the house, stepping over more pumpkin-shaped planters. The sound got louder as she got closer to the back of her house. Crazed stalker wanking it on her back door?

Nope. It was Conor. Slow dancing with a life-sized Dracula in his truck bed. And Dracula was getting frisky.

"What are you doing?"

He jumped and dropped Dracula over the side of the truck. "Damn. You're early."

"Shannon drives like a bat out of hell. What is going on?"

"Conor?" Shannon peered around the corner, one sneaker off and raised above her head. "What the hell? I almost called the police."

His brown leather jacket was dusty and covered with bits of fuzz. He jumped off the truck and ran a hand through his hair. Adelia's pulse pounded everywhere at once. She missed him so much. Every day was an exercise in pain and joy. Seeing him and not speaking. Opening her eyes in the morning and wondering if he was waking up with someone else.

"Sorry," he said. "I lost track of time. It's not quite done. Didn't mean to scare you. Not like that anyway." He hefted the heavy Dracula to the corner of the house.

Adelia looked at Shannon for answers. She shrugged. "Okay, well, it's not a serial killer. We're gonna go."

"What? Nooo," Jo said. "What's in the box?"

Shannon grabbed Jo's arm and dragged her away. Her VW Rabbit mewled to life, breaking the silence.

He smiled. "This isn't going as smoothly as I'd hoped."

"You're freaking me out. What's going on?"

"Can we sit?" he asked.

She nodded, clutching the black-wrapped gift to her chest

like a shield. He led her around the thicket of decorations to sit on her front step.

"This house is amazing," he said.

"Thanks. I wasn't sold on the stone masonry, but it looks pretty rad with the logs," she babbled. "The kitchen is gorgeous. And I cooked yesterday."

"What'd you make?"

"Grilled cheese," she said. "My therapist calls that a 'small victory.'"

He poked at the gift. "Open it."

She took a deep breath and gently pulled the ribbon decorating it. Her hands shook as she peeled the paper off. In the bottom of the box was a...shirt? She pulled it out. A grey Henley.

"This is, uh, roomy for me. But thank you."

"It's mine," he said.

She sat it in her lap. "Okay, you lost me here."

"There's a lot of stuff I wouldn't do because I was scared. Quitting Razzle. Starting my business. Fighting for us. I waited way too long for all of it." He shook his head. "Can we start over?"

Adelia fought for breath as the world spun around her. "But...it's been four months."

"Four months, eight days. A couple of hours. It's been awful." He licked his lower lip. "It took me a while to get it, but you were right. I can't ask for all of you if I won't give you all of me."

He took a shuddering breath and unzipped his jacket. He gently tugged her hand from the Henley and placed it on the bare chest beneath it.

"Oh." She pressed her palm to the dark hair and the heart pounding beneath it. With her other hand, her fingertips skimmed his ribs and torso, following the pattern of pale stretch marks crossing his chest, stomach, and hips like rivers on a map.

His abdomen jerked, as if her touch burned.

She shook, overwhelmed by what he was giving her.

"I've been running with my shirt off for the last week," he said. "I know it doesn't seem like a big dea—"

"It's a big deal," she said. Unable to stop herself, she leaned forward and kissed one mark, trailing her lips over it. "You're beautiful," she said. His quaking matched hers. She pressed on, touching him. Kissing him. "You always have been." His stomach contracted. "You always have been, Conor," she said, looking into his eyes. "You have nothing to be ashamed of and nothing to hide. You're the most caring, gorgeous man I've ever known and you always have been."

He threaded his hands in her hair. "I love you," he said, his voice shaking. "I've never not loved you." He stared at her with his wide green eyes and she felt like falling forever.

"Please say something. My nips are *freezing.*"

She burst into laughter.

"I've missed that sound," he said.

"What if we screw it up again?" she whispered.

"I recently read an interview with a brilliant musician who said, 'Be scared. Do it anyway.'"

"I've got to stop telling people that." She stared up at the clouds, her emotions too big for her head. "I don't know. It hurt so much before. I can't—" Panic blinded her. She stood, the shirt falling off her lap, and fumbled for her house key. She shot through the door and closed it behind her, leaning against it. The waterworks came on hard and fast. Thick, hiccupping sobs that choked her.

He knocked softly. "Adelia, let me in. It's okay if you don't want this. But don't cry alone."

Another wail broke free and she straightened and twisted the doorknob. He gathered her in his arms, cupping the back of her head. "I'm so sorry," he murmured. "It was too much pressure. I should have done it differently." He rocked her, and it only made her cry harder.

He held her until her sobs turned to soft wheezes. She pulled away from him but gripped his hand. "Look." She dragged him to the kitchen. "I try to keep it clean, but I don't always do the dishes, and sometimes I forget to empty the dishwasher." He gave her a confused shake of the head, so she pulled him to the bathroom. It was a clutter of hair dye kits and makeup. "I don't really know how to organize. I checked some books out of the library about it but I fall asleep when I read anything longer than ten pages."

Her bedroom was the last room on the left. She opened the door and showed him the piles of clothes on the floor. Her beautiful new lingerie strewn everywhere. "I'm messy." She turned and lifted her chin.

Understanding lit in his eyes. "I can handle messy."

"I can't cook. I burned that grilled cheese."

"I'll teach you."

She crossed her arms. "I don't want kids."

"Me, neither."

"I have toe hair."

"Me, too," he said, his smile making her heart puddle and pool out of her. "What else you got, Winters? I don't care about that stuff. We're not moderate, normal people. If we do this, we're going to fight and fuck and drive each other crazy, but we're also going to love each other like no one has *ever* been loved. That's the upside of being a little unstable."

His hands circled her waist and pulled her close. His lips descended on hers and all the puzzle pieces suddenly fit. He explored her, as though they were kissing for the first time. It wasn't a kiss that promised sex. It promised something so much better.

"I love you," she breathed against his lips. "I love you so fucking much."

He growled. "Why does it always turn me on when you swear?"

"I ruined you for the good girls."

"Say fuck again."

"Fuck," she whispered.

He groaned and bit her neck. "I missed you," he said, his breath hot in her ear. Swinging her around, he lifted her up and sat her down on the bed. Looking at the curtain-less windows he hesitated only a moment before sliding the jacket off of his shoulders.

Adelia couldn't get enough of touching him. She took her time, learning all the parts of him he'd been afraid to show. She stroked every line, every scar and mark that made him who he was.

When she tugged at his belt, he undid it slowly, never breaking eye contact. He slid off his pants and boxer briefs and she greedily took him in her mouth, reveling in his moans and the way his hands tightened in her hair.

"Stop," he said, his voice tight.

She looked up at him with questioning eyes. He leaned down and kissed her. "I need to touch you too," he said against her lips.

After that, they laughed and touched and stroked each other until they both trembled. Rolling onto his back, he pulled her on top of him. The sunlight, rippling off the river outside of the window, made patterns on his chest that she followed with her palms.

"Are you sure?" she asked. "About this? Us?"

He smiled. "I'm scared. But I've never been more sure." He dug his hands into her hair and tugged her close. His sweet, slow kiss was reverent, and in that moment she was consecrated in the burn of his gaze, her heart melting like molten glass, and shaped into something sacred and whole.

Biting her lip, she slid him inside and he moaned, arching his hips to hers. Taking control, she sat upright and rocked. He reached between them to stroke her, gentle and measured as her own pace. As she rode harder, he pressed his knuckles in just the right spot, rolling them against her, increasing the pressure and sending shocks of pleasure from her core to every part of her body. She fell forward and ground wildly against him. He surrounded her with his arms and met her rhythm. The sweet sound of their bodies collided like a drumbeat. A heartbeat. Lights danced in her vision and the pressure built until it had nowhere to go and no more space to fill. Conor drove harder into her and she nearly screamed when the pleasure broke her apart and put her back together. Conor clasped her to him and gave his own sharp cry of release. Quaking, he held her, whispering in her ear over and over that he loved her.

They stayed there for a long while, tangled together. She finally rolled off onto her side and he turned to face her. She cherished seeing his furrowed brow. The beads of sweat in his hairline. The redness of his lips. She traced his cupid's bow and he kissed her fingers.

All her life she'd lived like a fist, clenched so tight it hurt. For months she'd been unfurling, and now she felt those last tense muscles let go. The relief made tears gather in her eyes. They spilled along her lashes and down the bridge of her nose. And she did what she always did now. She let them fall.

"So, you're moving in, right?" she asked, sniffling. "Because I seriously can't cook for shit."

Conor stroked her jaw, catching her tears with his fingertips. "We're never going to do anything the normal way, are we?"

"Why start now?"

He kissed her softly, his laughter mingling with hers. "I guess I'm home then."

Home.

She'd grown accustomed to looking at her beautiful house and saying that small word. Feeling the weight of it on her tongue. Trying like hell to understand what it meant and why it mattered so much to her.

Now she knew.

Home wasn't made of timber or stone. It wasn't cabinets and countertops or coat closets. It was safety. It was love. It was a place to belong.

She snuggled closer into his arms.

It was him.

It was always him.

NOTE FROM THE AUTHOR

Thank you so much for reading this book!

When I started *How to Stay* back in 2014 all I wanted was to write *something different*. A bitchy heroine, a painfully shy hero, and jokes about toe-hair. But as time went on, *something different* started to look familiar. I never expected my own life to bleed so profusely on to the page, from a dysfunctional childhood in a small town, to body anxieties, to the feelings that came from living with my hoarder grandmother. But bleed it did.

I once told a friend that Conor was a type-A perfectionist who desperately wanted to let go of his artless life but was too mired in self-doubt to reach for his dreams. I remember how she slowly blinked at me without comment. I stared back at her and finally said, "Yeah, I just heard it too. Shut up."

Much like Conor, I eventually got my shit together and here is the result. Imperfect. Heartfelt. Laden with profanities. If you enjoyed all of that, you'll want to keep an eye out in 2020 for the next Bad Girls of Cherry Lake novel, *How to Dare*. It's about time Shannon Cooper got her own happily-ever-after, don't you think?

If you want to know exactly when Shan's book will drop,

you'll need go to my website https://christinamitchellbook-s.com and subscribe to my monthly newsletter. It's where you can find updates, bad jokes, b-movie recommendations, and subscriber-exclusive content like deleted scenes and more!

Anyhow, thanks again for reading this little piece of my soul. I hope you laughed, cried, and felt tingly in your nethers. And whether you loved it or didn't, I would be eternally grateful if you'd leave me an *online the webernet* review.

ACKNOWLEDGMENTS

This book wouldn't exist if I weren't surrounded by cheerleaders, mama bears, and violent bitches threatening me harm if I didn't finish it.

Biggest thanks to my hubs, Josh Mitchell, for never once minimizing this dream and never letting me minimize it either. You've always said, "This matters. We'll make it happen." I couldn't have done this without your endless support (and endless shoulder rubs). I love you more than sushi.

Thank you, Mama, for gifting me with all of the sass and swearing skills. They came in handy. Thank you for the encouragement, the flowers, and the no-bakes. I love you.

Meika Usher, my lobster. Thanks for the sing-alongs, fist bumps, victory twerks, advice, and hugs. Thank you for reading 800 versions of the first quarter of this book. You've stuck by me despite my anxiety, procrastination, tardiness, and generally being an anti-social fuck. You're a fantastic writer, a wild adventurer, and a brave bitch. Oh, and you've got a sweet, sweet booty. When I say I love you, it's not what it implies, it's guy love, between...two...guys.

Jeanne Ryan, for listening to me read the same damned

chapters for years. Thanks for believing that everything I write is wonderful. It's not true, but still, everyone should have a friend like you. I'm so glad Dave gave me to you all those years ago.

Louise Knott-Ahern, workshop queen, plot doctor, truth teller. I'd still be editing this book if you hadn't given me THAT talk. Thank you for believing in yourself and for helping others to believe in themselves too.

Jeannie Miernik, my quirky, brilliant, big-hearted activist friend. Your gorgeous prose will always be #goals for me. Without you and your crit this book wouldn't exist. Also, our creepy conversations are the best. I love you.

Victoria Solomon, your support and thoughtful critiques have been invaluable to me. Also, I can't stop thinking about that delicious black bean thing you brought to my house. You're an awe-inspiring person and a fantastic writer, and I'm so ready for the world to know that. Thank you for being my friend.

Esperanza, you're an old soul born of mermaid magic and restless summer winds, a fiercely loving sorceress who leaves strands of hair behind like confetti everywhere she goes. Your wisdom lives in my heart and in this book. Thank you for believing in me, pep-talking me, and biting me that one time.

Ladies of the Do! Erin King, thanks for the snort laughs and the generosity. I appreciate both your wisdom and your unshakable view of how one should bring up Dorito metaphors. Liz Zerkel, in a short time you've become a big part of my life. Thank you for the Snapchat convos, the sweet words of support, and for pimping me on your platforms. I can't wait to do the same for you. Yes Do, Motherfuckers!

Evatalia from Fiverr, thank you for creating a cover so beautiful I initially rejected it as being too pretty for a book that said the word fuck 113 times. Thank you to my sensitivity reader, Eryka Peskin, for your gentle teaching. Thanks to my fantastic editors, Jessica Snyder and Jami Nord. I'm grateful to you both for the pep-talks and hand-holding. Also, Erin King (you made the list twice) thank you for proofreading this book and not even charging me, despite my egregious misuse of commas.

Thanks to all those who been a part of my writing journey, whether it was specific help or just talking me out of setting this manuscript on fire: Alyssa Marble, Erin Bartels, Gina Mitchican, Jeanna Bini, Jesse Jones, Renee Clifton, Alicia Nash, Joanne Machin, Madeline Iva, and all the generous peeps in Binders.

A special thank you to someone who'll never read this. Lzzy Hale of Halestorm. You are a rock-goddess. If you hadn't opened for A7X and blown my mind with your voice and general badassery, my heroine would have been a boring-ass party planner instead of a rock star.

There are so many more. But I'll just say thank you to everyone who cheered for me, nagged me, or listened to me blather on about this book. I've held your every kindness in my heart and it has meant everything.

Lastly, to the substitute teacher at LCC who pulled me aside after class to talk about the personal essay I'd read aloud. You were only there for one day, but in the few minutes we spoke, you said something that profoundly changed my life. You told me that my abusers didn't make me strong. I was already strong and that's why I survived. I've carried those words with me for twenty years. Despite my not knowing your name, you are in every page of this book. Thank you.

CHRISTINA MITCHELL writes contemporary romances about damaged people who need (and deserve) happy endings. She drinks moscato from novelty mugs and spends her days listening to musicals, obsessing over Batman, and riffing on b-movies about genetically-modified sharks. She lives in Michigan with her hilarious husband, who almost never complains about the fuck-ton of glitter makeup she leaves lying around.

CONNECT ONLINE
christinamitchellbooks.com
facebook.com/christinamitchellbooks
instagram.com/sparkleyeti